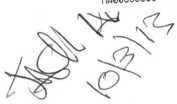

SECOND BIRTH

J F Althouse

THE WOLF PIRATE PROJECT INC.
DIVIDE, CO

This book is a work of fiction. Names, characters, places, and incidents are products of the author's imagination or are used fictitiously. Any resemblance to actual events or locales or persons living or dead is entirely coincidental.

A Wolf Pirate Book printed by The Wolf Pirate Project Inc., Divide, CO 80814

ISBN: 978-0-9822343-8-9
LCCN: 2013948250
First Wolf Pirate Project Inc. paperback printing 2013

Cover design by Brad Althouse

Manufactured in the United States

For information regarding special discounts for bulk purchases, please contact The Wolf Pirate Project Inc. at contact@wolfpiratebooks.com, or www.wolf-pirate.com.

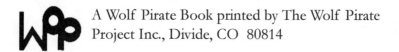

Second Sight and *Second Birth* are part of a seven-book series that takes you on what I hope is a plausible tour of our ancient past and future. Most of what I've written is based on library research, field study, and interviews. I have been asked how much of what I write is true. My books are fiction. The only way I could prove these events were accurate would be by witnessing them.

These first two novels are dedicated to an ancient army of 20,000 men and women who gave the ultimate sacrifice. Their courage and determination lives on in the men and women of our armed services.

Thank you for your interest and I hope you enjoy the series.

J. F. Althouse

Acknowledgements

The research done for *Second Sight* was the same I used for *Second Birth.* All the people I thanked in *Second Sight,* I remain indebted to. Here are some valuable new additions and second thanks to some wonderful people who continue to inspire and encourage me:

Wolfgang Sesmiolt, Nurnberg, Germany: *Herzlichen Dank für Ihre Hilfe.*
Bart P. Roelfs, Rotterdorf, Germany, and the excellent staff and crew from Uniworld: *Dank u voor het maken van een uitdagend onderzoek reis zo succesvol.*
To my fellow adventurers aboard the Royal Princess. Thank you for your enthusiasm and helping to make my father's first visit to Europe so memorable.
The staffs at the Nurnberger Welt Museum, Nurnberg, Germany; the Romisch-Germanisches Museum, Koln, Germany; the Kunsthistorisches Museum, the Welt Museum, the Wiener Stephansdom, and the National Library of Vienna, Vienna, Austria; the Hohensalzburg Fortress, Salzburg, Austria; the Museum Hallstatt, Hallstatt, Austria; the Zamecka Apartma, Cesky Krumlov, Czech Republic.
Val and Kareem Myett, Tortola, BVI, and everyone who assisted in the underwater research in the British Virgin Islands.
George Erikson, adventurer and author of *Atlantis in America,* for ongoing inspiration, friendship, and the prospect of new adventures and discoveries.
Kristen Lauria for volunteering to test read manuscripts, joining Jerry Mills and Darren Lambert.
All the indie bookstores that carried *Second Sight* and established the series.
Many fellowships and congregations for their support and encouragement, including Hope Fellowship in Douglassville, PA and Jarrettown United Methodist Church, Jarrettown, PA.
Ken K, Zach Bower, Kirby King, student Peter Chimera, the teachers and students of Christopher Dock Mennonite High School.
Daniel Frank Adamski, Jon and Heather, Brian and Laurie Smith, Thomas Medland.
The staff at Pocono Plateau Camp and Retreat Center.
Al and Mary Smith, Darren and Annette Lambert.
Ken Hamilton, Ian Burley, the students and alumni of SAVE.
Joe Gunn and the students and faculty of Indian Crest Middle School for their enthusiasm and encouragement all these years.

Whatever is has already been,

And what will be has been before . . .

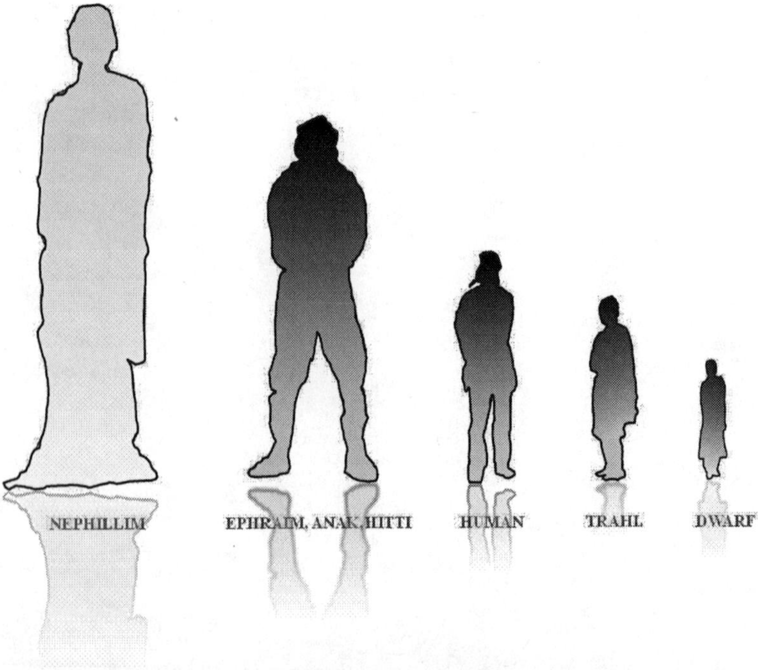

The races that existed on Earth at the close of the Second Age

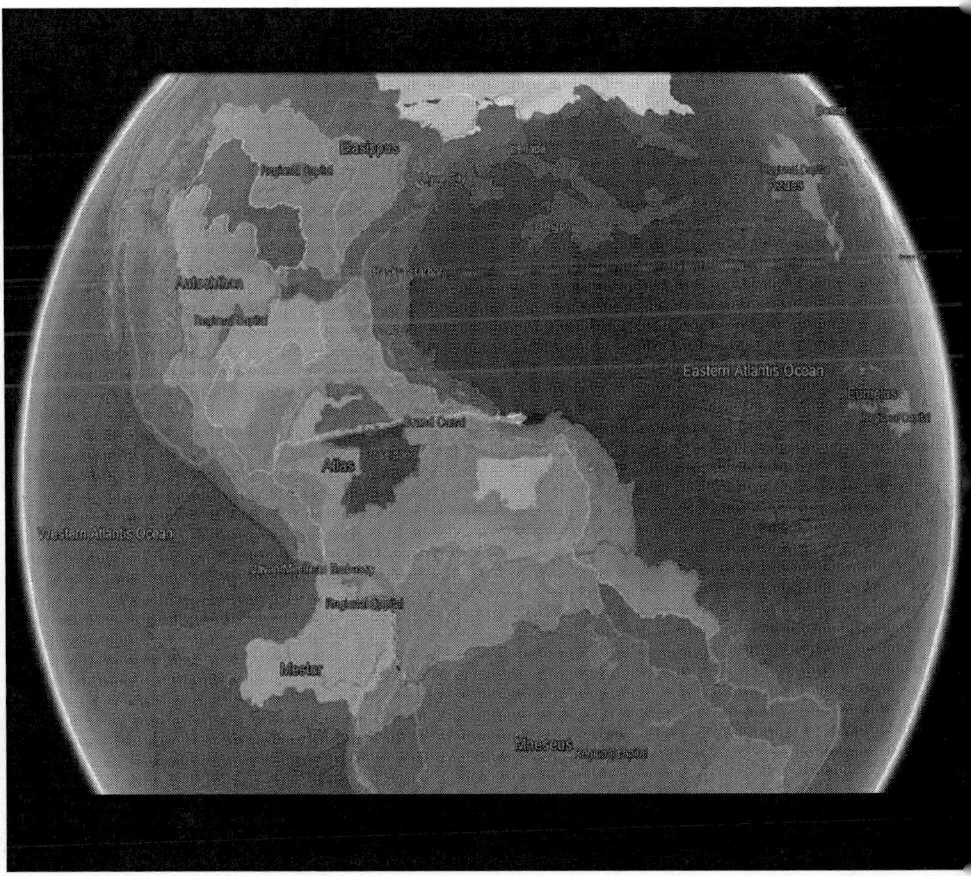
Basippos
Regional Capital
Autochthon
Regional Capital
Eastern Atlantis Ocean
Eumelus
Grand Canal
Atlas
Western Atlantis Ocean
Regional Capital
Mestor

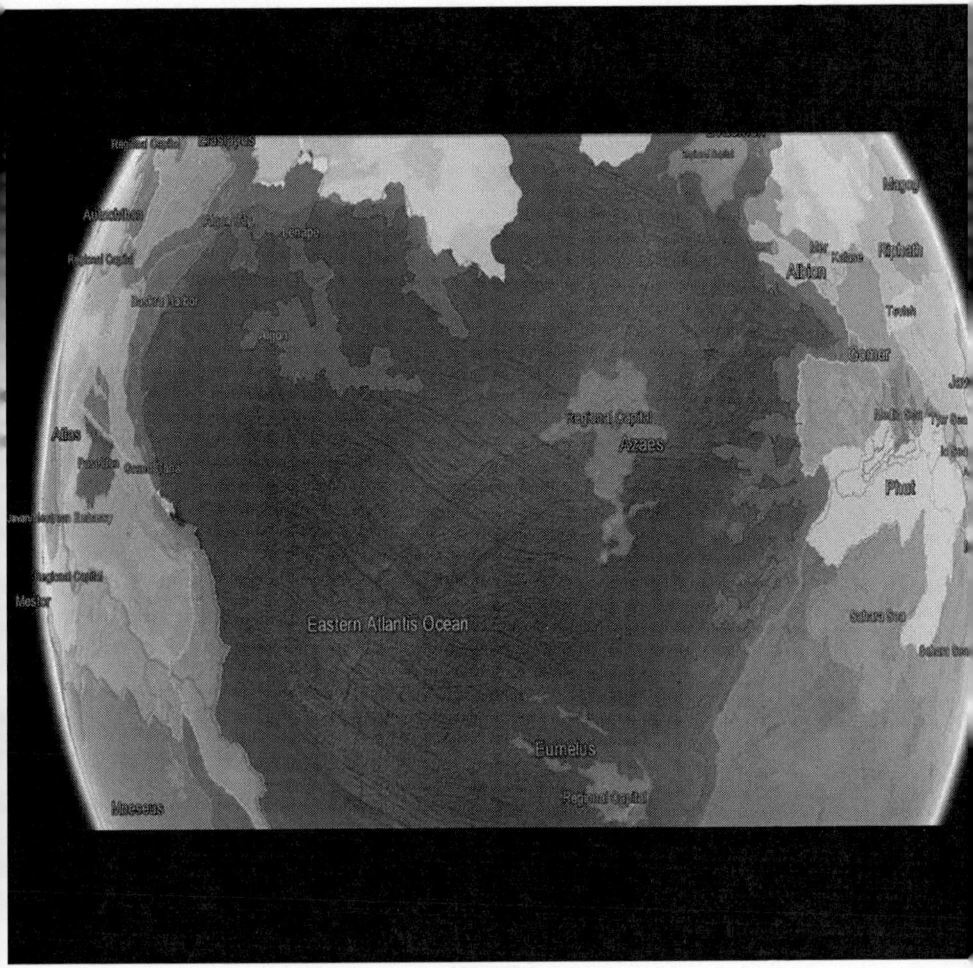
Regional Capital
Lenape
Algon
Magog
Riphath
Albion
Gomer
Regional Capital
Azaes
Atlas
Regional Capital
Mestor
Phut
Eastern Atlantis Ocean
Eumelus
Regional Capital
Maeseas

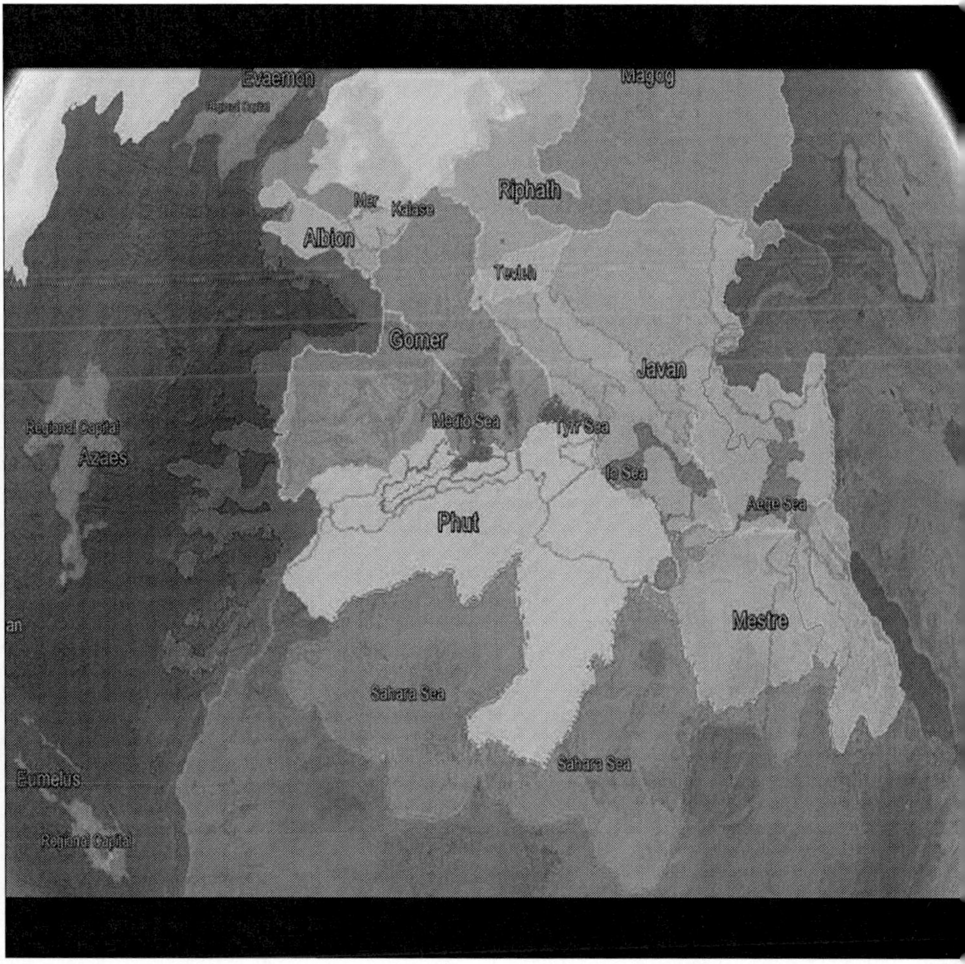
Evaemon
Magog
Riphalh
Mer
Kalase
Albion
Tevleh
Gomer
Javan
Medio Sea
Tyr Sea
Regional Capital
Azaes
Ia Sea
Aege Sea
Phut
Mestre
Sahara Sea
Sahara Sea
Eumelus

CHAPTER ONE

SARAH

I followed the path through tangled orchids and stepped onto the lava sand beach, my carry-on bag still slung over my shoulder. A weathered boulder twice the height of a man stood at the waves' edge in the shade of a mango tree. Shamel believed my husband would re-appear near that rock. How he knew didn't matter to me. The stone anchored me, an irrational hope in the face of so much uncertainty.

I surveyed the edge of the world. Waves rolled past volcanic cliffs. Silvered deadwood littered the shoreline. I felt like them, washed up on this beach, an unworthy survivor of the storm of storms, the end of the Second Age. Jordan had been the reason why I stood on this spot, still taking breaths after billions of people had perished.

I tried to tear my eyes from the turbulent horizon but couldn't. I should return to Shamel's mansion soon. Supper was at 1800 hours. He had adopted the Swiss custom of punctuality. A minute late and he would dispatch half his staff to find me. He worried so easily.

The latest refugees from the Second Age had fallen out of the sky and landed in the ocean, instead of on the beach. Some had drowned before we could reach them. Shamel had speculated that it had something to do with a stretching of the celestial chord between the ages. The sun and its dark twin were pulling apart. I feared I'd miss Jordan's flailing arms even though the sky hole hadn't appeared.

I brushed the tangled hair from my face and inhaled the salt spray as the surf pounded curling breakers across the brown sand. I dropped my backpack beside the boulder while a white-face monkey chittered from a nearby branch. The afternoon sun blinked through swiftly moving clouds, drifting toward its plunge behind the Pacific.

The ten-day trip to Paracas, Peru had been my chance to get away and recharge. It had been nice to visit Laura's home, meet her extensive family, and see the enigmatic El Candelabra for myself. But I felt far from recharged. My singular thought was to remain on this beach, keep vigil, and pull Jordan from the sea the second he hit the water. *Oh God, make him appear!*

Shamel had warned me it wouldn't happen quickly. Unlike the rest of us who'd torn the time fabric to flee to this age, Jordan had to retrace his cosmic trespass, mending his way home. Such a crossing could only happen with precision. He had to remain in the Second Age at least the same amount of time he'd been with me, from the moment he'd crawled out of the Embassy pond to the moment he'd sent me here.

That was the reality we understood from the Nephillim. But what if the Nephillim were wrong? They'd been wrong about other things. If it hadn't been for Jordan, none of us would be here, including most of the human race of the Fourth Age. Their ancestors wouldn't have survived if Jordan hadn't delivered the warning on top of the Sacred Mountain.

Would deliver. It was hard to remember time wasn't linear. It was square. All four ages happened at the same time, a cosmic swirl of interrelated events: past changing present, future changing past, present reeling through both. It only felt sequential, just as the dreamer of a thousand adventures discovers upon waking that he's slept only a moment.

Refugees of the Second Age were still arriving, with no rhyme or reason to their order. Shamel said it was because the journey was through a nexus, a bottleneck, a bead on a *migramah.* Pushing through that barrier required the force of will and the pull of others. When, where, and how we landed on this side was dictated by math nobody remembered. So far, seven civilians who'd jumped were unaccounted for, including Jordan and little Liv-ya. They could have appeared in remote places and not survived long enough for us to know. Or they could still be crossing.

I kicked off my travel sneakers, gathered my dress about my knees, and walked down the beach. The surf swept past my ankles and surged up my shins. I washed grime from my face, remembering the last time I'd been with my beloved.

I closed my eyes to see his face: Jordan carrying me to the Abyss, hurling me with the strength of desperation into the yawning mouth of the shaft, shouting as a tidal wave cleaved the clouds, "*I love you.*" The next moment, I lay in an English field, surrounded by sheep.

I wiped the surf from my face, smoothed my hair back, and stood up. Rhythmic splashes sounded behind me. Guess Laura had found me.

Relishing her concern, I forced a smile and turned. "Missed me already?"

A thin man in a rumpled business suit stared back at me. His trousers were soaked to the knees.

"Good evening, Your Highness," he said, his eyes sweeping hungrily over my body.

I backpedaled deeper into the surf. "You're the diplomat from the party."

He sneered. "You think you can escape us just by changing ages?"

A large wave smacked me across the back, hurling me toward him. He raised clawed fingers as if to impale me. I fought the tidal surge and tried to scream, but nothing came out. He lashed at my face.

"Stop," Laura yelled.

His fingers froze inches from my eyes, as if Laura had somehow thrown a rope around his wrist. His face was contorted in fear. He fought against the invisible restraint, cursing me while the undertow pulled me away. I sidestroked across the current and gave him wide berth, then struggled ashore as waves pounded the beach. He kept his eyes on me as I choked up seawater and staggered to my feet.

"Turn around," Laura commanded.

The man obeyed, cursing and spitting, still staring at me.

"Come to me," she said.

"No," he growled.

"You have no choice."

He lurched through the foam like a marionette with its head twisted sideways, until he stood obediently before her. She touched his forehead. "Be still."

He collapsed on the sand. Laura knelt beside him and spoke quietly. I stumbled to her side, heaving from the hard swim. Looking at him made me dizzy.

"Keep back, Sarah. I have to concentrate."

My legs buckled. I collapsed and knocked her over.

The young man sprang to his feet. Laura untangled herself and held up a hand. He froze at the sight of her spread digits, then turned and fled down the jungle path. His soaked pants flapped as he darted around a boulder.

"We have to catch him," Laura cried and took off after him.

I staggered behind her. "He's too fast."

I rounded a rock formation in time to see the man plow straight into Krax. Krax wrapped his arms around the man's waist and toppled him. In one swift motion, he grabbed the diplomat's collar with one hand and his pants with the other, and slammed him against the side of the rock. Krax placed his knee under the man's rear, lifted him, and leaned hard against him. He grinned as we caught up. "Hey, guys!"

The diplomat bucked. Krax pushed the man's face against the granite, his mouth contorted into a pucker. Krax panted back at us. "Good thing I followed you, huh?"

"Nice moves," Laura said.

"I never told you I worked in a psyche ward, did I?" He indicated his back pocket. "Babe, fish out my cell phone and call Shamel's security."

Laura motioned for me to keep back and approached the man. "That won't do any good."

The diplomat's eyes grew wide with fear. He struggled against Krax's hold.

Laura touched his forehead. "Be still."

His body went limp. Krax shifted his foot to keep him upright.

"How'd you do that?"

"Let go of him, honey."

Krax let go and the man fell. Laura followed him down, never pulling her hand off his temple. "What is your name?"

The diplomat's lips moved like a landed fish. "I am the assistant to the ambassador of Spain."

"I'm not talking about the person you've infected. What is *your* name?"

The chatter of the jungle went silent. The waves stilled. An unearthly chorus reverberated from his lips as if echoing out of a distant canyon. It clarified into words. "We are three."

"Names, *por favor*. Now!"

The man's lips spat out three horrible names I will never repeat. Even Krax, who couldn't possibly recognize these ancient terrors from Anakim legend, shuddered. Laura crossed herself and took a breath.

Three voices hissed from the unconscious man: one male, two female. "What are you going to do to us?"

"Send you where the Law requires."

The surf surged.

"No, let us go somewhere else!"

"There is nowhere else," Laura said sadly. The large breakers crashed on the rocks.

"Let us go into that iguana."

"It's time," she said.

"Noooo!"

Their cry was swallowed in whistling winds bending palms. Laura shifted her touch to the man's forehead and spoke too softly for me to hear. Pressure pushed me to the ground as if the world was retreating from these unseen creatures. I cringed at their collective violence, their rage. My heart felt like a stone. I collapsed in the sand.

The man thrashed. Laura kept her hand pressed against his head while he kicked and shook. Krax grabbed his legs.

"No, Krax!" Laura cried.

Krax gasped and went limp. The diplomat's eyes flew open. He ripped Laura's hand from his face and kicked Krax into the boulder. Laura grabbed one of the man's legs and held on as he dragged her across the ground, toward me. Her eyes were closed and her lips moved silently.

I tried to get up but my body wouldn't obey. The terror I hadn't felt since that last night in the Second Age flooded me now.

No, please, I prayed, *not now.*

"Praying … will … do … nothing," the voices hissed at me. "We will have you."

He desperately clawed across the sand. Laura held on like a stubborn anchor. He weakened and his fingers bled. A sick smile twisted across his face. "Jordan never crossed. Babla stopped him. We saw. We were there."

"No," I cried.

"Don't listen to them," Laura snapped. "They feed on lies."

The man seemed to gain strength from my despair. He lurched closer. Blood dripped from his eyes and ears. His grimace stretched into a triumphant smile. "The wave swept him away. He died in a sea of mud."

He lunged for my foot. Laura shouted something in a primordial language and he shuddered in agony, clutching his hand to his chest. "Others will find you." His eyes closed. "We are Legion. We … are … many."

He writhed in agony, then lay still, his fingers a hair's breadth from my foot. Krax moaned and rolled onto his back, holding his arm. "Oh crap, I think he broke my wrist!"

Laura crawled to my side. She pulled me away from the prostrate man. "Are you all right?"

I clung to her and nodded, staring at the diplomat from the safety of her arms. He breathed slowly. "How did you know to do that?"

"She's Catholic," Krax said, nursing his wrist.

"He's okay now; they're gone," Laura said. "He was infected with three Spirits of the Dead. He'll wake up and remember nothing."

"What he said about Jordan …"

"Were all lies, *kani,*" she insisted. "Spirits of the Dead say whatever they want to fool others into becoming like them."

"What if they were right?"

"Jordan is not dead," she stated. "How could they have seen what they claim and survived to tell it?"

"Because it hasn't happened yet," I said. A sudden breeze through my wet clothes made me shiver. "I'm so cold."

Laura laid me down. The palms shifted overhead. Sunlight and shadow danced before the sky. The palm fronds tinkled like glass chimes. A shadow drew near. It pulled me in.

"I can't move my wrists," I said.

"Sarah, hold still," Laura said from far away. Fluids began to drip on my chest. They started to burn.

"Jordan, wake up," I cried.

CHAPTER TWO

LEVI

We followed the medical convoy south over the final ridge between Tevleh and Javan. The healing encampment stretched the length of a busy airfield. Retrievers carrying wounded from multiple fronts hover-taxied to their assigned landing zones. Leg extensions pushed out from their hulls and dust billowed against the perimeter shields as the ship's landing gear pressed into the rippling grass. I looked back from my seat at the long train of incoming Retrievers. Their approach lights flared above the Tevleh Mountains, grim evidence of the desperate battle being waged on our border.

We landed in a priority zone next to a Critical Needs tent. Aizah, Diago, Aaron, and I escorted Jordan's battered body across the field, into it. We kept our weapons at the ready. This forward base was close enough to the fighting to feel the ground concussions through my armored boots. A healer I didn't recognize and his techs waited where the *Olympus'* Critical Care Team should have been standing. The techs swarmed to Jordan's side and transferred him to a waiting table, while the healer approached me and nodded.

"Where is the team from *Olympus*?" I asked.

"Aerial bombardment has delayed their flight. I will oversee the patient's treatment."

Healing equipment crawled overhead into position and dropped feeder tubes into his waiting palm. He slapped transfer clay onto Jordan's feet. Orange fluid coursed down from the equipment into the sticky mound. So far, he seemed confident in his work as he directed the fusing of bones and the regeneration of lost skin.

Aaron groused over what had happened at the rally point with the ambassador and the Mestrean Guardians. "I can't believe you let Numu take Suri."

"I had no choice," I said. "She revived at the jump point with no residual injuries."

"What were Numu and Amon doing in a battle support zone anyway?" Aizah asked.

"Same thing we were," I said. "Rescuing civilians who didn't belong there."

"Amon couldn't rescue his finger from a shut door," Diago quipped.

I turned and faced them. "Agreed, but what choice did I have? She's Mestrean. She's in Numu's charge. End of options."

Jordan groaned. The healer bent over his face and ran a fast scan.

"How is he?" Aizah asked.

"Not sure," the healer said, motioning to the techs. Privacy screens were moved into position. He pointed to a glowing boundary line around the warming table. "He's not responding to the feeders. I need you all to stay back, please, so we can work."

Aaron took Aizah's hand and drew her away. She bit her lip as Jordan's face turned ashen. "Why isn't he responding to the fluids?"

The healer looked at a floating display of Jordan's organs. "Does he have any residual wounds?"

"None, sir," a tech said. "All major organs are completely regenerated, but for some reason they're losing vitality."

"What would cause that?" another tech asked.

"Sit him up," the healer said.

They pulled Jordan into a sitting position, with his legs dangling over the floating table. His torso convulsed as he retched on the ground. Aizah and Aaron rushed to his side and held him steady.

"What's happening to him?" one of the techs asked.

"It's called vomiting," I said as they struggled to keep Jordan vertical. "It happens to primitives living on the ice."

"Why does it happen?"

"He's sick," Aaron said.

"What do you mean sick?" the healer inquired.

Aaron and I tried to explain Jordan's condition, how his body was under relentless attack by microbes mistaking him for a fresh corpse in need of decomposition.

The healer was unimpressed. "I read opinion papers concerning the premature aging of northern primitives. But I disagree with the conclusion. Microbes don't attack living tissue. He must have some other internal injury or having an adverse reaction to the fluids. We have to run tests."

"There's no time," I said. "If you can't treat him, I request you transport him to a facility that can."

"I'm afraid that's not possible."

I took a step closer, "Make it possible."

He tilted his nose at me. "I am in charge of this base and I have perfectly fine equipment and staff. The primitive shall stay. I'll figure out the appropriate treatment in due course. Now, kindly leave me to my work."

Aizah grabbed his smock and pulled his head down to her level. "He's not injured; he's *sick*. New medical term; learn it."

He struggled to free himself from her armored grip and she let him go at precisely the right moment. He toppled into a tray, scattering utensils with a crash.

"Oops," she said.

Diago's eyes were as wide as his grin. Aizah stood over the healer with a fist on her hip. She offered a hand to help him up, with the weapon attached to her wrist pointed directly at his nose. He hesitated to take her offer.

"Transport him now, or do I tell Athena why a very important citizen died because a ground-sucking healer refused a transport request?"

"You are being most unreasonable."

She tapped her open helmet and a com window came up. "Tell you what; why don't you complain to her directly and save time?"

His face paled as he waved her off. She took one step back, enough for the techs to rush in and help the healer to his feet. He straightened his smock. "Just what does her Excellency suggest I do?"

"Prep Jordan for transport to *Olympus*," I said. "Now."

"Use my only suspension chamber on this primitive?" he said.

"Where are you from, Healer?" Aaron asked. "Payahdon?"

He was shocked at the reference to the enemy's capital. "Certainly not. I am Senior Healer to the Phut High Council. I am on loan during this time of deep distress."

"That explains it." Aaron griped. "Primitives aren't welcome in your country."

"Who are you people?" he demanded.

"You follow current events?" Aaron inquired. "Embassies getting overrun? Royals rescued? Enemy capitals blowing up?"

The healer looked at me for the first time and did a double-take. "You're the Guardian who rescued the Princess and—" He looked at Jordan with dawning recognition, mouthing the Phutian equivalent of Anak. "He's the primitive who fell from the sky?"

"Correct," I said.

"The one everyone thinks might be from the future?"

"You're catching up," Diago said.

"Athena is counting on his knowledge of the future to turn this war around." I pressed my armored finger against the man's collarbone. "Now, are you going to prep Jordan for suspension or would you rather spend the rest of your life recharging heal sticks?"

"In a swamp," Aizah added.

"By hand," Aaron said.

"You heard them," the healer blustered. "Get this civilian prepped for suspension."

The techs scrambled. The screens slid aside and the transfer chamber walked through the gap.

"What's it doing on legs?" Aaron asked.

A tech grunted as they jostled it into position next to Jordan's bed. "Too heavy for just the floaters."

Jordan woke up and noticed the chamber as it lowered down even with his bed. He seemed to swallow back fear. Aizah wiped his face with a cloth and said something to him in Engel. I still struggled with the ancient dialect.

I motioned the rest of my team back so Jordan only had one person in view. Aizah talked to him compassionately as the techs went about their work.

"What is she saying?" I asked.

"She's explaining the suspension process," Aaron said. "I think."

"He doesn't seem too excited about it," Diago remarked.

"Would you be?" I asked.

"Have you been through it?"

"Once," I replied. "Not something I'd care to repeat."

Jordan became agitated, while Aizah soothed him. He reached for the open edges of the chamber and she snapped at him. He quieted and obediently kept his hands inside.

"Woman's touch," Aaron smiled. "Ten men couldn't have done that."

"I wish that healer had tried," Diago said. "Jordan's got excellent aim."

Jordan said something that included Suri's name. Aizah took his hand and spoke rapidly.

"He's asking about Suri now," Aaron said to me.

"I gathered that much."

"Suspension fluids are starting," Diago said. "This is where it gets cold, right?"

Jordan gripped her hand and whispered desperately. Aizah bent down to hear him better. She nodded and answered him.

"What's going on?" I asked. "What's he want?"

Aaron looked back and forth between Jordan and us. "No clue, Chief."

Aizah nodded solemnly and said something with finality, which Jordan seemed to accept. He let her hand go and lay still. She gently pressed his arm down and fussed with the sheet while she talked. Jordan had trouble responding. His body turned blue.

"I just remembered something," I said.

"What's that, Chief?"

"Diago, do you still have Jordan's backpack?"

"Yeah." He pulled it out from his weather cape.

I took it and approached the suspension chamber. The healer knew better than to warn me back. I unzipped the backpack and showed Jordan its contents. Then I put the backpack in the personal effects locker on the outside of the chamber. I pulled the drawing Jordan had done of his wife and daughter and placed it next to his head. He struggled to turn so he could see it. His neck cricked. I cringed, remembering how much it had hurt when I'd done it.

He strained to speak, his breath puffing onto the crystal side of the chamber. "Thank you," he croaked in my language.

"You're welcome," I said in Engel and touched his shoulder. He probably couldn't feel it but I felt compelled to try. He had a long path ahead of him. I prayed Athena would know what to do to save him.

Aizah gave him a Trahl kiss on the forehead, whispering something in his ear. The techs closed the lid. We stood vigil as the suspension process pulled him down into successive levels of near death. When the suspension process was complete, his body would contain less vitality than an acorn.

A commotion erupted on the far end of the tent. I spotted a flash of blonde hair race inside, followed by two civilians and an entourage of Mestrean Guardians in full battle armor trying to keep up without knocking stuff over.

"Stop giving me orders, Amon," Suri said. She skidded into the middle aisle, looking desperate. She swerved around one healing station and past the next, searching the faces of the wounded, cringing at those who didn't have faces.

Diago shouted and waved. Suri locked on him and bolted down the aisle, her hair sailing behind her sweating face. Healers and techs backed out of her way. Amon stumbled in her wake, babbling the whole time. Numu panted as he tried to keep up. To my amazement, the Mestrean Guardians trotted obediently in formation behind him, as if they were his private army. A new insignia was on their shoulder plates: a lion on a black background.

I flashed Ground Com about the situation. They advised caution. Things had changed in Mestre during my absence. The relations between the two ancient allies had become strained, partly due to the pair of royals racing toward me.

Suri spotted the suspension chamber and Jordan inside it. The healer extended his arm in greeting. "Your Highness, we are honored—"

She pushed him aside and pressed her face against the armored crystal. "Jordan! Jordan, can you hear me?"

"He can hear you," Aizah assured.

"He blinked his eyes," Suri said.

Numu and Amon approached. The Mestrean Guardians fanned out behind them, weapons charged. Aaron and Diago looked at me. I sent a message to their visors to stay calm but to keep their weapons ready.

"Good to see you're alive, Levi," Numu said with no trace of sincerity.

"You too, Ambassador."

He looked around the tent and then at the chamber. "What is that thing?"

"Suspension chamber," the healer said.

Numu took a step toward it and I politely blocked his path. "Keep away from the patient, sir"

Numu looked at the chamber, then assessed my glowing weapons. He held his ground, although sweat beaded his receding hairline. "Why is the chamber armored?"

"The suspension process reduces the inside temperature to near absolute cold," a tech explained. "It has to be armored to withstand the thermal stress."

Numu seemed nervous about something. "You Highness, we must go now."

"But Jordan—"

"He's perfectly fine. You must leave this good healer to his work."

"We have to get back to Mestre," Amon said. "The Ra is expecting us at court."

"So, go already," Suri said. "I'm staying."

"No, you're not."

That's sensitive, Aaron sent to my visor.

Amon grabbed Suri's arm and tried to pull her away. She resisted. Numu took her other arm. Aaron knew better than to interfere but Diago didn't. He rushed in and rounded on Amon with his fist. I grabbed him by the cape just before he connected with the back of the royal's head. I sent an alert to the other Guardians waiting by the Retriever. Aaron relieved Diago of his weapons and put him in a controlled hold with one arm around his chest.

The Mestrean Guardians swarmed to get between Amon and us. Javan Guardians materialized around the Mestreans. Weapons came loose from leg holders.

"Stand down, sir," I said to my Mestrean counterpart.

"You are threatening His Highness," he said. "We will fire unless you lower your weapons."

"This is Javan territory," I said, fighting the adrenaline to stay focused. "We're in charge of their security."

"You're wrong."

"Lower your weapons!"

"We'll not yield!"

"What are you idiots doing?" Aizah yelled. She pointed at the readout panel on the suspension chamber. "Jordan is trying to wake up. You're killing him."

Suri shook Amon and Numu off.

"Brother," I said, "Last chance."

"Everybody, just stop!" Suri yelled. "And stop aiming those things at me."

The Mestrean Guardians obeyed instantly. I nodded at the Javan Guardians. We lowered our weapons.

"They weren't aiming at you," Diago grunted through Aaron's glove.

"Quiet, Diago," she said. To Amon's delight, she took his hand and faced us. "I thank you, Guardians of Javan, for saving my life. I and my Guardians will now withdraw. Numu, order them to sheath their weapons."

"Order your Guardians?" Aaron whispered.

"Quiet," I said.

Suri cast a final look at Jordan. She touched her hand to her chin in farewell and walked away.

"Not a moment too soon," Numu said, looking pointedly at me. "May our paths never cross again."

"Don't count on it," I said.

Numu barked at the Guardians. They jumped like kept dogs and hustled out of the tent. The Mestrean shuttle lifted off while the hatches were still closing.

"Suri's in danger," I said.

"Jordan made me promise to guard her," Aizah said.

"Do it."

"Can I go, too?" Diago asked.

I looked at Aizah and she shrugged. Diago grinned and she smacked his shoulder armor. "Do exactly what I say."

"No hitting the prince," I said.

"Unless it's absolutely necessary," Aaron said.

Aizah and Diago cloaked. Diago's face was still visible when he turned and ran down the aisle. His head bobbed like a floating specter.

"Diago!" Aizah's disembodied voice shouted. "Helmet!"

"Sorry," he said and his head vanished.

The healer finished checking Jordan's suspension chamber and confirmed that he was okay. I looked around the tent. The other healers went back to work on their wounded patients. Retrievers continued to land and off-load more.

"Something's wrong," I said.

"Numu was in a hurry to get out of here," Aaron said.

"You scanned him for covert transmissions?"

"A dozen times while we stood here." He pointed to the scanner hanging above my head disguised as a vitality booster. "Not a peep."

"He didn't like that Jordan was in an armored chamber."

"Anak, we're about to be attacked."

I brought Ground Com up on my visor. *Attack imminent. Divert remaining inbound Retriever flights to other healing encampments.*

We see no sign of enemy—

The link went dead.

"Guardians, protect!" I yelled.

The Retriever pilots extended their shielding over the tent, while the Guardians around the healing stations spread their personal shields over the patients and staff. Jordan's healer and his staff huddled under the suspension chamber. Aaron and I held onto its sides as the sky turned to flame.

Aaron merged his suit's shielding with mine, encapsulating Jordan's chamber and the civilians huddled beneath it. A fire storm of ordinance ripped through the clouds and plunged into the field. The Retrievers' shields took the first blast. They sank under the impacts, great hulls shuddering within inches of the fragile fabric of the tents. A few of the deadly fireballs slipped between the ships' shielding, tore through the tent, and rained upon our weaker personal shielding.

Aaron and I took a direct hit. My armor buckled from the blast. Jordan's chamber staggered on its mechanical legs. The ground melted under our boots. Our shields insulated the doctors under the chamber but offered no traction as the ground became bowl shaped. I slipped and banged my faceplate against the chamber's viewport. Jordan's frozen face stared blankly at mine, his eyes the color of slate.

Aaron grabbed my glove and helped me regain my footing. The deadly ordinance poured through the weak spot in the Retriever's shielding, pounding Jordan's chamber with relentless precision. My faceshield displays sounded a chorus of warnings as system indicators plunged toward failure. I couldn't expend power to cool my suit. I needed all of it to shield the civilians. Sweat beaded my face as my body baked. The ground shuddered and heaved. It felt as though the earth might swallow us. My helmet insulated most of the noise, but the concussions hammered me.

The Retrievers shifted their positions and sealed the weak spot, giving me a reprieve. Without their help, our suits would have given out long ago.

Then a Retriever blew up. A fifty-foot diameter of patients, healers, and Guardians disappeared in a terrifying pillar of flame. The Retriever directly above us buckled. Its primary shielding failed. Its wings curled in the heat and the port engine exploded. The pilot slipped his flaming ship out of formation and stubbornly swept the sky with defensive fire until it crashed into a hillside and tore apart in a spiral of smoke-laced flame. The orange sky opened up above us in a torrent, as if some malevolent god now seized his chance to rend Jordan from existence.

My suit strained to hold back the withering concussions. Five seconds to its failure. I shut off my life systems, devoting all the remaining energy to the preservation of Jordan and the civilians. The action bought them forty additional seconds of shielding. I held my breath.

Thirty seconds to failure, the bombardment intensified. My starved lungs twisted in agony. Aaron's glove slipped from mine. The flames, the chamber, the civilians blurred and darkness took me.

Something pounded my chest. Cool, sweet air flooded my mouth. I greedily drank it in. I felt the familiar jolt of a heal stick injection through my neck portal and the rush kicked me back to life. A tech knocked on my helmet visor. I couldn't turn my head.

His voice was muffled. "Lay still, sir. Your armor's resetting. I'll be back in ten."

The armored healer bounded up the side of a curved cliff in a single twenty-foot leap. Where had that cliff come from? Where were Jordan, Aaron, and the civilians?

One by one, my suit systems blinked back to life. Data filled my faceplate. The civilian's life signs, including Jordan's faint signature, scrolled positive. My armor was frozen in a sitting position. I was in a crater of fused glass, with acid smoke tingeing the air. The healer and techs leaned against Jordan's upright suspension chamber, holding portable breathing filters to their smudged faces.

Aaron was sprawled to my left. He popped his helmet open and I retracted mine. "We cut that one close," he coughed.

"Confirmed," I said. "You okay?"

"I will be, as soon as my suit joints power up. My nose itches and I can't lift my arm to scratch it."

My joint assists came to life at the same time his did. Aaron jumped to his feet, furiously scratching his nose. I stretched to see above the lip of the crater and got an ankle-high view of what was left of the encampment. A five-hundred person, fully-equipped healing station had been reduced to twisted supports and smoking cables. Evenly spaced circles of grass where Guardian shielding had held dotted the enclosure, set amid a cratered field of ash and smoke. Each circle contained a healing station, healer, techs, and their patients. The civilians struggled to their feet and attended the others, ignoring their own injuries.

A lone fire suppression ship hovered above the encampment. When a piece of equipment burst into flames, the ship aimed its nozzle and fired a short burst of foam, extinguishing the blaze. Around the perimeter of the encampment lay the smoldering ribs of fallen Retrievers. An incoming supply ship made an approach for landing.

Aaron and I climbed out of the crater. At the top, Aaron flicked a burning ember off my shoulder plate. "That bombardment came from space."

"They were aiming at Jordan," I said.

"You're basing that on ending up in the deepest crater formed by fifty-one direct hits."

"Forty-nine," I said.

"You blacked out."

The supply ship drew closer. Six metallic legs extended. Hull lights shifted from hover-blue to landing-orange.

"How'd they target him?" Aaron asked. "He was shielded from surveillance ever since we bugged him out of Tevleh."

"Somebody provided the coordinates."

"Numu."

I nodded. "But he didn't stay long enough to be certain we didn't move him. Somebody else provided real time status up to the moment of bombardment." I remembered Numu's firm grip on my arm. "He put a bug on my armor."

"Anak, it's probably broadcasting again now that your suit is powered up."

He hand signed to me. *And listening to everything you say, Chief.*

I ejected from my armor. *Load my armor on the supply ship. Evacuate the crew and tell them to send it straight for* Olympus. *If my armor is being tracked, it will become a target. Load Jordan on the fire ship and go put out a fire somewhere. Stay silent until* Olympus *can get to you."*

Where are you going?

I pointed at the sky.

You'll need a fast ship.

Confirmed.

Don't see any, Chief. Whatever will you do?

Improvise.

I love improvising. What do you need?

The Dart file you took from Ground Com.

Don't know what you're talking about.

The file suddenly uploaded into my ocular. I grabbed spare armor, suited up, and spotted a gleaming hover car parked under an undamaged storage canopy. A Phutian Shield of State graced its tail. The healer who'd worked on Jordan was strapping himself in. My armor's assembler bots swarmed above my helmet.

"Is this your car?" I asked the healer.

"Yes, why?"

"May I borrow it for a couple of hours?"

"Why on earth—"

I pulled him out. "I'll take that as a yes."

I sent assemblers straight into the gleaming hood. The car imploded into a spinning ball of vaporized molecules. It hovered over the grass like a miniature solar system. I accessed Aaron's file and pulled up the necessary templates to turn the swirling mess into a Dart.

"That was a gift from the Phutian Council," the healer cried.

"Really?" I said, frowning at the readout of compounds from the dissolved car. "They didn't spend much on it."

The spinning mass swirled and jerked as dissolved tech, supplies, munitions, and nearby minerals mixed in. A Dart took shape. I retracted the canopy and jumped in as the tail fins solidified.

I touched my chin to the purple-faced healer. "I'll arrange for a replacement. Better get clear of this area, sir."

"That's what I was trying to do before you—"

I cloaked and rocketed into the clouds. The sky darkened

and flooded with stars. I kept communications off and anxiously watched as Aaron launched in the fire ship with Jordan's chamber onboard. Aaron cleared the ruined valley and flew northeast as if responding to a fire from a wild shot during the earlier attack. The crew-less supply ship with my bugged armor onboard raced straight for *Olympus*, remotely flown by the pilot hiding in the hills with the rest of her crew and the evacuated medical staff. I prayed our attackers would take the bait, shoot the supply ship, and reveal their location. My scanners showed nothing but stars and the smooth face of the crescent moon.

My Dart flashed an incoming weapons alert. Hundreds of plasma fireballs suddenly appeared above my canopy, raining straight at me. I winged over and punched the engines. One sliced my tail. I cartwheeled across the sky, twisting contrails before I brought the slim craft back under control.

"Voice response," I ordered the Dart. The ship was shaking too much to read the displays. "Where did that fire come from?"

"I don't know, darling. The attacker remains totally shielded."

Aaron had apparently customized the Dart's design to his personal preferences. "Next time, I'm drawing my own schematics."

I barely dodged a pair of fireballs by corkscrewing between them. The plunging fire converged as they dropped through clouds.

"Enemy fire is locking on the supply ship," the voice response advised.

"Where did it come from?"

"How should I know? I can't even get a gravity signature."

Minutes later, the supply ship was pulverized in a pillar of flame. What was left of the smoking hulk plowed into a mountain.

Rapid shots crisscrossed my ship's nose. I rolled out and took damage on a wing. Another wave of fireballs appeared as if crossing over an invisible threshold. They were so spread apart it was impossible to determine their origin. Every Retreiver in the vicinity of the ruined healing station became a target. The Retriever I'd sent back to the front—loaded with wounded—took multiple hits. Its shields succumbed and the ship plunged out of control, straight into a Guardian base.

A sickening fireball pillared from the center of the camp. The attacker rained additional hits on the base as if to be certain the target didn't survive. Hundreds of Guardian life signs vanished from my status display. Another fusillade rained to the Earth. These targeted all fire ships, including Aaron's hiding in a canyon.

Olympus diverted fighters to intercept. The nimble craft desperately shot at the incoming barrage as it swept across the length of the canyon. The deep rock walls exploded.

Aaron's life sign held steady. He flew the bulky ship though the canyon, barely ahead of the collapsing rock.

Ground Com broadcasted to all those listening that there was an enormous cloaking shield stretching hundreds of miles across the sky directly above Javan. They'd analyzed the complicated patterns of incoming fire and projected a possible location for the attacker. *Valhalla* and *Olympus* launched long-range air-to-space missiles at the shielding. Silent explosions mushroomed green and purple, outlining the sweeping oval of the immense barrier covering a third of the sky. Ground Com reported that the bombardment was ineffective.

Aaron's fire ship fled the canyon, escorted by a dozen of *Olympus'* fighters. All pretenses of concealment were over now. He flew straight for the Battle Mountain. One by one, the fighters sacrificed themselves, desperate to protect the tiny ship and its precious cargo. Jordan and Aaron were in peril and I was nowhere near the action. I needed a means to penetrate that shield and take out those weapons. Suddenly, I knew where I could find one.

I fled the shield and flew west, hopefully too small to be considered an important target. I arrested my forward motion over the Atlantic and watched the coastline south of the port city of Baskra. As I hoped, the night sky lit up and a slender shape hurtled into the sky. I matched velocities to intercept. The rocket's momentum from the initial ground cannon launch deteriorated.

I jettisoned my Dart and fired my suit's propulsion, aiming for the long hull midship. The air scoops opened on the side of the rocket to initiate internal propulsion. In five seconds, the onboard harvesters would suck in enough hydrogen molecules to manufacture propellant and ignite her engines.

The graceful rocket hull filled my faceshield. I grappled its side and cocooned my suit's shielding against the hull. The massive engines ignited. My teeth rattled as the ship ripped skyward. My suit's scanners indicated the craft was automated, devoid of crew. It angled and continued to climb, aiming toward the quadrant where *Valhalla's* missiles continued to hit.

Suddenly, my body felt like it was electrified. I gripped the insides of my armor gloves as the sensation plunged into my chest and shot out my toes. I was being flown through the shield.

When the sensation faded, I looked up past the nose cone. Where it had been empty space before now floated the massive hull of an ancient ship. My suit's scanners ran an analysis and chirped a match from an earlier mission. It was the other half of the starship hull Aaron and I had destroyed over Payahdon.

My borrowed rocket swept along the curved horizon of the ruddy colored hull. Blast holes testified to the pounding the mighty ship had endured before she'd broken in two and died. Fusing torches flickered from within the gutted interior. Thousands of Atlantean workers and their assembly ships buzzed about the titan with orchestrated purpose. The sun flared into view as my borrowed rocket cruised to the day side of the hull. Earth spread beyond her. Somewhere behind the curve of the hull, enemy fire hurtled through the rippling shielding, arching down into the atmosphere.

My oculars zoomed in on their target. Aaron flew a desperate zigzag course, trying to reach the safety of *Olympus.* Heavy fighters sprayed interceptor gunfire. A plasma shot got through and plunged straight for the nose of Aaron's craft. A Javan pilot winged over and stopped the hit with his fighter, vanishing in a blistering fireball.

"Come on, you piece of *drek*," I fumed at my sluggish rocket. "Get me in this fight."

The enemy cannons finally came into view, a long sweeping platform floating outside the ancient hull, attached by umbilical cords to hundreds of floating ammunition modules. Ephraim soldiers clustered about the throbbing guns.

My heart hammered. Next to the guns, within a specially shielded bubble, floated the strange alien gun I'd found in the nose section of this ancient ship. It was being maneuvered onto a central spot on the platform. Ground Com feared this weapon so much that on an earlier mission I'd been ordered to destroy it instead of salvage it. When I'd tried to blow up, it had reassembled itself, even after crashing into the heart of Payahdon. We never knew what it was capable of doing. Ancient writings were full of dire warnings but lean on specifics. Now Atlantis planned to use it on the Eastern Alliance.

I set my jaw. I knew from experience I couldn't destroy it but I sure as Anak would keep it from being fired.

I sent bots out across the hull of my borrowed rocket, found the proper penetration points and sent them burrowing. They flew to their assigned posts and took control of the flight systems. The automated supply rocket turned on my command. It vectored toward the platform, straight for the alien weapon. By the time anybody reacted, my improvised battering ram was too close to stop. All the guns were pointing the wrong way.

I clung to the supply rocket until I was certain my aim was right, then ejected, launching myself toward the ancient hull. Ephraim raced to get clear as the rocket plowed into the cannon array. Umbilical cords ripped loose from the munitions supply modules. The spurting hoses erupted and the modules exploded. The platform pinwheeled through the shielding, taking the alien gun with it.

Ground Com concentrated fire on the suddenly visible target and pounded what was left of the platform into oblivion. The alien weapon spun free of its bubble and tumbled into the atmosphere. I prayed Ground Com would recover it before Atlantis did.

My suit propulsion gave out but I was too far away to grapple the hull. A second weapons platform came into view as it opened fire. I watched helplessly as Jordan's ship and escorts came under heavy bombardment, still too far from the safety of *Olympus.* Atlantean fighters dove on the fire ship, using the attack for cover.

Olympus used its long-range guns with incredible precision to slice the enemy to pieces. One survivor broke through and peppered the fleeing fire ship before *Olympus* took it out. Aaron's ship trailed smoke, then its tail exploded. The momentum of my suit carried me into the hull as Jordan's ship crashed somewhere in the mountains of Magog.

I squelched my fury and focused on my mission. Jordan was in a heavily armored chamber. He might still be alive. I had to take out this installation if he was going to stay that way and find a way to disable the shielding so Ground Com could mount an effective attack on the enemy ship.

I grappled through the blast hole deep into the center of the ancient hull. My suit switched to gravity imaging. I shuddered at the sight. Within the hull swirled a helix of new construction. The materials were conventional: connected supply rocket hulls linked by umbilical passage tubes and cross-connected by a spider work of struts and trusses. The design was alien.

The hull rotated slowly on its axis, while the helix corkscrewed around me. My suit worked overtime cataloguing advanced tech finds. The Western Confederacy of Atlantis had outdone itself. The capabilities of this ship exceeded Ground Com's wildest dreams.

My suit finished its preliminary analysis of the enormous propulsion system being repaired in the stern of the hull. The impossible readout blurred as I focused on the exhaust cowlings, struggling with the impossible reality of their thousand-foot diameter.

"Anak," I whispered, "they built a star drive."

My suit chirped again. It had found the command and control center of the ship, a saucer six-hundred feet in diameter anchored to the forward section of the ancient hull. It was sheathed in rare orichalcum, a nearly indestructible metal not native to Earth. According to Nephillim legend, orichalcum had shielded the ancient starships of the First Landing. Their star drive engines had been scuttled and the technology erased to prevent Nephillim exiles from ever returning home.

I grappled through the struts and girders, fighting the vertigo induced by the swirling lines of linked supply rockets. Lights flickered from a metropolis of portholes. My suit scanners worked at mapping the living quarters, animal and horticulture zones, munitions stores, and manufacturing pods. They estimated the astonishing complex could sustain ten thousand souls in deep space for thirty decades. A thousand military personnel had already moved in but the civilian quarters were mostly empty. The munitions hold warehoused mobile armor, aircraft, and even a fleet of naval vessels.

Infantry weapons were stocked, everything from civilian pacification to heavy assault, sufficient to equip legions. Atlantis planned a long voyage and was going to pick a fight when they got there. I didn't have time to figure out why.

I grappled toward the command and control sphere. It came fully into view, a blood-red saucer buried in the woven tangle of gray girders thrown in sharp relief by the swiftly moving sun. A pair of fighters spotted me and dove, slicing through the maze of struts and rocket hulls. Their shots lanced the tangled construction. Debris whipped off my armor. The saucer loomed large, filling my faceshield. Stuff blew up behind my heels in rapid succession.

I loosed my bots. They raced into the hull and scanned the interior. If Aaron and Jordan had survived, Athena would need time to reach them.

My scanners identified the nerve center of the ship. Maybe I could disable the shielding systems from somewhere in here. Then Ground Com would have a chance to even up this battle.

I shot a grappler where my scanners said to. Incoming fire flared past my body, melting holes through struts and knocking robotic crawlers off their perches. I launched a dissolver charge into the curved hull of the enormous saucer. The charge detonated. A section of the hull cracked. I swung my feet around and hit the mottling surface boots first. A perfect circle of degraded metal cratered.

I fired my grapple into the breach and retracted through a maelstrom of escaping air and debris, then sealed the breach with one glove while dangling from the end of my other line. I dropped to the deck, my grapplers whipping across the dusty metal back into my armored wrist seals.

Smoke and dust swirled through the cavernous room. Alarms shrieked and emergency lights flashed in blurry halos. I had knocked out the power, thanks to my abrupt arrival.

The chamber re-pressurized. Data scrolled down my faceshield. Twelve-foot Ephraim officers were slumped in their harnesses before damaged displays. They had survived my intrusion and decompression but seemed disinterested in my presence. Others were strapped in front of flickering weapon consoles. Feeder tubes dangled from the ceiling into transfer clay stuck to their necks.

Chemicals dripped through the tubes.

My bots continued to scan the saucer. Life signs diminished the deeper they went into the heart of the enormous craft. Then the bots reached the center and chirped excitedly. They had found twelve human females. Ten were in hibernation, while two were in the process of being reanimated. By whom, I couldn't determine. There were no other life signs coming from the chamber. Being human meant they were hostages.

As the pair of women reached consciousness, their emotion markers jumped from passive to terrified. Suddenly, there were only eleven females.

I crawled past the closest giant. His yellowed eyes followed my movement before returning to his useless console. His erratic targeting display showed the lush hills of Javan, with the peak of *Olympus* centered in a fire-box solution. That he apparently lacked power to do anything about it stayed his wrinkled hand from shooting.

I slinked past other stations. The officers were alive but too weak to get out of their seats. One made what appeared to be a heroic effort to slide his hand over to a control and silence the alarms. The rest of them sat motionless, flickering displays illuminating their ashen faces. Their lips moved silently as they muttered into hovering coms. This was the brilliant force that had orchestrated the bombardment on the healing station?

I crossed the room and reached an exit portal. My roving bots warned that squads of armed and much more energetic Ephraim marines were on their way. The sliding doors were stuck half open, caught on a body strewn across the threshold.

I tossed a dozen dissolvers into the air and the consoles dissolved. The Ephraim stared at the spaces where the consoles had been and continued to mutter orders. The corridor beyond was dim and stank of garbage. Steam issued from a fractured pipe and bodies lay scattered along the deck. Some were breathing; most were not.

I grappled as fast as I could, racing down the curving corridor past flickering lights and rotting corpses.

"Lead, Ground Com."

It took half a second to realize Ground Com was talking to me.

I chinned the com and brought up a clear image of a Ground Com tech. The shields must be down.

"Ground Com, Lead"

"Mer has a firing solution on the enemy ship. Evacuate immediately."

"Tell them to hold fire," I panted as I alternated grapples down the curving corridor. "There are human hostages onboard."

"They know that, Lead. The Elder Council is ordering us to fire anyway. You must withdraw."

"You tell those overgrown Nephillim fossils to hold fire!" I shouted. "Give me time to rescue them."

Ephraim marines burst into the corridor and opened fire. I dissolved the floor and grappled through tangled piping almost as fast as my scanners could plot a path. The giant grunts raced along the corridor above me and shot into the floor. Blasts punctured behind my boots in rapid succession. My suit scanner got a clearer readout of the eleven women. One was a child six decades old. The rest were adults in their twentieth to thirtieth decade.

Military data suddenly scrolled beside one female outline. It was Jarell, a Javan Guardian, Special Missions class. I knew all the Special Mission Guardians. Her last assignment had been with me at the Javan Embassy in Atlantis, as an escorting double for the Princess Suri. When our mission in Payahdon had fallen apart, she and the other Guardian doubles had enabled me to extract the Royals and Jordan to safety by drawing enemy fire away from my air car. Ground Com had listed her as LDO, lost during operations. Anak if I was going to lose her to some eager missile-launching Nephillim.

Mechanized snipers crawled out of side chambers and swept the narrow pipeway. I ripped my weapon rods off my legs, slapped them on my forearms, and alternately fired with my free hand while grappling with the other.

"Advise you to get out of there, sir."

I recognized the voice and broke protocol. "Ten minutes, Joshua, and I can destroy this ship's systems from within and rescue the civilians. Then Odin can pound the ship to scrap metal to his heart's content. Ten minutes, that's all I need. You tell him that."

"Odin says it's your funeral pyre."

I dodged a blast coming through the pipes and swung around a hard corner. "Then good luck explaining to Athena why eleven Javans died, including an LDO."

I zapped him Jarell's data. There was a second of silence as I grappled closer to my goal.

"Delay execution of his fire command, Joshua. Do it for Jarell."

"I'm gonna be in a raft load of trouble for this, sir."

"Tell Odin you can't get a targeting solution. Blame it on sunspots. Be creative."

"I'll see what I can do, sir. Good luck."

"Understood. Lead listening."

"Ground Com listening."

I raced for the heart of the saucer. The corridor tilted and rocked. One minute I was grappling the ceiling, the next a wall. My scanners displayed the mayhem outside. The starship was being pounded by missiles rising out of the hydrosphere like shimmering geysers. Their sleek fins bore images of the four stars of Mer.

"Thanks for waiting, Odin," I groused.

My scanners diagnosed the attack. The starship's propulsion system was taking concentrated fire. Large sections of the stern and the unfinished engine cowlings caved away from the ancient hull. They pinwheeled through fleeing construction tugs. The tiny vessels exploded in a staccato of flashes against the black of space. Some incoming missiles deflected defensive fire and impacted closer to the bow; some penetrated and exploded with devastating effects.

Atmospheric alarms blared. Containment doors dropped in rapid succession, nipping at my heels as I grappled for my life. Minutes before I reached the entrance, my scanners swept the chamber holding the human hostages. I fired a spread of restrainer gel through the opening and dove into the room. A curved projection of a vast lake's shore reflected the late afternoon light from twin suns. Trees similar to willows swayed in a breeze.

The portal was swallowed by the projection, replaced by a

verdant valley that stretched miles to the foot of a distant forest. Artistically arranged along the shore were the furnishings of an opulent bedchamber. A creature dropped from one of the tree limbs. It had no appendages, just a long sinuous body covered in scales. It propelled itself across the mossy ground in an undulating motion. A thin red tongue with a forked tip darted rhythmically from its lipless mouth. It slithered toward me, then through me as if I was a shadow. The projected creature disappeared into the grass. Whatever it represented, I'd never seen anything like it.

I ignored my senses and relied on gravity imaging. A young girl approximately six decades old was hiding inside a storage compartment attached to a floating bed. I tried the door and opened it carefully. She was curled up at the far end, wearing a flimsy gown and crying, her tear-stained cheeks framed by disheveled blonde curls. Disconnected hibernation tubes hung from her neck.

"Is she gone?" she sobbed.

I motioned her to remain quiet and stay put.

The room shuddered from the impact of a distant missile. The projection faltered and died, revealing a plain curved room with furnishings arranged in its center. A circular bank of twelve hibernation chambers stood where the lake had once been. One was empty; the remaining were occupied by young women between the ages of thirteen to twenty-five decades. One chamber was damaged. A section of the curved crystal armor had shattered, leaving the occupant exposed. She was thawed but unconscious. There was no indication of the missing life sign I'd scanned earlier.

I recognized Guardian Jarell from her face tattoo and armor. That was the only way I could tell her from the others. Each woman was slender and in good shape. All had blonde hair and looked like Princess Suri.

The back of my neck crawled with unease. I remembered the meeting in Payahdon with the new queen. Babla had looked like Suri, too. Or, rather, Suri and all these women looked like Babla. Even the little girl resembled a younger version of the queen.

I kept my weapon ready and ran to the damaged hibernation tube. The design was an exact copy of Javan technology and the controls were security coded. The unconscious woman in it was dying. I undid the connections from her neck and injected her with a heal stick.

The room shook violently. Debris fluttered from the ceiling. Odin's missiles were getting closer.

I defeated the security locks on the control panel and activated the regeneration sequence. Each tube warmed and tilted upright. The bodies slid out. As fast as they cleared their chambers, I pushed military-grade heal sticks into their slim necks. They thrashed into hyper-consciousness.

I was gentler with the civilian from the damaged tube. She vomited on the deck. Once I was certain she suffered no internal injuries, I sedated and restrained her for carrying.

The little girl crawled out of the storage compartment. "Mommy!"

One of the women sat up and felt around. "Sophia!"

The girl ran into her arms. The woman hugged her fiercely, weeping and kissing the girl's tangled hair.

Jarell pulled herself to her feet and saluted me weakly across her scarred armor. Atlantis apparently hadn't figured out how to separate Guardians from their armor yet.

"Glad to have you back, Guardian," I said.

"Glad to be back, sir. What's our situation?"

"Dire. You know the way to the Queen's shuttle hanger?"

The deck heaved. A horrible screech echoed from somewhere.

"Yes, sir. The Queen brought us in on the shuttle."

I handed her one of my weapon rods, while I kept the other pointed at the door to the shielded chamber. "Any idea what made that noise?"

"No sir."

As if in answer to my query, a hidden panel in a wall swung open. A mottled hand with skeletal fingers gripped the panel's edge. Two-inch nails oozed yellow pus. A gold ring with a diamond inlaid image of a ten-headed dragon set in a royal wreath dangled from a clawed finger, held in place only by the thickness of a gnarled knuckle. The hand shoved the panel completely open. Out from the shadow crawled a hideous creature faintly resembling a human.

Flesh hung from its limbs like rags on swaying rope. It wore the tattered remains of a low-cut red gown, slit down one side to reveal deformed, vein-riddled thighs the size of my wrist.

The civilians screamed and shrank back.

"Is that the Queen?" I asked.

"I think so," Jarell said. "She didn't look that bad before."

An understatement, to be certain. What had once been a vivacious teenager only months earlier had deteriorated into a crawling corpse. Yellow-pocked eyes studied us. Babla's mouth sucked in strands of her unkempt hair. Her shriveled chest heaved desperately with each wheeze.

I maxed up the power setting on my weapons rod. "Get the civilians to the shuttle."

Jarell ushered the women out the portal behind me, while Babla bleated pitifully after them. She lurched toward me and I fired a stun round, causing her to collapse face first. Incredibly, she pushed herself to her feet and lunged again, her claws outstretched like two spiders.

"Don't let her touch you!" the little girl screamed.

I aimed point-blank at Babla's ruined face. She dropped to her knees, waving claws past her milky eyes. "Don't hurt me," she gasped.

"Guardian Jarell, are the civilians clear of this room?" I asked over my shoulder.

"Clear, sir."

I backed toward the exit, keeping the ruined queen at bay with my weapon. Despair creased her face. When I reached the exit, I grabbed the edge of the hatch. Babla's face screwed up in desperation. She charged me with astonishing speed, but I slammed the transparent hatch shut. She pushed back with little effect while the hatch sucked against the armored seals.

She pounded the clear door, her sobs muffled by the heavy material. Blood and pus smeared the armored crystal, blurring my view of her emaciated face. The women huddled on the far side of the corridor, and Jarell looked as shaken as they did.

"Keep them moving, Guardian," I said quietly.

"Yes sir. Sorry, sir." She motioned the civilians down a spiral corridor.

The hull shuddered. I steadied myself while Babla's bloodied frame bounced against the hatch. Her face smacked a spot between my gloves. "Don't leave me," she cried.

I studied her ruined bloodshot eyes. There was no hatred in them.

"Lead, Ground Com."

I was being hailed. I chinned my helmet com. "What happened to those ten minutes you were going to get me?"

"Are you clear yet? Say yes."

"Negative. I have the Queen in custody. Attempting her evacuation."

An abort signal just about pushed my eyeballs out of my sockets. I blinked and chinned the com again. "What did you do that for?"

"I didn't, command did."

"Put Athena on."

"She's not here."

"Where is she?"

"On a mission and monitoring the operation from a cloaked position."

She had to be hunting for Jordan and Aaron. "Status of mission?"

"Classified."

"Status, Joshua."

"The enemy might be monitoring."

"Now!"

"Fire ship destroyed," he blurted. "Civilian and Guardian are LDO. I'm sorry, sir."

Cracks spidered between my boots and up the bulkhead. The Queen of Atlantis, the woman responsible for Jordan and Aaron being missing or dead sagged beneath my glare. Bits of ceiling rained down on her ruined head. I wanted to open the hatch and separate that from her neck, but the thought dissolved as fast as it formed. Irrational compassion flooded me.

"Odin just launched some really big missiles, sir. Incoming on your position in three minutes."

I looked deep into Babla's face. She regarded me with resignation. Her litany of reputed deeds faded from my mind. Something told me she wasn't responsible for the horrors that had been unleashed upon my country and comrades. That certainty held its ground despite all the evidence I mustered against it. I couldn't shake its truth because the certainty didn't originate within me.

I knew of Babla's subterfuge from Aaron's account of their ill-fated encounter in the throne room of Payahdon, but this was no performance meant to entrap me. Her resignation to fate was real. I could see it in her shaking shoulders and sunken face. It wasn't fear of death that drove her to such a pitiable expression; it was shame. I was being counseled by a presence beyond this reality.

A sudden memory of scripture manifested to argue in her defense. *We do not fight against each other. We fight against spirits seeking our mutual enslavement and ruin.*

Babla had been a slave to something or someone, but she wasn't any longer. The tyrant appeared to have abandoned her. She was a broken soul, in need of mercy, no matter how ill deserved.

My jaw clenched. I came to a decision. "Protect all," I said and reached for the hatch release.

The inside of the chamber exploded. Babla's screaming face vanished amid the flames. Cracks spread across the portal's smoked swirling surface. I staggered back from the inferno, my scanner mercilessly detailing her agonizing death.

The women and I launched into space in the Royal shuttle and raced from the raging battle. The tugs and work crews defending the crippled starship allowed us to flee between their ranks, perhaps thinking Her Highness was aboard our craft. I kept my com silent and prayed for the Creator to preserve the illusion. We even had a brief escort from two Atlantean fighters before a pair of missiles from Earth destroyed them with Nephillim precision.

Secondary explosions rocked our transport as heavy artillery clawed through the thick First Age hull of the ancient starship, spewing fountains of spinning metal. The civilians cried out each time our shuttle was hit by debris. The hull spun and rocked. Our unused com went dead. Jarell did an expert job helping to control the transport, shutting down the failing systems before they ruptured. On a fraction of thrust power, deaf and nearly blind, our shuttle neared the enormous barrier that cloaked the starship. It was a phantom of its former strength.

I chanced a final look back at the disintegrating ship. It took multiple hits across the length of its cratered beam and broke into enormous pieces. I prayed a Retriever was on its way and set the controls to auto-fly, then motioned Jarell to assist with the civilians. Three would need extra protection in the event we were forced to land without any help.

Jarell and I took off our armor. Jarell let out the size of hers and suited up the girl and her mom inside, taking care to remove her weapon systems from the helmet. The third civilian was the woman from the damaged hibernation tube. My med scanner told me her body was deteriorating despite the heal stick I'd used on her. I made a mental note to get her to *Olympus* as soon as we landed.

We strapped the other civilians into the giant-sized seats and bunched padding around them. One of the women looked at me as I snugged her shoulder straps tight. "Are we going to make it?"

"We're clear of the fighting," I said. "A Retriever will find us and carry us home."

"Is that dangerous?"

"Routine. The ride is pretty dull, to be honest."

What was left of the ancient starship erupted, sending a ring of searing heat and debris across space. The blast boiled toward us. Jarell and I lashed ourselves to the deck. Brilliant light outlined the portholes.

Jarell attempted a grin. "So much for dull, sir."

The hull lurched and flipped. My lashings snapped. A bulkhead girder ripped free and spun into my face.

CHAPTER THREE

JORDAN

A long pool stretched to the foot of a man-made mountain, while a river thundered down its stepped flanks, plunging through wisps of cloud. I was carried to the summit by a giant child into a blurry garden. She danced across wet stone. Blonde hair, deer eyes, glittering silks, and smudged feet. With a skip and a twirl, her enormous cupid face orbited mine. A large red jewel shimmered between her eyes, hanging too low from a headband that was too large. She pushed the fiery jewel back above her soft eyebrows.

She took me deep into the garden. Her laughter echoed off a stone roof shading the summit. A square spring frothed at the peak's heart. I was flung high above cellophane-leaf trees. As I fell, another voice whispered, "Tell them to drink and live."

I landed in the giant girl's palm. She cradled me and placed me in a hole, then took off her jewel and laid it beside me. A stone slid across the hole, hiding her face, while her voice echoed, "Jordan, wake up!"

I tried to push the stone off but my wrists were restrained by thick straps. It took a moment for the remnants of the dream to fade. There was no stone, just impenetrable darkness. I lay on cold metal. My eyes strained to see something. My lungs sucked in air as if they hadn't inflated in ages. Why did it hurt so much to breathe?

I fought back panic. The scent of verdant mold hung heavy in the damp air; that and the smell of someone in need of a bath.

A harsh *clack* and a bank of lights came on, blinking rapidly on a vertical wall beyond my feet. My toes were silhouetted against the rippling lights. A hot mound of clay clung to my bare chest with tubes protruding from it.

A gust of warm air whistled past my face, splashing droplets that stung my eyes. The rhythmic lights glowed through my hands and outlined the restraints on my wrists. Where could I possibly be?

A sliver of light split the wall to the left. A tall door opened slowly, as if caught in a breeze, revealing a brilliantly lit space beyond and casting new details on where I was. Bottles and strange devices clinked like wind chimes. Flexible tubes attached to the clay on my chest swayed above my head, where burning fluids entered my body. The straps kept me from grabbing the tubes and ripping them off. Thrashing about did nothing to dislodge them. It only made the liquid drip faster and my chest burn hotter.

The door bumped against something with a reverberant boom. It sounded like I was in a chamber the size of a gymnasium. I forced myself to calm down. Whoever had opened the door hadn't shown themselves. Maybe nobody had opened it.

Right, keep dreaming.

I practiced my slow breathing, straining to get a bead on the intruder, and tried to remember where I'd been before here. My memory streamed back in chunks: a hibernation chamber, Suri crying, a picture of Lisa and Sophie leaning beside my face, and Diago trying to take Amon's face apart.

Before this place, I'd been in a field hospital. Levi, Aaron, and Aizah had been there, and Suri, too. She and I had almost froze to death on a primeval Alpine glacier. That's where I'd become gravely ill. Aizah had told the doctors to freeze me to slow down the progress of an unknown disease. Then they'd shipped me to Javan, Levi's home country, for treatment. Aizah had assured me I was in good hands, among friends. Looks like I'd been mailed to the wrong address.

Maybe the enemy had overrun the field hospital after I'd zonked out. They could have hauled me off as a hostage. That would explain the restraints and the lack of a friendly reception party.

I tried the restraints again and they slid a bit. The straps were anchored in slots that ran the length of my body. I could bring my wrists almost even with my waist.

A faint shadow wiggled somewhere off to my right. It looked like a man strapped to another table. He met my stare and said something weary and plaintive, a cry for help, perhaps.

The door slammed shut, sinking the room back into darkness. My table vibrated in time to heavy footfalls and labored breathing, followed by a cough high above my feet, hard and violent.

The blinking lights fluttered as the individual approached me, revealing a humanoid shape of enormous proportions. It wavered and then let out a huge sneeze. A slimy mass sprayed my legs. The creature sniffed back leftovers and thudded sideways to my neighbor's table.

A narrow cone of light beamed down on the man's body, while I was left in the selfish relief of its shadow. At the edge of the light, two long arms swayed above much longer legs.

The man gaped up at our visitor, then pulled feebly at his restraints. His skin was cracked and covered with sores. A jellyfish cluster of tubes dangled above him, dripping similar fluids into a similar mound of clay stuck to his chest. He choked and coughed. A long rod with a wet cloth tied to the tip swung down like a crane and swabbed his face with one gruff stroke. I marveled at the enormous hand gripping it, the palm as wide as my chest. This was no Ephraim. This was a much larger being. Was this one of the Nephillim I'd heard so much about?

The titan kept to the shadows and circled to the far side of my companion's table, moving with surprising agility and speed. A disheveled mane hung about his ears. It gave him the appearance of a super-sized Einstein. When I craned my neck to follow his course, a three-foot face swiveled in my direction. Luminous eyes focused on me for one intense moment. Then he returned his attention to my companion.

Huge hands grasped the end of the table and the man struggled against his straps, crying words I couldn't understand. The table tipped with one swift movement and touched the floor with a splash.

What I'd thought was a floor was actually the surface of a small pool just larger than our beds. The giant submerged the table to the point where the man's face was above the water. He thrashed against his restraints with the panic of the condemned. The tubes filled with deep red fluid and spilled out over the clay on his chest, which melted and covered him like a coating of syrup. He screamed until the coating poured into his mouth. Bubbles ballooned slowly as his back convulsively arched. Then, to my amazement, his body began to shrink. Like a camera zooming out, he diminished into the center of the table. The restraints slid along the slots and followed his limbs as they thinned and shortened

The giant pushed the man completely underwater. Violent splashes and bubbles churned. Then the water quieted. One final gurgle and the giant lifted the table back to its original height. Where a man had once been, a dripping baby now lay. The giant undid the restraints and manhandled the infant in one hand. It cried pitifully. He tucked it under his arm like a miniature football and walked off.

The spotlight abruptly winked out. The door opened and then closed. I waited ten long seconds in the darkness before I struggled wildly against my restraints. The more I struggled, the tighter they became. My foot knocked something over at the end of my table. Things went crashing across the room.

The sliver of light at the doorway reappeared. Heavy footsteps hurried toward me. I thrashed to free myself, but to no avail. The same giant approached the end of my table. Its eyes glistened in the darkness. Large hands grasped the end of my table.

"Please, no," I begged.

Then the table dropped.

CHAPTER FOUR

LEVI

Consciousness invaded my brain. I reeled from the chemically induced surge. Exiled memories from a dozen centuries lashed from their dungeons. The chemical wave receded, depositing another layer of despair over their accusing claws. I was marooned within the corporeal once more, the permanent jailer of an unwanted past.

"Are you okay?" a woman's voice echoed somewhere. It sounded like Suri.

I couldn't answer as I became aware of my body. My jaw was broken and my neck had been snapped.

I endured the heal stick pins-and-knives sensation as fractures knitted and organs jerked to life. I must have been seriously injured for the process to take several seconds. I remembered the explosion and the shuttle and those I'd tried to protect.

I fought to stay awake. My eyelids were as heavy as blast doors but I cracked one open.

A blonde in open Guardian armor floated above me, holding the spent heal stick. She was the little girl's mother. This I discerned from the little blonde head snuggled against her chest. The devastation of twisted bulkheads and sparking wires extended behind the woman's worried face. Consoles and flotsam drifted freely about them.

The queen's shuttle had lost its onboard gravity and taken severe damage, but the hull still held. The mother seemed uncertain what to do for me. The right thing was never to touch the wounded during regeneration. Important instructions I couldn't even imply by shaking my head.

She drifted dangerously close. "Can you hear me?" she asked as she reached for my face.

My jaw reset before my neck fused. "Keep back," I gasped.

She jerked her hand away. The sudden movement sent her weightless body into a slow pinwheel motion while my neck healed. I ducked her passing legs and the hard armor encasing them.

"Sorry," she said as her frightened face orbited mine.

I sat up, grabbed her legs to arrest her motion. Her daughter peeked out from the suit's collar and grinned. "That was fun."

Guardian Jarell had fared better than me. Her injuries were relatively minor. I gave her a half dose to regenerate her ruptured kidney and crushed legs. She grimaced as the green fluid bloated her veins. I waited until her eyes opened. They were the same color as Suri's but tinged with unspoken experiences.

"Are you healed?" I asked.

"Yes, sir."

We checked the civilians. They'd safely ridden out the blast in the shuttle's shock seats. Some were awake. The woman wearing my armor was feverish and agitated. I gave her a soother spray through the med port in the heel plate. She calmed down and went back to sleep. Jarell and I inspected the rest of the ship and found it inoperable but airtight.

"How long were we out?" Jarell asked.

I retrieved my suit tech drifting near a torn beam and queried the main unit.

"Sixteen days," I said.

"How did we survive so long?"

"Are you trained for space?"

"Only boots-on-dirt missions, sir." She sighed. "Until now."

Not many Guardians volunteered for space. Too many fatalities.

I sniffed an unfamiliar residue encrusting a vent and scooped up some of it, which I played the scanner over.

"Anak," I muttered.

"What is it?" she asked.

Some of the civilians had removed their restraints. I motioned Jarell to follow me to the nose of the shuttle to stay out of earshot. I showed her the substance while the scanner detailed its analysis on my oculars.

"What is it, sir?"

"A new kind of hibernation gel."

I sent part of the data stream to her oculars. Her eyes darted across the projected verbiage as I scanned the twisted bulkheads to confirm the substance had covered the entire ship.

"The hull was filled with this material until a few hours ago." More details scrolled down. "Our bodies were infused with it. The gel is partly organic. It kept us at a lower vitality level and fed us minimal nutrients to prolong our survival until rescue arrived."

Jarell glanced at the empty portholes. "Nobody seems to be out there trying to rescue us. Why did we wake up?"

"The system must have reached its functional limit."

My scanner reverse-engineered the manufacturing process and my heart hammered in response. The gel had been made from slaughtered dwarves. Atlantis was the unwanted home of several dwarf tribes.

I thought about the tiny families struggling on the platform in Gomer during the evacuation, their children smaller than my hand. The Western Confederacy of Atlantis had murdered thousands of dwarves to manufacture the substance that had filled this hull. And we'd eaten it. I kept this horror from Jarell.

"Ground Com doesn't possess this technology, do they?" she asked.

I sent the elimination command to my scanner's memory. "They never will."

"Why?"

"It's better if you don't know, Guardian."

"I respectfully insist, sir."

I couldn't refuse. I showed her the summary before I deleted it.

She paled and closed her eyes. "Thank you, sir, that's enough."

I killed the transmission and finished the deletion. It took a moment for either of us to move.

"I'll go scan again for Retrievers," she whispered, then flew to the nearest porthole. Stars framed her undulating hair as she gripped the curved edge of the six-foot window.

I foraged through my helmet tech and found the com unit. I gave Jarell a moment to collect herself before I joined her. We had a lot to do and discuss.

"Any luck reaching Ground Com?" she asked.

"No, their channels are being jammed."

An expanding cloud of space debris glittered across the sea of stars. Millions of fragments, from bolts to bulkheads, rolled by and collided with each other. I zoomed in. Battered shuttles, cargo rockets, and worker tugs tumbled amid the turbulent debris. I wondered if any held survivors.

"It's going to take Ground Com a long time to find us," she stated.

"Let's narrow the odds. You remember studying about early electromagnetic wave transmitters?"

"Ancient communication devices used at the beginning of the Second Age?"

I nodded.

She managed a smile. "I was told you invented them."

"You've been around Aaron."

"We met a few times on the Acropolis." And she showed annoyance with that. "He talked about you almost as much as he talked about himself."

We set to work rigging an old-fashioned broadcast beacon from scavenged materials. I linked it to a small power unit in my helmet. It chirped to life, broadcasting a simple pattern that repeated a coded Javan distress signal, embedded within the Western Confederacy's phrase, "Praise to the Queen."

"Maybe that will get Ground Com's attention before we suffocate," I said.

She nodded out the porthole, at the curve of the Earth. "Or go splat."

I looked out also. The horizon rose perceptibly.

"Looks like splat's winning, sir."

"Going toward Earth is better than going away from it."

"You always this optimistic?"

"Have to be, Guardian. When you give up, you start dying."

We resealed the mother and daughter in Jarell's armor. I made sure the wounded civilian in my armor remained sedated, then briefed the other civilians about the situation. I was impressed with how bravely they took the news. They confirmed our decision that the mother, daughter, and wounded civilian should be protected with our armor instead of any of them. If we crashed, those three had a better chance of surviving the impact, thanks to the inertia dispersing technology in the armor. If there was no child or gravely wounded civilian, I would have decided who got the armor by drawing straws.

Jarell and I strapped the civilians back in their seats. I prayed the effort might save them from the impact, then glanced back at the porthole. Earth now filled the entire view.

"What do we do, sir?"

"If you believe in the Creator, pray. If you don't, I suggest taking up the practice."

Smoke streamed from the edges of the shuttle's control wings. The hull rumbled as Earth's breath fingered its battered surface. In a few minutes, we'd be moving too hot and fast for a Retriever to save us. I steeled myself and prayed for a miracle.

CHAPTER FIVE

JORDAN

The table dropped with a sickening lurch and jolted to a stop. Water splashed over the sides and under my bare back. A hand as large as my face, with slender fingers the length of my forearm, gripped the strap holding my left foot. The hand ripped the strap free like it was made of paper, and then my right foot was similarly released.

Coughing echoed from the other side of the door as the giant glided around the table to work the restraint that held my left wrist, taking care not to injure me. The binding flopped free. The other restraint seemed to prove more troublesome for my benefactor. It twisted on itself and tightened. The large fingers worked frantically but got nowhere with the knot.

The huge door opened again, bathing the floor in harsh light. My rescuer retreated into the shadows while I strained to get my hand loose. There was a low grunt before heavy footsteps rumbled across the floor.

Blood dripped into my palm, lubricating the binding. I tugged until my wrist cracked, ignoring the pain. Then a light blazed down on my table. A giant's enormous face glared at me. His gruff voice growled, "What in Anak?"

He grabbed the edge of the table. Water splashed over the

sides.

My hand slipped free. I ripped the tubes off my body and flipped backwards off the table, beyond the lip of the pool, counting on finding the floor. It was there all right, but a lot farther down than I anticipated. I hit hard and slammed into some kind of cart. Metal and glass crashed.

The giant lunged at me but I ducked. His huge hand swooped by me like the boom of a sailboat. I staggered to my feet, my joints arthritic and my muscles burning. Yet I pushed past the pain and willed myself to run.

"How did this human get loose?" he demanded.

"I leave him alone for twenty minutes and you pull this stunt," a woman's voice bellowed from another part of the room.

"He's sick. He must be treated."

"Not this way," she said. They both spoke English.

"It's the only way to cure him."

"He's my human, not yours."

While I appreciated her concern, I wasn't in the mood to take sides. I was nobody's science experiment, thank you very much.

The open door beckoned. I stumbled toward it like a moth to a flame, with thumping and jostling behind me.

"You're letting him escape!" he shouted.

"You bet I am," she said.

A young giant leaned through the doorway. "Hey, everything okay in here?"

I darted through his legs, across plush carpeting and out onto a sidewalk.

"Stop that human!"

I staggered into a supersized urban jungle. Lots of giants standing next to the door at a counter twice as high as my head. They held plates of food the size of beach umbrellas. A few looked down at me with consternation. A female giant screamed. Food rained down on the sidewalk in large gloppy piles. A plate shattered. I leaped as a four-foot-long shard skidded under my feet. Oversized hands reached for me. I dove between legs and fled across a street into the bustle of a more oblivious crowd.

The light illuminating this weird scene was a horizontal sliver of daylight at the end of a very long boulevard. My eyes adjusted to it as I ran. I was in a cavern sheltering a city. The road was dimly lit. Judging by the length of the side streets, the city sprawled for miles. Air cars the size of blimps silently glided over my head. Square courts with high walls sat in the center of each intersection. They came to the waists of giants walking on the sidewalks. Shafts of bright sunshine, diced into patterns by grills, beamed upward as spotlights. Acres of lush vegetation hung in cradles, basking in the illumination.

Giants hurried past me in every direction, most too busy to get to wherever they had to go to notice me. I dodged them and crossed the brightly lit square. Those closest to me looked down and gasped as I darted past. Being the only human on the street probably had something to do with their reaction. That and that I was as naked as Adam.

Heavy boots slammed the ground in a rapid cadence, coming in my direction. There was no time to ponder embarrassment; I fled from the stomping.

"Stop him!" voices yelled. "Stop the human!"

The mouth of the cave was as wide as the horizon and seemed just as far away. Those chasing me took one step for every three of mine, gaining on me with each jaw-jarring stride. I was a block from the exit. There was a sunny meadow out there and a forest beyond. Something told me that if I got outside, I'd be safe. I ran until my lungs ached.

A big hand swooshed across my back. I dove headfirst into the sunlight. My pursuers stopped cold.

"Anak, now what do we do?" one of them moaned.

I rolled to my feet and tore across the meadow. I skirted ponds and dashed into a grove of saplings a bit taller than my head. The sun was low in the sky. I considered it relative to the horizon. It was rising. Ten o'clock, maybe, although its light was intense. That or my eyes were messed up from having been frozen.

I darted from cover and put more distance between me and the cave's exit. When I reached a thicket of substantial pines, I stopped and caught my breath, chancing another look back, squinting hard against the morning glare. Nobody followed me.

I ran to the end of the meadow and up a hill into heavy woods, where I took time to look over my shoulder. I'd just emerged from a huge mountain. Its flank was covered with crumbling temples and thick forests. A waterfall cascaded down overgrown terraces and ended in a final ribbon of silver that splashed near the cavern's exit.

There was movement at the cave's entrance. A cloaked figure emerged into the bright sunshine and carefully surveyed the meadow. I flattened myself behind a dense thicket and willed my body to be invisible. Not even a Ranger could spot me in this cover.

The figure locked onto my position as if I was painted orange and walked straight toward me. A burst of fog billowed over my pursuer like a canopy and a breeze shifted its cloak to reveal a long flowing gown beneath. It was a woman, but was she giant or human? With only a flat meadow for contrast, I had nothing to judge her height; at least until she reached the saplings. They came to her knees.

I retreated up the hill, slipping on wet moss and leaves. The woods thickened as I climbed. Closely spaced trees, steep slopes, and maybe a river in the next valley if I was lucky would slow the behemoth down. This was going to be easy.

Despite her size, which I estimated to be about eighteen feet, her steps were silent and graceful. As I ran for the ridge, she quickened her gait. Then her voice echoed across the meadow. "Wait, Jordan, I'm not going to hurt you."

Her voice was musical, her words kind, and I recognized her by it. It was the same voice that had laid claim to me in the laboratory.

I crested the ridge and pushed through a tangle of bushes. Beyond was blue sky and—

"Jordan, no!"

The ground suddenly gave way. I grabbed an overhanging branch and arrested my fall. Rocks and chunks of dirt tumbled down the face of an enormous cliff. Clouds obscured the view below me.

I hauled myself back up onto the ridge. The giant lady was already at the foot of the slope. I wasn't trapped yet. I studied the cliff and considered the available handholds. Maybe I could free-climb down its face.

Then I saw something that defied explanation. The clouds parted. The cliff clearly ended a mile down but there was no valley floor to meet it. Instead, more distant clouds issued out from under its base like an ocean of fog. The rocks I'd dislodged plunged through them like specks of pepper. The clouds thinned and parted, revealing forests, cities, and a harbor far below, complete with ships the size of rice. I had done a lot of high altitude jumps. That harbor was two miles down. The surreal landscape I stood on scrolled beneath my feet like a miniature tableau. This mountain was airborne.

CHAPTER SIX

SARAH

The wind hissed, skimming our Land Rover with a stream of sand. The parked vehicle was canted beside a sandblasted garage on a shadowed dune, buried up to the hubcaps. Beyond the battered vinyl siding spread a vanishing suburbia. Only wind-torn roofs and skeletal bedrooms remained visible above the advancing dunes. The home of this detached garage clung to life forty feet away. The façade had been wind-worn down to the bare wood. Tattered shingles clung to twin gables as stubborn oak leaves would to bark-less branches. Rusted gutters banged against long-shattered windows. Beyond the stark trapezoids of shade caused by the garage and the home, the sun vitrified all.

A gust of wind howled viciously through a hole in the garage's roof. Two small children huddled beside me, their tiny heads wrapped against the storm. Only clear blue eyes peeked out from scratched goggles. They cried and grabbed my legs, and my arms instinctively encircled both of them. My mind burst with an epiphany: *These are my children.* An impossible reality I embraced with abandon.

They were frightened for good reason. We were taking a great risk by lingering so long here. I looked anxiously at the house. A man's form glided past a window frame, outlined by copper sunlight. My heart caught in my throat at the sight of him.

This had been his hometown. A town on the outskirts of a dying metropolis called Philadelphia. The dunes were much higher here. Only the skyscrapers were still visible, those that hadn't fallen over in the initial blast.

How did I know this?

Tree limbs, their bark long since stripped and their trunks half buried in sand, clawed skyward. They marked where the old roads lay hidden. In a few more years, the trees and roofs would be hidden. Then this town would sleep beneath an ever-deepening, ever-hardening wasteland, crushed and forgotten by the few who ultimately survived the catalyst of this global siege, a celestial legion the ancients had called the Stream of Heaven and its poisonous centurion, Wormwood.

Jordan crawled out of the upstairs window as a squadron of lumbering transports rumbled overhead. The enormous aircraft descended in a single line, their engines briefly drowning out the storm. The Mexican insignia of the eagle clutching a snake blazed from its wings. Wheels swung down and landing lights flared. I remembered a metal landing strip set up on the edge of a detention camp a few miles east of here. We'd skirted the perimeter of the camp to arrive here undetected. All able-bodied adults had been conscripted into expeditionary forces. Their children were being held in safety centers where the Western Confederacy of the Americas sustained them, provided their parents fought bravely in the East.

My skin crawled at the thought of being captured and our children indoctrinated by those self-righteous bureaucrats. My husband was still considered a citizen of this country-turned-empire, despite my Swiss status. He watched the planes land, rippling cross-shaped shadows across the sand. To their right, a dust plume billowed. Vehicles were coming from the airbase.

I shouted a warning. Jordan pulled his head scarf into place and pushed through the wind to reach me. The plume grew larger. They were coming fast. Had we been spotted?

Jordan scrambled around the garage and stared at me as if he saw me for the first time. Looking into his eyes calmed my nerves and steeled my resolve to survive. I hugged him fiercely and heard the words come out of my mouth, "We'd better leave. Another patrol is coming."

He looked at me as if he was confused. His mouth opened and said words, but I heard no sound. The lead vehicle burst over the nearest dune. Soldiers leapt from the sides as I tried to scream.

I abruptly sat up. Like lights coming on in a theatre, my bedroom materialized and replaced the desert. Jungle noises silenced the shouts of soldiers. Rain dripping off the tile roof replaced the gunfire. I was back in humid Costa Rica, in my mountain villa overlooking the Pacific coast and the sleepy town of Quepos.

I shut my eyes and struggled to remember what I'd seen. It couldn't have been a dream. I could still feel the sand in my boots and smell the fumes of the transports. My eyes were still adjusting from the blinding sun. I'd traveled the *Migramah* and gone to a place and time as real as this. A time in the future where I was with Jordan. He was my husband. We had two children, a three-year-old son and a two-year-old daughter.

"We named them Diago and Athena," I whispered.

Doubt wormed through me. I hugged my knees, letting my sweat soak the sheets. I whispered the words of the Berbai. "Faith knows what is not yet made, illuminates what is not yet seen."

"Jordan comes back to me," I whispered. "He comes back." I squeezed my eyes as if to push back my fears. "We have children."

I suddenly felt someone in my head, reminding me of the terrible reality of time and place when ages climax. When the two suns neared, all things happened at the same time and all times happened in the same place. What was, is, and would be became one tangled reality. Jordan's peril, my prayer, and our future hung in a wild balance: solid, shattered, victorious, and overwhelmed. A single thought could tip the balance into chaos or stay the celestial landslide. A feeling became a thought and acquired a voice.

Protect him now.

"How can I protect him?" I cried, wondering who or what I was arguing with.

Guide him there. Here we'll bear. Ignore the call, he will fall.

A downpour drowned the night. I shut the terrace doors to muffle the pounding of the rain. Dropping to the floor, I counted how many days it had been since Jordan had vanished down the shaft in Giza. Then I recalled the number of days he'd been with me in the Second Age. I subtracted the difference. Where was he now and what was he doing? My hand went to my heart. Mestre!

I sank to my knees so my head rested on the glass coffee table. I remembered to relax and let the author of the strange message guide me. My thoughts and dreams fell into a current. A vast river, full of lizards. I spotted him, lost and frustrated. Shadows criss-crossing over him.

"Jordan, follow me," I whispered.

This was crazy. I was praying about a past event I'd only heard about as if its outcome could be affected. A pain welled up in my heart. I gasped at the urgency. This was not insane; ignoring my heart would be.

I plunged into Jordan's reality. The scene sharpened in complete detail. I found him, where he was supposed to go.

"Honey, come east."

Jordan hesitated. He looked in the direction I wanted him to.

"Go," I moaned.

He took a step.

"Hurry. I'm waiting for you."

CHAPTER SEVEN

JORDAN

No wonder she'd been taking her sweet time to capture me. I was on an island without an ocean. Trunks snapped and trees toppled. The giantess was coming for me.

I clawed back onto firmer ground. She spotted me and froze. Her enormous lips trembled as she exhaled a cloud of mist. She was three times my height, cloaked in a hood and fog like the third spirit in Dickens's *Christmas Story*, but a spirit with decent curves.

The fog flowed up the hill and spilled past me, over the cliff. She motioned with a twelve-inch finger as if coaxing a puppy. "Jordan, come away from the cliff. You're making me nervous."

"Yeah, that makes two of us."

"You could fall."

"No kidding."

"Come down." She pulled back her hood. "I promise I won't hurt you."

My mouth dropped. Scratch the Scrooge analogy; this was no Specter of Death, not unless Death was a twenty-foot tall Miss America finalist. Miss Texas, to be specific. She was stunning with sweeping cocoa-colored hair and solid blue eyes. I hid my lower half.

She glanced at my spread hands with clinical disregard and took a giant step backwards. "Come down, please."

I'd sooner step on an IED. But, then again, I wasn't keen on cliffdiving, either. Maybe I could dodge her and make a run for the mountain. Its flanks looked climbable, lots of places to hole up.

A pair of strange looking aircraft hovered into view beyond the peak. Shouting echoed from the meadow. Ground forces shrouded in fog made a slow methodical sweep. Running wasn't an option now.

She spoke softly into her hand. "He's with me, keep back. He's frightened enough as it is."

Something told me I could trust her. I ripped a leafy branch off a tree and took a step down the hill. She backed off as if to reassure me that she meant me no harm. I didn't believe it, but for the moment I was out of options. I took another step.

"That's good," she said softly. "You can do it." She sounded like she was talking to a four-year-old.

"What exactly do you want with me?"

"I'm trying to help you."

He's my human, not yours.

"I don't need anybody's help."

She put her hands on her hips. "Jordan Anthony Wright, you're in no condition to be on your feet. Stop arguing with me and get down here. *Now!*"

My reaction surprised me. I stumbled down the hill, her eyes following my progress. But then I came to my senses and ducked behind a tree.

The ground shuddered when she knelt on the other side. She sighed in relief, sending a warm breeze whistling past my face. I smelled apples and cinnamon.

"Thank you," she said from the other side of the trunk. "I realize it's hard for you to trust me."

I chanced a look to make sure she didn't move. "I saw what your hairy friend did to that other prisoner."

Her left eyebrow arched. It was as long as my hand. "That was a patient, not a prisoner. And that hairy friend is Odin, a great scientist and the head of the Nephillim Council. And my father."

"That doesn't give him the right to experiment on people."

"The patient was a primitive from the northern wasteland. He suffered from premature aging, similar to your condition. Odin saved his life by regenerating his body back to its original birth state."

"Was that what he was going to do to me?"

"Yes."

"He's nuts."

"Occasionally."

"You're his daughter; why should I trust you?"

"I freed you."

"Why was I there in the first place?"

"Excuse me if I was a little busy with all this." She indicated the aircraft orbiting nearby and the floating mountain in general, then pulled a bundle from her sleeve. "I brought you the clothes Levi attached to the hibernation chamber."

Her hand swung down on an arm as long as a ladder. My clothes sat folded in the middle of her huge palm. They'd never looked so good since I'd bought them. But I hesitated taking them. Her fingers could crush me like a bug.

She rolled her eyes, "*Spassee*, take them! I'm not dropping them in the dirt. It took forever to restore them."

I snatched the bundle from her, and she carefully pulled her hand back, her eyes fixed on me. I dressed quickly, ready to jump back if she tried anything. All the artwork I'd studied in museums showing giants next to humans, all the oversized steps and doorways I'd measured, all the religious writings I'd read recounting a race of super-giants intermingling with humans and having spawned the half-giants I'd been running from were living proof the Nephillim really existed. Once again, I was without my camera. If Krax was here, he'd be so excited, he'd put his feet in his sleeves.

Her ten-foot-long hair swayed in a sudden breeze. "I straightened Odin out after you, um, exited. He offers his apologies."

"Not accepted."

"He was only trying to regenerate you."

"Not interested."

Her eyebrow arched. "I agree. That would be inconvenient for you." She paused. "And a certain princess, I understand."

I missed a button. "Excuse me?"

She shooed away a giant wasp orbiting my head. "That was quite a show you put on. You run fast with no footgear, or anything else, for that matter. Half of *Olympus* is still in shock over your exposition."

Did she say *Olympus*? I snapped my pants. "Who are you?"

"Where are my manners? I'm Athena."

"The goddess Athena?"

"Anak, no! Just Athena, thank you. Athena Ray-Odin, if you want the formal version."

"And Odin's your father."

"Yes."

"The one who wanted to turn me into an infant."

"Unfortunately."

"This is *Olympus*?"

"Yes. Why, is something wrong?"

"It's not what I expected. Where I come from, mountains are attached to the ground."

She didn't seem to hear me. Images of faces materialized in the air to the left and right of her head. She stepped away and answered quietly, as if she had a cell phone in her brain. The faces stayed with her like shoulder angels while she paced with a nervousness hinting that a lot of stuff was going down.

I remembered what little I'd learned about Athena since I'd come to the Second Age. According to Aizah, Athena was the leader of Javan, and Levi and Aaron worked for her. She ran the war against Atlantis. This giantess had a lot more important things to do than chase a naked human around her floating mountain. Why hadn't she just sent those foggy goons standing by in the field to capture me?

"Are any ships surviving reentry?" she said to one of the faces. "Can we intercept?" She nodded. "Launch all remaining flights."

Half a minute later, a thundering boom sounded from below the cliff's edge. A flight of four aircraft shot into the sky. Five seconds later, another flight launched. I itched to see how they did that. I pictured the old Swiss tunnel bases and hurried with my shoes.

Athena looked down as I finished. "Much better."

She pressed her hand to her ear, I guess to take another call. As she listened, her face screwed up. "Are you sure it's Levi?"

Levi was in trouble?

Ignoring my caution, I drew nearer to see if I could overhear what they said about him. Athena's free hand reached down and maternally encircled me. "How long before the shuttle hits the atmosphere?" Her fingers tensed on my chest. "Oh God."

Levi was in space? What was he doing up there?

"Launch the heavy Retriever. Rescue pattern Omega … I know it's dangerous … What?" She let go of my shoulders and smacked her forehead. "How did we lose a Retriever? Aaron did what? How did he get out of heal bay?"

The sky flashed and rumbled. "Hello? Hello?" She pulled a device from her ear and hurled it away like she was aiming for the next continent. It hit a tree and ricocheted at me. I dove to avoid it.

"Sorry." She picked the device up, examined it, and shoved it back in her ear.

"Something wrong?" I asked.

"First, you run off; now Aaron's missing." She fumed as she fussed with the earpiece. "I've never had this much trouble with humans before." She tapped her ear and nodded as if she was talking to someone else again. "Mmm, I lost you … Yes, defensive fire on all incoming debris. Don't let anything hit the ground!" She covered her eyes and nodded hurriedly. "Yes, I meant scan for life signs in the debris first, then fire." She pulled the device from her ear, looking frustrated and uncertain. I'd seen that look a dozen times in the faces of new officers.

"You're new at this," I said.

"In all previous conflicts, Mer headed the Eastern Alliance. With Mer crippled, Javan has to step forward." She steeled her shoulders. "What I lack, I gain from those I trust." She looked at me pointedly. "Jordan from the future, can I trust you?"

Blurred flashes rippled the clouds, accompanied by a building roar. Alarms echoed across the valley. Weapon fire popped and hissed from positions scattered around both flanks of the mountain. The ordinance appeared self-propelled, changing vectors before plunging into the cloud ceiling. Something big exploded, blowing a hole through the clouds. The concussion hammered my chest. Tree limbs shook and leaves fluttered to the ground. Athena's face hardened and she scooped me up before I could react.

Olympus' fire teams lanced the sky as flaming objects dropped through the clouds. They weren't meteorites; the things broke apart like damaged aircraft, shedding glowing debris below *Olympus'* horizon. One cluster struck the side of the mountain's peak, smashing a temple off a ledge. It tumbled to the base, tracing a fiery trail through the trees.

Athena bundled me against her chest like an infant and I struggled uselessly within her grip. She ran across the meadow with ten-foot strides. Her ground forces converged to give her escort, while the cloud canopy that had been protecting her struggled to keep up. Her chest heaved against my face as she panted from exertion.

"Put me down," I shouted.

"I can sling you over my shoulder and hold you by the ankles if that makes you feel better."

"Where are you taking me?"

An aircraft swung overhead and shielded her as she ran. A chunk of twisted metal hit the aircraft, spun off it, and struck a tree. The trunk splintered as the tree toppled over the edge. Ground personnel used hand weapons to shoot at other debris spiraling in. Fire popped up everywhere. Athena shifted her hold to carrying me like a football as she made a final mad dash into a small canyon, surrounded by a dozen armored giants. A paved path down the center led into a cave. Her escort's boots echoed in the wide tunnel.

Inside, she turned to the squad. "See to the defenses."

She blinked once and the images of talking faces floated back into place. She steadied her gait and cradled me in her arms. When I struggled, she flexed her forearm, inducing a squeeze that could crush my guts out of my throat. I got the hint and relaxed.

Sunlight filtered up through cracks in the cavern floor. The path wound down through a series of massive ledges connected by a lacework of stalactites and stalagmites. Plants crowded on the ledges and dangled from the ceilings wherever patches of sunlight played. The foliage was translucent and appeared fragile. Their leaves were pale blue; the blooms and fruit soft pastels. A transparent animal darted across a rubbery branch.

We skirted a series of circular ports, each the size of the Holland Tunnel. Hot steam billowed from the openings, while water dribbled from the lips and misted away.

"Cover your ears," Athena said.

A thunderous boom and then four gorgeous gleaming God-can-I-please-fly-one aircraft roared over our heads and shot out the farthest opening. They flew away in a classic four-finger formation and vanished into the flank of a cumulus cloud bank.

As Athena descended, the bow of *Olympus* became discernible. We'd descended several dozen cascading ledges. When I looked up, I saw their edges were aligned, forming a grand curving sweep of a hull. We were on the starboard side of a mineralized carrier with a mountain for a superstructure.

Athena kept her bounding double-time pace as *Olympus* plowed through clouds with the grace a Nimitz Class spreading the sea. By the time she reached the lowest ledge, I felt like stir fry in her arms. Vertigo had already set in a half-mile earlier. Now she hurried along an uneven path through a thick garden.

Boy, I needed to puke, but I fought it back and tried to ignore how the scenery pitched and rolled as she leapt from one ledge to the next. The bottom of *Olympus* was a massive upside-down landscape of ledges above the sky and distant valley. Sunlight filtered up through the crevices. Inverted forests of pale blue and translucent green swayed from the ceilings, filling every square foot of the lit surface, all competing to grow. Long grasses brushed my face, feather soft. Glowing insects and iridescent birds with glass-like wings darted through the rushes. Through windswept partings, I spotted shafts extending upward into the mountain ceiling. Vast mirrors, cut in complex shapes and arranged in artful clusters, hung beneath them, reflecting the sunlight into the shafts. Were these the light shafts I'd seen during my run through the city?

I finally couldn't resist. I leaned over Athena's massive forearm and vomited.

"Oh, Jordan," she said and stopped. She steadied me with one hand and grabbed a finger full of some flowering vines. Orange blooms swung down under my nose. "Breathe deep."

I did, while she got another call. Her fingers crushed the flowers.

"Keep searching," she said to the caller. "Let me know the moment you find either of them." There was a long pause as she listened. "I know. Yes, you're right; we can't give up hope. I'll be on the summit shortly. Have the flights extend their search patterns as deep into the debris field as they can safely go."

Things didn't sound good for Levi and Aaron.

My vertigo passed. The edge of the path gave way to a wide ledge bounded by a panoramic sky. Clouds paraded past in an endless chain. Athena carried me to the edge, where I could look down. There, the clouds broke ranks, revealing distant forests and tiny villages dotting rolling valleys. The harbor I'd seen from topside lay far to the stern, shimmering in the midday sun.

"Cool, huh?" Athena said sadly. She needed a break.

"You're kidding? You say cool?"

She appeared confused. "You do say that word, don't you?"

"How would you know? We just met."

"You talked during thaw out; answered my questions."

"Like what?"

"Eating habits, military service, movies you like, where you've been, who you've met. I think Kate is attracted to you, by the way."

I felt violated. "What else did I tell you about my personal life?"

"I already knew about your wife and daughter. Levi briefed me. And you volunteered your opinion of Kate before I could change the subject. I promise I didn't press any further. Privacy is important to me."

"Thank you."

"I need to carry you a little farther, to a place where you can rest and finish your recovery." She gestured to the hanging forest as she took me across the terrace. "This is why I wanted Levi to bring you to me when I learned you had taken ill. These plants will help you fight off the microbes trying to decompose you."

"I saw water plants growing in caves under Mer that looked like these."

"Yes, they're similar."

"And in the Sanctuary."

She sighed, "Those were the really important ones."

"Why grow them here? Can't they survive out in the open?"

"They're First Age plants we germinated from seeds found in Odin's Vault. They can't survive without protection until we complete restoration of the atmosphere."

"What's wrong with the atmosphere?"

"We're still missing the hydrosphere."

"The what?"

"The Nephillim Council has been evaporating ice into the atmosphere for centuries to restore it, but it's still too thin. Sunlight continues to strike the ground, creates ozone, and wipes out fragile portions of the biosphere. These plants need a fully restored hydrosphere, maintained by a fully carbonated biodome to survive in the open."

I wondered if I should break it to her that their science project had apparently failed, given that we didn't have anything resembling a hydrosphere in my time, much less a tenth of the flora and fauna this age supported. But she was having a bad enough day as it was. I was, too. Vertigo came back and agitated the contents of my stomach.

She ducked through a gate and led me into a compound of pillared marble homes and sweeping patios bounded by ponds with transparent bottoms. It was very Greek, in a floating, upside-down, Twilight-Zone kind of way. She presented me to a woman who looked like a governess with attitude. The woman regarded me as if a lizard had just been brought into the house. I could tell she and I weren't going to be climbing trees together or singing about our most favorite things anytime soon.

She took my hand between her thumb and forefinger and squeezed just enough to let me know she meant business. "Hold still."

Was she kidding? Struggling would have dislocated my shoulder.

I swallowed hard as she reached into her pocket. Scratch the governess persona; I knew that clinical look. I was in worse trouble.

Gigantor was a nurse.

Her hand plucked something out of her pocket. Instead of the expected eighteen-inch-long syringe, she pulled out a flower and shook it vigorously. I got a blue pollen shower as a result. Warmth coursed through my battered body.

"You should be feeling better in a few minutes," Athena said.

"Is the patio supposed to spin?"

"Maybe he needs more." She pulled a flower off the ceiling and shook it over my head. I sneezed.

Nurse Ratched frowned. "No, madam, that's for dwarves. He needs more of this."

They shook half the garden over my head like a salad in need of seasoning. After enough pollen had fallen to fertilize Ohio, something in the mix started to work. The floor stopped spinning. Everything looked colorful. I felt happy, verging on invincible. The Woodstock generation had probably channeled Nephillim pharmacists.

The effect soon started to fade and sanity reasserted itself. I felt violated again. This was the last time anybody was going to pollinate me without checking the warning labels on the stems. But, to my relief, the vertigo didn't return.

Athena and Nurse Ratched held a post-op consult and narrowed my treatment down to a three-bloom combo for future dustings, eliminating the plants that put me on the magical mystery tour.

"Now, understand, this is not a cure," Athena said. "First Age plants are not as effective as Odin's solution would have been. Your body is too badly damaged for just pollen to cure."

"I'm not interested in Odin's solution."

"You made that quite clear. Therefore, these flowers are your only choice. As long as you stay on *Olympus*, you will remain healthy."

"You mean if I leave, I get sick?"

"Sick in a week, dead in two."

"I'm trapped here?"

Her eyes flared as wide as her nostrils. "The last thing I want you to feel is trapped."

I flared back. "Yeah? Well it's not working."

She stared at me for a while, pursed her lips and nodded. "You're right, no one should be kept against their will." Her hands spread twelve feet apart. "In a way, we share the same fate. I am just as trapped as you are."

"Very funny."

"I cannot venture into the sunlight without protection. It is too intense for me. That is why Nephillim live under the icecap and in the mountains. When we visit the surface, I have to wear the equivalent of a spacesuit because of the ground ozone."

"I guess I see your point."

Her face softened. "Once you're stronger, perhaps we can take short excursions off *Olympus.* Maybe visit a certain princess in Mestre?"

Did Nurse Ratched just laugh? No, it had to be gas.

"We are not far from the border of her country," Athena said.

"I told you about Suri?"

"Yes, you talked about her several times."

"How is she?"

"Not married yet."

I didn't realize how anxious I was to hear that piece of information. Athena's hint of a smile indicated approval of how I felt. Which was what? Okay, I missed Suri. Not just, Golly, wonder how she's doing. I mean pit-in-the-stomach, have-to-find-her-now-or-I-won't-be-able-to-breathe missed her.

Formulating that thought cemented my resolve. I had a mission and it didn't involve staying here. Floating mountain, warrior giantess, and terminal illness be damned, I had to find her.

A fish breached the surface of a nearby pond with its yard-high dorsal fin. Waves lapped over the edge. My mind raced. First, I had to figure out how to get off this mountain without dying on impact.

"There is one more thing I must tell you. Keeping it a secret any longer would be unfair to you." Athena looked earnestly at me. "Please understand it was an absolute necessity."

Her eyes glistened when they blinked. Was she starting to cry? I held my breath as her enormous hand brushed the side of my face like a skillfully maneuvered backhoe. "I simply couldn't allow someone else to take on the responsibility. Who knows what would have happened to you?"

"What are you talking about?"

"It only makes sense. People would be upset if a human toddler was left to roam about Javan uncared for."

"How did you know I was—"

"How did I know you were only three-and-a-half decades old? Please, credit me with some rudimentary intelligence." She put a hand to her forehead as if to re-board her train of thought. "I had no choice, really. I had to move fast. There were many volunteers, hundreds who actually wanted you. All were *completely* unqualified. So few Nephillim can have children anymore. Just because they are desperate doesn't qualify them as parents, especially in your case."

Oh, for the love of fish crackers, please tell me she didn't do what I think she did.

She paced the terrace. Her thirty-two-inch feet rhythmically bounced the fish out of the water. "And there wasn't time to get your permission. The Council was moving uncharacteristically fast." She looked at me as uncertainly as she had when she'd given orders to her defensive forces. "Given the circumstances, it really was the only solution to your dilemma."

"Dilemma?" What was I, an oil spill?

"Of who should care for you," she said. "Oh, the Council debate was so tiresome. Especially the sticky issue of ..." She waved her huge hand as if to bat the issue away. "So I ended the debate. They were quite pleased with my offer. Even Odin came around." She leaned over and unexpectedly suctioned my forehead with a saucer-sized kiss.

"Offer to do what?"

"To adopt you."

"Wait a minute."

"Your name is now Jordan Ben-Odin. It's customary to be named after one of your fathers, your *grandfather,* as you would say. Sorry, he's the only one left in our family. I had no choice."

Flaming debris roared past the bow of the mountain. Athena's ear buzzed. "I'll be right there."

"They found Levi?" the nurse asked.

"Maybe." Athena put her free hand to my backside and slid me into the nurse's perimeter.

"Gee, Mom, leaving already?"

"I'll be back as soon as I can. Don't let Odin in," she called to the nurse as she bounded down the path. "I don't want any more experiments done on him."

"No, madam."

"And watch him. He's very spirited for a toddler. Don't let his adult appearance fool you."

That did it. I was out of here.

My prison warden scowled and planted her girth across the path. I spun on my heel and paced the edge of the pond. There had to be a way off this flying rock that included surviving.

Debris rained down hard. The larger pieces were taken out with amazing intercepts by Athena's air force. A massive explosion lit up the clouds, flaring to life like a second sun. Shadows lengthened across the valley, then faded as the fireball spent itself out across the sky. A dull rumble echoed through the heavens seconds later.

I looked back at the giantess. Her hand was at her ear. She spoke worriedly to someone, while debris of the metallic spaceship kind dropped through the clouds. Important life-and-death stuff was happening. Instead of being able to do something about it, I was sidelined as a casualty of the situation.

I finished my circuit of the pond as far as the path would let me before I reached a thorn bush barrier marking the farthest point of the mountain's prow. Fog billowed ahead. Threads whispered past my body and wet my face. It was fresh water, very cold. A new rumbling sound grew as *Olympus* cleaved through the fog.

"Come away from the thorn bush," my baby-sitter called. "You'll catch a chill in that mist."

I saw what caused the rumble. It wasn't fog; it was spray from a waterfall. *Olympus'* prow cut across the panoramic edge of the falls, affording a breathtaking view of the green curve of an enormous river rolling over an infinitely wide cliff. The falls were ten times wider than Niagara and plunged a mile down to the valley's floor.

Olympus crested the falls and flew upriver, its raging torrent much closer to the flying mountain's underbelly than the valley had been. But not close enough to do a leap off the bow and survive the plunge.

A wisp of translucent blue fluttered briefly into view. Apparently, there was a whole lot of garden vine growing nice and long under the terrace I stood on. Could that fragile stuff take my weight long enough to repel down?

My warden called. I only had one way to find out, unless what's-her-name was willing to volunteer to take the plunge for me.

I timed the swaying movement of the vines. They were hundreds of feet long. Nurse Ratched called again. I had to wait until the vines were swaying in the right direction. I felt the ground shake as she ran toward me. Not enough time to wait. Heck with it, I jumped.

CHAPTER EIGHT

LEVI

Earth's sweeping curve beckoned below, pulling us to destruction. Debris from the starship flamed past the portholes and fractured into iridescent sprays as gravity and atmosphere ripped the skin from the girders and the bulkhead from the deck, dismembering the queen's creation in a furnace of friction. I estimated our rate of fall by comparing the curve of the porthole to the steady flattening of the Earth's horizon. We only had minutes before annihilation.

Jarell's nose pressed against the bowled glazing. She looked up, spotted something, and fixed on it. Her irises flashed as she engaged her oculars and pointed at a speck crossing the face of the moon. "Sir, what do you think that is?"

I zoomed in. The remains of the starship rushed into focus. It tumbled slowly across the moon. Reflected light formed a halo around the oval hull as the great sweep of the smooth lunar surface slid behind her.

"It's what's left of the queen's starship," I said.

"The bombardment must have pushed it out of orbit."

"Not much is left of the ship except the command saucer and some structural tethers."

"You can see that much detail?" she asked. "My oculars can

barely tell it was a ship."

"Ground Com upgrades your oculars when you volunteer for space." I fished a link out of the satchel holding my helmet tech and linked her into my eyes. "Take a look."

She pressed her temple and her eyes widened. "Wow. Maybe I'll sign up for space after all."

"Looks like you already did."

As the derelict rotated, the sun revealed a sobering view of the devastation caused by Odin's missiles. I thought of the thousands of Atlantean soldiers and civilians who'd died, and inwardly railed against the insanity of Nephillim methods of war; particularly Odin's predilection to counterattack with such devastating force. Precision could have been used on the starship's weapons platforms instead of carpet-bombing the entire hull. Lives could have been spared. Now, only the red saucer that comprised Babla's command quarters had survived, thanks to its orichalcum skin and its location deep within the ancient hull.

Twisted metallic tethers sprang from a common anchor point on the rim of the saucer. They fanned above and below the ship in great arches, reaching into space like three enormous arachnid antennae. The tattered assemblage rotated slowly against the backdrop of the moon, while the sun flashed off the weathered metal.

Jarell gasped. The remains of a forbidden starship built from forgotten technology—the pride of Atlantis—turned the color of blood as daylight bathed its orichalcum skin. One metallic tether curved high above the saucer as it tilted to form an oval. The remaining pair of tethers swept beneath it as if bent by a stellar wind. The oval shape and curves briefly formed a browed eye that seemed to regard us as prey. The illusion would have been comical if it had been anything other than this vessel that created it. The eye drifted directly over the center of the moon, continuing its rotation and ending the illusion.

"Anak, did you see that?" Jarell said.

"Almost wish I hadn't."

Another speck of light flashed, not far behind the saucer.

"Now what?" she asked.

I zoomed in. "It's a rocket. More following behind it."

The stream of rockets appeared as they emerged from the moon's dark side. Their shape and function were unmistakable.

"Are those Mer or Atlantean ships?" she asked.

"I can't say from this distance."

"Maybe they're looking for us."

"As long as they're friendly."

I disengaged the connection and shut off my oculars. I wished Aaron was here. Guardian Jarell was not someone I knew well enough to share what I'd just learned, information that even Ground Com might not even be aware of. The convoy coming behind the moon was a fleet of Mer construction vessels. They had to have been positioned behind the moon ahead of the attack. Odin was repairing the command saucer, but why?

Jarell remained oblivious to my musings, her attention on Earth. The horizon had flattened ominously. "We're being pulled in, aren't we, sir?"

"Confirmed."

She handed back the ocular link. "What can we do?"

"If it was just us, we could suit up, bail out, and land in our armor."

Her eyes flickered sideways at the frightened civilians clustered at the far end of the shuttle, to the mother and child safely tucked in her armor. Her eyes calmly met mine. "Not an option."

"No," I said.

She floated over to the mother and daughter. The eyes of the other civilians strapped in the giant seats followed her. She reviewed the suit's systems with the mother, then she floated back, steeling herself. "Will the rest of them survive?"

A massive explosion erupted high above us. Secondary blasts flamed deep into space.

"Anak, what was that?" she asked.

I zoomed in with my oculars. The explosion dissipated, revealing the remains of a lifeboat. The engines were a mangled memory. The crew cabin was intact but spinning wildly. Lights glowed from the portals. Hundreds of small meteors whipped past the helpless vessel, narrowly missing the hull. Most were so small my oculars barely detected them. Some were as large as the lifeboat itself. Oblong and ragged, they coursed the inky sky, eclipsing the stars in a rhythmic staccato. I zoomed in on the portals. Terror-stricken faces of Ephraim civilians screamed silently back at me.

The hull spun into the path of an object twice its girth, took a direct hit, and sliced open at the bow. The doomed ship recoiled from the impact, spewing a death spiral of bodies and equipment. I shut my eyes and gripped the bulkhead. The distance from our shuttle spared Jarell from witnessing the carnage, yet I felt her stare.

"What happened?" she asked.

"A shuttle blew up."

"What caused it?"

"Meteors flying through the debris field."

"How many?"

Another explosion sent shadows chasing across the interior of our shuttle.

"That was a tug," she said. "It was closer."

"Where are these things coming from?" I murmured, moving to the opposite side of the hull and staring out, zooming to my ocular's full limit and switching to gravity imaging. What had been empty space suddenly framed a celestial stampede: a seemingly endless river of meteors and comet fragments: small, deadly, and all hurtling above us at incredible speed.

"Are they going to hit us?" Jarell asked.

"They're following a tight vector a thousand miles above us. I think we're safe for now."

"I don't remember learning about a giant meteor stream around the sun," she said.

"It isn't orbiting the sun. It's cutting across the solar system."

"Sir, zoom back and look at that patch of space."

I did as she said. The black sky was crowded with stars, except where she pointed.

"You see it?"

It looked like someone had erased a swath of the sky, leaving a thin streak of pure black. The stars weren't missing; something was blocking them.

Before I could analyze the phenomenon, light filled the portals.

The civilians covered their eyes in the searing glare, while the hull shuddered as gravity pulled us down nose first. The stars vanished behind flames. In a few minutes, we would too.

CHAPTER NINE

JORDAN

I cleared the jagged bow and dropped through a billowing mist over a thundering river. The roar from the falls drowned out all else. Dangling vines flew past me in a blur.

I spread-eagled and tried to glide under *Olympus*, into her hanging garden. A gust of wind hurled me into her lush vegetation, until I was enveloped in a curtain of blue. I clawed at the fragile ropes and they disintegrated in my hands like spider webs. As I plummeted into denser growth, they tangled about my body and slowed my rate of descent, maybe enough to survive.

I looked down. Big mistake. A blue bug the size of a mattress hit me. It splattered against my face. I spit out bug guts, blinking through whipping masses of foliage. Leaves flapped from my arms and thighs like streamers. Fortunately, my collision with the bug did the trick and slowed my fall. I broke clear of the vegetation in time to tuck and hit the river feet first, no faster than a high dive.

I sank deep and tumbled in the grip of the current, exhaling. When I saw which way the bubbles went, I followed them back to the surface. My head broke clear just before my face smacked a boulder. I gripped its slippery flank as the current fought to reclaim my body. Then my feet touched the bottom. I pushed hard against the current and forced myself into an eddy. Water plants—the normal, substantial green kind—protruded from the opaque shallows. Branches and debris floated among their thick stalks. So did a flotilla of crocodiles. I counted a dozen blocking my path to the shore. They rested half submerged, periscope eyes checking me out.

I took a breath and reminded myself that most animals in this weird age didn't attack people. But this was my first encounter with ancestors of Fourth Age crocodiles. The smallest one was thirty feet long, snout to tail. Hard to assume these monsters were tamer than their flesh-eating descendants. To get to shore, I had to wade through them. Going back was not an option.

"Assume I must," I muttered.

I carefully waded toward the shore, trying to remember how that Australian guy had done it on television. The crocs pivoted, keeping their snouts pointed at me. A forty-foot behemoth went under and followed.

"Nice crocodile," I said as I waded the remaining distance to land.

A huge snout nudged my back. I sucked in air, tried to keep calm, and reached a gravel beach of tangled brush shaded by swaying palms. Super-croc beached his six-foot girth at the water's edge and watched as I climbed out. He snorted, then reversed engines.

The sun was to my right, high in the sky and directly south, upriver. That meant it was noon. I'd landed on the west bank of what I hoped was Suri's home town. I had to find an elevated position and do some recon. If this was the capital of Mestre, I should be able to spot something architectural to indicate where the palace was located.

A park lined the river, with a busy street and town beyond. Alarms sounded as the flying mountain came about, arcing majestically to the east. She had glided about two miles south of my position, at an altitude of a thousand feet, judging from the scale of the trees hanging off her cliffs. I was able to take in her port-side profile, a flying island with a Matterhorn peak thrusting above her forested hills. Her hull was made up of pockmarked cliffs and lacework caverns from which trailed curtains of blue vines. My giant baby-sitter from Athena's apartment was probably having a Nephillim-sized cow by now.

Silver shapes flashed sunlight as they launched from the cliffs. Was Athena's air force deploying more assets to intercept incoming debris or was she sending out a rescue party for her adopted human?

The sleek craft banked sharply and ripped straight toward me.

"Rescue party," I murmured. "Sorry, not attending."

I crawled up the bank and ducked behind what appeared to be a trash can. People lounged and chatted on the grass. Crocodiles and other bulky unrecognizable amphibians lounged around them, probably waiting for a treat, like a twenty-inch hoagie or a small goat. A substantial croc sidled up to a family of three. It stopped at their feet and opened its jaws. The father reached into the beast's mouth and rubbed its tongue, while mom and daughter smiled.

"No way," I whispered.

A throaty grunt came from behind me, followed by a familiar nose nudging my backside. My forty-foot friend from the river was back. His fist-sized eyes blinked above an enormous reptilian grin. His jaw hinged open, revealing a tooth-lined gullet large enough to swallow a Volkswagen.

I squirmed around the trash can. He followed, swatting his tail against an oversized lemon tree and raining fruit down on my head. I crab-walked backward as he advanced, snapping up lemons along the way. Laughter came from nearby loungers.

I got to my feet and went to a bench near the young family, trying to keep calm as my unwanted friend followed. The little girl walked right up to the monster's snout and touched his nose. He stopped dead and tilted his mouth open. She stooped down on all fours and rummaged around his teeth while her mom and dad beamed proudly from the bench.

The croc held still as the girl found something and started tugging. She needed better footing and reached deeper inside. She grabbed his tooth and pulled with all her strength. Something came loose and she flopped backwards. The croc started to lower his jaw but stopped short of her head.

Mom called and the girl backed up. The croc's jaw finished closing the same time mine did, while the little girl simply walked up to her mom. She opened her hand to reveal a piece of slimy green fruit. Her parents approved as she grinned triumphantly, then stuck the fruit in her mouth.

Mom and dad gave a gasp and quickly pulled the mess from her teeth. As she fumed, her mother gently spoke in a language I hadn't heard before. Probably saying something like, "We don't eat the giant crocodile's yucky food, sweetie."

One of *Olympus'* planes winged over the bench, its shadow rippling the uneven bushes. They'd decided to search both river banks.

I waited until the jet vanished over the rooftops of the town, then dashed across the street, ducking under the silent air cars and apologizing in Javan to the annoyed drivers. The city was crowded with humans of every imaginable hair and skin color. There were Trahls, half-giants, and some of the tiny people I'd seen in Gomer walking on elevated sidewalks that kept them from getting stepped on.

One of Athena's jets cruised above the traffic. I retreated into the shade of a columned porch filled with street vendors. A twelve-foot guy tapped my shoulder like a hammer and babbled something, holding a three-foot parrot out for my inspection. I touched my chin, said no in Javan, and backed off.

The jet slowed until it was parallel with my position. Were they tracking my footprints? My DNA? My bad breath? I had to get off this street and find cover.

CHAPTER TEN

LEVI

The deck tilted under my feet as gravity took the deadly lead in a dance I desperately wanted to sit out. We were being pulled into the atmosphere with no sign of rescue. Mother and daughter were buttoned up in my armor, peering tearfully through my helmet visor. I lobbed restrainer gels over stress cracks in the hull as flames licked outside the portholes, while Jarell double-checked the civilians' seat straps. The hull moaned as if it sensed its impending demise. The deeper we plunged, the louder her anguish.

The ship was uncontrollable. We had a means of calling for help but Ground Com didn't respond to the com unit from my helmet. Something had continued to block it since my foray on the starship. All we had was the makeshift beacon, but I had no confidence that its simple electromagnetic signal would get through.

The downward plunge pressed me against the warming deck. After centuries of relying on the protection of my armor, the pressure was unnerving. Flames writhed past the viewports in an angry torrent. Jarell somehow kept the beacon broadcasting, licking her scalded fingers as she twisted connections that flew apart with each shake of the hull.

The makeshift device smoked, then caught fire. I pulled her away as it flared. We crawled back to the civilians and huddled beneath their giant shock seats. The bow glowed red. Remnants of equipment and consoles hanging from the ruined cockpit melted into twisted, organic shapes. Some of the women cried; others uttered prayers to their deities. Anak, what I wouldn't give for a dozen more suits. There hadn't been time to forage the starship. My fault. I'd lingered with Babla.

This wasn't my first ride in a disintegrating spaceship but it was the first time I couldn't evacuate. Loud wrenching noises started near the bow, carried along the beam, and cracked behind us. Pieces of the outer hull shielding wrenched free and sliced through the tail wings. One must have sheared off because the ship rolled into a starboard spiral. All of us were plastered against the hull, unable to move. The mother held her daughter and stared sadly from my borrowed armor. The injured woman inside Jarell's appeared unconscious. Spittle and blood tracked her cheeks.

The hull slowly bent midship. One of the consoles exploded. Was this finally it?

The fact that I contemplated death jarred me. After so many centuries of begrudging my long-lived condition, I shrank from the yawning reality of imminent death. I sensed Jarell beside me, remembering the rescue mission in Payahdon, her decoy team veering away in a matching air car and disappearing between two Atlantean rafts, taking a pair of enemy fighters with her. She had been a decoy for the Princess then and a resourceful comrade during this mission. Like most Guardians in the field, I hadn't attempted any social contact on the Acropolis beyond what protocol required. It was hard to see the value of socializing when I would outlive every friend I made. But now, stripped of all protection, bereft of hope, and surrounded by strangers, I couldn't face death cloaked in the solitude I'd used to survive my artificially long life.

I'd heard that tough missions had a way of lowering social barriers. The prospect of mutual death eliminated them. This was the closest I'd come to testing that theory.

"It's been an honor serving with you, sir," Jarell rasped through the smoke.

I leaned closer and made brief eye contact with her. Her set jaw and clenched hands told it all. She was steeled, ready for the end.

Something in me gave way. I put my arm around her. She leaned against me, as a daughter would hide in the comfort of a father.

"The honor's mine," I said.

The ship wrenched over violently and Jarell was thrown from me. I slammed into a seat strut. Pain shot up my side. The intense light from the portholes confirmed that we were fully in flames. I hoped the three civilians stuffed in our armor would survive. I prayed for a miracle for the others.

The ship steadied and my tethers took the pressure from my body. Something pulled me toward the cockpit.

"What's happening?" Jarell demanded.

"We're slowing down," I said.

"How's that possible?"

The flames thinned. The silhouettes of heavy grappler prongs shifted outside the portholes, then shuddered as they suctioned onto the hull with heavy bangs. The hull slowed significantly, although we continued to fall.

A distorted voice echoed through the hull. "This is *Olympus* Retriever Flight Delta Epsilon Heavy. Respond if able."

The civilians cheered.

"Delta Epsilon, we hear you," I shouted.

"Is that you, Chief?"

"Aaron?"

"Of course. I mean, aye, sir. Always wanted to be able to say that. Sorry it took so long. I got banged up during approach. What's with all the supersonic meteors up here? My ship got pasted."

"Where's Captain Octurius?"

"He couldn't make it."

"Who's piloting the Retriever?"

"I am."

"Where's the pilot?"

"He couldn't make it, either. Anak, hang on, something just broke off."

One of the grapplers snapped. We were thrown sideways under the seats.

"Don't worry," Aaron said, "I still got a spare. Stupid meteors wrecked the rest."

The replacement grappler clanged into place and the hull steadied. Unfortunately, our rate of descent increased.

"I was in healing bay when word spilled that you were in trouble," Aaron said.

"How's Jordan?"

"Thawing out and telling your mother his life story. Reminds me of how you were so sharing when they popped you out of your cocoon."

"Where's the captain, Aaron?"

"All the good crews are tied up at the front."

"In other words, you stole a Retriever."

"I'll give it back."

"And you have no crew?"

"Boarding was a little rushed, what with security upset and everything."

"That ship isn't designed to conduct rescues during re-entry. It doesn't have sufficient shielding for what you're attempting."

"Why is that, Chief?" Aaron asked as if we were back on the Acropolis, sipping beers and discussing hypotheticals. "You'd think Ground Com would have had the foresight to design a vehicle for this kind of situation."

Flames thickened as we increased speed. The grapplers turned bright orange and started to slip.

"I was afraid this wouldn't work," Aaron said. "See? That's why you need me, not one of those greenhorn goat ropers. They'd have really messed this up."

The grapplers snapped. My stomach lurched and the women screamed as we free fell.

The massive bulk of the Retriever rocketed past the portholes, eclipsing the daylight as it shifted beneath us. The deck shook as it made contact under our hull. We slowed and leveled out, but we still fell. Aaron's engines must have taken damage in the strange meteor stream. Flames shot out around the much wider hull of the Retriever.

"There, that's better," Aaron said. "Yeah, so like I was saying, I can't believe Ground Com would buy Gomer-built Retrievers when there are Javan shipyards perfectly capable of designing superior machines."

The port side of the Retriever burst into flames. A main engine sheared off the massive hull and whipped past the shuttle. We fell faster.

"See what I mean?" Aaron said. "That never would have happened to a Javan ship. I understand the need for international trade to hold the Eastern Alliance together, but buying substandard equipment is ridiculous."

"Is he on medication?" Jarell asked.

"Probably," I said.

"I heard that," Aaron said, sounding peeved. "They gave me a lot of medication in healing bay. Makes all these controls just so confusing to read."

The Retriever's remaining engines intensified their thrust as Aaron tried to compensate for the loss of the other one.

"How did you break out of healing bay?" Jarell asked.

"The nurses were very cooperative. Hey, I recognize that voice. Is that you, Patrice?"

"It's Guardian Jarell, sir."

"Didn't we go out once?"

"No."

"Impossible."

Propellant harvesters spewed plumes of vapor from the sides of the remaining engines. They were dangerously overheating. Aaron jettisoned another engine. It exploded a second later.

"Aaron, do you actually have a plan that includes our survival?" I asked.

"Anak, there go the other engines," he replied as he jettisoned the remaining pair. They shot off sideways in a double helix and exploded like miniature suns. We punctured through layers of cloud, hurtling toward a lush forest. The women were hysterical.

"Aaron, eject! Land in your armor."

"Didn't have time to grab it while the healers were chasing me," he said.

"You're flying a ship without armor?"

"Look who's talking."

"Of all the stupid–"

"Don't worry, Chief, I have one more idea. But you might not like it."

The Retriever fired its maneuvering thrusters and slipped out from under the shuttle, taking station a thousand feet to our port. I felt the familiar lift of an antigravity beam slow our drop. The Retriever vanished beneath us as it continued to free fall in a trail of flame. Aaron had sacrificed his power to keep us aloft.

"There's a mobile repulse battery racing to get in range of you," Aaron said. "This antigravity beam should be able to slow your drop long enough until it gets here. It'll take over and repulse you down for a soft landing."

"Your Retriever will crash," I said.

"That's probably why I designated this phase of the operation as Plan C."

"Aaron, I–"

His voice was fuzzy with static. "Don't start, Chief. You'd have done the same for me."

It was suddenly hard to speak.

"Do me … favor?" he said.

"Name it."

"When you … back to … Acropolis, lift a glass … my memory."

"I'll buy a round for the whole barracks."

There was no response.

"Aaron?"

Our hull suddenly lost the antigravity field. Jarell quickly wiped back a tear and gripped the seat struts. A few seconds later, our shuttle was captured in another field. A woman's voice resonated inside the hull. "Rescue vehicle Alpha, this is MRB Delta Beta. Stand by for soft landing in twenty."

"Understood Delta Beta. Thanks for the assist." I tried to hold it together. "What's the status of Delta Epsilon Heavy?"

"Impacted and cratered. No life signs." There was a pause. "We're sorry, sir. Understand he was your friend."

"The best." I whispered.

They brought us down slowly while fire ships doused our smoking hull. We soft landed and *Olympus* Rescue swarmed the hull, instantly dissolving the hatch. I stumbled out and searched the horizon through stinging eyes. Flame-laced smoke coiled upward a mile beyond the forested hills.

Jarell found me waving off a pursuing healer. She hesitated, taking in the distant scene. I didn't know what to say and didn't feel like trying.

"I should check on the civilians," she said.

"Very well."

She turned to go, hesitated, and pivoted. She snapped a full salute across the chest, then to her chin. "Thank you for saving my life, sir."

I returned the salute appropriate to her rank, once across the chest. "Carry on, Guardian."

She nodded and walked off. I returned my attention to Aaron's billowing pyre.

I had to see the wreckage for myself. Judging from a familiar mountain range to the south, the crash site was beyond the Phut border. Relations were strained between our nations since they'd initiated a trade agreement with the West. Crossing without cloaked armor might prove risky just to prove the obvious.

"So what," I muttered and set off toward the woods.

I'd only gone ten feet when I slammed into something invisible. I leapt into a defensive stance. Had Phut sentries acquired cloaking ability?

"Hold on, Chief," Aaron's disembodied voice said.

He materialized in front of me, holding a flight helmet in the crock of his arm. He was dressed in nothing but a patient's gown. "I'm all choked up after hearing what you said to the Battery Commander. I'm really your best friend? Anak, you have to get out more."

"What are you doing here?"

"Don't act so disappointed."

"How did you survive the crash?"

"Who says I crashed?"

A gleaming Dart materialized above us.

"You flew the Retriever remotely from the Dart."

"Of course."

"You didn't tell me."

"You didn't ask. Those were great words, Chief. Thanks."

"Why didn't you get help?"

"I had no choice. The Retriever crew was gearing up to save you but not thinking it through. Probably would have gotten heroic and sacrificed themselves. I couldn't let that happen, so I linked their ship to my Dart and launched it before they could board."

"Your Dart has somebody else's name stenciled on the fuselage," I pointed out.

"Okay, so I borrowed that, too. Anyway, I flew their Retriever with my Dart, and, well, you know the rest."

"Well done."

"Sheer genius, you mean."

"No, genius would have included not crashing Athena's heavy Retriever."

"You'll buy her a new one with the gazillion credits you have piled up."

"Why would I do that?"

"Out of gratitude for me saving your hide again." He glanced at the shuttle. "Looks like Jarell's got things under control. How about we get out of here?"

"Athena's upset?" I asked.

"Yeah, more than usual."

"Let me retrieve my armor first."

Aaron begged a flight suit off one of the fire crews on our way back to the shuttle. When we were within eyeshot of the civilians, they spotted us, abandoned their healers, and came running.

"Wow, a Princess Suri look-a-like contest," Aaron said as the jubilant women reached us.

I was surrounded by blond hair and reaching arms. Aaron was left gawking with the healers.

"Levi, the lady's man," Aaron said loud enough for me to hear. "Who'd'a thought."

Apparently too much to bear, Aaron inserted himself among the women. "Hi, I'm Aaron. Yes, I'm with him. Actually, I was the one who rescued you. No, no thanks is necessary. That's what we do. Oh, gosh, you didn't have to do that. Well, okay, one more.

What's your name again?"

The mother and daughter came up to us as Aaron diverted the other women. "May my daughter thank you?" the mother asked.

I got an eager hug the mother had to pry loose so I could breathe.

"You okay?" I asked the child.

She nodded and tugged on her hair. "But the lady in your suit isn't."

"Is she hurt?"

"She has monsters in her."

A commotion erupted around the opening in the hull. A Guardian flew out of the shuttle. He hit the ground helmet first and flipped over. Weapon fire lanced from the shuttle exit. A second Guardian bounded out, ducking the shots. My insignia was on the arm plate. It was the wounded civilian. Apparently, she felt better now.

She slid down the crumpled wing of the shuttle into the makeshift healing station. A healer tried to approach her but she fired my grappler though his chest. He crumpled over. She retracted the prongs, taking part of his lungs with it. Every Guardian, including Aaron and I, charged her. The Guardian she'd slugged out of the shuttle rolled over and pulled his leg weapon free. She stomped on his chest, ripped the weapon from his glove, and raced for the woods. The rest of us opened fire with restrainer gel. She fired back with blistering accuracy, deflecting every shot, dodging every lunge, then fired my grappler long-range into the woods as if she'd done it her whole life, retracting and cloaking as she fled. The Guardians grappled after her. A flight of Darts whipped overhead and vanished over the trees.

"What in Anak was that all about?" Aaron asked.

"I don't know."

"Maybe an allergic reaction to the heal stick," a healer offered.

"She was given a military grade before we landed," I said.

"That could explain it," the healer said. "Especially if she was Berbai. The rush lasts longer in them."

"She's heading for Phut," one of the other Guardians said.

"Anak, send intercepts," Aaron said. "She could hurt a lot of people before that stuff wears off."

Healers were working on their fallen comrade, fusing his chest back together. I found the little girl. Her mother looked more shaken than she was.

"I need to ask your daughter some questions. Is that okay?"

The woman nodded. I knelt down while Aaron chatted with the mother. "The sick lady in my armor who just flew away," I started. "What did you mean when you said she had monsters in her?"

"The wrinkly lady put them in her," she said. "She tried to put them in me, but it didn't work."

"How did she try to put them in you?"

The girl curled her fingers into a little claw. "She tried to scratch me."

"Did she?"

She shook her head. "She was too slow. I ran around the room and she got tired. She puked green stuff and I hid in the bed cabinet. She tried to scratch me, but I crawled all the way in the back, where she couldn't reach. She got mad and called me bad names." Her eyes widened. "You want to hear them?"

"No, that's okay. What happened next?"

"She busted one of the sleeping tubes and scratched the lady that got sick. She just hit the glass with her fist and smashed it!" The girl thrust her little fist through the air. "Then monsters came out of her nose. They crawled up the tube and started going inside the other lady's nose. Blood came squirting out of it. "

"What did they look like?"

"Smoke," she said.

"How many?"

"Lots of them. The biggest one went first. He's the leader. The others argued about who got to go next. The littlest one had to wait the longest. They were almost all in when they heard you coming. They made the littlest one go back inside the wrinkly lady."

"Why?"

"They were really scared about you seeing the wrinkly lady. The little monster had a hard time making her crawl. She didn't want to hide in the other room and close the door. The monster tried to get back to the busted tube but it was too far."

"What happened to him?"

"He went like this." She curled her hands up in the air, like smoke dissipating.

I didn't know what to ask after that. As strange as her story sounded, somehow it resonated. I remembered Jordan's antics in the Throne Room in Payahdon, his inexplicable assault on the Queen when she'd tried to touch Suri. Maybe the myths about First Age beings infecting others to unnaturally prolong their existence had some basis in fact. Perhaps such an infestation had happened to Babla. Could she have gained ancient knowledge and tech-craft because of the infestation? Had she paid a price for her new-found skills? Her body had deteriorated rapidly; perhaps it had been drained by the demands of a parasite living inside her, or a colony of parasites if the little girl was accurate. Was that the fate Suri continually dodged by avoiding contact with whatever had been inside Babla?

Aaron found armor for both of us. It felt good to be suited up again. Two Darts were issued, along with Athena's request for our immediate return to *Olympus*. I had a lot of reasons not to abide the request. I wanted to join the search for the civilian in my old armor. My gut told me it was imperative she be found and contained. Unfortunately, explaining such an imperative would be impossible to my logically minded mother.

"Ready to go?" Aaron asked.

"We have to help find that civilian."

"Too late, Chief. The search just got called off."

"Why?"

"The lady was quick with the grapplers. She crossed the border into Phut already."

"Since when is that a problem?"

"Since Phut activated that trade deal with Atlantis. They went neutral on the war. No Eastern military allowed on their turf."

"So we go in stealth."

"Ground Com doesn't want to risk an Alliance crisis over a civilian who is clearly not interested in being rescued."

"She's important."

"How so, Chief?"

I hesitated.

"You don't believe that monster-infecting-human story the kid told you, do you?"

"Maybe."

"You're going spooky on me, Chief."

Aaron had called the Western Alliance by a different name. I used that to change the subject. "The West is called Atlantis now?"

"A lot happened while you were floating up there. The West controls both sides of the ocean now, including my favorite stretch of beach in Gomer. Phut is neutral, and all those little costal countries Athena set up for refugees from Baskra have been invaded and subjugated. The West figured they were big enough now to name themselves after half the planet." He made a derogatory gesture with his thumb in front of his nose. "All hail Atlantis."

"Unbelievable." I walked away from the Darts and headed for the woods.

Aaron watched me, then sighed and followed. "Could I at least get a shower before we go breaking international law again?"

"No, that civilian has to be found." I scanned the border for patrol locations and gravity imaged any cloaked units. The grapplers were adjusted too short. I maximized their range.

"I got the oak tree," Aaron said as he snapped his visor down.

We cloaked and grappled into the woods, racing for the border.

We scoured the east half of Phut, ducking patrols and linking with Javan sympathizers village by village. No one had seen the woman in my armor. It was as if she'd vanished the moment she'd crossed the border. None of our covert assets in the Phut military had any leads, either. We then acquired cloaked Darts and flew over the rest of the country, all the way to the enslaved coastal countries. Still no sign.

Phut patrols got dangerously lucky, clustering near where we were searching, as if they had acquired the ability to defeat Javan cloaking technology. I made the frustrating decision to abort the search and return to *Olympus*. Something told me if the Phut military had figured out we were in Phut, the woman would also, which meant the monsters inside her would, as well.

It dawned on me then that Javan's fight was not with Atlantis. Something far more dangerous was using the largest empire on Earth for purposes unknown. If I couldn't find the infected woman in my armor, Suri would be at risk. I had to up covert security around her as best as possible without violating Mestrean sovereignty. I had to figure out who these ethereal beings were that were infecting the leaders of Atlantis, the enemy within the enemy. Once infected, could the victim be freed from them?

We flew east over the Sahara Sea, our wing tips perfectly aligned and only a thumbnail apart. Aaron looked my way into the sun. His faceshield turned opaque as he pointed down. I nodded. We dropped, leveled, and skimmed the sparkling ocean. Mountainous green waves rolled beneath our retracted skids, then blurred as we punched the engines.

There was no logic to such an enormous sea existing on top of the Mestrean/Phutian Escarpment. No rivers fed it; dozens of waterways drained it, rushing through carved canyons and cascading over cliffs to plunge a mile into the immense Javan Valley. Layers of ancient shorelines etched the canyon walls, a testament to its steady evaporation. During my lifetime, the Sahara Sea had receded by a hundred feet, supporting the argument that it had been formed during prehistory, the by-product of a massive global flood. According to the myth, that epic drowning had deposited ancient glaciers here. Its waters had seeded high altitude seas that now drained from rain-less plateaus.

Had the so-called Flood inundated the entire world as the stories recounted? Because of what I'd seen in Tevleh, it was easy to believe enormous waves had crisscrossed the planet during ancient times, casting vast sheets of ice over impossible heights. But I couldn't give quarter to the belief that a spontaneously created ocean could submerge an entire planet. My math said it was impossible, given the resources at hand. Earth's mountains were too tall and her oceans too shallow. Where would the enormous amount of additional water have come from to drown mountains five miles high? Where could such water have receded to?

We crested the eastern shore and whisked into central Mestre, slipping under a formation of Battle Mountains, the Nephillim ships. They'd been on a dual mission: guard the western border of Mestre shared with troublesome Phut and intercept pieces of Babla's ship that continued to rain erratically upon the region.

One of the Battle Mountains was missing. *Olympus,* Athena's flagship, was seven hundred miles east, plowing clouds over the Mestrean capital. Her main guns fired intermittently into the sky, taking out high altitude space debris. Why was she out of formation?

"*Olympus* is flying low and her search screens have been deployed, Chief."

I patched into Ground Com's situation board and studied the dispatches. "Somebody fell off the mountain."

"Who?"

I plotted *Olympus'* plane formations on my canopy display. "Nobody's saying."

"That means it's somebody important."

"The fact that civilian flights are restricted from the search grid reinforces that hypothesis."

Aaron glanced across the narrow space between our canopies. "They're not trying real hard to find this person, Chief. All the flights are clustered on the western edge of the city when they should be spread across the search grid."

"That doesn't make sense."

"Look at the flight pattern."

Aaron posted a diagram on my canopy as we banked around a hilltop village. Warnings flashed on my canopy indicating that I was approaching a restricted search and rescue zone.

"They're flying in concentric curves," Aaron said. "North to south, arcing east across the river into the Government District."

"Like driving a herd of animals to the palace."

"Or maybe one person."

We crested the western outskirts of the capital and banked north towards *Olympus*, away from the search grid. The warnings vanished from my canopy. The Battle Mountain's triangular profile stood out sharp against the azure sky.

"I wonder what your dear mother is up to?" Aaron quipped.

"Not sure. She's not answering my queries."

"Still mad you didn't visit her on your last rotation."

We veered to *Olympus'* stern, avoiding the active starboard launch tubes. Nephillim couples braved the outdoors on shaded terraces protruding from the stern. One couple had a young son, a heartbreaking rarity these decades. He saw us coming and waved. We rewarded him by corkscrewing past the stern at full speed and winged north over the Javan Valley to queue up for a landing.

The sight of my adopted homeland swelled my heart. My mother had founded Javan and Mestre as an experiment in human nation building, a project that had infuriated the West. The half-giant nations of Payahdon believed the only good human was an enslaved one.

We orbited the lush countryside. I steeled myself for my confrontation with Odin. He had never accepted his daughter's decision to adopt me and my baby sister after she'd found us shivering and bleeding in the basement of our parent's destroyed home in Berbai. My sister's death from her wounds was met with his clinical disregard. I had grown up in Odin's mansion in Mer, learning to steer clear of him. The increasing tension between the half-giant West and the human/Trahl/dwarf East had escalated. I'd joined Athena's Guardians to do my part to serve and protect all, including her contrary father. He and I maintained a tacit truce for the sake of our mutual enemy, the West.

Recent events in space threw new doubts on my standing with Odin. Why had he ignored my distress beacon and left those civilians in peril on that shuttle? Odin must have heard the old-fashioned distress beacon from my shuttle. I'd built it from a design I'd recalled from his vault scrolls. Had he intentionally wished us to die during reentry? After centuries of coexisting with the reclusive codger, the answer was automatic. Of course he did.

According to Odin, the goals of the Nephillim superseded any other race, especially human. What was he up to? Why was he repairing the Queen's command saucer? My gut told me that celestial black smudge in the sky had something to do with it. The strange stream of meteors and comet fragments emanating from its gullet was the core motivator of all the West had in play, including the dogged pursuit of Jordan and Suri. I felt it to be important because the West had been concealing the phenomenon with the shielding from the starship.

I needed answers but Odin wouldn't be forthcoming with them. There was only one place I could unearth them, but it wasn't on *Olympus*.

As we winged over and turned south, a gigantic ball of fire punched through the clouds. Shadows radiated behind city towers and sentinel trees as the flaming hull section from Babla's ship dropped with deadly intent. Crossfire swept in from three directions as *Olympus*, aided by two heavy cruisers stationed over Tevleh and Magog, desperately sliced at it. The flaming mass shredded under their relentless bombardment. It vanished in a cloud of ash less than a hundred feet from the ground.

"Cut that one close," Aaron breathed. "How much more of that metallic garbage is up there?"

"That ship was huge. Too bad we couldn't have dissolved the old hull from the inside before Atlantis got their claws on it. The East will be busy for months intercepting the pieces."

"Yeah, with no help from the West."

We banked high over the grassland and lush forest of southern Javan and leveled into an approach vector back toward the towering Mestrean cliffs. I lined up with the flashing red dot that represented *Olympus* on my canopy display. She was twenty miles upriver from the Mestrean Falls, deploying the rest of her search flights as fast as she could spit them out of her launch tubes. The sun broke through the clouds and flashed across the thundering wall of water. My faceshield shaded to compensate. We crested the falls and raced upriver, separating our wing tips for landing. The triangular profile of *Olympus* grew.

"Dart Flight, Ground Com."

"Ground Com, Dart Flight," I responded.

"Cleared for landing port-side tube Alpha. Welcome home."

"Thanks Ground Com. Looking forward to a shower," Aaron

said.

Under normal protocol, flight operations landed all incoming aircraft from the control summit instead of the pilots. This was to protect *Olympus'* volatile Operations Deck. But our service record yielded us the privilege to land our own aircraft. We roared into tunnel Alpha and plugged the landing circles dead center before the deck officer could even get his batons up. He shook his head, lowered his arms, and stifled a grin.

Aaron popped his canopy the same time I did mine. A hundred feet in front of us, a Retriever hovered into the loading end of a starboard launch tube. The catapult grabbed the extended launch heel as the Retriever cycled its heavy engines for takeoff.

I jumped to the deck and Aaron landed beside me. We both snapped salutes to the officer.

"Look who's Deck Officer for the *Olympus* now," Aaron yelled as the catapult hurled the Retriever out the starboard tube. "What happened? *Valhalla* still mad they lost the Fleet meet?"

The deck officer turned red and returned our salutes. "Sirs, Athena requests your presence on the Peak."

"Understood," I said. "What time?"

"Request was immediate, sirs."

"We just went through some rough *drek* up there." Aaron jerked a thumb toward the rocky ceiling. "Can I at least get a shower?"

"Sorry, sir."

"I smell like Anak's armpit."

"Yes, sir. I noticed that, sir. Lift to Peak is straight ahead, past the repair bays."

"I know where the stupid lift is," Aaron grumped and fell into step beside me.

CHAPTER ELEVEN

SARAH

Jordan had briefly admitted his crazy dive off *Olympus* to me with little detail. Tonight, I saw all of it in my dreams. While the night creatures of Costa Rica chattered beyond my balcony, I felt the sickening rush and saw the vines blur as Jordan plunged into the great river that had once bisected Mestre's capital; a river that had shifted east at the end of the Second Age and survived into the Fourth, now renamed the Nile.

I followed Jordan as he searched for me in the past. He struggled to find his way through streets and plazas I knew from decades of visits. I couldn't tell if I was praying, wishing, or guiding him, but with each step he took, I urged him closer to where I'd been waiting.

At some point in the night, I actually fell asleep. When I woke, I tried to envision Jordan but without a glimmer of success. I sensed forcing the connection between us was futile. It happened on its own, following a rhythm beyond manipulation. I accepted the premise that we were connected. I struggled with the fear that I wasn't seeing the past; I was seeing Jordan's present. A present that was as changeable as mine. I hugged my knees in my large bed and prayed my heart out for him.

Carlos's wife suggested at breakfast that we celebrate my return and make a day trip to the beach. I welcomed the diversion. To my delight, Krax and Laura joined us. Perhaps they worried about other infected strangers who might be stalking me.

We piled into the SUVs and drove to Quepos, where we took the boat ferry from the beach across the tidal wash to the peninsula. It wasn't really a ferry, just a man with a flat-bottom boat. He poled fifty feet through the swirling tide to a path marking the entrance to Manuel Antonio National Park. Clouds heavy with rain drifted low over the jungle, winking rays of morning light as they passed. White-faced monkeys skittered and leapt through orchid-heavy boughs, keeping a sharp eye on our shoulder bags and the food they held.

Carlos's large family required two boat trips to cross. Despite all of us helping, the youngest boy managed to accidently fall into the water and get happily soaked.

Anticipation of the view ahead spurred me up a familiar path through the jungle. We crested the hill and took in the breathtaking expanse of wild beach. Crashing waves and low-hanging trees swept along the great arc of sand. Families picnicked beneath the bent trunks, shooing away white-faces bent on thievery. We found a vacant hollow in the trees with low-swaying branches shading smooth sand and a pair of three-foot iguanas. The surf was quieter here than at the Quepos beach, buffeted by a volcanic seawall of rock thrusting up from the waves like the fins of a sea serpent. Trees tenaciously grew from its crevices, washing their limbs in the surging sea.

A fallen tree provided ample seating. Laura and I chatted while Krax went exploring with Carlos, his wife, and most of the children. Nina, Carlos's youngest daughter, stayed behind and nestled in my lap. I absently stroked her hair just as I'd done with my little cousins, Becca and Liv-ya, so long ago. I remembered the first time Jordan had met them. My heart warmed at the memory. Why couldn't I have relived that happy memory last night?

"*Senora* Sarah," Nina whispered with a secretive look on her face. "Tell me again about the … the …" She wrinkled her face in concentration, rolled her eyes, and said, "*La montaña sagrado.*"

"Sorry?"

She sighed with dramatic exasperation, *"Usted y Jordan."*

Laura laughed. "I think she means when you and Jordan first kissed."

"Sí!" Nina giggled. *"Cuando él te besó!"*

I smiled as I began to describe that wonderful evening on the pyramid. But then I suddenly found it hard to breathe. Impossible images flooded my memory as if someone had invaded my soul and splashed obscenities over my past. They attacked what had been, wrenching it away and forcing a new what-was. Their terror tore at my sanity. The altered scene played out over and over, taunting me with its terrible outcome. My body stiffened as if to hold onto the last shred of what had been. I fought to bring it back.

"No," I cried. "That's not how it happened!"

"Ow, you're squeezing me!" Nina cried.

"Oh God." I released her into Laura's arms and tried to get to my feet. "I'm sorry. I have to go."

Laura shifted Nina to her other hip and stopped me from rising. "Wait."

I barely heard her. The altered memory played out again, this time horribly real. I battled its emergence, as if this was the final pass that needed to cement its existence. I flew as if I were a spirit circling the Sacred Mountain, spiraling to the summit, hunting for Jordan as he ran.

I fell off the log. The beach hardened into a stone slab. I was on a garden terrace. Jordan kissed me. The moment was so achingly real, so serene, I almost missed the invasive change: an assassin lurking in the translucent leaves. He raised his weapon.

"Jordan, get down!" I screamed.

"Sit back on the log," Laura said from somewhere far away. "Take a breath."

The assassin fired.

CHAPTER TWELVE

JORDAN

The fact that I'd done a nose dive off a flying mountain into a raging river started to register. Why had I act so recklessly?

Reason One: Nobody was going to imprison me, protect me, or adopt me. I hadn't traveled thirteen thousand years into the past just to become somebody's project or prodigy.

Reason Two: I was going to find Suri and … well, I was going to find her. Reason Two was still in development.

Both reasons had mandated an immediate departure from *Olympus*. Lacking a courtesy shuttle or a bean stalk, I'd jumped. Now I had to evade capture and find a high position to recon my surroundings. I might be down here for a while before I accomplished my mission. I had to locate a secure place to take shelter, preferably near food and non-lizard-infested water sources. If this was Suri's home, with luck I might be able to spot the palace from here. During my fall, I'd glimpsed just how big the place was. It spread to the horizon in all directions. Finding the palace, much less her, was going to be tricky. Was she really going to marry what's-his-face?

I stowed that thought. No way would she settle for Amon. She'd sooner marry a rock. I just hoped I ranked higher than a rock. I didn't know how she felt about me. We'd become friends during the insane field trip halfway around the world, from Atlantis to here.

Good friends, in fact; maybe even a spark of something more. The one time I'd finally gotten the nerve to tell her how I felt, she'd been unconscious. It was during a battle on a glacier and she'd just fallen off a cliff. Bad timing.

I scouted along the buildings facing the river and found a tall ziggurat-shaped structure with a lush roof garden overlooking the river. It looked like it might be an apartment complex or hotel. Kids chased each other along its layered balconies. The lobby sported the Mestrean version of a glass elevator. I decided to skip that and hunt for the stairs. They had to have them.

Wrong. I gave up and chanced the lift, enduring a two-minute ride facing the doors, my back to a cluster of moms, dads, and kids. A toddler pulled river grass off my pant legs. He looked like he was three decades old—my age.

Sunlight and shadows rippled across the translucent doors as the elevator slowed. A feeling hit me. Something was wrong. Suri was afraid.

That was crazy. How on Earth could I possibly know what she was feeling?

The thought grew into a certainty. My heart pounded. I could see her. She was standing on the edge of a terrace, ready to give up. But give up on what?

Give up on you, moron.

The doors opened and the children bolted into the sunshine. The parents chased after them as they raced to a playground in the middle of the roof garden.

I found the front parapet and wedged in between a cluster of trees. The city straddled both sides of the river, more on the west than on the east. The river raced north to the crest of the falls, throwing up waves against bends where the current struck the shore. The billowing spray of that massive waterfall shrouded clusters of tall buildings rising on both banks. Five arched bridges of different designs stitched the city together.

The riverfront was festive. Garlands swung from balconies and street musicians entertained gatherings of people. Shoppers navigated through street markets, clutching satchels of brightly wrapped packages. Parents had babies wrapped in hip carriers or floating in front of them in colorful wheel-less strollers. Toddlers skipped alongside or hovered around their parents on tethers like animated balloons. The strangest thing wasn't the hairstyles or attire, nor the variety of races or the Jetson-style child-carrying tech. It was the lack of old people. Except for the kids, everyone appeared to be in their twenties. Were Numu and I the only people on the planet who looked like we were pushing forty?

There was a substantial plateau beyond the eastern outskirts with more prominent buildings covering the summit. A tall cloud billowed behind the imposing structures. Maybe another waterfall was on the other side of the plateau. If this was Amon's capital, that's where his dad, the Ra, would put his palace, up high and looking almighty. My heartbeat quickened. Odds were that's where Suri would be.

Olympus crossed my field of view. Its massive shadow blanketed the river and rippled over the eastern quarter. It was cruising north toward the falls. Athena's aircrafts seemed to be engaged in a search over the western part of the city. They flew in diamond patterns of four, weaving in a north-south-north serpentine, steadily shifting toward me.

A short couple came down a garden path and approached the rampart. I held still in the shadows. What appeared to be a camera fluttered in the air and followed the couple's movements like an excited hummingbird. They faced it and smiled, posing for a picture with the river and *Olympus* in the background. Their heads had the characteristic elongated skull draped with shimmering auburn hair, just like Aizah, Aaron's on-again/off-again fiancé.

I wondered what she was up to. I'd made her promise to guard Suri. After what had happened in the medical tent, that probably made that promise challenging.

I smiled, remembering the confrontation between the Javan and Mestrean Guardians while I'd been put into deep freeze. Prince Amon and the venerable Numu had come to take Suri back to Mestre for their long-awaited wedding. She hadn't looked like she was all that interested in the idea. She'd hesitated, and Amon, charming as ever, had tried to drag her out of the tent. Lots of yelling had ensued and weapons had come out. Suri had ended it before it had gotten fun. She'd agreed to go just so everybody wouldn't start gluing each other to the ceiling. Aizah had been one ticked off Trahl when they'd left.

Yeah, she'd keep her promise. She'd shadow Suri like a second skin. But if Suri caved in to Amon's advances, Aizah wouldn't do anything to stop it. Guardians were like the U.S. military. They protected civilians from outside threats, not stupid decisions.

Did these festivities mean there was something important going down, like a royal wedding? I had to find her.

Athena's aircrafts continued the methodical grid search over the city behind me. Cone-shaped beams issued from their undercarriages and swept the rooftops. Scanners, I suppose. None scanned the east side of the river. That probably meant they knew which side of the river I'd come ashore.

Olympus glided over the bridges like a jagged *Hindenburg*. A crowd gathered to watch. She came to a full stop a mile north of my position. Her shadow covered the full width of the river. Watercraft resembling hovering jet skis circled across the turbulent waves. The drivers waved excitedly.

The searching aircraft turned to make a pass down the waterfront. Those scanners would sweep over me if I didn't get moving.

I took the elevator down and paused at the exit of the building. A diamond pattern of jet-shaped shadows zipped down the boulevard above the clogged traffic. Drivers looked up in succession as the swiftly moving shadows darkened their cars. Then the shadows stopped.

I held my breath. The gleaming crafts descended like silent Harriers. How could they know I was here? Maybe I'd been bugged and they were tracking my signal. But why sweep the entire city? Why not just rush in and lasso me?

The jets hovered at an altitude of twenty feet and shifted over the park next to the river. Armored Guardians dropped down and swept the grounds with thin metal devices. They were hunting in the general area where I'd come ashore. If I'd been bugged, they would have pounced by now.

A crowd gathered to check out the hovering aircraft. The

bridges were clogged with folks looking up at *Olympus*. Nobody was flying over the east bank yet. I grabbed a hooded tunic hanging on a hook in the lobby, covered my head, and headed uptown toward a bridge.

The sun slipped low over the city, bronzing the rooftop gardens. I hiked up winding streets in the midst of a boisterous Mestrean parade. It was a challenge to keep my bearings in these narrow streets flanked by tall construction. The city lights brightened ahead and music echoed off the buildings. Cheers erupted, followed by applause and whistles.

I used the fading sunset on the rooftops to keep me oriented east. That was the direction of a wide hill in the middle of the eastern half of the city. A large complex of government-like buildings covered its summit. I bet my limited time before I got sick again that the Ra's palace was one of those buildings. Patrols of Mestrean Guardians were stationed at the intersections, carefully watching the crowds. I remembered their uniforms from the confrontation in the medical tent. They wore armored uniforms similar to Javan Guardians, except their insignia was a gold lion instead of the Javan silver eagle. They also packed more weaponry than I'd seen Levi or Aaron carry. Their visors were up and they were clearly on alert: heads on swivel, faces expressionless, eyes watching everything.

I'd taken the extra measure of camouflaging myself with a party headdress I'd borrowed from an intoxicated reveler several blocks back. I wrapped his scarf around my face and shielded my eyes. I had to remind myself that this ancient time was about a hundred years more advanced than my own. We had facial recognition capabilities back where I came from, which meant they might have that and more. From what the Javan pilots were doing back on the river bank, it looked like they could follow DNA traces on the ground. Hopefully, this mob would obliterate my trail.

The crowd flowed into a wide plaza, affording me my first view of the hill and its official looking complex since seeing it from the rooftop next to the river. It exuded age and power from every statue, column, and fountain.

"That has to be it," I breathed.

The crowd bunched up in the plaza. People milled sideways, craning to see past headpieces that stood motionless in the jam. I wormed my way through to get a better view. Mestrean Guardians on mounted golden stallions manned a formidable barricade bisecting the plaza. Their uniforms were regal and ornate. They could have given the Queen's Mounted Guard at Buckingham Palace a run for their money, but they didn't hold rank as cleanly and their horses stamped impatiently. Maybe they weren't called out to do crowd control very often. Maybe this was a rare event, the eve of a royal wedding?

A stream of fancy air cars flowed behind the stamping hooves and glittering armor, depositing VIPs on a red carpet. The crowd pressed against the barriers, eager for a look between the horses, cheering and screaming with each new arrival. I remembered when I'd been in Nice and had seen a crowd of pedestrians go nuts over a French celebrity. He could have been an accountant to me. Seeing these people cheer as the VIPs exited their cars seemed just as strange. I had no clue who they were or what they had done to deserve the accolades. For all I knew, they were just rich people. Would an ancient visitor to my age make the same assessment at a Hollywood gala?

The crowds cheered as the apparent who's who of Mestre greeted their fans with dramatic nods and swooping touches to their chins. Some touched with both hands and gushed to their fans. After the love had been sufficiently shared, Guardians with loads of medals ushered them through an ornate stone arch rivaling the entrance to Payahdon's inner citadel.

I saw movement above the crowd. Small devices floated in the shadows above the glare of spotlights, gliding along the length of the barricade. Were they devices to scan the civilians? Maybe I'd been spotted.

I backed away from the barricade. I didn't plan to crash this party through the front door, anyway. I headed north up the closest street bordering the base of the complex. There, I reached a higher vantage point and kept a nervous eye on the sky for scanners. To an arriving visitor, the gate would appear to be the only access up to the complex on the plateau. But a place this big would have multiple entrances, a logistical necessity. Trash, hired help, and dignitaries doing undignified things would use side doors. Breaking into this monstrous place would be risky, leaning toward insane, but I was determined to try. It wasn't the first time I'd barged into a secure building. On those occasions, I'd been part of a highly trained team that had planned, prepared, and rehearsed the operation until the cows had come home and died of old age.

I studied the endless buildings and fortifications spanning the imposing escarpment. Back in the city, I'd been fairly lucky in navigating the winding streets to reach the plaza; almost as if I'd had a guide. Now that my objective was in sight, I felt less confident.

I steeled myself, remembering my goal: find Suri and if she wanted to leave, provide whatever means I could to extract her, thus saving her from what I hoped was a shotgun wedding. Nobody should be forced to do anything they didn't want to do, especially when it came to marriage. I didn't presume to be a replacement for Amon but I was her friend in the deepest sense. Whatever she wanted I would make happen … or let happen.

"Whatever she wants," I said and resumed my course north in search of a side door.

The buildings diminished. Vacant lots appeared the farther north I walked along the escarpment. Past the city rooftops, massive ornamental structures continued to present themselves in full glory along the summit. Fifty Versailles Palaces could have fit in the space.

The Mestrean Palace had to be up there. I'd been counting paces to estimate the distance from the main gate, noting landmarks and avenues of escape. A plan formed as I took in the details. I'd find Suri, and if she wanted to skip the wedding, I'd bug her out to the falls, where I'd let one of *Olympus'* search planes spot me and beg a ride back to Athena before the bad guys caught us. Athena had shown approval for my feelings for Suri. I was gambling that her approval included a willingness to risk ticking off an entire country.

Why would Suri agree to marry Amon anyway? She'd tried to explain it once. For some insane reason, she thought he was her only prospect. In my age, a woman like her would have dozens of guys trying to build up the nerve to court her. An old-fashioned word that didn't get used much because it was synonymous with another old-fashioned word: commitment. Was that why I was here? Was I risking my hide to compete for her hand?

"No, get that out of your head," I said. "You're just a friend."

I pictured her reaching out to me on the raft, asking me to dance.

"A really good friend."

I felt her tears in the snow cave. I smelled her hair brushing my face.

I wrapped my arms over my head and clenched my fists. "All right, maybe I love her."

I walked faster. A quarter-mile north of the gate, the ground vibrated with the rumbling of heavy machinery. It sounded like a promising infiltration point. Noise and disruption made great cover.

The din came from a construction site that stretched east all the way to the foot of the plateau. Large mechanical devices with big claws swung back and forth, ripping boulders out of the side of a cliff. I searched the distant edge of the site. A rush of excitement came over me. I suddenly knew how to get into the palace.

I spotted what looked like a break area. I grabbed a worker's smock and slipped through the orchestrated chaos.

How to Infiltrate a Construction Site

Rule One: Act like I'm supposed to be here.

Rule Two: Act like I know where I'm going.

Rule Three: Don't play with the giant claw machine.

I went past a couple of workers bent over a slab of granite. One held what looked like a supercharged drill with a toothed cup at the end. The other appeared to be explaining something to the man holding the drill. The man with the drill set the cup on the granite and grunted something at the machine. The drill spun so fast the cup became a blinding blur. Gas shot from the tool's housing and doused the granite in a mist. The blurry cup bit into the stone like it was made of butter. A second later, the man backed the drill out of a six-inch hole.

I'd read about unusual drill holes found at Giza in the late 1800's by the British surveyor, Petrie; unusual because machined cup drilling hadn't been in use yet, the Industrial Revolution still being in its infancy. Or was it in its second infancy? I'd read Christopher Dunn's fascinating theories of how the bore holes might have been made by the equivalent of ancient ultrasonic drills.

"Looks like you guys were right," I whispered.

I passed the outline of a foundation large enough to support a structure the size of a small town. A team of uniformed men stood in the bottom of the foundation with a floating model of the finished project rotating in the air next to them. It was a model of an immense pyramid. Work teams were pouring molten granite into shimmering form work seemingly made of smoke.

"Wish you could have seen this, Krax," I said. Wish I had my camera. Sigh. Something else to sketch that nobody would believe if and when I got back home.

By the time it took me to walk the length of the pyramid foundation, ten feet of wall had been added to the structure. I was watching a construction process that might have been used to build Egyptian pyramids and Inca fortifications, an incredible process involving poured-in-place stone. Since we didn't have the technology in my age, the mere idea of such a method existing in the past was too hard for scientists to swallow, despite fibers protruding from rock indicating that it may have been used.

I hurried through material storage yards, keeping my objective in sight. Artificial light steadily increased as dusk settled over the city. A long line of construction workers followed a path that wound up to the top of the plateau. I hung out at the base, casually watching for the right worker to come by. It took a while, but he finally showed up.

He looked tired and was carrying lots of heavy equipment. I slipped into line and worked my way up behind him. When he stumbled, I tapped him on the shoulder and motioned to let me help carry some of his stuff. He nodded and I shouldered the heaviest pieces. He touched his chin and said something that sounded like a blurred version of "Thank you" in Javan. I coughed, touched my chin in response, and faded behind him a little to hinder further conversation.

Up top, guards stood post. They kept watch but didn't appear to be on as high alert as the squads down in the city. Important people gathered along a wall overlooking the construction site. More than a few guests seemed to be enjoying their refreshments too much. The guards tried to manage the thickening crowd and prevent them from getting too close to the edge. More distractions and noise for the guards. Outstanding. This might actually work.

I took a breath and pressed on, keeping close behind my new friend. As expected, there was a security point at the top of the path. My friend and I entered the checkpoint together. One guard checked him while another stopped me and asked something. I coughed hard and pretended as if it was too hard for me to respond. My friend noticed and said something, pointing at the tools I carried.

They let me through. Twenty feet into the crowd, I handed the tools back to my friend and slipped away. It wasn't exactly James Bond, but hey, I was inside.

I spotted a plain building with multiple doors and small windows, clues that it might be the workers' housing. Then I found an open window to a bedroom, which proved I was right. There was a closet with men's clothing in it. I picked out pants and a smock that looked formal enough to navigate the party without attracting attention. The clothing automatically adjusted to fit me. Very cool.

I headed for my objective: a brightly lit, heavily colonnaded mother-of-all-palaces. I found a crowd of inebriated guests heading for the entrance and inserted myself in the middle of them. I helped steady one guy over a large step at the entrance. He slurred incomprehensibly at me. I nodded back and laughed as he staggered up a set of wide stone stairs. Music and conversation rose in volume as we climbed. The final rays of sunset shot through a massive arch flanked by gold lions. It beamed from a pillared hall long enough to land a Cessna on.

A thousand people danced under glittering lights. An imperious ornate stage thrust from the north wall, arranged with a tableau of important-looking people presiding over the crowd or posing to be noticed. If Princess Suri and Prince Amon, the future rulers of Mestre, were anywhere in this massive hall, they had to be up there with the VIPs.

My heart raced. I took a deep breath and forced myself to relax. The place had to be saturated with surveillance devices watching for anything out of the ordinary. I carefully made my way closer to the platform, using my drunken buddy as cover. He didn't seem to mind as long as I kept replacing his empty goblet with a fresh one along the way.

I steered close enough to the stage to check faces. Some large ugly guy with a gold headpiece sat on a throne in the center of the platform. That had to be who Amon called the Ra. He looked like he could be Amon's father.

A tired-looking woman wearing a ton of jewelry sat next to him on a smaller throne. That had to be mom or the latest substitute. Ambassador Numu stood next to the Ra, waving his arms in his usual theatrical gestures as he pontificated. He was being ignored and didn't seem to notice. He'd packed on some extra pounds since I'd last seen his old bald self.

Everyone in this room, with the exception of the Ra and Numu, appeared to be in their twenties. In the center of a cluster of fawning ladies, each who could have landed a multi-million-dollar modeling career in my age, was a very happy Prince Amon. I scanned the rest of the stage for any sign of Suri, but she wasn't there. I backed away into the crowd and made a careful recon of the rest of the enormous room.

An hour later, I spotted her. Those slender arms, the curve of her back, and the shimmering drape of her hair spreading across her bare shoulders like a soft mantle were unmistakable. Gold and red ribbons were woven throughout her flowered hair. She stood alone on the steps, her lovely profile turned away, staring out at the distant glittering city.

A dozen Guardians were clustered about her in a tight perimeter. Plainclothes types were discretely positioned in a thirty-foot circle, pretending to talk to other guests. They were easy to spot because of their herculean muscles under their fancy dinner smocks and the way their eyes constantly scanned the room. I was as close as I could get without being scrutinized. Surely, they'd been briefed on my appearance so they could shoot the instant they made a match. It started to sink in just how lucky I'd been to get this far.

My heart pounded as I formulated my next move. Now that I knew Suri's location, I could create a diversion at the opposite end of the hall. A small fire fueled with alcohol and drapery would do the trick. The place was all stone. The fire would make a bunch of smoke and billow straight up, leaving plenty of air for the crowd. I could light a rope fuse and be back here, ready to spirit Suri away when the crowd broke through her guards. As long as she stayed on those steps.

A couple of women joined her. She nodded sullenly at their words. Back on the platform, Amon continued to enjoy the glamorous groupies fawning over him. He seemed oblivious to Suri. She deserved better than that, but did I stand a chance of being that guy?

She turned from her friends and pushed the hair out of her face. My heart froze. There was a gold wedding band on her finger. I stared at it, my world imploding. This was the *after*-wedding celebration.

I stared for too long, long enough for her eyes to lock on me.

One of the guards noticed her gasp and followed her gaze. I ducked and faded into the crowd, cursing my stupidity. Had he made me?

Silent and smooth, the guard parted the crowd and came straight my way, moving slowly so as to not disturb the party. Other guards on the balconies leaned over the railings and looked in my direction. The exits filled with guards. The place had gone into lock down.

I skirted the dance area and headed for a window in the wall. Expansive gardens and paths were a bone-crushing hundred feet below. A balcony hung below the next window fifty feet down the wall. I could jump to it and free climb the masonry to the ground. Maybe.

Guards converged on my position. I skimmed the wall, heading for the window, but plainclothes Guardians got there first. They held devices in their hands, concealing them from the guests as they aimed in my direction. I ducked and felt something hot hiss over my head.

Someone grabbed me around the neck. I struck his head. It was like hitting cast iron. My assailant manhandled me through a square hole in the wall where a moment earlier it hadn't existed. The plainclothes rushed forward. A thick stone panel swung shut in their faces.

It was pitch black except for a distant red light flickering at the end a sloping passageway. My rescuer shifted his armored grip so one gloved hand covered my mouth. I didn't like the feel of it. I struggled and banged my head against his faceshield, but my assailant still dragged me down the passageway. We reached the end and he pulled me into the darkness. A stone panel scraped open to reveal dim red light, then slammed shut after I was through. As we descended long ramps, I wondered if my captor was friend or foe. Until I was certain, I had to assume the latter.

He stopped and relaxed his grip. When he did, I ducked and rolled. He grabbed my leg, pulled me back as if I was a toy, and sat on me. His helmet lit up, revealing a determined and oddly familiar face.

I realized who was crushing my gut with his butt. "No friggin' way."

He looked like Carlos from the restaurant in Costa Rica, a much younger and healthier version of the out-of-shape, chain-smoking version I'd come to know and love. But his face was unmistakable.

He placed his palm on my chest. "*Teha* Jordan." He touched his own chest. "*Shua* Baak."

He didn't speak Spanish but his voice was unmistakable. What was Carlos doing here introducing himself as if we were meeting for the first time? He'd saved my neck and seemed to know exactly where he was taking me. If he'd wanted to do me harm, he'd have left me in the hands of the imperial goons upstairs. I decided to trust him now and sort out the rest later.

We walked in silence through a labyrinth of narrow tunnels. As we did, he stopped at intersections and held his hand to his helmet, nodding and answering back to somebody. He was being directed somewhere.

It suddenly hit me what was happening. Anak, he was probably taking orders from Athena! She was telling him where her air force would rendezvous for my extraction.

Now wasn't the time to bolt. I'd be lost down here and probably captured by someone worse. I bided my time.

After another hour of walking through a labyrinth of tunnels, the floor leveled. He pushed a massive stone panel open. It swung on stone pins as if it was made of balsa wood.

We stepped outside. Stars shimmered through trees heavy with the smell of fruit. A smooth-faced moon descended full and orange. It vanished behind a wall. We were in a garden far from the construction site. The faint glow of lights tinted the sky to my left. That would be north. The moon hovered above the wall in the opposite direction. I was on the east side of the plateau, on the other side of the city and river.

I searched the sky for any signs of approaching aircraft and scanned the walls for any openings. I'd have to examine them by feel, maybe find a hidden panel like the one we'd just went through. If there was some way I could disable Carlos without injuring him, maybe rub fruit juice in his eyes, I could make a run for it and …

My heart sank. What was the point? Suri was married. I was going to be sick in a few days and dead in a week if I didn't go back to Athena.

Carlos—Baak—motioned me over to a bedroll spread out on a carpet of sweet-smelling grass. He handed me a plate of food and drink. Apparently, we were spending the night. That didn't make sense. Why not bug me out under the cover of dark?

We had a brief meal together, eating in silence since we couldn't talk to each other. Carlos cleaned up the remains and showed me the different types of fruit hanging from the trees. I'd been in this age long enough to recognize a lot of them. Still, I didn't feel like eating, but he was insistent that I stuff myself. Yep, it was Carlos all right.

I picked one of my favorites, one that tasted like soft beef jerky.

There was a small pond and stream in the far corner with a hedged area. An outdoor privy. Once I used it, he pointed to the bedroll, "*Cyschu,* Jordan."

I guess that meant he wanted me to sack out. The man had risked his life to save mine back at the palace. Regardless of how this ended, I owed him. I nodded my thanks. "*Brosheleau*, Baak."

"*Brah-la,* Ad-Jordan." He nodded lower, the sign of a friend, then retreated into the darkness.

The night peepers stopped chirping as the stone panel scraped shut. A few seconds later they resumed their melodic rhythm. I waited a few minutes, then got up to check the panel. It was closed tight. I was alone.

Something told me I didn't have a clue about what was going down. I asked that something if it would mind filling me in. Then I remembered the strange voice in my head before I'd awakened on the *Olympus*, the one that had told me to go tell everybody something on the mountain. What mountain?

The bedroll thickened and warmed around me. I was exhausted from the day. I dreamed about a pyramid-shaped mountain with clouds girding its middle and Suri's voice calling me. I forced myself to stay awake and stare at the cold stars through the trees. Stupid dreams and voices in my head were no comfort. I was tired of seeing things and thinking they had any meaning other than that I was deluding myself. I was tired of this stupid adventure.

Abort mission. Take me home, Mom.

I fell asleep and dreamed of nothing.

It was a horrible night. I woke up constantly. I thought I heard movement, grabbed a stick, sharpened it against the wall, and kept it ready beside the bedroll. I climbed back in and feigned sleep but put a rock under my head to keep awake. If there was an intruder, my best chance of overpowering him was surprise. Let him think I was asleep, then attack from close up.

Fatigue from the day and a full stomach of meat fruit must have pulled me back to sleep. While I was out, I got hit on the head. I jerked awake and felt sticky mash in my hair. Smelled like pear.

Morning pastels overlaid the remnants of the night. Stars dotted the zenith. My eyes felt like lead and my bones ached. Not good signs. I recognized the initial symptoms of the ancient disease dogging me. Probably the reason I hadn't been able to stay awake during the night. I only had a few days before it would immobilize me.

Branches rustled in a slight breeze. My hand curled around my feeble weapon. I moved into a crouch and backed into the shadow of the wall. High above me towered the east face of the plateau. The multitude of columned buildings slowly took on color in the predawn light.

I watched for movement between the brightening trees. Sunrise struck the summit. The reflection illuminated the garden with rapid intensity. There, beyond the trees, a dead branch shifted on the grass.

The intruder was cloaked. He was too clumsy for a Guardian. None of Levi's people would give themselves away like that. I steeled myself and wondered if he was armored. Swinging this stick in his face wouldn't do squat, but it would feel good trying.

A warm wet breath blew in my ear. I ducked and swung. My stick shattered on invisible metal.

Aizah materialized, laughing. She wore scratched-up Javan armor. Multiple displays flickered around her retracted helmet, shading her impish smile. Both weapons on her shapely legs were armed and glowing. She'd been leaning against the wall, her hand on her hip, probably the whole time I'd been trying to get a bead on the other intruder.

"That's no way to greet a friend." She pushed off the wall and stretched, swishing her auburn mane. "Good reflexes with the stick." She brushed remnants of it off her forearm.

"How long have you been here?" I asked.

"Never left your side."

"That explains why I kept hearing things."

"Don't insult me." She jerked her head toward the trees. "I *never* reveal. That was Diago. He couldn't stop eating."

Diago materialized in the grove, wearing new Javan armor and grinning sheepishly behind his visor.

"Nice suit," I said. "No longer a recruit, I see."

Aizah translated and Diago nodded proudly.

"Right," she said. "You know what the hedge is for. The pond is heated. Here's fresh clothing."

I took the clothes and trudged to the hedge.

"We're on a tight schedule," she stated. "Do be quick about it."

"I'm in no hurry to get back to *Olympus*," I said.

"Understood, Commander," she said sarcastically. "You have ten minutes before the transport arrives. Regardless of your condition at that time, I *will* extract you. Understood?"

Resistance might be futile but I was going to do it anyway, just to tick her off. I slowly washed and dressed, counting Mississippis.

"Jordan, it's time to—"

At the last possible second I stepped out from the privy hedge, fixing the last clasp on my tunic. She rewarded me with a raised eyebrow and an annoyed smile. Diago laughed.

They grappled me over the wall. We hiked into a forest of date palms, juniper, and wild orange. Diago took point, while Aizah brought up the rear. Their weapons were out and glowing.

"When did you first spot me?" I asked.

"The moment you dove off *Olympus*."

"Really? Gee, thanks for all the help in the river."

"I was two miles away, guarding Suri as promised. Besides, you were perfectly safe. There's a barrier that catches people foolish enough to get caught in the current and conveys them to shore. You could have waited and then walked out."

"What about the forty-foot crocodile?"

She fought a smile. "The water lizard only wanted you to clean his teeth."

"Where are we going?"

"You'll find out."

"Bad answer. Diago, where are we going?"

Diago looked at me and shrugged his armored shoulders.

"Great, you still don't speak English."

"Engel," Aizah said.

"Whatever."

We reached a road. An air car with camouflage netting hovered in the shade of a grove. Four Javan Guardians materialized from the woods. It was clear what was happening. I was being bugged out with enough security to make sure I didn't try anything stupid, like escape.

Aizah pointed her weapon toward the car. "Do get in."

I was going back to *Olympus*, willing or not. Actually, I didn't care. There was no point staying in this stupid country. There was no point to anything now.

The car lifted and silently flew east through the forest. Suri's palace disappeared behind swaying palm fronds.

CHAPTER THIRTEEN

LEVI

Aaron grumbled as we ducked under the organic hull of a Dagger III hovering in its growth cradle. He didn't even seem to notice the nutrient scoops, although he always checked out Ground Com's latest toys.

"You *are* in a bad mood," I observed.

"We should be lounging on the cliffs of the Acropolis by now, clean and fed."

Aaron mentally spiraled downward after a tough mission. Bathing, followed by eating, brought him back.

Normally, teams got a day of toes in Acropolis grass before going out again, but Athena's urgency might be fed by the same foreboding that was clawing at me. Seeing that blank streak in space had rattled me. It had felt evil, right down to the core of my gut. Something was coming that would make this war look like a training exercise. Time was its prey, but I had nothing to anchor that conclusion down other than emotion and some obscure stars.

"Just because your mother is three times taller than us doesn't give her the right to order us around."

"Adopted mother," I corrected for the umpteenth time. "And she's not ordering; she's asking. Probably has a good reason."

"Are you turning silver or something?"

I swatted his armored back.

"Lift's just a little farther past that pretty Dart."

"I know where the lift is," I said.

His grin was back. "Let me hold the portal open for you."

We rode the clear tube up through the core of the mountain. I never failed to marvel at the view. Solid rock blurred past us, flashing successive views of hollowed-out caverns that held the city. *Olympus* had fifty-three such caverns constructed within the bowels of a severed mountain, lifted from the ranges of Him-Aalaya two hundred centuries ago, using fantastic organic machines salvaged from a First Age vault discovered beneath the Acropolis. After the massive *Olympus* and her eleven siblings had been commissioned, the machines had mysteriously died and disintegrated, fading from memory until they became only a legend. Many of the caverns assigned for living space showed signs of expansive new construction. The antiquated style of Elder architecture was unmistakable.

"That must be housing for the Nephillim refugees from Mer," I said.

"Wonder how the war's going up north?" Aaron commented.

"Mer must be operational again."

"And you know this how?"

"The missiles that took out Babla's starship launched from the Northern Hemisphere. Mer is the only northern base where such advanced technology could have originated."

"This is why I like hanging out with you. I feel so much smarter."

"You'd have found out once we checked in with Ground Com."

"I don't know. They seem to be in the dark about Nephillim operations more often than not these decades. Especially Odin's escapades. I hear he's gone completely rogue."

"Agreed."

"Why? What do you know?"

"I'll tell you when I'm confident we're not being listened to."

The lift shot up through the narrowing throat leading to

Olympus' Peak. The view shifted to a spectacular outside panorama through a series of wide portals spaced perfectly to match our rate of climb and give the illusion of one stationary portal. Fleets of cumulus clouds, normally trailing far beneath *Olympus* when she cruised at optimal altitude, formed a solid ceiling. Flaming debris from Babla's massive ship punched through like orange branches, splitting. Each tumbling piece threatened Mestrean villages and eco-restoration zones. Aaron pointed out the Ra's royal game preserve. A couple of smoking craters scarred its wide expanse.

"Wonder why your mom's got *Olympus* flying so low over the capital?" Aaron mused. "Her garden's practically scraping the ground."

"Not necessary for intercepting that debris."

"Either she's losing it or it's extremely important," he said. "Exposing her seed garden like this? Ground ozone's going to murder those plants."

"Hence the lack of bath and food."

"Can't be that important," he joked.

I zoomed in on the western horizon, checking the positions of the other Nephillim Ships of the Line. They were buried in the clouds at eighty-five hundred feet.

"The *Valhalla* and *Pericles* have joined the formation on the Phut border," I said.

"How many does that make in total?"

"Five on station."

"Anak, that's a lot of fire power guarding one border. I haven't seen the *Valhalla* since that scrape in Azaes. And me without scanners," Aaron groused. "My oculars burned out during reentry. If I was on the Acropolis, they'd be fixed by now."

"Odin's probably got a lab. He'd be happy to work on you."

"No thanks." He smirked, tapping his forehead. "No telling what he'd stick in here. I can't imagine having him for a relative. How do you do it? Athena must be ready to toss him off *Olympus* by now."

"The idea is occasionally voiced."

The lift came to an abrupt stop. I straightened my collar seam and made sure my helmet had retracted neatly behind my ears.

Aaron watched. "Nervous?"

"Preparing," I said.

"Try not to blow your top too fast this time, Chief. Overbearing giants or not, they're still your family."

"Didn't exactly have a say in the matter, did I?"

"Who does?"

The portal sighed open and we stepped out. We were on the Peak, a circular command center carved within the circumference of the final hundred feet of *Olympus'* granite summit. It was surrounded by an expanse of forty-foot windows. Here Athena conducted affairs of the State. The displaced Elder Nephillim of Mer apparently conducted theirs, as well. Eleven of the most powerful leaders were clustered at the bottom of a sunken amphitheater known as the Furies. I recognized their enormous faces protruding above the rim. Athena stood beside her father wearing outdoor excursion robes designed to protect her against the sun's exposure. Odd. My adopted mother was a stickler for proper attire. This had to be quite the emergency for her to dress in such a way before the Elder Council.

The giants watched a real-time projection hovering comfortably at their eye level. Voices reverberated from the projection and echoed around the enormous room. Aaron and I reached the rim of the Furies and descended a few steps until we were at head level with the Nephillim.

Athena made brief eye contact with me. She seemed pleased that I was here. I nodded my greetings. She lightly touched her heart, an unexpected emotional gesture. My most recent scrape with death must have rattled her.

Without thinking, I returned the sentiment. It must have rattled me, too.

Aaron watched the three-dimensional scene with intense interest: a close-up of Jordan riding in an air car accompanied by a team of Javan Guardians.

"Jordan's awake!" Aaron exclaimed.

"Quiet, Guardian," Odin's voice rumbled.

"Nice to see you, too," I muttered.

Athena shut her eyes.

"Is this projection happening in present time?" I asked.

Athena nodded.

We watched a live image of Jordan, Diago, and other fully suited Guardians through the oculars of another occupant in the car.

"Who's transmitting this?" Aaron whispered.

The broadcaster suddenly panned the stern of the car as it fled through a palm forest. In the background stood the Ra's palace atop the Citadel. Aaron and I had been there many times in the past, usually uninvited.

"Before you landed, we were treated to a nice view inside the old Sanctuary Garden," Athena said quietly.

"Was it occupied at the time?" I asked.

"Jordan apparently spent the night under Diago's and Aizah's guard."

"How did he get there?" Aaron inquired.

"Broadcasting inside a Sanctuary is illegal," I said.

"Monitoring the human was necessary," Odin growled. "We have to find out what he knows."

"What exactly are you trying to learn?" I asked.

"Our future," one of the other Nephillim croaked.

"Future? How would a primitive from the north know anything about the future?" Aaron demanded. "And while I'm still on the subject, how did Jordan get there?"

Odin waved us off. He crossed his massive arms and squinted at the projection as if to shut us out.

"I have determined from cellular examination that Jordan is from the future," Athena said. "Through him, Father hopes to learn what the Fourth Age remembers about our war with Atlantis. Tactical knowledge that could help us win this conflict."

"We could have had everything we needed by now if you'd let me finish healing him in the lab." Odin waved a huge arm through the projection. "None of this foolishness would have been necessary."

"You were going to regress Jordan to an infant so you could mine his memories," Athena said.

"We need what is in his head." He scowled at the images. "Thanks to your meddling, I'm forced to employ this ridiculous method."

"Including breaking Sanctuary law and invading a person's privacy," I said.

"We had no choice, Guardian," Odin grumbled. "We must find out what he knows as quickly as possible."

"Why not just ask him?" Aaron said. Indignation edged his tone.

Odin glared at Athena. "After the human's experiences this morning, I doubt he would ever trust a Nephillim again."

"Wonder what he means by experiences?" Aaron muttered to me.

"Jordan must've damaged his lab and escaped."

"Sweet."

"The two of you are here only by the thinnest of consideration to my daughter. Remain quiet or I'll have you removed."

Athena motioned to us. "Guardians, perhaps you should join me on the bridge."

We followed her. Aaron looked over his shoulder at the projection. Jordan was asking the person who was broadcasting a question. *"When did you first spot me?"*

"The moment you dove off Olympus."

"That's Aizah's voice," Aaron exclaimed.

"Really?" Jordan replied to Aizah. *"Gee, thanks for all the help in the river."*

"Jordan jumped off *Olympus*?" I asked.

"It's a long story," Athena muttered.

"What's going on?" Aaron demanded. "Aizah would never agree to transmit from a sanctuary."

"Odin implanted a device in her oculars. He sees and hears what she does without her knowledge."

Aaron's face turned as red as mine.

We passed through a garden foyer leading to the Battle Bridge of the *Olympus*. Athena engaged mobile communications with her vast military forces via her com implant as we approached the armored doors. I was given access to her transmissions and followed the streaming data. My fuming comrade trudged beside me. Aaron seemed to realize the intimate implications of Aizah being monitored by Odin. I couldn't blame his anger. I was seething, too. When had he implanted her oculars? A few days ago? A few years? Who knew what Odin had observed whenever Aizah thought she was alone? When Aaron and Aizah thought they were alone?

Did you know about this? Aaron finger signed to me.

No. I signed back.

He signed with an angry flourish that knocked a hanging plant off its holder. *Odin's lucky I'm a pacifist.*

I caught the plant. *True, but Aizah isn't.*

He laughed through his anger, earning a questioning glance down from Athena.

CHAPTER FOURTEEN

JORDAN

The swaying palms grew taller the deeper we flew into the forest. Their ten-foot wide trunks played host to a rainbow of exotic orchids and cascading blooms. I approximated our speed to be one hundred and twenty miles per hour. It was incredible that a vehicle could travel so fast and make no noise.

The driver kept her heading slightly left of the rising sun. She and the entire team were on alert. They said little, kept their heads on swivel, and quietly pointed out things to each other. When anything moved, a Guardian would sign with a slight flick of an armored hand and the others would acknowledge with a grunt or a nod. Fifteen minutes and thirty miles later, if my math was right, Aizah casually glanced at Diago and did her raised eyebrow thing. Diago refrained from eye contact with her, put a glove to his mouth, and coughed. Aizah looked straight ahead and readied her leg weapon without looking down.

Diago slid back out of her field of vision and sidled up to me. He changed a setting on his leg weapon and activated the targeting sight. Something interesting was about to happen. This time I was in on it. Outstanding.

We slowed and plunged into a thick vine-draped forest. Aizah looked starboard and tapped the driver on the left shoulder. The car dropped to within a few feet of the ground.

The sky barely showed through layers of green. We skimmed a still pond, snapping rushes, then glided over a stretch of black sand beach bounded by a broken boulder wall to the left. Shadowed ruins scarred the forest floor. Aizah took a deep interest in the far side of the pond.

Diago motioned for me to grab the rail. He pantomimed the two of us leaping over the side. Was I ready, his expression seemed to ask. I nodded.

Without taking her eyes off the shore, Aizah lowered her left hand to her ankle. She signaled Diago three fingers, then two, then one. I followed his lead and rolled low over the rail, taking care to stay out of Aizah's peripheral view. I cleared the car and dropped into tall grass. I rolled through it and flattened face down, keeping my eyes on the receding car. Diago slid up beside me. One of the Guardians in the rear of the car gave us a discrete wave.

The car whispered down the shoreline, keeping close to the stone wall. Thirty paces east, two men—one a Guardian, the other a civilian dressed exactly like me—darted out from the wall and vaulted aboard like shadows.

Diago motioned that I should stay put and remain quiet. The car turned south and accelerated over the pond, vanishing into the forest on the eastern shore. After a minute, during which Diago's lips moved as he counted to himself, his face brightened. He yanked his weapons free and smacked them once on the ground to get them glowing. The kid was eager.

He motioned me over the wall and we melted into the forest, following a game trail that wound between a series of ruins. A tall jungle towered above crumbled stone buildings with immense windows and entryways. The air smelled of rich earth and wet stone. A family of saber-toothed lions passed us. One of the cubs batted and chased my shoelaces until the mom grunted.

After an hour hike, we came to a dramatic clearing: a rectangular granite plaza as large as a city block. Heat shimmered off its flat surface. Diago pointed to the far side, where some kind of temple or mansion edged the plaza with trees growing through its ruined roof. He indicated that I should head there.

When I stepped out into the open, I looked back. He didn't follow but urged me to hurry. Then he hastily saluted and vanished.

"Okay, now I'm officially confused," I muttered.

The sun peaked through the tops of the dense foliage. The door of the massive building was slightly to the left of the sun. I was still facing east. Feeling rather exposed, I hurried across the clearing.

CHAPTER FIFTEEN

LEVI

Olympus' Battle Bridge was a swarm of activity. A full complement of Ground Com staff manned their consoles, each somber and determined as they directed legions of Guardians locked in battles across dozens of countries. Couriers crisscrossed the circular room, ducking under the central view-res cluster to save on travel time. Classified messages followed each courier in a train of scan-proof bubbles, while the view-res cluster had one hundred active displays projecting toward various departments.

Joshua—the staffer I'd chewed out during my foray on the Queen's starship—stared up at his screen, frantically guiding a Guardian squad caught in an ambush. The squad was dashing through smoking buildings, evading incoming rounds seconds before they impacted, thanks to his guidance. They broke free of the burning town and bounded for their extraction point

A fire storm of rounds blanketed the entire valley and Joshua had no solution. The eruptions drowned out the Guardians' screams, right before the transmission was cut. Joshua shut his eyes and took a breath. A new transmission transferred to his screen. He called up the scanners for data and poured himself into the next emergency.

The ribbing Aaron and I gave Ground Com whenever we were

in the field was merely stress release. When they were off-duty, kids like Joshua never had to pay for their drinks.

In a blinding blitz, the Western Confederacy of Atlantis had invaded the East. It had conquered all the coastal countries and enslaved their populations. Mer had been pounded nearly to extinction. Mighty Gomer was on her knees, her cities in smoldering ruins. Phut had left the Alliance, feigning neutrality. Chi and Indra in the Far East had refused to join the struggle, trusting Atlantis would sate herself with conquering the Alliance and leave the Far East alone. Javan, Mestre, and a few inland countries like Magog were all that remained of Athena's crumbling Eastern Alliance, her grand experiment in human civilization. In spite of all the bad news and anguish, the overall situation was strangely stable.

"Anak, we're holding them," Aaron muttered.

"They're hesitating." I pointed at a monitor. "Look at that beach landing on Mer's coast. Twenty heavy walkers deployed, but forty are still sitting in the landing rafts."

"Maybe their command and control has been disrupted since the Queen died."

I pointed at the section monitoring enemy transmissions. "Ground Com's listening to command chatter."

"Is it the King?"

I shook my head. "The Payahdon console is idle. The orders are originating from somewhere else." I zoomed in on some of the consoles and read the staffers' lips as they relayed intercepts to other stations. "Somebody is ordering the West to focus attacks on secondary targets with reserves and follow-ons held back."

"Why in Anak would they do that? "

With the Net still compromised, communications had been rerouted through ancient ground lines crisscrossing miles beneath the surface, which Ground Com had derived its name from. I glanced at the LDO display—Lost During Operations—above a carving of Rahn and Deuca, patriarchs of the Nephillim and human races. The display listed three thousand four hundred and thirty-three names. I knew every one of them.

"To the Fallen and the Lost," Aaron said.

We saluted in precise unison to the fullest measure: palm and forearm snapped silently across our chests, pivoted slowly to our lower lip. My mother waited for us to finish before she indicated the lift to her command dais overlooking Ground Com. "Please join me."

"Who is in command of the West?" I asked as the personal lift conveyed us to her elevated station.

"I thought it was Babla," she said, her eyes forward, glued to the shifting displays on the view-res. "At least until Odin blew her starship out of the sky. Then it appeared as if no one was in charge, until those strange transmissions started coming in a few minutes ago."

"What about the King?" Aaron asked. "Isn't he in Payahdon with his generals?"

"Payahdon went silent as soon as the Queen left for her starship," Athena said. "One of our teams infiltrated Old City a few days later. The generals were dead or dying in their mansions. The King was rotting in the palace."

"Assassination?"

"If you define having one's heart eaten out of one's chest an assassination, yes."

"Anak," Aaron exclaimed.

"They found a fissure under the bed. Someone had broken in through the floor and bore up through his bed. His heart, lungs, and spine were devoured as he slept. It happened over a month ago, while the Queen was still in the city."

"The LDO shows the team was wounded during the mission," I said. "What happened to them?"

"They made it to the Retriever but something injured them. Weapon, poison, I can't find the source. They're all catatonic. I am having difficulty keeping them alive. Their symptoms are similar to Jordan's, only far more aggressive."

"What is going on with Jordan?" I asked. "How did he get off *Olympus*?"

She told me what had happened after he'd thawed. I had a new level of respect for his resourcefulness and a deepening concern for his recklessness. His motive was obvious, though.

"He must really have it bad for that princess," Aaron said.

The hint of a smile briefly colored Athena's face as she concentrated on a Nephillim-sized multi-monitor hovering above her station. It displayed the illegal transmissions coming through Aizah's right ocular that Odin and the other Elders continued to monitor in the Furies.

Aizah looked down at her armored legs. Thigh weapons glowed on attack setting. I caught a glimpse of Diago. He looked proud in his new apprentice-grade field armor.

Don't stare at it too long, kid. Better to focus on what's hoping to blow your young carcass out of it.

Aizah must have noticed the same thing. She barked at Diago. He snapped back to scanning for threats. The view shifted as Aizah looked back at Jordan. He seemed frustrated and watchful. Probably wondering about the developing situation, what threats they were trying to evade and what Aizah planned to do with him. That had been his attitude all the way from the embassy in Atlantis to the snows of Tevleh: the reluctant civilian-eager combatant.

I read the Confidential Mission Brief in the secure message bubble floating beside the transmission. Interesting plan Aizah and Athena had cooked up. Interesting because it was devoid of any mission extraction point. Had other command staff seen this? All it contained were plans and logistics for extracting Jordan from the palace and transporting him east. But east to where? A remote pick-up point? Another safe zone like last night's stay in the garden? Why go to all this trouble moving him around? *Olympus* had sovereignty of the air, including the stale variety coming out of the Ra's palace. *Olympus* was the strongest battle mountain in the fleet. Why didn't she just glide in and extract Jordan from the Sanctuary while the Ra slept off last night's festivities? Mestrean Guardians wouldn't shoot at *Olympus*, no matter how much the Ra blustered. Their Javan brethren were onboard.

Aaron seemed as puzzled as I was. A voice inside me said to stop worrying.

I remembered the words I'd heard inside me as I'd watched the sphere of light deposit Jordan in the embassy's lake. Something vastly more important than this war was in motion. The welfare of billions of lives depended on its successful conclusion. Its culmination was at hand. If I tried to control it, it would vanish like a dream.

I watched Odin's illegal view-res transmissions with gathering apprehension. Jordan had to get out of the air car.

"Jordan has to be released," I whispered into Athena's ear.

She glanced back at me, her face partially blocking the air car racing through the forest. "I know that."

I gave her a questioning look.

"You're not the only one hearing voices in your head," she said.

Aizah and her team scanned for threats as they plowed through the Ra's Forest Reserve. Then Aizah glanced down at her uniform and straightened something that was only done when one assumed nobody was watching. She clearly had no knowledge that Odin had implanted a monitoring device in her ocular.

"How long have you known Aizah was illegally implanted?" Aaron asked.

"Same time you found out," she said.

"She has to be warned that Odin's monitoring," I fumed.

Athena's fingers danced over inputs next to the image. "She just was."

Aizah suddenly looked straight ahead, at the back of the driver's helmet. The image held that way for a few seconds. Then she looked over at Diago. He'd been staring at her feet. He glanced up quickly, then lowered his visor.

Aaron grinned. "He was watching her hands before she looked over. She finger-signed him. Something's going down."

"She's releasing Jordan," I said.

"Watch the display," Athena chided.

They flew over a long pond. Aizah looked straight ahead again. Then she looked to the right, far enough that Diago wasn't in her field of vision. We were treated to a long boring study of the opposite shore as Aizah zoomed in on various bushes and trees, as if looking for hidden threats.

"I bet he's not sitting next to her anymore," Aaron said.

My mother nervously tapped her arm console an inch away from a glowing command marked ABORT. The car lowered to within jumping distance but maintained its speed. Aizah kept watch of the far shore, keeping Diago completely out of view. Suddenly, the car banked south over the water and raced into the trees. Aizah looked back at Diago's seat. A Guardian with recruit armor and faceshield sat in it.

"That is definitely not Diago," Aaron said.

"Extra beer for you tonight," I said.

Aizah looked back at Jordan. He was slouched in the seat, his tunic hood pulled over his face as if he was asleep.

"And that's definitely not—"

A priority call flashed on the air car's monitor. The request to acknowledge showed Odin's enraged face.

"I wonder if he realizes Aizah's on to him," I said.

Aizah focused on her armored hand, formed a fist, and slowly extended her middle finger at her right ocular, the ancient curse of wishing the recipient to become a finger-less archer.

Aaron snickered. "He does now."

"I didn't know Trahls were acquainted with that expression," Athena said.

CHAPTER SIXTEEN

JORDAN

The weathered structure towered fifty feet above the granite plaza. Creatures darted along draped vines. Brilliant plumages flashed as birds took flight.

I stepped through the ruined portal, into a roofless hall infused with age. Something told me if I kept going, I'd find granite stairs.

Worn stone steps sprawled precisely as I remembered them: cracked and upheaved where a root sixteen feet in diameter had pushed through in its quest for daylight. The roots were taller than me. They curled and twisted into a massive sprawling ruin of broken walls and toppled columns that dwarfed any I'd seen before.

I clambered down two mammoth roots, dusted the bugs off my chest, and surveyed the side of what I'd thought was a plaza. The plaza was just the top face of a single cut stone towering a hundred feet out of the ground. The forest floor had grown up against the west end, concealing its bulk. It was lower along the east face, offering an astonishing view of its sloped facade. It was a definite contender for *The Biggest Things I Saw on My Trip.*

I envisioned this monstrous slab free of jungle encroachment. This was no plaza; it was a mastaba, the burial mound of a king. But the mastabas I'd studied were flat-topped earthen mounds a fraction of the size of this monster. What ancient king merited the construction of a tomb cut from a single stone the height and breadth of a baseball stadium?

I ran my hand across its smooth surface and pressed my ear against the cool edge to sight along its length. The jungle was reflected within the surface as clear as a mirror, evidence that the face was a perfect plane machined for a thousand feet without the slightest defect.

"Who made you?" I wondered.

A memory flashed of falling down an endless stone shaft. Carved faces had flown past me, each slightly different from the next. They'd superimposed themselves on each other as I fell, laughing at my query. *What a silly question to ask*, they'd said.

A wide granite walk broken up by invasive trees led east from the mastaba toward a ruined structure hiding in the shadows of the towering forest. I stepped through the crumbled entrance into a silent room as tall as a gymnasium. The marble and gold inlaid floor had cracked and upheaved from aggressive trees. Flowered vines draped surviving ceiling beams. Large patches of roof lay broken over tumbled stone columns, through which filtered sunlight. Antechambers beckoned beyond the crumbled walls and gaping windows. Steps, doors, and sills were all three times human proportions, indicating that the Nephillim had once lived here.

The place was as familiar as the stone stairs had been. I'd played here once and hadn't been alone. I tried to conjure the elusive memory, but it hid beyond the periphery of my mind.

I should have turned back, signaled Diago, but for some reason I didn't listen to my training. I felt like I was reliving a dream and it might dissolve if I deviated from the script. Because of that, I closed my eyes and relaxed. An image formed of the ancient occupant of this home: as tall as Odin, but with a kind face and attentive eyes, intensely curious.

"He was bald," I said.

I walked deep into the ruin, leaving the sunlight to grope through the deepening shadow. There, I heard the most beautiful sound far behind me.

"Jordan, where are you?"

I retraced my steps as fast as I could without tripping over anything. Suri stood in the entrance under the flowering vines, her back to me, a shaft of sunlight illuminating her beauty like a nymph in a Renaissance painting. She'd changed clothes since last night's gala. She was now wearing a simple robe cut to calf-length for ease in walking. A breeze lifted her long blonde hair.

"Hi," I managed.

She spun around to face me, then gave me a nervous smile that made my heart pound. She stood rooted within the sunlight, her hands clasped with her eyes glued to mine. "Jordan."

I ran, oblivious to everything. I tripped over some debris and planted my face in the ground. Lying there, I heard her footsteps. She reached down to help me up, then brushed the dust off my tunic. Her hands were warm as she fussed with the folds of my sleeves. "Are you hurt?"

Her wedding ring flashed in the sunlight and my heart sank. I pulled back to concentrate on a clasp on my tunic. "I'm okay."

"Sorry." She stared at the floor, then around the room, and finally back at me.

Everything I'd planned to declare to her dissolved. I bottled up my love and forced it back down. Any hint of how I felt was supremely inappropriate now that she was married.

A sickening epiphany dawned on me. I now knew why Aizah and Diago had gone to all this trouble to spirit me here, even though Suri ran a huge risk meeting me. This encounter had been arranged so we could say goodbye before I was forcibly returned to *Olympus.* I experienced a new personal record for despair.

Suck it up, Jordan. Married or not, she's still your friend. Be hers.

"You are unfrozen," she said.

"Yes."

"Did it hurt?"

"Not much."

She nodded, as if I'd just delivered a full medical report. *Come on, Jordan, get with the program. Let her know this is okay, even though it's not.*

"I'm glad," she said. "I was so worried. I heard the hibernation process can be frightening."

My heart skipped a beat. When seconds mattered and it's the

last time you're going to see someone, you don't start with a casual conversation.

I tried to relax and go with it. Her eyes were locked on mine. My brain melted into a soppy mess. We were a foot apart but it felt like a mile. It took an eternity to make my mouth work again. "How did you … Who told you I was here?"

"My informants told me you were on the *Olympus*." She indicated that we should start walking. "I thought I would never see you again. Then Aizah said she saw you in the city last night. I thought she was mistaken. But then I saw you in the palace and I …" She took a breath. "How did you get Athena's permission to leave *Olympus*?"

"I didn't. I jumped."

"Oh, you jumped." It took her a second for it to register, then her eyes flared wide. "You what?"

I thought she was going to slug me, but to my surprise, she threw her arms around my neck and hugged me hard. "Are you crazy?"

I wanted to tell her yes, I was crazy about her, that I'd have fallen twice as far to be with her; but what good would it do? Instead, I gently pulled away.

She brushed her hair back as we headed down the stairs into a tunnel. It got dark fast. Her hand found mine and led me through the void. It was a good thing she was there. She walked with a purpose, dodging obstacles I would have tripped over. She acted like being together was natural. Did she know what her closeness did to me?

"You could have been killed," she echoed. Her hand squeezed mine at the last word.

"*Olympus* was flying low over a river," I said. "I caught the vines to slow my fall and landed in the water."

Her hand released mine. "The River Iterah! You could have been swept over the falls."

"It has a barrier."

"In disrepair."

"Really?"

"There are many rocks."

"Yeah, they hurt."

"Oh Jordan!" She sounded like she was either about to chew me out or start crying. Change the subject, man.

"You seem to know your way pretty well down here," I said as she zig-zagged through an imperceptible jog in the tunnel.

"Mmm," she said. Apparently that meant yes.

"Is this designed to confuse trespassers?"

She took a breath. "You're trying to talk about something different because I'm upset with you."

Subtle she wasn't. "Yes."

We stopped at a spot where sunlight penetrated a fist-sized hole in the ceiling. Her eyes danced over my face as if she was drinking me in. "Forgive me, I haven't seen you for three weeks. It feels like much longer. Much has happened in the meantime."

She made my heart hammer. I had to look away to keep from blurting something inappropriate to someone else's wife.

"I played down here when I was a little girl," she said. "Now I come when I want to get away from Amon. He doesn't like the old places."

"Lucky me," I blurted. Oops.

"You like old places?"

"That's how I got here, remember? I was crawling under an old pyramid."

"Cool. Would you like to see some more of it?"

"You're saying cool now?"

"I like that word very much. You said it many times when we traveled."

Sunlight heralded the end of the tunnel. The harsh light beamed through gaps in a blocking wall. Suri slipped through a narrow fissure without smudging her dress. I was a little wider and had to crawl through a larger gap near the floor. Despite my more polite protests, she insisted on helping me up and wiping the grit off my clothes.

We were in the middle of a substantial city ruin. Beyond the toothed skyline of stone and gold, a familiar sound thundered.

"Are we near the big falls?" I asked.

"Oh no."

"What's that sound?"

"Water falling."

"In other words: a big falls."

"Not exactly."

"What do you mean?"

"Ayah, stop asking!" she exclaimed. "I'm trying to keep a surprise for you."

"A surprise?"

"One more question and I will run away," she teased.

"I doubt it."

She darted down a crumbled lane.

"That wasn't a question," I shouted after her.

I chased her into a wide plaza with a short step platform in the middle. She jumped up on the high spot with her arms outstretched. There was apparently no need for caution or concealment anymore.

"Why did you jump off *Olympus*?" she asked.

Man, she didn't give up. Didn't she have a clue? I could have given her a long report about the weirdness that had happened on *Olympus* but none of that was the reason why I'd jumped. Looking at her, feeling her hand, married or not, I would have to tell her or I'd regret it the rest of my life. Now. If only I could get it out the right way without making her uncomfortable. But, God, the way she was looking at me …

"Um, because I wanted …"

She took a step closer. "Wanted what?"

Two men in full body armor chose that moment to leap onto the platform. They were armed with long staffs that glowed. One yanked Suri away from me, while the other kept the business end of his staff pointed at my chest. I could barely see his face through his reflective helmet, but I could tell he wasn't smiling.

"Laoh tehav Ra-He!" the taller one snarled in an electronically enhanced voice, complete with impressive echo. He pulled Suri behind him as if to shield her.

Suri yelled at them and struggled to extract herself from the man's armored grip. They yelled at me, aiming their crackling staffs inches from my face. I remained like a statue and hoped Mestre had a non-lethal weapons policy.

A heated exchange occurred between Suri and the taller one. She seemed to be winning the argument, especially when she said something with the finality of throwing down a royal flush. The guard repeated it timidly as a question.

She yanked herself free. "Mmm."

They flipped open their visors. The look on their faces was better than Krax's when we'd driven over the commandant's bird-bath.

Suri snapped something that sounded like *atten-shun!*

The short guard bumped into the tall one as they tried to form a two-person line. They swung their staffs to a vertical position, the short guy narrowly missing a statue.

I stared at them in disbelief. One was Carlos and the other was a younger version of Shamel, Krax's mysterious benefactor who'd bankrolled our expedition to Egypt. Carlos attempted to imitate the statue while Shamel looked me over with narrowed eyes. He didn't seem to recognize me.

"This is Baak," Suri said, pointing at Carlos.

"We've met." I flicked a two-finger salute off my eyebrow.

"And this is Shareb."

Shamel bowed stiffly, muttering something.

"They apologize for their behavior. They thought you were a trespasser."

"Why did they think that?"

"This place is forbidden."

"But I was with you."

She looked away evasively. "I'm not allowed to be here, either."

"But in your case, they pretend not to notice?"

"Usually." She glared at them.

"So why did they attack me?"

"They thought you were threatening me." She waved her arms at her wincing bodyguards. "I told you I was meeting Jordan here! You almost shot him!"

They looked at her blankly.

"Uh, they don't speak English," I offered.

She looked at me, muttered to herself, then said something to them in another language. They did their best to look contrite as they saluted across their chests and hurried out of the plaza.

"That's why you come here," I said. "To get away. It's the last place anyone would look for you."

"Mmm."

"Doesn't Amon get mad when you slip away?"

"Only when he thinks he's supposed to."

"But with you two just married," I started.

She looked at me as if I'd grown a horn out of my forehead. "What makes you think that?"

I forgot about breathing. "You're not married?"

"No."

"But what about that?" I pointed at the ring on her finger.

She put her hand to her mouth to hide her laugh. "That's what they wear in your age when you marry. You thought it meant the same thing here?"

The sun suddenly brightened and the ruins looked less ruined. The dynamic duo came back with food and drink. They peppered me with small talk and Suri translated. They acted like two uncles checking out the new guy their niece had dragged home. Shareb reminisced about Suri when she was little. He told me how she'd constantly escaped the palace nursemaids, scampering through the ruins while half the guards tried to catch her.

When lunch was finished, Suri asked Shareb and Baak something. They looked appalled and vigorously shook their heads. She repeated her request, pleading to Baak, who looked like he had the potential to cave in first.

"Spu-esa, Baak? Ayah spu-esa!"

Spuesa sounded like *spassee,* which was please in Javan.

Shareb firmly said, *"Va dav!"* and made a sweeping no gesture the same time Baak sighed and nodded yes. Shareb noticed him out of the corner of his helmet and swatted the back of Baak's head, flipping his faceshield back in place.

"Shareb? Spu-esa?"

Shareb gave her a long lecture, wagging his hand like an Italian for emphasis. Suri dutifully nodded, saying, *dah-ee* a lot. That meant yes in Mestrean. From Suri's expression, it was clear Uncle Shamel was telling her not to forget to do this, that, and be home by ten. When he finished the safety lecture, she gave me a triumphant look and grabbed my hand.

"This way," she said.

Shareb and Baak escorted us east out of the plaza. I leaned into Suri and asked, "Are you getting them in trouble?"

She glanced back at them and smiled. "No more than usual."

We hiked about a mile. Baak got Shareb talking and eventually chuckling over something. Back in Costa Rica, Carlos was sad, somber, and all business. What was he doing here in the past, younger and happier, acting like an Egyptian Costello?

We reached a wall constructed of bus-sized polygonal stones. It reminded me of the Wall of the Crow, only a lot taller. Shareb and Baak stopped and spoke urgently in whispers to Suri, as if I could understand them.

"Dah-ee, dah-hee," she impatiently repeated to each sentence.

Baak pulled out a wrapped bundle from behind a wall. It contained a heavy tunic, legging wraps, and gloves. He carefully got the tunic over her, fussing with the folds that somehow stuck together, and she slapped the leggings on. Then he gave her a pair of slit gloves I remembered wearing when we'd been in the mountains.

"You've done this before," I observed.

"Oh, many times," she said. She thought for a moment, then looked at me with concern. "I'm sorry I don't have any coverings for you. There was no time. I didn't know you—"

"Don't worry about it." I said, waving her off. "It's my fault for dropping in unannounced."

"Mmm," she said, not getting the joke. She gave Baak and Shareb each a hug, which got them all embarrassed. Then they noticed me grinning. Their chuckling ceased and they snapped to attention. After that, they pivoted and marched north.

We reached an opening in the bottom of a wall, where Suri crouched to crawl through. She stopped to look back at me. *"Vah-ya tu, Jordan"*

The light seemed to fade and a chill swept my body. I'd heard those words two times before: on a wild beach in Costa Rica and during a freak sandstorm in Giza. I'd read those words in a mirror, scrawled backwards in a book. Suri was the ghost girl. Somehow, she'd called to me from the past, and somehow I'd heard her.

"Are you okay, Jordan?"

"Fine. I'm fine. Let's get vah-ya-ing."

As we crawled under a wall that was hundred feet thick, I got the impression I'd done this before, deep under the limestone and sand of Giza. I fought back the urge to tell her my revelation. The last thing I wanted her to think was that I was crazy.

When we reached the other side of the wall, we stood up. Suri brushed me off again. I barely noticed. Thunderous water obliterated all other sounds. To the east was a towering cloud of mist. A wind kicked up and the mist stirred. It parted and I stared.

At the end of an immense reflecting pool towered a massive pyramid. Waterfalls thundered majestically down its stepped flanks. Clouds girdled its midsection.

"How do you like your surprise?" she yelled in my ear.

I don't know what overwhelmed me more: the most astonishing architectural sight on Earth, the opportunity to stand here and experience it with Suri, or the fact that I'd already seen it?

That which I'd long forgotten rushed back to me with crystal clarity. A childhood fantasy in my bedroom keep, forged with my eyes shut, fingers in my ears, the desk hard against the door and my toy soldiers bouncing from their firing positions as my drunken foster parents pounded on the door. I was a five-year-old orphan again, desperate to be somewhere else. In my imagination, I'd created a fantasy world and hid there every time they'd come for me. When I was old enough to run away, I forgot that world. Yet, here I stood, every stone and pool exactly as I'd imagined it. I had been here many times in my mind, with a young girl who looked a lot like Suri.

CHAPTER SEVENTEEN

LEVI

Athena's eyes narrowed as Odin ranted from the monitor. "You sabotaged my efforts to extract vital information from this human."

"How would you like being turned into an infant, Father?"

He ignored her, as usual. "You colluded with a renegade Trahl to release him into the wilds of Mestre."

"When did our people start condoning the imprisonment of other races?" she demanded.

"We have the right to ensure our preservation."

"That is why he was sent to us," she said, crossing her arms. "He must be free to carry out his mission if our world has any chance of surviving the cataclysm."

"You sound like a priest," he spat.

"Thank you," she said. "His coming was foretold. You read the scroll yourself. *Make straight the path so the child may lead us.*" She held up her hands. "Jordan is a three-and-half-decade-old child."

"A bedtime fable. Thanks to your silly romantic notions of a higher power directing this chaos, our only chance of learning our future scampers about in a Mestrean wilderness, doing Anak knows what."

"He came here for a reason. Our meddling puts him in jeopardy."

"This act of insubordination forces the Council to question your loyalty to our people. We tolerated your experiment in human nation building because it provided us opportunities to test weapons and measure progress with terra-restoration. But now the Trahls and dwarves resist our authority. I had Aizah under my control and you turned her."

"Try asking her the next time before you secretly tap her oculars." And she motioned the communication to an end.

Odin turned crimson. "I am not finished with you, young lady."

"I'm busy with a war."

She cut the audio. Odin's face shook as he silently shouted. Nephillim-sized globs of spittle flew from his contorted mouth as his image faded.

Applause broke out behind her. She turned around and shot Ground Com an annoyed look. They quieted, but the pride on their faces remained fixed.

"That took guts," Aaron said.

"If he's so displeased with my command, he can walk home." She hailed the ship's captain. His face appeared above her console. "Captain, I advise bringing *Olympus* to a heading of ninety-two degrees. You should advise *Valhalla* and *Pericles* to remain on station with the rest of the picket line. Your speed would be best at nominal, altitude at one mile. You would not want to upset the Ra while flying past his palace."

"Agreed, Counselor," he said and his image faded.

"What's happening?" I asked.

She took a deep breath and whispered "Remember that bedtime story I read to you when you were little?"

"Which one?"

"About the prince and princess going up the mountain to gather water?"

"What about it?"

"It wasn't a story."

CHAPTER EIGHTEEN

JORDAN

The pyramid commanded the horizon, a mist-shrouded forest to its left and a sun-sparkled lake to its right. At its base stood six golden pyramids in two lines, flanking a reflecting pool that stretched longer than a runway. Those structures were small by comparison to the artificial Everest behind them. The air rippled above their perfect flanks of gold. Musical chords reverberated from each, pulsing in rhythm with the breeze. Suri's words, *Vah-ya tu,* echoed within this otherworldly symphony. Those words were so similar to the little Spanish I knew. How could it possibly mean the same? *Follow me.*

She took my hand and urged me on.

An ancient age using higher technology than mine, the inhabitants speaking languages close to those in my age despite a time/space chasm of thirteen thousand years. The mental boundary between my former past and this present collapsed. My past was this present's future. This present was my past. What was would be and what had been hadn't happened yet. Which affected which?

I felt truly and completely lost in the face of this impossibly familiar structure, set adrift with nothing to hold onto. Only Suri's friendship felt real. When she took my hand, the mental abyss receded.

"Are you okay?" she asked.

Not really, but could I admit that if there was no time to explain? Despite all my hopes to the contrary, I sensed my time with her was about to end. This was the logical place for a rendezvous with *Olympus*. It was big enough. The stupid flying mountain could come bursting through the mist at any second.

"I apologize," she said. "You've only recently been thawed out. Maybe we should sit and rest a little before we climb the Sacred Mountain." She nodded toward the tallest pyramid.

I craned my neck to stare at the top. It could take all day to climb that thing. She assumed we would be together that long. My hopes lifted. "I'm ready whenever you are."

Her smile radiated as bright as the pool sparkling beyond her hair. "Are you sure?"

We stepped out from the shadows of the perimeter wall. They surrounded the entire complex. I remembered that. But what memory might that be?

Then those memories burst loose and flooded me. I remembered things I'd imagined as a kid. What I saw and what I remembered were either both figments of my imagination—meaning I was insane or dreaming—or both were reality.

As I chewed on those choices, a strange sense of comfort grew within me. Suri's other hand slid up my forearm as she steadied herself while navigating a tree root. I had only one choice. This was reality. As real as my childhood bedroom; as real as the life I'd lived, shared, and lost before I'd fallen into this age.

We walked under the shade of swaying hibiscus branches heavy with fruit and flowers. The path ran straight, paved with smooth interlocking stones that were smaller than I remembered and tightly fitted, yet broken up by ancient tree roots. I kept my mind open to remember my dreams. Memory fragments continued to flow as if eager to reunite me with my childhood. In my dreams, my feet never touched these stones. I'd always been carried, but who had carried me?

We reached the beginning of the long rectangular pool. The water was the color of milk. A multitude of water plants festooned with flowers crowded the edges. They grew thick and wild, their spindly roots reaching over the stone ramparts of the pool's walls. Waterfalls cascading down the steps of the pyramid filled the reservoir. Judging from the height of the hibiscus trees, the commanding structure was a half mile away.

Water sluiced from the pool on our end through simple cuts in the stone, coursing serpentine rivulets into the gardens. Large stepping stones protruded from the surface of the reflecting pool, set in a perfect line that ran back to the pyramid's base. They were square, each large enough to hold a dinner party and spaced a healthy leap apart. The most distant ones faded from view, lost in the glare of the sun and the mist from the falls. I didn't need to see the ones closest to the pyramid to know they'd be saddle-shape, worn from water crashing over them for thousands of years. The ageless-ness of the place was obvious. It had been built, stood over the years, fallen down, and been forgotten long before I'd been born. But I knew I'd been here before. This was the nexus of all I'd seen since I'd jumped from *Olympus*. Everything from the city—the palace, the ruins, the pool—all had brought me to this structure.

I suddenly remembered the rest of my dream. There was something on the other side of this mountain, a massive enigmatic statue of a lion sitting on top of an enormous pedestal of sloped black stone. In my age, it had lain for millennia, buried under desert sands, exhumed centuries before my birth. Early carvings in Egypt depicted its massive stone pedestal as large as a mountain with smooth unscalable sides. Because of the pole shift, the statue had rested southeast of this structure. In this age, it faced directly east, greeting each perfect sunrise. The only way to see the statue would be from the summit of this pyramid.

I eagerly followed Suri as she sprinted the length of one stepping stone and leapt across five feet of water to the next.

CHAPTER NINETEEN

SARAH

I awoke in the front seat of Carlos's Rover, my head on Laura's shoulder, facing the passenger window. The nightmare on the beach flashed within the late afternoon sun as its beams played between coastal villas and clusters of tourists. We were returning to Shamel's estate. Krax's long black locks swayed every time he swerved to miss a pothole. Laura brushed my own hair back from my face. While she did, I fought to keep the connection with Jordan open, but his image receded with the distant breakers.

"You feeling better, kiddo?" Krax asked as he ground a gear.

I nodded within Laura's embrace.

"We're taking you to a hospital," Laura said.

I pushed a strand of sandy hair behind my ear. "Please just take me home."

I didn't want to be distracted by doctors. I had to reach Jordan again. Somehow, I knew the nightmare had been more than a memory of the past. I'd been connected to Jordan as he lived out events in a present I remembered as a past. A present bending toward a horrible outcome far different from what I remembered.

I squeezed my eyes shut, trying to will the nightmare back. Grip it; restore it to what had been. Jordan did not—would not—die. But my efforts seemed futile. Instead of seeing Jordan, I saw the inside of my eyelids.

"You must not try to fight," Laura whispered in my ear over the roar of the engine. "Just pray."

The sun was low on the Pacific by the time we reached the mansion set in the coastal jungle north of Quepos. After living seven years in this age, I still had a hard time remembering to call it the Pacific. In our age, both oceans had been called the Atlantic. North and South America—the former homes to five of the ten nations of Atlantis—were a massive island in the Atlantic's center, with the empire's enormous capital of Payahdon sprawled between Jamaica and Nicaragua. The twin islands of Antarctica and the submerged islands west of Ireland surrounding the Azores and between Cape Verdes had been home to the other five nations.

Krax slowed to a stop behind Carlos's Rover. The older boys jumped out and helped the guard open the iron gates. The Land Rovers turned into the estate, crunched over the gravel drive, and stopped beside a trickling fountain.

I got out of the car and stepped through a thick mahogany door, into the cool of the marble foyer, and heard singing echoing to my right, in the conservatory. Shamel's staff ushered us to the rear of the mansion, out onto the trellis patio and down the path to the beach apartments, where fresh clothing, hot baths, and cool beds awaited those too weary to join our host for a late afternoon tea. I showered and changed in Jordan's apartment. It was exactly as he'd left it when he'd flown to Egypt. I'd brought back the few possessions he'd left in the hotel in Cairo and arranged them as best as I could remember.

The only thing missing was the photo of Lisa and Sophia. It had been stolen from the hotel. When the staff had been questioned, I learned Jordan had hidden emergency money in the back of the frame. The thief had apparently disposed of the evidence to avoid fingerprints. I thought about the sketch he'd drawn on the Baskra sailing raft. I remembered what he'd done with the drawing and buried my face in a towel.

Laura ducked her head in the door. "Ready for tea?"

I turned and folded the towel on the rack. "Are you?"

She took a breath and looked up the path at the glassed conservatory. The silhouettes of my fellow survivors milled around beyond the windows. This was the first time Laura and Krax would be introduced to them.

"I am a little nervous," Laura said.

"You have nothing to fear."

"They're refugees from the past, like you?"

"Thanks to Jordan. And because you're his friend, the thanks we owe him, we owe you, as well."

We walked up the path arm in arm. Krax waited in the foyer before a pair of servants holding the grand glass doors open. He was canted sideways, his hands leaning on a cane, nodding in time to the melody of an old song from my childhood. The singing had a lively tempo.

"I recognize that hymn," Krax remarked as he accompanied us through the doors. "Sounds like Handel."

The head butler greeted us in the spacious chamber, a two-story vaulted room with lancet windows towering between shelves of books. Shamel was seated along a long wall, where he could take in his favorite view of the sunset over the wild Costa Rican beach-scape. He was surrounded by refugee children charming him out of his sweet biscuits, as usual.

Many who had escaped the end of the Second Age were here. It was the first time I'd seen them since I'd revealed my identity to Krax and his friends. Many were successful business owners or members of governments, having parlayed our age's knowledge into prominent positions of private and public service. We were a kind of beneficial network, a band of civilian Guardians quietly watching over our adopted age.

My friends looked understandably nervous about being revealed to Fourth Agers, as we sometimes called the people of this time period. This was still new to us, having people from this age know that refugees from the Second Age lived among them. Two refugee families were former Mestrean priests and priestesses of the Ancient Temple of Shan-Ti. They'd landed in this age three years before me, even though we had started the journey less than an hour apart. They'd formed families, adopting orphaned children who'd traveled with them. I was anxious to hear how their children fared in this age. Premature aging seemed to be striking the young harder than the adults. They were maturing much faster than what was normal in the Second Age.

Shamel's wine-tea steamed on a mirrored tray while his withered hand waved like a pendulum in time to the chorus being sung around the airy room. It was delightful to hear the old songs, even though the pyramid chords were missing. Carlos, Laura, Krax, and I slipped into empty wicker chairs and settees. Some of Carlos's children clustered around him. The others had run off to find their mother in the kitchen. Many busy hands around the room wove yarn in an elaborate creation that came from our age, the ancestor of the Arabic *migramah,* or macramé. It stretched a quarter of the way about the room, from chair to sofa to floor mat to window seat. They wove in time to the hymn.

I joined the singing, as did Carlos and his family. Carlos's older children had found places among the weaving, their nimble fingers joining the dance through the strands that kept time with the song.

Krax bent over his cane to watch one of the younger women work. She was newly married and suckling her first son under the folds of her mother robe. When I'd arrived, she'd already been here two decades and had aged to adulthood in a tenth of the time it would normally take in the Second Age. It was hard to believe she was the same little girl I'd known back in Javan.

Krax nodded as she tied off a complicated knot. Her little son stared wide-eyed up at his nose.

"Far out," he said, his grin pushing his glasses temporarily into their proper position.

She cringed in delighted surprise and hid her mouth properly as she laughed.

"My name's Krax. What's yours?"

"Becca."

He stuck out his hand. Becca took his finger tips with her free hand and nodded.

Laura timidly attempted the melody, weaving her soft voice into the chorus. When it concluded, we applauded her contribution.

Shamel properly introduced us to the other guests. He plainly told Krax and Laura that the guests and staff were refugees from the Second Age and apologized for not having divulged the information sooner. Krax simply said "Cool. That song sounded familiar. What was it?"

"A children's morning song," Shamel said.

"We used to sing it in the temple to greet the sunrise," I said.

One of the women nodded at the shared memory. She had been a young acolyte in the temple. We had played dolls on the East Altar, where the sun had warmed the stones and the lion statue had blocked the morning breeze.

"The song is still sung today," Shamel said. "It is called *Awake My Heart*, a folk song attributed to Estonia."

"Amazing that it lasted thirteen thousand years," Krax said.

"It didn't," Shamel said. "Like all art and science, the end of our age dealt a blow to our culture. The song was lost within three generations."

"Then how did the Estonians learn it?" Laura asked. "Did you teach them?"

Carlos started to laugh, but his wife glared at him. He coughed and looked at his feet.

Shamel picked up the section of the *migramah* laying across his lap. "This is how they learned it." He winked at the children clustered about his feet.

A staffer came into the room and whispered in Shamel's ear. He nodded in approval and looked expectantly at the only solid wall in the room. The staffer swept his hand in an arc and an image appeared on it.

"News from Egypt," Shamel announced.

I recognized the view from my early morning briefing with him and Carlos. A three-dimensional image of the excavation work under the Khafre appeared on the wall, focusing on a team of white-suited explorers being lowered through a fresh hole in the thick granite floor of the shaft.

"The Egyptians have reached the bottom of the shaft," Shamel said.

"Nobody went poof?" Krax asked.

Shamel shook his head. "They did not experience the phenomenon that sent Jordan into the past. They've been drilling into the floor of the shaft and have penetrated a chamber beneath it."

"What kind of chamber?" Laura asked.

"Officially, they are keeping all discoveries quiet," one of the staffers said.

"They have discovered the library vault," Shamel said. "We will attempt to convince the Egyptians that they have found everything and all further exploration is unnecessary."

"How many more chambers are there?" Krax asked.

"Two, each more important than the first. They are rectangular and carefully hidden so finding one does not result in the discovery of the other two. The chamber they've penetrated holds the tablets of knowledge, carved on small *stellas* of solid gold and stacked vertically on stone shelves. We are hoping the other two chambers are not found. They are separated from the first by a hundred feet of bedrock. The access tunnels are carefully plugged with the stone of the exact same mineral vein as the bedrock, rendering the tunnels invisible to present age technology."

"Why are you hoping they don't find them?" Krax asked.

"Because of what they contain."

"Which is?"

Shamel's tired eyes suddenly flared with life. "Some things are not meant to be found. They reveal themselves at their own choosing."

"You would be referring to the legend of the weapons that don't rust and the glass that bends," Krax said.

Shamel sipped his wine-tea.

"How do you know what's down there?" Laura asked.

Shamel seemed to deflate as the question passed through him. He dabbed his lips with a starched linen napkin. "My dear, I know more about what waits beneath Giza than any human from your age or mine."

The others paused in their weaving as he continued.

"I was Commander of the Palace Legion when the Ra came into power. He was young then, arrogant and foolish. Drunk with power instead of hungry to serve." Shamel paused. The shadow of the palms played across his tired eyes. "He called for me one morning and I arrived sooner than he expected. I saw something I should not have seen."

"What did you see?" a little girl asked.

"Something that will not be spoken so it does not continue to harm," he said. "The Ra was quite embarrassed and then furious. I think he even wanted to kill me. But because of my rank and service to the Ra's father, instead, he stripped me of my rank and banished me to guard the ruins of Rahn. I spent thirty decades exploring them." He smiled at me. "That is, when I wasn't otherwise engaged following a little runaway princess intent on climbing the Sacred Mountain."

I blushed.

"Sacred Mountain?" Krax echoed. "That's a Mayan term for pyramid. You're talking about a pyramid in Egypt. I mean Mestre."

"Correct," Shamel said. "The Navel of the Earth, the tip of which you and Jordan rediscovered beneath the Khafre."

"I've heard Egypt called the Navel of the Earth before," Laura said. "The Khafre pyramid is the Navel?"

"No, it is just an edifice that marks where the Navel is buried," Shamel replied.

"Why is it called a navel?" Krax asked.

"That is a question that will be answered at the end of a very terrible time," Shamel said. "I pray those decades are not soon upon us." His thin fingers grasped the *migramah*. "You asked how an ancient song could be lost only to be relearned thousands of years later." He flattened the long strands of yarn on his leg and pulled two apart. "Let this strand represent your age and the other mine. The Second and Fourth Ages are parallel to each other, like the opposite faces of the Sacred Mountain. The First and the Third are the same way. Usually, the twinned ages are far apart. Sometimes they draw near. And at very special times …" His fingers slid to where the two strands gathered in an intricate knot encapsulating a tiny red bead. "… they touch. It is during these embraces that our ages dance. It happens when the sun and his dead mother draw closer in their eternal dance."

"Excuse me?" Krax said.

"The sun shares a binary orbit with the dead star it was birthed from," Shamel said, looking slightly disappointed. "After all the hints I've given you, Krax, surely you surmised that?"

Krax grinned. "Not a clue."

Shamel held his head as if he had a headache. Some laughed. Then Shamel looked up again. His eyes grew bright as he searched the children's faces. They beamed back with enthusiasm. "When the sun and his mother draw close," he whispered, "wonderful things happen. Certain children from each age … touch." He looked at me fondly. "Very special children."

"Jordan and Sarah," Laura surmised.

Shamel nodded. "Among others. Some explain their contact as an imaginary friend. Others think they're having wild dreams. But the contact is real. Much crosses between the ages when the universe brings them near each other. Jordan and Sarah did what any two children would have done when they saw each other: They played together. They saw each other's worlds. They taught each other poems and dances."

"They learned each other's songs," Krax said.

"Or their language," Laura said.

Shamel's eyes glistened. "That which is has been already. That which will be has already been. For the Creator forever seeks what has passed away. Wars and disasters may erase knowledge." He held up his part of the *migramah*. "But restoring it is child's play."

He looked out the large windows to the sea. The sun hung low over its sparkling waters. "It is time to go down to the beach and sing the sun to sleep."

CHAPTER TWENTY

JORDAN

The pyramid and falls seemed to levitate above a mist cloud. A rainbow arched from its tip to its base, beckoning me east. The sun warmed my back as Suri and I raced the length of the pool, vaulting over the shimmering water and landing on granite stepping stones barely protruding above the water's surface.

Suri set a challenging pace, yet we raced side by side. Something ancient and wonderful was happening. Something I'd seen before and forgotten, a fantasy borne in the heart of a frightened boy. I shed much with each stride. As we neared the base of the pyramid, its cleansing mist bathed me, wiping away everything I didn't want, leaving me with one fact and emotion. I was beside Suri and I was happy.

In my dreams, I remembered seeing the pool from a distance. I hadn't been alone then, but my feet had never touched the ground. How had I moved?

The memory flowed back to me, buoyed upon a thousand details I'd forgotten since childhood. I hadn't run then, but had been carried, tucked under the arm of a giant toddler. She'd scampered through the trees, keeping her distance from the water, following a shaded path between the pool and flanking pyramids, a secret way that kept her hidden from a gentle guard who'd searched frantically for her. His deep-throated voice pierced the falls' thunder. *"Tehav Ra-he!"*

The memory of that phrase caused me to hesitate. Suri leapt ahead with the grace of a ballerina, her willowy legs outstretched, her body arching over the water, landing on the next stone. It was a long run, compounded by the hurdles, yet she seemed to embrace the challenge with the stamina of a track star.

The musical chords I'd heard coming through the walls of the pyramids emanated from their sloped faces. A blend of tones as if wind blowing across a thousand empty bottles was perfectly blended in a fantastic complexity. Each pyramid offered its own complete song. The melodies ebbed and surged as we ran, echoing off each other's facades, a symphonic canyon modulated by breeze, stone, and water.

I kept my eyes forward to keep from nose-diving into a stone. We ran past the final pair of pyramids with the crescendo following in our wake, as if heralding our arrival before the massive waterfall. We stopped mere yards from its thunderous splash.

Suri leaned into my ear and shouted, "This is called the Sacred Mountain of Mestre."

Her water-glistening eyes danced across my face as she sought my reaction. "Magnificent," I said.

She flashed a smile, her lips only inches from my mouth while her hand found mine. When she turned to face north, her hair blew across my face, washing me with a lilac scent. The tiny flowers in her hair had begun to bloom.

A footbridge crossed the pool beside the wall of crashing water. Unusable stepping stones extended beyond the bridge, into the thundering stream, their surfaces saddle-worn. Why had stepping stones been built where no one could walk?

Enormous steps set in the sloped face of the pyramid extended up both sides of the falls, continuing behind the water. I wondered if the two sides were really a singular staircase the waterfall bisected. For all its grandeur, the design was similar to platform pyramids in Java, Guatemala, and St. Louis. I even remembered seeing one entombed beneath the Giza Plateau. It had been much shorter, with toppled columns and deeply worn steps in the center. When I tried to remember more details, the memory seemed a million years away and as many miles distant.

Suri tugged on my hand. Her lips brushed my ear when I leaned down. "Race you to the top," she shouted. She pointed to the stairs to the left. "You go up those. I'll climb the ones on the right."

My heart hammered as I gave the summit an appraising look. It had seven major tiers, subdivided by many more, with hundreds of steps scaling each tier, the highest blurred by swiftly moving clouds. The steps were steeper than a schooner's rigging.

"What's the matter?" she laughed. "Afraid you'll lose?"

I rubbed my chin for effect and leaned over to reply. "No, just wondering how long I'll have to wait 'til you catch up."

She gave me an open-mouthed expression that blended into a laugh. Then she tensed.

"What's wrong?" I asked.

She pointed. "Somebody just ducked behind those trees. It might be the Ra's bodyguards."

"You're sure?"

She huddled against me and nodded frantically.

"Stay calm," I said, pushing her protectively behind me as I tried to spot movement where she indicated. As I searched, I fashioned a plan: We would withdraw south over the bridge. When we got off the pool, we'd make a run for the opposite woods.

I turned to explain that to Suri but she was gone. My heart pounded. Then I spotted movement beyond the waterfall. Suri had dashed across the bridge to the staircase on the right of the waterfall. She blew me a kiss and darted up the stairs.

"You're so fried," I said and sprinted up the left side.

We climbed opposite sides of the thundering waterfall for two hours, Suri always a dozen steps ahead of me. Speed gave way to concentration. Clouds of mist reduced my world to a slippery staircase, foaming water the color of milk tumbling down between us. Suri lithely pulled herself skyward. She took a break, pivoting her slim body sideways to take in the view in my direction. She pushed her long hair past her shoulders as I came up even with her.

She smiled, her chest heaving from exertion. I remembered dreaming of making this climb many times, carried by a giant girl.

The steps had been much larger. She'd dropped me once and I'd tumbled down several steps to land facedown on one of the terraces. Fortunately, in dreams nothing hurts. The girl had frantically climbed down and scooped me up. She'd smoothed out my robes and searched for any injuries. I remembered her face then, that of a child but as large as my whole body, smudged with blue streaks across her forehead, her hair the color of gold woven with glittering ribbons.

Suri untangled the ribbons in her hair, saluting me as if she was a Guardian, then continued climbing. An impossible idea emerged as I watched her scale with the energy of a child.

We reached the summit just as the sun began to set. I pulled myself onto the worn stone platform where an enormous ceiling hung twenty feet above me. The city spanned the horizon with the palace mounted at its center. The sun's rays shot through the city towers, through the palace, and across the ruins in long shadows.

Olympus crossed my line of sight, her trailing garden briefly veiling the sun. She sailed majestically past the palace in a long lazy arc. I feared she was coming about, changing course to an easterly heading.

A garden of translucent blue plants filled the summit platform, crowding the little space where I sat catching my breath. The species appeared similar to those growing in Athena's upside-down garden. The source of the falls seemed to originate somewhere deeper in the garden. It flowed with the consistency of milk before tumbling over the edge with a dizzying effect.

Suri knelt on the other side of the channel. She scooped a handful of water and drank greedily, then motioned for me to do the same. It was warm, slightly honey-sweet, and thoroughly satisfying.

Stone paths edged the channel with footbridges arching over the water at regular intervals. A single slab of granite stood on a forest of stone pillars. It shaded the entire garden. The eaves were ragged and wind-worn, hinting at a tremendous age.

Thanks to Athena's brief tour of *Olympus'* upside-down garden, I was pretty certain I understood at least one of the functional purposes of this elevated garden. Perhaps this pyramid had been designed to protect these fragile plants the same way Athena's *Olympus* protected her upside-down garden: keeping plants higher than the ozone and shaded from direct sunlight.

Something resembling a translucent mouse skittered over my foot before darting back into the undergrowth. I remembered translucent fish swimming past enormous water plants under the mountains of Mer. They'd been living in a vast underground system of cisterns, safe from the sun and ozone, fed by a pyramid that erupted a strange light when our little boat had passed.

Suri waved at me from across the channel. "Wait there and I'll cross over."

I nodded. She picked her way gingerly around the heavy growth clustered along the channel and disappeared into the garden. I followed her progress by the swaying of branches and the scattering of translucent insects and birds.

Was this sacred mountain one of many ancient sanctuaries for fragile First Age plants and animals Earth's natural biosphere couldn't protect? The need to protect fragile plants was familiar to me. Most of my age's food and medicinal plants required human cultivation in order to survive. The gingko had been down to a single tree until it had been rediscovered and cloned into a vast agricultural industry. The honey locust tree had been desperately trying to reproduce faster than it died, producing copious seed pods that fell and rotted on the ground with only two percent germinating. Then a Dutch botanist had figured out a way to coax the seeds into geminating at a much higher rate by using acid to breach the shell casings and trigger the soft pulp to life. These trees and many others had been on the verge of extinction before mankind had intervened, salvaging their nutritional and medicinal benefits. But what had caused Earth to become hostile toward her most fragile occupants in the first place?

Suri reappeared from behind a gleaming palm. Her eyes found mine and my pulse quickened. It felt as though she'd been doing that to my heart for years, even though I'd only met her a few months ago. Other weird notions raced through my brain, namely how this garden was familiar to me. In fact, I felt I knew this garden well enough to be a tour guide. Suri was familiar to me, too, as if we'd grown up on the same street. Maybe that's because we had.

There, I said it. Don't know what it meant but I had to face my twisted reality and prove myself right or wrong. Might as well dive into the metaphysical abyss instead of stare at it all evening.

Suri lithely stepped across the nearest bridge to join me. "What do you think?"

"I think I've been here before."

Her confusion changed to a nervous smile. "You're saying words that make me laugh, like you did in the snow cave."

"I know this garden. From the falls all the way to the …" I hesitated; all the way to what?

Her disappointment was obvious. "This was my big surprise."

She wiped perspiration from her face with her sleeve, smudging blue pollen across her forehead and sending the ribbons in her hair glittering. Just like so many times before. My final doubts went over the falls.

"Who showed you this garden? Was it Athena?"

"No." I grabbed her hand and led her into the garden. "You did."

"That's impossible."

It all came back to me. Every visit, each time with a slightly older, slightly more adventurous giant princess. Why she'd been so big began to make sense.

"Up ahead is a bench where you sang to me," I said.

We rounded a bend in the path and passed the bench. It was smaller than I remembered. Encouraged, I walked faster. Suri looked at the bench with wide eyes.

"You held me on your lap and tried to teach me your language, but I could never say anything. My mouth wouldn't work."

"I don't understand," she said.

I took the left at the third fork in the path. "Up ahead is the tree you tried to climb to get yellow apples. But the limbs are too high. I laid on the ground and watched you jump. You got so mad, you kicked the tree. It shook and a big apple fell on your foot. Then you cried."

"I was little when that happened," she said.

We reached a place where the path widened into a half circle. "Me, too. I think we were about the same age, five." We had curved back toward the channel. "Actually, you were five decades and I was five years old, but you know what I mean. We were both kids."

Stone benches edged the clearing. Flowering water tubers floating on the river channel rustled as we passed, releasing milky white clouds into the water. I steered her into the middle of the patio and grasped both her hands. "And this is where you danced."

She let go, retreating to the bench. Her legs hit the seat and she plopped down, a hand over her mouth. "How did you know that?"

I stepped off a stone in the center of the circle. "I saw you. I was a little boy the first time it happened. And you were a little girl."

"I came here alone."

"No, you didn't; you brought me with you." I knelt in the center of her dancing place. My memories guided me to a particular stone in the patio. There was no mortar around its edges. "I had dreams about a little girl who was as large as a giant. Only now I realize she wasn't a giant. I was tiny." I pried the stone up, exposing a shallow hole, where I pulled out a bundle the size of a loaf of bread.

Suri rushed over and snatched it from me. "Nobody knew about this. I never told anyone, not even the guards." She tenderly opened the bundle and exhumed a doll. The covering slipped from her fingers and drifted to the ground. She checked the doll as if I might have damaged it, then caressed its worn face. "My mother made this for me when I was born. He's the only toy I had before the Ra claimed me."

She stared at the doll's faded expression, gently smoothing the tattered pants and little tunic that looked exactly like mine. What were the chances I'd be wearing the same clothes? Zero. The abyss deepened. I didn't care. I had nowhere else to go. I embraced the drop.

"Handsome guy," I said. "What's his name?"

"Horez. It means flying god." She blushed. "I tried flying him off the pyramid once."

"I remember. I almost puked."

"I don't understand."

I took the doll and carefully placed him on the bench. "This is where you put him when you danced, right?"

She nodded. "The crack in the bench helped him sit upright."

"You were a good dancer." I took her hands again, her face worried with confusion. "You twirled in the sunset and your gown sparkled." I stared at her forehead and suddenly remembered. "You wore a jewel."

"How do you remember this?"

I reached down in the hole again. There was a second wrapping. This time, I handed it to her. "It was red."

She opened it, revealing a blood red oval-shaped jewel set on a gold chain as fine as a woven thread. "It's my betrothal diamond."

"May I?"

Her eyes fixed on mine. I carefully opened the gold chain. It unfurled into a delicate headband.

The diamond faceted her face as I lifted it to her forehead. "Fits a lot better now that you're all grown up."

She blushed as I fastened the strands around her head.

"I'm not supposed to wear this yet," she said.

"You wore it for that guy," I said, nodding back to the little doll.

Her finger went to her lip. "He insisted," she said playfully.

"You spun around with one hand holding onto the headband."

She laughed. "I was afraid my diamond would fly off the pyramid like he did."

"I figured you were a princess when I saw you wearing this."

"I am the *Ra-he*," she said sadly.

"Right! Ra-he. That's what the guards shouted whenever they were looking for you."

"I was running away from Amon. The guards were worried I would try to climb the Sacred Mountain and hurt myself."

"Amon tried to take your doll away. You told me that just before you hid it."

"Amon was mad that I liked a doll more than him."

"You danced one last time and then put it in that hole so Amon wouldn't find it."

"Amon was afraid of heights."

"You always looked sad when I saw you."

"The Royal Court was upset that the Ra had arranged for me to be Amon's bride. The other princesses were jealous." She nodded at the doll. "He was my only friend." She held the little doll to her cheek and closed her eyes. "He felt so real." She looked at me as if for the first time. "It was you …"

I nodded.

"I thought I made you up."

"I thought I made you up," I echoed.

She laughed and wiped a tear. We stared at each other. Then, somehow, we ended up in each other's arms.

Vertigo hit me out of nowhere. I felt the early symptoms of the disease emerge. I kept my worries to myself and struggled to hold her as the memories flooded back. The only difference between them and the present was Suri. My imaginary friend had grown up with me.

Somehow, we had been joined across the gulf of time and space, two lonely children pulled together by unknown means. We shared safety in this ancient sanctuary. Back then, I could only watch her as through a rippling of glass. Her dance had entranced me. I would stare at her through the little window into her world, my bedroom fading behind me, wishing so badly that I could cross into her world to be with my only friend, free to explore, share, and live.

My joy overcame my infirmity. I took her hand and we danced.

CHAPTER TWENTY-ONE

LEVI

Olympus vectored northeast, ascending to the cloud ceiling. Even from this distance, the Sacred Mountain felt close enough to touch as we cruised east. The setting sun bathed the sky crimson.

Athena glanced across the bridge to helm control. "This is close enough. Hold and maintain."

"Agreed," replied the helmswoman. She turned to her pilots. "Hold and maintain."

The mighty mountain clawed the clouds and became a fixed point one mile northeast of Jordan and Suri. It was farther away than I would have anchored.

"Why are we stopping here?" I asked.

"To give them privacy," Athena said.

"For how long?"

"As long as it takes."

"They're exposed. A cloaked squad should be deployed on the summit."

"Aizah and her team are waiting at the base of the Lion. Diago is in position next to the north pool."

"That's not enough."

"For now it is."

"The entire Palace Guard is searching for the Princess. They'll be searching the ruins any minute now."

"I cannot send additional assets," she said.

"Why not?"

"Because I was told in a dream not to."

"You know you can't rely on—"

"Don't even start. You've been having dreams, too. Aizah told me."

I looked accusingly at Aaron.

"Can I go take that shower now?" he said.

"Yes, Aaron told her about your visions," Athena said. "That's what one does when one is in a relationship. And Aizah was moved to tell me. I'm grateful she did. It encouraged me to act on what I'd seen. Jordan was meant to leave *Olympus* by his own devices, find Suri, and end up there." She nodded at the view-res of the summit.

"What do you mean *meant to*?" I asked. "You knew Jordan was going to jump?"

"I monitored him the entire time."

"You let an injured civilian jump off a Battle Mountain at cruising altitude—"

"I descended to a thousand feet over the river."

"Oh, excuse me; that's much safer. He now wanders the capital."

"He knew to go east."

"You told him?"

"He ascertained it for himself."

"You let him risk capture in the palace, walk across the forbidden Mastaba Tomb of Rahn in full daylight, nearly get his head blown off by an incompetent Ruin Guard, all so he could go Sacred Mountain climbing with the betrothed princess of Mestre, which would anger the future Ra of Mestre and jeopardize the loyalty of our only remaining ally in this war?"

"Yes."

"Why? What could possibly be so important that you would risk my civilian that way?"

"He's not *your* civilian."

"About that shower," Aaron prodded.

The night sky lit up with a sudden bolt of green light. It shot through the roof of the Sacred Mountain. The enormous beam punctured the clouds, illuminating their underbellies with otherworldly swirls of light.

Aaron sighed beside me. "Never mind."

CHAPTER TWENTY-TWO

JORDAN

"I dreamed that you played with little toy men armed with weapon rods," Suri said.

"Plastic army men."

She pointed her fingers like she was shooting. "You went like this: *Choosh! Choosh!*"

"Well, yeah, that's what army men do when they see bad guys." When she fingered the little doll in her lap, I said, "I always saw you through his eyes."

"Remember when you pretended your bed was an air car?" she asked.

"Actually, it was a rocket ship. I was trying to save you from those girls pulling your hair."

"Amon's cousins. They did that every morning." She looked at me tenderly. "You saw that?"

"Darn right I did. I was ticked."

"What does ticked mean?"

We talked for hours, our legs dangling off the edge thousands of feet above the forest. High cloud cover from the Javan Valley drifted north over the cliffs of Mestre, forming a solid ceiling above the six pyramids and reflecting pool. The pyramid's song echoed up through the waterfall. The descending sun dipped beneath the ceiling and cast Suri in dramatic shadow, highlighting her beauty as the forest faded into dusk.

Suri carefully wrapped her doll and wedding jewel in a satchel and tucked the satchel into her dress. She hugged her knees, her face peaceful in twilight's wash. The symphony of the pyramids quieted. As the land readied for sleep, the lights of Ra's palace came on, extending a twinkling line on the horizon, with the softer lights of the city beyond. The sun vanished and the pyramids ceased singing altogether.

"That was beautiful," I said.

She gripped my hand. "Pause for it."

"You mean wait for it?"

"Mmm."

The closest pyramid suddenly burst with lightning.

"Holy cr—"

The pyramids on either side ignited. Great arches of lightning lanced across the reflecting pond, sparking the other three pyramids to life. The clouds and the pool reflected the staccato chaos. The crackling bolts crawled like sidewinders down the flanks and spread across the ground, flying with the speed of gazelles under the palm trees. The forest glowed in concentric waves, rolling all the way to the horizon.

"First time you've seen pyramids awake?" she asked.

"Roger that."

"This is an okay place to watch, I guess. But down there is more exciting."

"Exciting? Are you crazy? You could be killed."

"Don't be silly. Your hair sticks out and your clothes blow around, but it doesn't hurt; it just feels funny." She spread her arms dramatically. "Jordan Wright, I present Athena's gift."

"What exactly are they doing?"

"Making tomorrow's power."

"For Mestre?"

"For everybody."

I let that sink in.

"How do they do it?" I asked.

"Flogs me."

"You mean beats me."

"Flog means the same thing, doesn't it?"

"Maybe you should stick to Engel and go easy on the American for a while."

The fragile creatures inhabiting the garden skittered away or flew off, occasionally orbiting us for a look. One of the larger animals gave a high-pitched twitter. It looked like a squirrel whose internal organs glowed like an anatomy lesson. Its little heart was beating as fast as mine.

I took a chance and slipped my arm around Suri's shoulder. She grabbed my hand and nestled against me. A different kind of electricity coursed through me.

"I wish we could stay here forever," she said.

"Anywhere with you would be fine by me."

She searched my eyes. "What's wrong?"

"Is Athena planning to take me back to her mountain?"

She nodded. "And I'm coming with you."

"What about Amon? Aren't you supposed to be getting mar—"

She kissed me hard. "Does that answer your question?"

All I could do was smile before her lips sealed mine. Bits of leaves fluttered on us. The garden creatures were going bonkers. A troupe of translucent squirrels raced around the branches and ripped up leaves.

"What's gotten into them?" I asked.

Deep in the garden, something rumbled. The fragile plants swayed. A bolt of green light shot through a square opening in the thick stone roof. We were bathed in swirling emerald light that branched across the ceiling, dripping liquid light over our heads. Suri stood as if to leave.

"Suri, wait."

"It's so beautiful"

She started to walk toward the light. I got up to stop her and the swirling light captured my attention. It was intoxicatingly beautiful. I started to follow. Suddenly, somehow, I heard Suri's voice behind me.

"Jordan, get down!"

I instinctively ducked. A tree exploded next to where my head had been. Suri was knocked off her feet. Successive trunks shredded as the unseen attacker fired a wide spray in our direction. I dove on top of her and pulled her into the undergrowth.

We crawled behind a stone bench. The fire was coming from aircraft hovering beyond the pyramid. Their sleek forms eclipsed the city lights as they winged over us to take up another position. Shots hissed inbound from the north, splintering branches and dropping fruit onto our heads. Flashing lights outlined the hulls of bulkier aircraft. A landing party was on its way.

My mind raced. The summit of the pyramid was about five hundred feet across. Assuming it was square, that gave us five acres of heavy growth. We might be able to evade but we couldn't stay.

"We have to get off this pyramid," I said. "What's on the other side of the summit?"

"There are four rivers flowing from a spring in the center."

"Where that green light is coming from?"

She nodded. "There are bridges next to the spring. We can cross there to get to the back of the pyramid."

"Let's go."

"But it's forbidden to go near the Sacred Spring."

"Since when does the word forbidden worry you?"

I earned a frightened smile for that.

The center of the garden contained a sizable clearing. Vine-covered altars and worn statues rimmed its edges. Carvings covered the pavement. A square hole in the stone roof framed the green column of light and revealed the night sky. Precisely below the roof opening, a spring churned in a square pool. The swirling green pillar emanated from the pool's depths. I kept my eyes averted from the light to prevent a repeat entrancement of earlier. Four channeled rivers gushed out of the pool, flowing north, south, east, and west, each the width of a two-lane road. Four bridges spanned the four channels a stone's throw from the spring.

We darted over the north bridge, ducking as shots hissed overhead. As we crossed the channel, the current frothed like a living thing. The green light swirled and the river heaved, cresting above the bridge like a miniature tsunami. The churning rapids rushed through the railings and grabbed our legs. I gripped Suri and pulled her across the bridge. We leaped to dry ground and the river instantly flattened.

"How did you do that?" Suri asked. The garden was different in this quarter. Kind of like Canada meets Gumby.

"Flogs me."

Shots hit the railings, ricocheting past my ear. We darted through translucent rubbery conifers and wispy ferns. Angry voices shouted straight ahead. They were hitting us from all sides. I pulled Suri down, rolled us into heavier growth, and pressed my finger to her lips. She got the message and laid still. Beams of light swept through the ferns, missing our heads. The beams bounced and sharpened as the intruders neared.

We slid under a berry bush. I rolled on top of Suri to hide her with my tunic. A squad of armored Mestrean Guards ran past us, heading for the center of the garden. They were probably planning on cutting us off at the bridge, not realizing we'd already crossed it.

I waited until we were clear, then led Suri through the woods. We reached the channel flowing east, keeping enough garden between us and the edge of the pyramid to stay hidden, while several aircraft continued to pan searchlights over the east side of the square structure. There was no sign of troops on the other side of the channel.

I tested the river with one foot. The milky water was waist deep and dangerously swift. Massive blocks of stone stuck out of the current, arranged in long lines spaced five feet apart. They were designed to keep the river turbulent and prevent silting, like an Inca irrigation ditch. With luck, I could lay headfirst in the current, grab one stone upriver and use a stone down river as a foothold.

I patted the surface of the channel wall. "Lay on your back."

When she did, I straddled her. "Put your arms around my neck. Wrap your legs around my thighs and hang on tight."

She hugged me.

"Tighter," I said. "Put your chin over my shoulder, tight against my neck."

I lifted her off the ground and stretched for the first stone.

"Watch down river. You see anyone checking out the channel, bite my ear and take a deep breath. I'll submerge us for a count of thirty. You okay with that?"

She nodded against my cheek.

I crab-walked off the channel wall and lowered us into the steady current. Water poured over the back of Suri's head, leaving her mouth free to breathe. Her hair swept over her face, parting at her nose. I shimmied across the channel. Before long, Suri bit my ear and sucked in air. I submerged below the waterline.

The surface became milky white as a beam of light swept over us. Suri stayed calm for the full count, then I came back up and continued across the channel. I lifted her out of the far side of the river.

A beam caught us just as we rolled into the bushes. Shouts, whistles, and lights swiveled our way. The beams bounced and grew, converging on us from every direction.

"Anak," I cursed.

Suri clung to me and sobbed as Mestrean Guardians burst through the foliage. I was ripped from her. She screamed and clawed at the armored limbs carefully holding her. Me, they weren't so gentle with. I got thrown to the ground, kicked in the gut, then my wrists were encased in restrainer gel. Two Guardians hoisted me to my feet by my forearms.

"Thanks for ruining a great evening, guys," I said to their faceless helmet shields. They gave no indication they heard me.

I tested the restrainer gel. Suri would probably be shipped back to the palace. I belatedly realized sitting with her on the edge of the pyramid, in full view of the distant palace, might not have been the brightest idea. It was a safe bet this country had extremely good surveillance. If Amon had seen me kiss her, I'd probably be marched to the edge of the pyramid and pushed off.

They took us back to the center of the garden. The green glow from the shaft of light intensified as we neared the bridge. I remembered what had happened the last time I'd crossed it. Maybe I could use it to my advantage.

CHAPTER TWENTY-THREE

LEVI

Clouds ripped past our cloaked aircraft, a stripped-down Retriever with less armor and a lot more speed. Gravity imaging painted the summit of the Sacred Mountain a bright orange on my canopy. Suri and Jordan were outlined in red. The hundred and eight heavily armed Mestreans were dark green. Their orderly movements back to their transports indicated our approach had not yet been detected.

"Lead, Ground Com."

"Ground Com, Lead," I said.

"Civilians have been captured."

"We noticed," Aaron said.

"Numu brought a raft-load of Guardians just to capture two civilians," I muttered.

"Did you pack extra heal sticks, Chief?"

"Why? We're not getting hurt."

"Yeah, but they are."

"Good point."

I heard Aaron crick his neck before he whipped his helmet armor over his face. "You okay over there?" I asked.

"Just missing that shower," he said.

"Keep your head in this."

"Always, Chief."

I snapped my own helmet into place. "Aizah and her team are pinned down. Diago, too. But they haven't seen through our cloaking yet."

"Good. If Mestre knew we were coming, freeing the civilians might take longer."

"Not on your life."

"I said might."

The floating readouts inside my faceshield dimmed to compensate for the darkness. I watched a real-time image of the Princess struggling with her captors. The imaging came from a spy embedded in the Mestrean Palace Guard. He was an old friend from before the reign of the present Ra, risking his life to monitor and broadcast back to Ground Com. He kept his recording ocular on Suri. She kicked a Mestrean Guardian in his armored backside.

Aaron laughed.

"Thirty seconds to jump," I said.

"Confirmed."

I leveled out while Aaron checked his grapplers. Then something suddenly exploded. The view of Suri tilted and showed a sideways view of the bridge. Brilliant blasts incinerated nearby vegetation.

"Lead, Ground Com. Weapons fire. Civilian hit."

"Idiots," Aaron shouted.

"Lead, Ground Com. Identify casualty."

"Jordan ben Odin," I said, gritting my teeth against what I'd just witnessed.

Aaron pounded his control panel. "He was in custody and the Mestreans shot him."

"He's still alive," I said. "Bleeding out, though."

"Come on, you goons, heal stick him," Aaron shouted.

I pushed the Retriever to its limit, nearly shredding the cloaking field. We ejected and skidded across the roof of the Garden, straight for the hole in the stone ceiling and the pillar of green light.

CHAPTER TWENTY-FOUR

JORDAN

The goons carried me onto the bridge. As I hoped, the square pool erupted like a wizard's caldron just as before, when Suri and I had crossed it. The river surged toward my body, flooding the bridge up to the Guardians' waists. The guards were swept sideways and I fell free, although I landed in the current, plastered against the floundering guards. They were pressed up against the railing, their legs in my face.

My wrists were still bound but I clamped my fingers on a weapon rod and yanked it free. I blasted a hole in the railing and tried to worm though the opening.

Armored hands grabbed me, then hurled me to the clearing beside the pool. I still had the weapon as I rolled to my knees, aiming at the nearest Guardian.

A searing blast hit me in the chest and sent me sliding across the pavement on my back. Suri screamed from somewhere far away. My head hit something hard and everything turned bright green.

CHAPTER TWENTY-FIVE

LEVI

Aizah and her team broke through and landed on the eastern edge of the roof. They bolted for the center, enemy fire slicing past their helmets. The shaft of green light flared and surged high into the night, as if sensing our approach. Aaron and I dove into the space between the light and the stone edge.

It was as if I'd jumped beside a tornado. The light hurled me head over heels across the garden, over the Mestreans. Aaron tumbled through the air beside me, while the Mestreans opened fire. I recoiled from their impact and fired restrainer gel across their skirmish line. Aaron and Aizah crawled up next to me and engaged those still shooting. The rest of Aizah's team was pinned down on the roof. The pillar of light had thickened so much it blocked the opening.

Jordan lay crumpled against the edge of the pool, blood flowing from a horrible chest wound. I sheathed a weapon and pulled out a heal stick.

"Aizah, keep them busy," I said.

She and her team tried to draw fire while Aaron and I ran to Jordan. Aaron kept his armor between me and the Mestreans' shots. He fired both rods and staggered from multiple hits, while I dove for Jordan.

The pillar of light surged and twisted violently. Luminescent tendrils raced across the ceiling, raining green brilliance down upon all. The garden seemed to come alive. Every tree straightened and every leaf broadened, each growing under the spectral shower. Weapons sputtered and died. Restrainer gel evaporated.

I slid beside Jordan's body and pounded the heal-stick into his chest. Green light whipped between him and me. The stick vanished before the tip could even touch his skin. The light wrapped around my legs and pulled me away. The beam pulsed and wove about his body, wrapping him in a translucent coffin of radiance. The light let go of me.

I hurled myself at Jordan but it was as if the light encasing him was made of stone. Aizah pounded the barrier, screamed, and threw a heal-stick at its undulating flames. The stick vanished as Aaron pulled her away. My helmet display pronounced Jordan's condition with grim finality.

When it was clear that weapons were useless, all shooting ceased on both sides. The light continued to thicken around Jordan as if guarding its prey. Aizah clenched her fists and wailed like a wounded she-lion, and Aaron held her. Suri fought against the Palace Guardians restraining her.

"Let me go!" she screamed.

They released her, their eyes transfixed on the swirling pillar. Suri bolted through the milling Guardians and cried, "Jordan, oh God, Jordan!"

Amon chased after her and snagged her arm. "It's over. You're safe now."

She kicked him where it counted. He doubled over. She sprinted for Jordan but Diago caught her in his arms. She threw him off. I grabbed her next and held on as she kicked air.

"It's no use. We can't get to him," I said.

She was close enough to see his chest had been blown open. Various organs hung horribly in view. Her fist went to her mouth. "No, no, no."

I held her while she sobbed. Numu pushed through the Guardians and past Amon, who was hunched over, moaning. He approached me, his substantial middle arriving first. "Guardian Levi,

I am placing you under arrest."

The captain of the Mestrean Guardians stood beside him. His eyes briefly met mine.

"Captain, I order you to arrest this man for trespassing," Numu said grandly.

The captain turned off his weapon and attached it to his leg. "Not tonight, Ambassador." He slapped his fist across his chest and angled it to his chin. I returned the salute.

"Guardian," the captain said.

"Captain," I returned.

"I'm sorry for your loss."

"Who fired at the civilian?"

"It wasn't one of mine, I can assure you."

The pillar of light ceased its stately rotation, while the base thickened around Jordan's corpse. Luminescent strands emerged from its sides and stretched across the stone ceiling. They draped above Mestrean and Javan Guardians alike, wraithlike branches laden with clusters of radiant stars. The stars broke apart and fell upon us, splashing our armor with embers. The Sacred Spring and her four rivers went silent, as if giving audience to my fallen brother entombed within its roots.

Then Jordan's mouth opened.

Thunder echoed far away. I was a kid again, standing under the protection of my father's cape, watching a spring storm gather over his vineyards. I smelled the rich earth of my homeland; felt the warm Berbai sun beaming through heavy clouds; felt my father's large hand on my shoulder; the pain of his death.

The thunder passed. Whispers issued from Jordan mouth, growing into the cadenced verse of my childhood tongue.

Aizah moved to my side. "That's not his voice. It's like someone else is talking through him."

"Which is probably why his lips aren't moving," Aaron said.

Others seemed to hear the strange whispers, too. They raised their faceshields, looking confused. Numu was red with anger, apparently oblivious to the phenomenon.

"Captain," Numu bellowed, "I order you to—"

The Mestrean captain, my old friend, ignored him. Numu began to curse. He suddenly clutched his throat, gaping like a fish, unable to speak any further.

The Mestrean Guardians stood shoulder to shoulder with us, their weapons hanging at their sides or discarded on the pavement. They stared at Jordan's mutilated body, apparently hearing what I heard: a warning delivered with deep concern, like a father pleading to a child. I retracted my helmet to hear it better.

"He's speaking Mestrean," one of the Mestrean Guardians said.

"No, it's Phut," said another.

"You're both wrong," Diago said. "It's Algonian."

Amon snaked through the crowd to Suri. He tried to hold her hand, but she withdrew and fixed her eyes on Jordan. Amon stared at his rejected hand as if he was uncertain what to do with it.

"Can you understand what he's saying?" he asked.

Suri nodded.

"I can't. It sounds like gibberish."

The voice coming from Jordan overwhelmed my senses, washing through me like a torrent. Images of destruction rode the current. The horror they portrayed cleaved me. I shut my eyes in anguish, a futile action. The vision flowed unabated. I looked again at Jordan's damaged body.

A shifting form, vaguely human, knelt beside him. The stranger turned his head to regard me. With inexplicable certainty, I knew he was the one speaking to me, projecting his words through Jordan's lifeless lips. I felt his despair over Jordan's violation, his wrenching concern for the wellbeing of all present, particularly for Amon and Numu. He spoke of our world's imminent demise.

I recoiled at the predicted devastation. Billions of lives would be crushed, buried, burned, and drowned; our cities swept into molten chasms boiling from the sea, swallowed in enormous whirlpools like toys.

These things will be, the messenger said, as if responding to my unspoken protest. *Their course was chosen by your ancestors long before the Second Age, the inevitable consequences of an ancient war. Lands will be swept into oblivion; the oceans upended. Earth will be mortally wounded. Mars will die.*

What is the point of telling me this? I thought angrily.

His pain collided with my rage and swallowed it. *The weak and helpless will be sent to you from every race and every land. Lead them to refuge. Those deemed worthless in this age will be sovereigns in the next. Pray they learn to serve, not rule.*

The messenger bowed low. I felt another presence, infinitely greater than the blurry shade attending Jordan's corpse. The blaze of this new arrival's countenance dropped me to my knees. I cowered from the sheer weight of his examination. I sensed the others fall beside me.

Guardians of Mestre and Javan, do you accept this task I give you?

His voice pierced as metal through gossamer. I understood the enormity of what he requested, the sacrifices required. Of course I was up to the task. But why did my world have to end in the first place? Was this, as my soul sensed, the author of all creation addressing me?

My outrage flared. The specter of a billion horrible deaths was too much to ignore. Protect all, harm none. That had been my creed. A life's path that stemmed from following him.

I cried out to my maker. *Why are you letting them die?*

He did not respond.

Why won't you stop it?

The messenger attending Jordan's body jerked his head and met my stare. *Why won't you?* He shook with frustration before he continued. *Choose to gather the weak. Lead them to safety before there are no choices left to be made.*

I woke to darkness. The swirling pillar of light was gone. The pool bubbled gently as if nothing had happened. Guardian shoulder lights came on, crisscrossing the clearing. Aaron and I stared at each other. Aizah followed Suri as she stumbled to Jordan's body. A crowd clustered where he lay. Aaron looked as though he'd been through Hades and back; and I felt the same.

"Orders?" Aaron asked.

"We should gather Jordan's remains and …"

The words wouldn't leave my throat. Aaron retracted his glove. His bare hand clasped my shoulder until I could control my grief.

"This is why Jordan was sent?" I asked. "To be somebody's stage prop while delivering a warning?"

"Could have just sent a view-res," Aaron muttered.

"Aaron, get over here!" Aizah shouted.

We pushed through the crowd.

"Impossible," Aaron whispered.

Jordan was seated upright against a healer's armored chest. His legs were spread and feeder tubes were in the bottom of his feet. His chest was fused with baby pink skin framed by his seared tunic. He stared at Suri as another healer waved a diagnoser over his regenerated skin.

Suri pressed Jordan's hand to her face, tearfully laughing as he joked with her. Amon stared red-faced as she Trahl-kissed him on the lips.

I got down on one knee beside the healer as he finished his scan. He showed the results to his colleague, who blew through his teeth in apparent astonishment.

"How did you bring him back to life?" I asked.

The healer shook his head slowly. "I didn't."

"Maybe you got that heal stick into him, Chief," Aaron said.

"Maybe," I said, but I felt different.

Jordan said something to me and Suri translated. "He said you're a sight for sore eyes."

"Does he remember anything?"

Suri asked Jordan. Her eyes looked puzzled when he finished. "He says he wasn't here."

"Where was he?"

"On a beach with two men and a little girl."

"He gets a vacation and we get orders," Aaron quipped.

Suri translated for Jordan. He smiled weakly and slumped into her arms. She worried over him.

"He's fine," a healer said as if to reassure her. "He's just had a long day."

"Yeah, dying takes a lot out of you," Aaron said.

Suri gasped. Aizah swatted Aaron's armor.

"What?" he said.

The healer administered a sleep paste under Jordan's nostrils. "This will help him rest during the trip back to Javan."

"I'm coming with you," Suri said.

"No," Amon squeaked.

She ignored him. "Is that allowed?" she asked me.

"Certainly not," Numu blustered.

"Of course it is," I said. "Don't you agree, Captain?"

The captain of the Mestrean Guardians bowed to Suri. "The summit is neutral ground, as ordained by Athena. Her Highness is free to claim asylum and safe passage to Javan."

Numu wagged a fat finger up at the unflinching captain. "I will have you arrested for this insubordination."

"That would be a grave mistake," Athena's voice thundered.

"Oh good, your mom's here," Aaron said.

Olympus' running lights blazed to life beyond the eastern edge of the garden. Dozens of heavily armed fighters de-cloaked, weapons glowing. Numu gawked in their glare.

Numu's palace bodyguards struggled to fire their weapons but they dissolved in their armored hands. Their armor powered down, trapping them inside. Aizah pushed past the helpless men and aimed her weapon at Numu.

"Aizah, don't," Aaron said.

She glued Numu's boots to the pavement. "That's for endangering Suri and Jordan." She spun and kicked him square in the gut. He toppled into the gelatinous trunk of a fruit tree. Golden apples rained down on his head. "That's for being a pompous *rukta*."

Aizah sauntered back and took Aaron's hand, glaring at Amon as she passed. Aaron flicked a two finger salute off his chin. "Tell your dad we said hi."

We boarded *Olympus'* bow. Suri and Jordan were taken to the healing bay. Aaron, Aizah, and I leaned against trees as *Olympus* reversed engines and glided backwards past the obsidian pedestal of the Resting Lion. The flying mountain came around to make for Javan. I zoomed in on the garden with my oculars. The prince stared back from the edge, his fists clenched.

*****

Later, I looked down through the breaks in the pavement of Athena's apartments. *Olympus* had taken station over Suri's family village in the Lake District of Javan. Athena's hanging garden swayed lazily in the spring winds. Beneath their fragile vines spread the enormous branches of the village tree. Its three-foot-wide rose blooms were past their peak. Thousands broke free on a gust of wind and drifted earthward. Hints of green colored the silver bark. Five hundred feet below their protective ceiling, the streets and rooftop terraces of Suri's village formed a spiral collage that hugged rolling hills. These were my people, refugees of a tiny country west of Phut, considered low priority by the Nephillim, erased during a border war with the Atlantean half-giants, the war that had killed my parents. I remembered my baby sister shivering in my arms as we'd hidden in the bombed basement of our destroyed home, hiding from Odin and Athena. They'd been exploring the ruins after the truce, discussing their finds as if my people's wrecked possessions were scientific curiosities.

"What are they going to do to us?" my sister had whispered as Athena carried us back to their ship like a couple of strays. Her eyes fluttered from fever.

I pulled her into my arms. "Don't worry; I won't let anything harm you."

"Promise?"

Odin hadn't been able to save her. He hadn't invented the heal stick yet.

I squeezed back the memory of her death as I looked down on Jordan's new home. I'd overseen his transfer to a remote cottage on a ridge overlooking the village. Suri wanted him with her, while Athena had insisted on keeping him on *Olympus* for treatment. Suri had refused. The cottage was a compromise, far enough away to avoid disturbing the villagers and out in the open so Athena could regularly douse Jordan with pollen.

Suri and some of her family kept vigil at his bedside between treatments, waiting in the foyer while the pollen dissipated to keep their clothes clean. A group of Suri's younger siblings had hidden under his bed during the last drop. There were no ill effects to the children from exposure, so I didn't intervene.

I took no chances with Jordan's security. Aizah, Diago, and two dozen of my best Guardians kept watch around the cottage and surrounding fields. Suri requested that we remain cloaked and avoid disrupting the civilians' lives any more than we already had. Athena had agreed. *Olympus* and the orbiting patrols I'd insisted on had disturbed the village enough. I'd countered by pointing out that Ground Com was monitoring a spike in coded chatter between Phut and the West ever since Suri and Jordan had arrived in Javan. In my opinion, the couple remained a valued target to Atlantis.

Athena's nervous bustling in the food garden brought me out of my reflection, her enormous arms picking fruit high above my head. She was my adopted mother and had likely saved my life, but she and her kind had not saved my family.

Aaron came out of my apartment, toweling his head. "Anak, those are sweet digs you got there, Chief. The bathing room is enormous."

"Thank you," Athena called from the terrace garden. "You're welcome to stay there anytime. They're hardly used."

Aaron looked at me and mouthed 'ouch.'

Athena entered carrying a tray of watermelons, her face the picture of stress. "Isn't this nice that we are all together again?"

Odin groused beside the looking-through pond, as I'd called it when I'd been a child. Its transparent bottom showed a rippled view of the lands below. Athena nudged him with the tray. He startled and seemed to notice her for the first time.

"Aren't they nice?" she said.

He fixed his eyes on the fruit. "Decent specimens."

He accepted a watermelon from her, held it between two fingers, and bit half of it. Pieces hit the water, exciting the fish. He popped the rest into his mouth and glared at me. "I listened to every syllable that primitive grunted last night. Pure gibberish, but you say you understood it?"

"Every word."

"What language was it?"

Aaron spoke up, "He was speaking Javan, sir."

"And Berbai-nachi," I said.

"At the same time," Aaron finished.

Odin's eyebrows lifted four inches. "Berbai what?"

"My mother tongue," I said. "I'm from Berbai, remember?"

Odin waved my retort away with a massive hand. I felt the breeze.

Athena set the tray down and looked eager to steer us away from the subject of her controversial decision to adopt me. "It wasn't gibberish, Father. Ground Com detected a complex pattern in the sounds coming from Jordan's mouth."

"Of course it was complex," he snorted. "The signal came from the old Net."

"Excuse me?" Aaron said.

"Knowledge system buried inside the Earth," he explained. "Existed before the First Landing. Devilish thing to study."

"Because Father can't find it," Athena said.

"It's there, all right," he said. "Until yesterday, it was nothing but background noise, impossible to pinpoint. Then that primitive opens his dead mouth and it turned on. Fourteen hundred overlaid signals simultaneously channeled into his brain and out of his mouth."

"And were you able to trace it back and narrow the location of this Net?"

He muttered something incomprehensible and resumed staring at the pond.

Athena looked at us. "You both understood the message?"

Aaron nodded along with me.

She sighed. "I wish I'd been there. We heard static on the summit. What did Jordan say?"

"That there would be a global war," I replied.

"Well, that's prophetic," Odin said. "Or should I say pathetic? What does he call what's happening now? A global disagreement?"

I ignored him. "There were visions with the message."

"Diago saw a seven-headed monster with three horns rising out of the sea in the West," Aaron offered. "It strikes the Eastern Alliance."

Odin laughed. "Seven heads and three horns? Obviously, it's Atlantis invading the Eastern Alliance; which, if you haven't noticed, has already happened."

"Seven heads?" Athena mused.

"The seven nations on the main island, of course," Odin said.

"The three horns are the outer islands?" Aaron asked.

"Evaemon, Azaes, and Eumelus," Odin said, spreading his massive arms. "Use your heads. He's obviously talking about this war." He snorted. "Some prophet."

"There are other details that refute that," I said.

"Since I couldn't make sense of that noise, perhaps you'd care to enlighten me?"

"The attack starts after a truce." Aaron said.

"After signs appear in the sky," I added and looked pointedly at Odin. "You wouldn't know anything about that, would you?"

Odin glared. I felt the heat rise in my face.

"When I was in Babla's ship getting my backside blown out of the sky by your overzealous missiles, I noticed a—"

"You would have been perfectly safe," Odin interrupted, "if you'd moved quicker."

"Father!" Athena said. "You knew he was on the ship when you launched?"

"I had no choice."

"What do you mean?"

His watermelon-stained mustache tangled with his beard as he pressed his lips shut.

"I saw something before I hit the atmosphere," I said. "Something that blotted out the stars. It wasn't there the last time I was in space."

"What is he talking about, Father?" Athena asked.

"Nothing."

"I disagree. I think it's something so important you were willing to let civilian hostages die in order to keep it a secret," I said.

Odin didn't erupt into anger and start breaking things as I expected him to. His face sagged beneath his mane as if a great weariness settled over him. He reached for Athena as if to touch her face, but she flinched. He retracted his hand and sighed. He stared at Aaron and I. "Don't be too sure of this supposed doomsday message. Your race has been obsessed with predicting the end of this age ever since it started. Only Nephillim of science have the skills to glean what's true and what's fable."

"That's supposed to impress us?" Aaron said.

"Stay your tongue, human." He pointed skyward. "You couldn't possibly fathom what waits out there."

"The Stream of Heaven maybe," I suggested.

Odin turned in a huff, knocking a melon off the tray. "I'll be in my lab, trying to do something productive."

Athena watched him vanish through the leaves, then sighed. "Care to explain what he's talking about?"

"I will. Promise me you'll maintain security around Jordan and Suri."

"Why would they need it in Javan?"

"Promise me." I pressed. "Please."

She nodded and I touched my chin in farewell.

"Where are you going?" Aaron asked.

"To find out what Odin knows."

"He's not going to tell you," Athena said.

"I wasn't planning on asking."

CHAPTER TWENTY-SIX

JORDAN

I sat up, sweating. Soft fleece cratered under my elbows. I lay on a four-poster bed on a stretched tarpaulin. The fleece smelled of lanolin.

The room had no roof. Instead, loose netting hung from thick branches crisscrossing above the eaves. Morning light played shadow games through dangling moss and star-burst flowers. Orchids cascaded to within a few feet of my face. These were serviced by a hummingbird the size of a crow. He darted in and inspected my nose. His great wings thrummed like a lawn mower.

Apparently satisfied that my nostrils didn't require siphoning, he darted to another flower. I lay back and took inventory of my body, vaguely recalling the beating it had taken. Everything was still attached and nothing seemed broken.

Nectar-loving creatures invaded the room in large numbers as the morning brightened. They zipped past my face and orbited the bed. A simple wooden chair sat beside the arched entrance to a shadowed hallway. A multicolored shawl hung over its back. Small windows afforded views of a brilliant flower garden. A substantial wooden door with black hinges hung partly open at the far end of the room, revealing another large room with glazed tiles and tall windows covered in flowing curtains.

"So where am I this time?" I asked.

I remembered the night on the Sacred Mountain. Javan medics working on me while Suri held me. The doctor had rubbed goop under my nose that smelled like modeling cement. Everything had gone fuzzy. He must have sedated me. What had happened after that? Had I gotten evacuated?

I sat up and sneezed. A cloud of pollen puffed off my body. The same stuff from Athena's upside-down garden.

"Oh God, please don't let this be *Olympus*," I whispered.

I sneezed again, so hard I shook the bed. Children's voices giggled beneath me. Then somebody poked me through the bedding.

"What the heck," I exclaimed. I slid over to the edge and reached under it. That triggered a chorus of squeals. Little bodies evaded my probing. I withdrew my hand and waited until someone got brave enough to poke me again.

"I know you're down there," I teased.

Girly giggles were followed by shushes from a few boys. I estimated five targets. As expected, I got poked again. I snagged a hand and someone hollered. I let him go. Three boys and two smaller girls poured out from under the bed. The boys found their footing first and darted for the door.

"Hey, wait a minute," I called.

The boys fled and the door swung shut, latching in the girls' faces. They struggled to lift the big lever, crying out rapid sentences. Maybe I wasn't on *Olympus*. Odin wasn't keen on humans running loose.

I swung my legs around and sat on the edge of the bed, my hands up to indicate that I wasn't aggressive. They backed into the corner as if I might shoot them. "I won't hurt you."

They probably couldn't understand me, but I hoped my tone would calm them. Surprisingly, it worked. They stopped sniffing and stared back at me with big eyes.

"Dahbrey," I greeted in Javan, touching my chin with my fingertips.

"Dahbrey," they chimed in gentle singsong, as if manners were so well ingrained in them the response was automatic.

"Jordan," I pointed to myself, then at them. *"Etu?"*

They could have passed for Suri's kid sisters. I wondered if they were. I repeated my name and gestured to them to tell me theirs, repeating *and you?* in Javan.

"Becca," said the taller one. "Liv-ya," said the other, scratching her ear.

Becca was a sable-haired, blue-eyed five-year-old; Liv-ya was blonde, doe-eyed, and maybe three. They were dressed in matching knee-length dresses with multicolored leggings and sandals, fresh smudges on their knees from crawling under my bed. I wanted to ask them if they knew where Suri was, but I didn't know how to say it in Javan. I slid off the bed, took a step sideways, and backed up to a chair.

"Suri?" I pretended to be looking around the room. "Is she here?"

Vertigo hit me. I slumped on the chair. The girls marched right up to me. Becca poked my chest. "Jordan."

"Suri tu-en cha," Liv-ya nodded importantly.

"Tu-en Suri cha." Becca added.

Tu meant you. *Tu-en* was a verb meaning you do something. No clue on what *cha* meant.

"Tu-en Suri cha?" I tried.

They covered their mouths and giggled.

"Vendah," Becca exclaimed.

Vendah meant no. Actually, according to Suri, it meant less than yes.

"Tu-u-u-u-en Suri cha!" Liv-ya corrected, poking my chest for emphasis. Maybe *cha* was the short form of *cha-nahee*, meaning darling, honey, sweetie, etc.

"Tu-en Suri cha-nahee!" Becca pretended to hug somebody.

Yep. "You ladies wouldn't happen to speak English, would you?" I asked.

"Cha-nahee! Cha-nahee!" Liv-ya chanted gleefully, squishing her nose back and forth to imitate a Javan kiss.

"Didn't think so," I said.

I'd made two new friends. They began chattering away in Javan, pointing to different things in the room, offering incomprehensible descriptions and trying to get me to repeat their words. After a few minutes, I called time out. "Girls, thanks. I mean *brosheleau*."

"*Botta!*" they chorused.

"I wish I knew how to ask you where Suri is," I muttered.

"She's planting." Liv-ya giggled.

Becca clamped her hand over Liv-ya's mouth. "You don't say that to company," she scolded.

What the—?

"Hees nah comfanee," Liv-ya complained through Becca's digits. "Heeffs her boyfrenn."

"You speak English?"

Liv-ya yanked Becca's hand away. "Of course. Suri taught us yesterday."

"You learned English in a day?"

"Yes."

Becca rolled her eyes. "Liv-ya's telling stories. Mother Habi has been teaching us ever since you got here." She stared at Liv-ya. "Suri helped us *review* yesterday. Remember?"

Liv-ya swished her hand past her ear, which I guess meant *what's the difference.*

"Why didn't you tell me sooner?" I asked.

"Sister said you needed practice learning Javanese," Becca said.

"Lots of practice," Liv-ya shook her head sadly.

"By sister, you would mean …"

"Me," Suri whispered in my ear.

I jumped out of the chair. Becca and Liv-ya burst out laughing. Suri had been hiding in the shadows of the hallway. She wrapped her arms around my neck and rubbed my nose. "Welcome home."

The girls hid their expressions behind their hands.

Suri released me, put her hands on her hips and glared at them. "You two are very late for school."

Apparently *Ahh!* is the same in Javanese as it is in English.

CHAPTER TWENTY-SEVEN

SARAH

We gathered with Shamel on the beach. The sun broke below the clouds and cast a fiery glitter upon the churning waves. The children darted to the surf's edge and scared the birds off. Becca tied her dress about her knees and held her infant on her hip to keep the fresh foam from the breakers from dousing them. She'd been a little girl of only six decades when she'd jumped. She'd landed on this beach many years before I'd arrived. How Carlos had found her was a miracle.

The sun kissed the turbulent horizon, painting the underside of the clouds a deep rose. Krax leaned on Carlos's oldest son for support, since his cane was useless in the soft sand. He chatted with Kate, who'd arrived late. Her phone flashed and she squealed in delight when she read the number. She pressed the phone to one ear and covered the other as she spoke into it.

"It must be Greg," Laura said. "Carlos says they talk constantly."

"But he'll only be away two weeks," I said.

Laura took my hand. "Lucky her."

Shamel and Carlos sat on a weathered tree trunk beached in the sand. Laura and I joined them. The children darted about the beach in the darkening shadows as stars peeked through the fleeing clouds. Weather changed quickly here.

Kate slumped down beside us in a huff, snapping her phone shut. "Wouldn't I be talking to Greg and the phone goes dead."

"Guess he'll have to survive on only four calls today," Krax said.

The sky suddenly flashed. I craned my neck to see if I could find the constellation Orion. As if summoned, the Hunter's stars appeared from behind a cloud, shimmering in the hot, wet air.

"Another storm?" Laura asked.

"No," I said as my heart raced. "Look at Orion. The middle star is fading."

"Could just be a cloud," Krax said.

"I know, but look. See? Now the star is completely gone."

We stared intently at Orion. The other two belt stars vanished, as well. Shamel spoke rapidly to Carlos.

Another flash that lingered too long to be lightning caused the children to stop running and look up. They cheered excitedly.

"Would somebody please explain this?" Kate said.

"Someone is crossing," I replied.

Carlos slapped his thighs and stood. He shouted to his kids. The younger children came to him; the older ones ran to a shack and grabbed equipment. Shamel pulled out his armored phone, tapped a single button, and spoke tersely in Javan.

A blue haze formed around Orion by the time I heard the thumping of Shamel's helicopters. Flashing red and green lights leapt over the coastal palms as the choppers came up the beach. One circled over the ocean a quarter-mile from the beach where the ocean had begun to glow a dim green. The other approached the shore, guided by Carlos's flashlight. The youth were waiting with snorkels and fins. Landing lights coned the knee-deep water. The helicopter dropped an inflated raft into the surf, and the children clambered aboard, yanking the motor to life. Soon, the nimble craft bounded across the crashing surf.

"I can't believe it might be happening," I said, choking back my excitement.

"Do you think Jordan is coming?" Laura said.

"It's a little soon, but I'm not complaining." I laughed as I watched Orion for the signal, the one I'd seen so long ago from an air car in the Embassy.

The raft charged across the ocean under the watchful searchlights of the choppers. The first helicopter was on station, orbiting a pronounced circle of glowing green light.

"Everyone should now cover their ears," Shamel said.

The children huddled around Carlos with their little fingers obediently in their ears. Staff and medical personnel hurried down from the mansion. The middle star of Orion reappeared from wherever it had gone. It grew to the size of the moon. A shaft of light punctured the center with the swiftness of a flaming sword. Then it vanished.

I blinked to clear the after-shadow from the corners of my eyes as the raft eased into the center of the fading oval. House staff handed out night-vision binoculars to the adults. I zoomed in on the rescue in time to see a person being pulled out of the water. Once the refugee was on the raft, he was then hoisted into the helicopter.

My heart sank. The person was too small to be Jordan.

I felt guilty for my reaction. Another refugee from the Second Age had escaped a horrible death. I said a prayer of thanksgiving for whoever we had just plucked from what I still called the Western Atlantic.

The raft and escorting helicopter remained in the ocean to hunt for a possible second arrival, while the other helicopter headed for the beach. Staff had cordoned off a landing zone with flares. The chopper hovered over the center, high enough to lessen the sting of blowing sand, while the medical team ran to the edge. The helicopter carefully lowered its newest passenger, who was carried in the arms of Carlos's jubilant son.

A cheer went up among the staff. It was a young girl, maybe four decades old, wearing tattered Javanese sleeping clothes. She clutched Juan's soaked life vest.

I dashed up as the medical team received their patient. They checked her vitals as I brushed back her wet hair and felt a surge of relief. I spoke to her in Javanese even though she knew English. "Oh, darling, I thought you were lost!"

"Suri?" she said.

Becca knelt beside me, still holding her baby. "Liv-ya, you're alive!"

Liv-ya darted her eyes from me to Becca, then to the baby and back to me again. Confusion and fear twisted her face.

"It's me, Becca."

Liv-ya closed her eyes as if to shut us all out.

"She doesn't recognize you because you're all grown up," Shamel said. "See how she hasn't aged? For her, it was only a few minutes ago she fell down the shaft and started her journey across the gulf to this age."

"But … she was right behind me when I jumped," Becca said.

"Maybe she couldn't leave as quickly as you thought," I offered. I prayed whatever had delayed her hadn't stopped Jordan from crossing.

"She doesn't know you arrived decades ago and have grown up since," Shamel said.

"This is joking talk," Becca cried. "Liv-ya's my sister. Of course she would know who I am." She touched Liv-ya's face. "It's me, Becca. Don't you recognize me? Are you hurt? *Tu-en tua?* "

Liv-ya kept her eyes tightly shut and began to cry.

CHAPTER TWENTY-EIGHT

JORDAN

Suri slipped her hand in the crook of my arm. We left the cottage and stepped into the morning light. Wisps of fog lingered around the wet stone walls. We walked down a dew-covered path that led to a school flanked by waving ferns the height of sailboats. Liv-ya and Becca scampered ahead to check out oversized butterflies drying their wings in a patch of sunlight. Suri intercepted Liv-ya, who seemed to be having trouble keeping the hair out of her face. She pulled out a pair of small gold spirals, and with a quick twirl, wove them neatly into Liv-ya's hair above her ears.

The field thinned and gave way to a long rock shelf overlooking a sweeping valley, which was populated with enormous trees. Suri pointed at the closest one, about a mile away. "That's my village. My people are called the Berbai."

The sprawling village looked as if they'd sprouted from the base of an immense silver-trunk tree. Its stately canopy towered over the flat-roofed cottages as a benevolent guardian, topping out in a teardrop tangle of massive branches thick with leaves.

"There are five more villages farther up the valley," she said.

"Your people are Berbai. I thought this is Javan," I said.

"We're refugees."

As we walked, the other villages became visible on the horizon, each marked by a tree. It reminded me how Mayans always centered their villages around the mighty ceiba trees.

Suri handed me her people's version of binoculars, explaining she didn't like implants. I zoomed in on the other settlements. The Berbai were spaced beside two milky white streams that curled along the valley. Larger trees on more distant hills loomed beyond those. Their canopies spread wide and draped boughs like willows. The glittering trace of a city skyline stretched below their swaying limbs. Beyond the skyline, a towering mesa defined the northern horizon. Shafts of sunlight lanced the clouds and etched across the jagged cliffs. Silver lakes lapped the foothills, sparkling where sunbeams swept their placid waters.

Out of habit, I checked around for threats. I felt exposed without Aizah or Levi in the neighborhood. Maybe they were keeping watch, just being stealthy about it. Yeah, that had to be the case. There was no way they'd leave Suri and me un-escorted after last night, even in their home country.

I spotted a pair of Athena's aircraft making a wide orbit and relaxed a little. I suspected her mountain was hiding up in the clouds somewhere, probably right over us.

Suri pointed to the city under the giant willows. "That's our capital, Deucalion. I'll take you there later, after we . . ." She paused in mid-sentence, as if she was afraid to finish. "Unless you're feeling tired and would rather rest. That's okay, you know. Athena said you might be worn out by this afternoon."

"I feel fine, actu—"

"Oh, but please go. We don't have to stay the entire day. It isn't a very large city, not like Ra's. And it's not nearly as noisy. Rather quiet, really. You like old things, don't you? You did when we were traveling. Remember when we hiked in Tevleh and you saw Shem's Knowledge Pillar on that mountain? You wanted to examine it. I'm so sorry we couldn't walk to it because of how deep the snow was." Her eyes flared. "Because of those walkers! Anak, they were frightening. I never thought we would get away from them."

"Yes, I was interested in studying the carv—"

"If we went to the city, you'd be so pleased! There's a duplicate of both of Shem's Pillars in the city, the brick one *and* the stone

one! They're not old, but all the carvings are exactly the same. I think it would be great to see, don't you? Unless you wanted to see other things first."

"Whatever you think—"

"My fathers think you should see the Senate. They're in special session for some reason." She stooped down to pick a blue flower from the path. "They think we should hear them argue." She buried her nose in the bloom. "I guess I'll do it if you want to."

"Well, actually, I'd—"

"The Second Landing! You *must* see that. That's where Rahn crashed. One of my cousins is a scientist at the site. No, wait, two of them are. Anyway, the one can get us into a cave they're excavating. He said they found a piece of one of the Nephillim ships preserved in mud-rock! Then there's water skating—"

"Slow down, Suri," I said, stopping her on the path. "I'm here because I want to be. We have all the time in the world."

"Do we? The things you were saying the other night suggest otherwise."

"Frankly, I don't remember what I said."

She wrung her hands. "I just want you to be happy here and feel at home."

"And maybe you're a little nervous about me meeting your parents?"

She lowered her eyes and blushed.

"If nothing else, they'll see how much you mean to me," I said.

She smiled, then hurried to catch up to Becca and Liv-ya. She pointed out each new creature that flew, darted, or hopped off the path. I remembered the guided tour of the White House our unit had taken when we'd shipped home. Krax had gotten a kick out of the perky intern leading us around like we were sixth graders on a field trip. The memory of her walking backwards down the ornate hallway, pointing out things to us, merged with this surreal hike down the ridge.

We stopped to eat a wriggling flower Becca had picked. A red bird as big as a cow bombed the path and we inched around the gooey mess. Anak, did it ever smell.

The fact that this world didn't seem as weird as it did when I'd first landed here made me hopeful I could finally unpack my troubles. I was used to long tours in faraway places, feeling like a drifter. Maybe, with time, I could let this place seep in and become a home.

Did I want it to? Suri acted like we would marry soon and yesterday on the pyramid had signaled our engagement. That had been some engagement party. My eyeballs still smarted from the fire flashes. How could she bounce back so fast? Yesterday, I had my chest hollowed out; today, I had a beautiful, fascinating woman chattering happily on my arm and two future nieces that looked like they took cute pills every decade.

A long shadow swept across the path behind us. *Olympus'* rocky bow broke from the cloud cover and cruised into view, rippling the clouds in her wake.

And I had a giant adopted mother. I could use a few minutes to adjust.

A gust of wind blew Suri's hair. I smelled her flowers as she turned toward me. She stood up on her tiptoes to rub her nose against mine. Adjustment complete.

"And after we see the gardens," she said, "I thought we could visit one of the dance arenas in the evening. They make the gravity lighter so you can dance on walls. Unless you're tired by then. I hope you're not; I've always wanted to go." Her hand snugged tighter around my arm and her head burrowed into my shoulder. "Now that I have a good dance partner. We'd need a fifty-hour day to do all of it. So, we have to narrow it down a bit. What do you think?"

"Excellent plan," I injected while she took a breath to reload.

Her eyes smiled behind her breeze-blown hair. "Which part? The water skating is better in the afternoon when there aren't so many people on the lake. Gets choppy in the evening when the long necks start diving for fruit. Most visitors love the Deuca museum. It's world famous. "

"Did you say Deuca?"

"Yes, does that sound good?"

Deuca was the Greek name for Noah. Did that mean the Javans

had a museum dedicated to Noah? And had they really named their capital after him? Plato seemed to hint at it. The Deuca museum won the pole position on my bucket list.

Suri studied my face and nodded once. "The museum it is."

We crested a bump in the ridge. The path broadened as it merged with two others, one from the valley down to our right and the other from a tangled woods up to our left. People walked the path ahead of us, now paved with wide smooth stones. The walkway threaded down the hill into a crumbling city ruin. The sweeping curve of a forum came into view. People in many dress styles, from simple to flowing, were settled about the seats. Children clustered at the bottom, sitting on cushions or tufts of grass protruding through the ancient paving stones. A young couple was seated on stone benches, leading a discussion with the children. They looked like all the other adults in the forum, fit and trim and in their late twenties. I tried to ignore that many of them would be older than Marco Polo if they lived in my age. It wasn't hard. I had come to grips with Suri being just shy of three centuries old.

We crossed a worn threshold marking the rim of the forum to a knot of people waiting for us near the crest of a long staircase. They beamed at Suri as we neared, occasionally making eye contact with me. I guess they waited until we closed the minimum required distance before they initiated greetings. In America, that was about ten feet. In the Sahara, it was about a hundred.

At twenty feet, they nodded and touched their chins. I followed Suri's lead and returned the greeting, taking care to make eye contact with each. If this culture was anything like others I'd navigated, the greeting moment was crucial. Knowing the language paled in comparison to knowing the customs. When we say, "thank you," we expect a "you're welcome" in return. These folks expected eye contact.

They were very happy to see Suri and spoke in hushed whispers so as not to disturb whatever was happening below. Suri introduced me, translating their polite questions and welcomes. Then they got chattering in Javanese and left me in their wake, catching up with Suri during her long absence.

I stood politely until Liv-ya and Becca tugged on my sleeves.

They led me to the steps, where I stood with them hanging on my arms, looking down at the children clustered around the two teachers.

"Is this your school?" I asked.

Liv-ya rolled her eyes.

"What did you think it was?" Becca giggled.

"Oh, I don't know. I thought maybe it was a place where I was supposed to tickle you." I pretended to lunge for her belly. Her eyes flew wide and she fled back to Suri, ducking behind the folds of her gown. The other grown ups excused themselves and walked off. Suri rejoined me with Becca holding onto her hair ribbons.

"Ouch, Becca, *fruuli*, that hurts." Suri shook her head at me. "Honestly, Jordan, you're as bad as the children."

"Well, technically I am a kid."

"Yeah, he *is* a kid," Becca parroted.

Liv-ya swung on my arm. "A big, hairy kid."

The girls skipped off ahead to check out a foot-long bug crawling on a pillar.

"Guess they're okay with me being a freak of nature, huh?" I said.

"You're no more a freak than I am," Suri said.

"Excuse me?"

She looked like she'd let that slip without thinking. "Let's get them down to the school."

She clearly didn't want to talk about it. I left it alone and made a note to bring the subject up again during a more private moment.

This place was enormous. I was a hundred and fifty feet from a semicircular stage. The seating tiers angled down as steep as a ski slope and probably could hold five thousand people. The acoustics of ancient forums in my age were incredibly perfect. This one was no exception. Sound carried far here. Even from this distance, I understood the faintest whispers coming from the children.

Liv-ya hesitated at the first step. It was a long way down and her little legs weren't built for the task. She looked at me expectantly and held out her arms. I scooped her up and swung her around on my back. We descended the long steps to the stage. She sang as we bounced down the risers.

"Awuba, Jamaica, ooo I wanoo ake you, do bahmuda, bahama come on pitee mama, Key lawgo, montego baby, why don't we go ..."

"What the heck are you singing?" I asked.

Liv-ya swung her head past my ear, her breaths wetting my face. "Isn't it just the coolest song you ever heard? Everybody likes it."

Becca tugged on Liv-ya's leg. "You're not singing it right."

"Yes, I am."

"No, you're not. It goes: Aruba, Jamaica, ooo, I wanna take you ..." Becca finished out the stanza perfectly and went on through the rest of the song. Liv-ya chimed in half a note behind her as Suri caught up to us.

"Beach Boys," I said as she took my elbow. "How is it they're singing the Beach Boys?"

She hid her smile. "Ask Diago."

We finally reached the stage. Liv-ya hopped off my back and plowed through the other kids to hug the teachers. They were introduced to me as Eldest Father and Mother.

Eldest? The mom looked like Suri's twin sister and Dad looked like he could bench-press Mom with one hand. They chatted with me in English—Engel, I mean—and introduced me to the other students. The kids were keenly interested to know where I came from. They guessed the usual: a primitive northerner who traded in First Age tech I'd dug up from those Nephillim polar vaults I kept hearing about. I told them plainly that I was from the future.

Suri looked like she was going to fall over when I said that. What would be the point of telling them differently?

The kids got excited. Eldest Mom and Dad looked like they'd swallowed moldy sausage but bravely kept smiling. Questions came flying. The possibility that I was a time traveler made a splash. What age did I come from? Was it the third, fourth or fifth? I wondered how they knew there were three more coming.

A parent retrieved a ball the kids had been playing with and handed it to me. It was a rubbery globe of the Earth, complete with mountains and valleys in relief. You could have handed me the keys to a Jag and I wouldn't have been as excited. After looking at fuzzy map displays on air car consoles and at YOU ARE HERE placards in cities, I was finally looking at the whole Earth.

Anak, it was different. The Andes and Rockies were missing, and water was missing, too. Lots of it. The Gulf of Mexico, Mediterranean, and Caribbean were valleys. The ice cap was over Greenland as I'd theorized. The east coast of what would be the United States had an extra hundred miles of real estate where it should have been the Atlantic Ocean, the beaches sitting on the edge of the continental shelf. New York had a big fat peninsula that hooked all the way down to Bermuda. Both the Pacific and the Atlantic were called the Atlantic. Guess these folks believed coming up with one name for the Earth's ocean was plenty.

The Azores were as big as England, and the English Channel was a valley connecting France. The South Pacific islands were all connected. You could walk from Australia to Thailand. Western Australia must have been darn chilly because the ancient Aussies were stuck with the South Pole sitting off their west coast.

All this I pointed out in careful detail. The class went viral. Every student standing tried to ask a question. Even some of the parents were on their feet.

Suri tried to extract me from the mess, but Eldest Father and Mother waved her off. They seemed committed to what was happening, as if none of us had a choice but to play this out until we all got to the bottom of it.

Eldest Mother handed me something resembling a gooey crayon in a metal holder and asked me to draw what my world looked like. I sketched in missing shorelines, mountains, and seas on the globe. Folks got quiet when I drew water over the Caribbean Valley. They gasped when I did the same to the Mediterranean. I explained that the Atlantic and the Mediterranean were connected by a sea passage. They called it the Heracles Pass, a high altitude ravine that led from the Atlantic coast over and down into the Mediterranean Valley. I explained that in my age only a couple of peninsulas survived. One was called the Rock of Gibraltar, the other Ceuta.

Parents in the stadium clamored to speak. Eldest Mom and Dad looked like they'd seen enough. I guess hearing that where they were sitting on would be a thousand feet underwater didn't go over well. They looked pointedly at Suri. She sprang to my side, said something anxious, bowed, and yanked me from the circle while I was in mid-wave.

"What was that all about?" I asked after we were out of earshot.

"What do you think? You just told them Javan will become an ocean. Ever since you came, people have been whispering that the world might be coming to an end. Now they will shout it. They see the meteors falling every night when they used to come only once a decade. All the villages are saying the Serpent is returning."

"Serpent?"

If Suri was angry with me, she let it drop as her own questions got the better of her. What was the sea level in my age? Which land masses had the most diversity of wildlife and which had the least? What mountains were similar between my world and theirs? I began to understand what she and the others were probably after. The Javans were way past the question of whether or not their age was ending. They wanted to know when, how, and where to go to survive it.

The more we talked, the clearer it became that there was only one place on Earth that could provide sanctuary, a place both the Fourth and Second Ages considered a wasteland. In a doomsday scenario, any piece of unaffected ground, no matter how inhospitable, is prime real estate and worth fighting over if it means the sky won't come crashing down on you. In their case and ours, it was the Middle East. Armageddon would have nothing to do with oil, but everything to do with getting to safe ground and eliminating the competition if they got there first.

Suri took my hand and sighed. "I am sorry for asking you so many questions."

"Sorry I caused such a ruckus in class."

"It wasn't you; it was the topic." She forced a laugh. "People have been worrying about the end of this age ever since the First Age ended. And that was twenty-six hundred decades ago."

"Can we stop talking about it?"

Her fingers encircled my forearm. Her grip was tight. We had all the time in the world to be together. But what if the world was running on empty?

CHAPTER TWENTY-NINE

LEVI

The Elder Council held their relocated assembly in Athena's forum aboard the *Olympus*. The Nephillim relics lounged about the circular rings of stone benches, shamelessly eavesdropping on a projected conversation between Suri and Jordan. My armored gloves reflexively clenched as my anger mounted. Odin stood with his nose practically touching the image of the conversing couple walking arm in arm along the path near Suri's village. Jordan's voice echoed about the circular forum with embarrassing clarity. I counted heads. All twelve Elders were present, with the exception of Apollo.

Odin huffed at Jordan's description of an implied mass extinction happening in his past, our future. "That can't be true. The primitive can't possibly comprehend a global catastrophe. He's simply describing a localized tidal wave or earthquake that affects the ice or tundra. To a primitive, such a minor event would feel global."

"Oh, come, Father, of course he means the entire world," Devana chided. She lay across the top tier, her head propped up on her elbow. "Consider the tech found in his satchel and the equipment he wore when he landed in the lake. He's clearly a civilized traveler and not an ice-scraping primitive."

"But it would take a cataclysm massive enough to destroy eighty percent of the planet's biosphere to wipe out every human symbiotic plant," Durga exclaimed. She swung her enormous head in my direction. "Levi, what say you of this prediction? You've been with the human longer than us. Is he sufficiently knowledgeable of his time to be accurate on this topic? Is he describing a future cataclysm as large as the one that ended the First Age?"

"The more important question is when did a private conversation become public fodder?" I shot back.

Durga's eyes flared. "Ever Athena's minion."

"Protest noted and tabled, Guardian," Ares yawned.

I crossed my arms and fumed.

"I trust Jordan's words," Zeus said from a seat far below Devana. He cleaned his weapons, watching the projection intently. "That little human knows what he's talking about."

"You realize what it means if he's accurate, don't you?" Demeter posed. "Centuries of work restoring the First Age biosphere becomes a fool's errand if Earth ends up as he describes."

Odin snorted. "Accurate? He's a primitive, end of discussion."

"But his tech," Devana repeated.

Odin waved her remark away. He had never favored her opinion. No wonder she spent so much time in the wilds of Indra studying animals.

"If he's not worth listening to, why invade his privacy?" I said.

The projection blurred from sudden motion, then clarified. Aphrodite blushed. "They're embracing. Your son has a point, Odin. We shouldn't be watching this."

"Adopted son," Odin corrected.

Jordan and Suri leaned in to rub noses.

"That's enough for me. I'll be in my chambers." Aphrodite raised her perfect arms and floated above the Forum. She glided over the others and landed lightly beside me, patting my head like a child. "I don't know how you stomach him sometimes, Levi."

Her eight-foot strides took her out of the chamber faster than I could have run, her shapely body swaying slowly under the folds of her thin robe.

"Is it true the primitive is only three decades old?" Dionysus asked.

"Athena ran tests during his thaw," Devana said. "Sister says he's between three and three and a half decades old."

"But he looks so … old," Dionysus said.

"Athena says most of his people don't live past the age of nine."

"Only nine decades? But that's before puberty. How do they breed?"

"They mature unnaturally fast. Most of the women are pregnant by the time they're two, some at one and a half."

"Children birthing children," Dionysus whispered.

"And ruling nations," Ares added. "No wonder they have so many wars."

"That is ridiculous," Durga huffed. "Where are the Nephillim in their age? Why aren't they shepherding the rabble?"

Zeus finished cleaning his weapons and slapped them into braces on his muscled forearms, then pulled down his sleeves. The tips glowed blue under the folds of his robe. "It would appear from the interviews Athena conducted during Jordan's thaw that human food plants aren't the only things that become extinct before the Fourth Age." He looked around the circle. "We do, too."

CHAPTER THIRTY

JORDAN

We hiked beside a swift stream. Worn stones provided natural stairs along waterfalls splashing over moss. Suri didn't say much. She held my hand and kept her eyes focused on the next wet rock. As we neared the valley floor, meadows gave way to shaded woods draped in pastel orchids. The scenery helped calm my nerves. I was still coming down from the questioning at the school, regretting the reaction I'd triggered in Suri and scaring the kids. Their parents looked like I'd slapped them. What had I been thinking? Obviously, I hadn't. That was the problem. I'd had an audience and run with it. They'd hung on every word. What conclusions would they draw? What bad decisions might they make if my answers were wrong?

Was this world going to be destroyed by a global disaster? It had to be, based on what my messed up age looked like. But was it a sudden erasure or a slow decline? It had to be sudden. How else could so many creatures and plants go extinct all at once? How else could oceans rise without completely eroding the islands they inundated? The Mediterranean would fill a thousand feet in a week based on the seabed borings Ryan and Pitman had taken. The evidence in my time indicated that this age's end would be swift and brutal. But had my people—children by Second Age standards—interpreted the evidence correctly? These folks seemed to think so. So did I. Heck, last night on the pyramid, while I was having a serious out-of-body experience, somebody had simulcasted imminent doom through my mouth in a dozen languages. Maybe their end was coming, but when? Next week, next century, next millennium? The timing was important. Waiting year after year in a bomb shelter for the big one to drop gets old.

Suri took my hand to steady herself as she stepped over a wet log. A bigger question for me was how much time I would have with her.

God, if you're taking requests, I'd like to sign up for the extended tour, please: marriage, kids, grand kids, great grand kids.

Anak, I was tired of what I knew about the future. I was walking through paradise with the possibility of a new life and new love. The last thing I wanted to know was when this would go *pfffft.*

The path leveled and curved away from the stream. Forest noises clacked and sang deep in the woods. The sun fingered through laced branches. Suri's hand lightly explored my back.

Ignorance was feeling good. If the Berbai had any more questions about the end, I would beg off. It could be centuries before all the bad stuff happened, maybe millennia. Was it such a crime to sit out further speculation? They'd spent dozens of centuries trying to put their world back together; why should I be the doomsday guy raining on their efforts to rejuvenate the First Age. Or, as some called it, the Age of Noah?

I came from Suri's future and it wasn't a bright one. Compared to this paradise, my age sucked. Restoring the world back to the way it was before Noah and his zoo had boarded the ark wasn't happening, folks. Thanks to me, they were just now realizing it.

A waterfall of some intensity echoed through the trees. Suri's fingertips finished their reconnaissance over my shoulder and made camp on the base of my neck. I got goose bumps from her touch.

Becca and Liv-ya tackled my legs. Liv-ya had a streak of mud on her chin.

"You guys got out early?" I asked.

"No, silly, school's done," Becca said.

"You mean finished," Liv-ya scolded.

"That's how Jordan says it," Becca whined.

"That's because people in the future don't know how to speak Engel properly," Liv-ya said.

"Oh, and you do?"

Suri interrupted their argument. "Tell Mother I am bringing Jordan to the village."

"But we want to walk with you," Liv-ya cried.

"Doesn't the stupid village know he's coming already?" Becca asked.

"Becca, don't say stupid."

"But stupid sounds cool," Liv-ya said.

"Girls, please tell Mother. The village doesn't know how close we are. It would be sad if Jordan arrived and people weren't ready to welcome him."

Both moaned, but a few seconds later they were racing. Suri and I followed at a slower pace. The path widened and sunlight rippled over the soft grass. I picked up the pace a bit, a habit of walking fast, I guess. Suri kept up for a short way.

"We're close to the village now," she said.

"Yeah, I hear a crowd."

"I have a confession to make." Her fingers slid around my elbow and tugged me to a stop. She faced me shyly. Her hands rested lightly on my chest as she looked up with those incredible eyes. "Mother already knew when we would be arriving."

"If your mom already knows I'm coming, why did you send the girls ahead to tell her the same thing?"

"So we could do this." Her arms catapulted around my neck.

It was a simple hug: me burying my face in her neck while she hung on me. She drew back and we nose-rubbed. The practice was growing on me. Eskimos clearly didn't do it because it was too cold to kiss.

"Cha je tu," she whispered in my ear.

I didn't need to speak Javan to know what that meant. "I love you, too."

She sighed and relaxed against me. I was overwhelmed with feelings, all aimed at her. *God, if this age has to end, could you at least postpone it?*

Sounds of a crowd drifted up the river.

"Guess it's time to meet the rest of the village," I said.

"Dah," she sighed.

We passed a spring gushing under a smooth rock. The stream flowed as wide as a driveway before it joined the river. I knelt down and reached for the water, but Suri pulled me back. "What are you doing?"

"I was just going to get the grime off my face before I met your relatives."

"Don't you see the color of the water?"

It was cloudy white. She pulled a small implement out that expanded into a thermos-sized cup. She dipped it in the flow and handed it to me. "Drink."

I did, and it went down smooth and sweet as cream. Her land flowed with milk and honey. The phrase was literal. Go figure.

"This is the same stuff that came out of that spring on the Sacred Mountain," I said.

"The valley is watered by it. This stream feeds my village. We try to keep it clean." She pointed at the cup. "You're allowed to drink uphill from the village as long as you use this instead of your hands."

The trail opened onto the valley floor. We were half a mile from the village but a crowd waited at the perimeter of stone pavilions and pastel cottages.

I heard a familiar rumble above us. *Olympus* descended out of the cloud deck, letting off blasts from her port side. The expulsions were violent enough to puncture the clouds and send them swirling. I spotted movement left and right of us.

"What's wrong?" Suri asked.

"We're being watched."

Something metallic wobbled in the grass, followed by a sneeze. I threw a clod of dirt. It puffed against the ground a couple of feet shy of my target. Diago's head popped up. He waved sheepishly. Heavily armed Guardians, platoon strength, materialized around us.

"Ven-dah," Suri sighed. "What are they doing here?"

I recognized Aizah's curvy shape under her armor and face

gear. She stood with another Guardian, both wearing command insignia.

I waved. She flipped up her faceshield, snapped a chest salute back, let a sly smile slip, and vanished. The rest of the platoon cloaked with her. Diago ducked back into the tall grass.

"Don't suppose we'll get better privacy in the village?" I asked.

Suri looked crestfallen. "Were they watching us the whole time?"

"Probably."

"Why?"

"It happens when you're a celebrity."

"What's a celebrity?"

"A person who can't sneeze without ten people writing about it."

"I don't understand."

"Neither do I."

We continued walking.

"Are they still out there?" she whispered.

"Hard to tell." But then I spotted a stalk move. "Yes, they're maintaining a perimeter about fifty feet away."

The path narrowed between some brambles. I let Suri move ahead and noticed the backside of her fancy gown was grass stained. When I mentioned it, she twisted around to check and groaned. "I fell asleep on the grass waiting for Athena to finish treating you. Now I'll have to change after I drop you off."

"Drop me off where?"

"At your house."

"I have a house?"

"You can wash up when you get there. I laid out clothes for you."

She was picking out my clothes already?

"You can't go to the party looking like you rolled around inside an obassca flower."

"I don't know, sounds like fun. What's the party for? Some kind of holiday?"

She looked apprehensive, then apologetic and annoyed in quick succession. "It was my youngest mother's idea. I hope you don't mind. They're so thankful you saved my life in Tevleh and helped me escape the Ra, they feel a celebration is in order."

"Escape the Ra?"

"My family was upset when I accepted his invitation to live at the Palace."

"Why did you go if you didn't want to?"

"That still isn't obvious to you?"

"Uh, let me think. No."

She sighed. "You are either very kind or blind. I went because it was the only chance I had of meeting someone. That is, until I met you."

"You're kidding. You thought Amon was your only shot at a husband?"

"We had a lot in common."

"The only thing you have in common is that you're human. And for Amon, that's a stretch."

That pulled a smile out of her. "You're bad. I thought he was my only choice. Then you appeared and … Well, that's why my family is having a party. They want to thank you."

"For letting you hit me with a car?"

"Please don't tell my mothers. I'll never hear the end of it."

"You have more than one mother?"

"Of course; don't you?"

I had to think about how to answer that. "Okay, technically, yes." Then I thought a moment, fighting the apprehension. "It's been a while since I've been to a family gathering."

"You're not worried, are you?"

As long as she didn't send me out for last minute supplies. "Me? Never. How big is this party?"

"Just my parents and siblings," she said cautiously.

Something spooked her. She probably assumed I got nervous around a large family. I didn't care if she had fifty relatives; I'd lived on a guided missile frigate. Two hundred and twenty-seven of the best people I'd ever want to meet. So, she has a set of moms, maybe a dad and step-dad. I'd already met her kid sisters. Worst case scenario: triple that for other siblings and step-sibs. Total damage, I was about to be gushed over by eighteen people. Meet her family? Bring it on!

"Do you have any brothers?" I asked.

She looked at me like I was nuts. "Of course."

Ha, I thought so. They were probably older, too. That would explain the tomboy in her. "How many? No, wait, don't tell me. You have three."

"I have six hundred." Several seconds later, she asked, "Is something wrong?"

"That's a lot."

"Are you feeling sick again?"

"Just getting my head straight. Wow, six hundred brothers and sisters."

"Six hundred brothers. I have eight hundred sisters."

"Holy—"

"I told you I had a big family."

"You have *fourteen hundred* siblings?"

"Actually, I have six hundred and twenty-seven brothers and eight hundred and forty-one sisters. I rounded."

Adapt and conquer. "Do I get to meet the cousins, too?"

Her face lit up. "Yes! But Mother Habi—she's eldest—didn't want to overwhelm you by inviting all the relatives at once." She covered her mouth. "Oh no, Habi will be distressed if she finds out you wanted to meet everybody at the same party. Please tell her you are grateful she split the introductions up? Besides, you'll get to meet my cousins at the Gathering."

"Gathering?"

She hesitated just a moment. "It's like the Introduction Party except ..."

"Except?"

She looked at the ground. "I wanted to ask you last night but I didn't know Athena was going to take so long treating you. I thought I could sneak in and talk to you after she left." Her hand slipped off my arm. "You don't have to agree if you don't want to."

"Agree to what?"

She wrung her hands. "It's a Berbai tradition, although no Berbai has walked where you have before. You should have had extra time to prepare. No, probably not a good idea to have the Gathering yet. I should request a postponement. You didn't know what it meant. How could you?"

She veered into the tall grass, off the path and away from her waiting relatives. "When I told my mothers what happened, they just assumed everything should take place as soon as possible. Oh, Anak, I'm so stone-skulled sometimes. Now you're going to be upset."

She double-timed it across the hill through the grass, paralleling the edge of the village. I ran to catch up. *Olympus* blasted her starboards and veered to stay over us. This girl could cover ground when she wanted to. She was knocking over stalks taller than her thighs.

She started talking the moment I caught up with her. "I was too excited. I shouldn't have said so much. Otherwise, they wouldn't have assumed it was official. It's all my fault." She waved her hand back at the village. "Now everything is happening so quickly." She came to an abrupt stop and spun around. I just about smashed into her. "It's because I'm old. That's why I went to Mestre. I'm the only sixth generation who isn't … Oh Jordan, I'm so sorry. Please don't be mad."

"I'll be anything you want if you'll just tell me what you're talking about."

"It's just that nobody ever … I mean, all my life, I never thought … *Oh-Ayeee!*"

She fled at flank speed. I sprinted hard and passed her with difficulty, cutting her off. "It would really help if you finished sentences."

"Sorry."

"What is this Gathering for? Talk; I don't bite."

"The Gathering is where a man and woman announce their betrothal," she explained. "If you back out, it won't be like what happened to Aaron and Aizah. You're safe because you didn't officially ask me." She groaned. "But you did put the betrothal jewel on my head." She paced, tramping a mini-crop circle around me. "But you didn't know what it meant. We were just doing things that made us laugh." She looked at me. "But it felt real, didn't it?"

"It felt real my whole life."

"Now everything is all mixed up and crazy again. When I'm with you, why does the world feel both perfectly balanced and upside down?"

"I understand that perfectly."

"I just never felt this way about anybody. I actually started hoping what you said last night meant you wanted to …"

I left her hanging a little. Maybe I shouldn't have. The woman was a mess, but this was way too much fun.

"Get married?" I asked.

"Pretty silly, I imagine. Don't worry, when we get to the village, I'll tell my mothers I was presumptuous and ask them to call off the Gathering. They'll understand you need time to adjust and decide."

"No pressure."

She put up both hands. "I'll tell them the news while you're washing up"

"Sounds like a plan."

We hiked back toward the path. Everybody including the *Olympus* tagged along. Athena must have been punching stalactites off the ceiling by now.

"So, this Gathering was going to be our betrothal ceremony? Just out of curiosity, how do Javans propose?"

"Berbai," she corrected. "My people come from Berbai."

We reached the path. I stopped and turned her toward me. *Olympus* let off some blasts to slow down. A swirl of cloud went overhead. Diago and his squad were downhill doing crowd control. A lot of people seemed to want to come up the path.

"Would you like to see how guys in my age ask girls to betroth them?" I asked.

"Now? But the village is waiting."

"Come on, you'll like it. And it would mean a lot to me."

She sighed. "Be quick."

I stifled a smile. I got down on one knee and took her hand. "First, he kneels."

"Is the man asking the girl's stomach to marry him?" she said, hiding a laugh with her free hand.

"Pay attention, please. Next, he looks her in the eye and says something like, 'Suri, I love you with all my heart and soul.'"

She stared at my hand holding hers.

"Maintain eye contact please."

"Sorry."

I took a breath. "Then he says, 'Suri, will you marry me?'"

Her lips parted. Her eyes darted around my face but no words came. I waited as the blood left my foot.

"This would be the part where the girl answers."

"Sorry." She blinked a lot. "What was the question again?"

"I just asked if you would marry me."

Her eyes got big. "Are you really asking me or are you trying to say things that make me laugh? Because if you are, it isn't working."

Her English degraded when she got nervous. I filed that away for future reference. "I promise I'm not trying to be funny."

"You're really asking me?" Her lips parted. "You are."

Somebody in the crowd shouted her name. She looked down the hill. Four people had broken away from the waiting throng to hike up the path: two women, plus Becca and Liv-ya skipping in the lead. The women waved to Suri. She waved back with both hands, bouncing up and down.

"Those are two of my mothers," she said happily. She gave me a hug and sprinted down the path, twirling once to face me, her face aglow, "You asked me to marry you!"

She reached her mothers and plunged headlong into their outstretched arms. They looked like they were the same age as her. She chattered happily with them and the women burst into squeals. Becca and Liv-ya jumped up and down like pogo sticks. The women steered Suri to the waiting crowd. She freed one hand to wave back at me and shout something. I couldn't make out what she said. Aizah materialized next to me.

"I guess she said yes," I said.

"Nice work," Aizah said. "Maybe you could give Aaron some pointers."

"Where is he?"

"Taking a much needed shower. Then he accompanies Levi on

another assignment."

"So much for bonding time for you two."

She waved me off. "We're fine. You're the one who needs help. I thought my family was big." She studied the crowd with Suri flowing through knots of well-wishers, and shook her head. "Speaking of bonding time. It appears your bride-to-be is going to be busy with greetings for a while. Half the Berbai must have shown up."

The rest of Aizah's squad appeared around us. They flipped their faceshields open. I recognized a couple of them from the Payahdon evacuation. It was good to see them alive. I touched my chin and they snapped horizontal palm and finger salutes against their chests.

"Glad to see you and the former princess alive, sir," said a Guardian bearing a striking resemblance to Suri. The name on her sleeve read: *LLERAJ*. Which, reading right to left, was Jarell.

"You speak English," I said.

"Engel, sir. Once we figured out you spoke the same language the Trahls used for field code, the Javan Guardians began studying it."

"I'm honored."

Aizah gave me an appraising sniff. "You should bathe."

"Suri said they gave me a house in her village. Maybe it has a shower?"

"No need," Jarell pointed. "We'll throw you in the lake if you're in a hurry."

"And even if you aren't," Aizah said.

"No fair. You have power-assisted armor. Any of you ladies know where my house is?"

"We'll take you," Aizah said. "Great location, conveniently near the residence of the Senior Parents."

"The walls are like paper," Jarell added.

"As long as the bathroom works and comes with instructions."

"You still don't know how to use it?" Aizah asked with concern.

"I've been on the run since I got here, remember? The only bathrooms I've seen since the embassy are the backside of trees."

"Must have been chilly in Tevleh. You'll like the one in your house much better."

"You care to explain how to use it before I get there?"

"As soon as I get a free moment."

"We're so busy guarding you right now," Jarell said.

"Exhausting," Aizah added.

"Oh, come on."

Jarell smirked. "He still doesn't know what the rings are for?"

"Nobody took the time to tell him."

"That's terrible, leaving someone in the dark like that."

"Never mind, I'll figure it out," I said. "Lead on, I have fourteen hundred relatives to meet."

"They only become your relatives if you are permitted to become a citizen," Aizah said.

"Didn't know about that."

"A lot of things are happening faster than normal," Jarell said. "Try to keep up."

"How do I become a citizen?"

"First, you have to master the rings," Aizah said.

"Seriously, how do I do it?"

"They give you a test and if you pass, you're made a citizen."

"And you're allowed to marry Suri," Jarell added enthusiastically.

"I can't marry her if I don't become a citizen?"

"Relax," Aizah said. "It's a portion of sugared bread."

"You mean a piece of cake."

"Really?" Aizah tapped her helmet. "Ground Com had that idiom completely mistranslated. Well, regardless, shall we meet your fourteen hundred future relatives?"

"Fourteen hundred and sixty-eight to be precise," Jarell corrected.

Aizah checked her heads-up display. "Make that fourteen hundred and sixty-nine. Congratulations, Jordan, it's a baby brother."

CHAPTER THIRTY-ONE

LEVI

With Jordan and Suri tucked away in separate houses, Odin no longer had a conversation to eavesdrop on. He glared at Athena's status report clutched in my fist. The rest of the Nephillim Elders appeared regally bored.

"My daughter was supposed to deliver that," Odin groused.

"She's pressed with ongoing operations associated with the war," I said. Actually, she'd had enough interaction with her father for one day and had bribed me to volunteer instead. I agreed on the condition that she grant Suri's request to have Jordan stay in her village instead of sequestered on *Olympus*. I think the idea of keeping some distance between Odin and Jordan had motivated her to agree.

I delivered her report on the war with Atlantis, long on fluff and thin on detail. As expected, Odin bombarded me with questions that Athena made clear were not to be answered. After his actions in space, I didn't. Those of us trying to defend ourselves without turning into blood-lusting animals didn't want the Elders knowing anything their twisted synapses might use to justify annihilating more civilians. We understood the West had an orbiting starship full of weapons aimed at our homelands. Of course, it had to be dealt with, but that ship had been full of civilians who'd had families they wouldn't come home to. Odin didn't care. He seemed to enjoy the opportunity to launch whatever First Age marvel he hadn't tested yet and blow the Ephraim into oblivion.

"Civilian deaths based on density and diversity of organic matter in the orbiting debris field is estimated at fifteen thousand six hundred. It is probably higher since many civilians were vaporized during the attack or burned up falling back to Earth." My body shuddered as I relived the explosion. "The public outcry from Payahdon over the deaths of so many innocents will no doubt strengthen their resolve to win this war."

Odin chuckled. "You call them innocents? Amusing euphemism for scientists and engineers working toward your country's destruction."

"Their families were threatened with torture if they refused."

"It was providential that I intervened and blew that ship up, or your tiny Javan would be a smoldering memory by now."

"I defeated the shielding, destroyed the primary weapons platform, and rescued the hostages. All that remained was the second weapons platform. Instead, you destroyed the entire ship. Your excessive actions inflamed the West and hardened their resolve."

That sent the other Nephillim swarming to Odin's defense. How dare I accuse them of war mongering? What chance did Athena think she had of defeating the Western Confederacy without their help? When was Ground Com going to give the Elders better tactical information so they could help us minimize future casualties? In other words, their blunder was our fault. We didn't help them target accurately.

The bigger the being, the larger the ego. I absorbed their venting with stoic calm. When they finished, I stated that I would convey their concerns to Athena. Odin huffed and waved me away like unwanted litter. The frustration on their enormous faces was palpable. I knew what ate at them. Their pain explained their motives but didn't justify their actions.

Numerous funerals had already been held on *Olympus* for Nephillim babies. So few survived their first year. These tragic occasions drilled home the fact that for all their might, all their smarts, and all their technological muscle, the so-called Sons of God—the

First Born—were an endangered species trapped on a planet with a severely damaged biosphere, the result of a war their ancestors had instigated during the First Age. The slow but steady decline of their race had spurred Odin and the Elders to pour all their energy into terra-forming the Earth back to its original condition: boring miles into the ground, using the heat to melt the ice caps and shooting the vapors into space in a massive effort to restore the hydrosphere; and genetically preserving First Age species in sealed and elevated sanctuaries for eventual reintroduction. After five hundred decades of this effort, the first sign of hope had emerged. A thin hydrosphere had begun to materialize over the North Pole. Then a human named Jordan had come along and announced in multiple languages that they would ultimately fail. The golden paradise of the First Age would not be resurrected. The planet would continue to sicken. The Nephillim would become extinct.

I finished my report and saluted. Odin already had his back turned. How did a race deal with impending demise? In Odin's case, by ignoring it.

Zeus nodded grimly. The women looked away with their hands hiding their mouths. I turned on my heel and left the room.

Aaron waited for me in the corridor, leaning against a column. He was peering out of the heavily shaded windows at the clouds sweeping under the bow of *Olympus.* He was freshly scrubbed and once again looking his confident, immaculate self.

"You finished in there, Chief?"

"No, but they're finished with me."

He pushed off the column and fell in step. His armored boots echoed in cadence with mine. "Odin hammered you hard?"

"Nothing he hasn't hung on my neck before."

"I could have delivered that report in ten seconds: The West is running out of armies. We're running out of restrainer goo. If we make more goo faster than they make new armies, we'll win. I will now ignore your questions."

"I'll ask Athena to let you deliver the next report. You'll need weapons when you face them."

"Sweet."

"How's Aizah feeling?"

"Better since Athena pulled Odin's surveillance bug out of her eyeball."

"Must have hurt."

"Never saw a Trahl smash so much furniture before."

"And how are the two of you doing?"

"Don't know."

"Sorry to hear that."

"I heard a rumor," he said to change the subject.

"Can't trust those."

He nodded at the doors leading to the Peak. "Ground Com thinks Athena's brewing another special mission. Very secret. Wouldn't happen to be this trip you're about to take?"

"If it's so secret, how did you find out?"

"Athena has to stop recruiting Ground Com personnel of the female persuasion desperate to meet me. So, when do you fly off this floating dirt clod?"

"Not until I get a shower and my armor refitted."

"Where are you going and do you get to blow stuff up?"

We reached the crew level and headed for a secure room. I used a handheld device similar to the one Athena had rigged to find Odin's bug in Aizah's head. Satisfied the room was not transmitting our conversation, I continued. "Up 'til now, the West has been waging a world war with only a fraction of their forces."

"I know, forty percent. So what?"

"Why would they do that?"

"Because they're dumber than Anak spit."

"Opinion noted but not accepted."

"They're dumber than Odin?"

"Their tactics make no sense. Every border war the West has launched since Athena colonized the East, they've always come at us with everything they had, counting on overwhelming numbers to beat our superior weapons. They targeted small countries, hit hard, and plundered before we could drive them back with First Age tech. This war is different. They've attacked on multiple fronts, infiltrated our Net, deployed a cloaked spaceship for air superiority, located Mer, and still held back significant assets, denying themselves a decisive victory. They left Mer intact and allowed us to reestablish tactical communications. They've reached the borders of Mestre and Javan, but they don't amass for invasion. They're conducting skirmishes instead, bleeding both us and them of equipment and soldiers. If this continues, both sides will grind down to nothing."

"Not much of a world war, is it?"

"Why would they do that?"

"I'm sticking with the dumber-than-spit theory." He focused on my face. "But I see you're not buying it."

I shook my head. "I think Odin knows their plan and isn't talking. One thing is clear: He doesn't care who wins this war."

"You're kidding."

I stared at him.

Aaron frowned. "You're not kidding. Why wouldn't he care?"

"That's my mission. Find out what's more important than winning this war, learn the West's next move, and glue them where they aren't expecting."

"And end this war?"

"Stop it cold." I clenched my fists. "And spare a lot of families on both sides."

"Where are you going to search for this secret war-ending information?"

"Mer."

His face dropped. "You're not thinking of breaking into Odin's Vault, are you?"

I nodded.

"You're insane, Chief. He'll fry you."

"Not while he's distracted."

"You don't know your adopted father very well, do you? The term distracted doesn't apply."

"Odin's camped out thousands of miles from home, engrossed in Jordan's every syllable. All he seems to worry about is when the end of this age is coming."

"He doesn't believe in that stuff."

"Of course he does. All his bluster back there in the Furies Forum was just cloaking. He is more concerned about the end of the age than anyone else on the planet. Why else would he be repairing the Queen's spaceship?"

"What?"

"I'll explain later. Breaking into Mer is possible. Odin is sufficiently distracted. He's more intent on learning what Jordan said during his thaw instead of seeing to Mer's defenses."

"What about the Council? Somebody in that group is going to notice."

"How? They're here; which means they're not there. The only Council member missing is Apollo and he's never home."

"A lot of motivated Trahls will be guarding Mer. Penetrating it will be impossible for a typical Guardian." He grinned at me. "But only slightly challenging for an atypical Guardian."

I narrowed my eyes as we turned a corner and headed for the officer's bath.

"You're really going to break into Odin's super-secret tech vault, Chief?"

"Say it louder. I don't think the cave people on Mars heard you."

Aaron slapped me on the shoulder. "Count me in."

"Already did."

CHAPTER THIRTY-TWO

JORDAN

The Guardians escorted me to a stone arch that announced the entrance to the village. Suri was somewhere deep in the crowd. Aizah sent four Guardians grappling to rooftops. The remainder spread out and vaulted the village wall, cloaking in midair. Aizah and Jarell stayed with me, walking slightly to my rear. The three of us entered the crush of exuberant relatives and well-wishers.

"Where's Suri?" I shouted through their clamor and reaching hands.

"Don't worry about her," Aizah said. "She'll find you."

Aizah and Jarell politely negotiated the crowd while I touched my chin a zillion times in greeting. Aizah consulted her heads-up display to navigate the bewildering maze of neighborhoods and plazas. She led me down a winding street of compact homes and shops. Children waved shyly behind their parents standing in open doorways. Many greeted me in English with a lilting accent. The village was a lot larger than it had looked from the ridge. Above us towered the canopy of the enormous village tree. The base of the trunk came into view as we crossed a spacious market square. The roots sprawled in vast serpent-like coils across the plaza. Those segmented the village into wedged districts. We walked under a root arching high above a cafe. A profusion of orchids hung from its mossy underside.

After an hour, we arrived on the other side of town and came to the ornate entrance gate of a new home. Hints of an immense façade peeked through cascading growth. The vines seemed freshly planted, each stem carefully tied to brackets that extended up the walls, splaying off the roof. Aizah spoke quietly into a carved face mounted on a post. The gate swung open and she waved me through.

A shady garden path led to a door tall enough for a Nephillim. Twelve freshly painted columns supported a sparkling glass portico. Aizah spotted a sticker on one of the columns and peeled it off. I asked to see it. It looked like an advertisement for whoever had made the column. Jarell looked up at an open window above the door and whistled. She put her hands on her hips, then retracted her helmet.

"He said the house would be big," Aizah murmured, retracting her own helmet.

Before I had a chance to ask who "he" was, the other Guardians materialized and formed up behind us, attaching their weapons to their legs. Some pulled bits of vine off their armor. Diago and the group he was assigned to came around a hedge. The door latch clanked and lifted. Jarell smoothed her hair. Aizah picked a caterpillar off my shoulder, while the heavy wooden door swung inward, revealing an important-looking human.

"This is Suri's father," Aizah said.

He solemnly invited us in. I think that made the third of Suri's fathers I'd run into so far. How many dads could one girl have?

He gave us a tour of the front portion of the home—correction, mansion. There were three living rooms, one large enough for a basketball court. The place was furnished in a mish-mash of styles, including Spanish Colonial, Egyptian, Walmart, and local yard sale. Everything looked and smelled brand new, even the yard sale items, which had been crafted to look worn. The kitchen sported a pantry with boxes of familiar American foods, all favorites of mine. I picked up the Cinnamon Life Cereal. The large print was clear but all the small print was a blur. It was as if they'd copied my memory of the box. Could they have matched the taste?

Suri's father-number-three led us past the bedroom wing on our way to a glass conservatory the size and style of Longwood Gardens in Philadelphia. The crystal glazing of the windows afforded a faceted view of manicured grounds and ponds. A five-acre pond had curved stone stairs on one end, while a solitary willow swayed on the summit of a hill, partly shaded by the canopy of the village tree stretching high above it. The grass looked as though it had sprouted a week ago.

I was introduced to the Village Elders, who rose from chairs as we entered the room. They were all related to Suri. One of her cousins presented me with my old backpack and indicated that I should open it and inspect the contents. Almost everything was there: my camera, compass, iPod, even my trowel. The only thing missing was the drawing I'd done of Lisa and Sophia. Levi had placed it in the hibernation chamber before I'd been frozen. Maybe it had been lost or damaged somewhere on *Olympus.*

I nodded my thanks and slung the backpack over my shoulder. Diago selected a large apple from a dish, studiously avoiding my eyes.

"Well?" Aizah asked.

"Well what?" I said.

"You don't seem impressed with your quarters."

"They want me to stay *here*?" I whispered.

"Of course."

"I'd need a GPS to find the bathroom. Can't they just give me a cot in somebody's cottage?"

"Like Suri's, maybe?" Jarell teased.

"But where would we stay?" Aizah asked.

"Yeah, what about us?" Jarell inquired. "We want to swim in the pool."

"Honest, ladies, this place is too big."

Suri's father watched from the other side of the room. Either he didn't understand the conversation or he chose to stay out of it.

"I can't stay here. I'd be taking advantage of their hospitality."

"Not when you own it," Aizah said.

"Excuse me?"

"This is your house," Jarell said. "You bought it last week."

"What? How?" I thought for a moment. Of course. Step-mom's twelve-inch fingerprints were all over this. "Athena did this."

"Not exactly," Jarell said.

"Then who did?"

Aizah called over to Diago. He ignored her and concentrated on his apple. Aizah dramatically cleared her throat. A Guardian standing behind him nudged him in the back. Diago glanced sheepishly at her. She crooked her finger at him and he obediently shuffled over.

"You were supposed to tell Jordan before we got here," she said.

He stared at his feet. She sighed, then nodded at my backpack. "I believe you have a device that records music and videos. It is called an iPod."

"Yeah, so?"

"While you were thawing out, Diago borrowed it. He took it to the capital and showed it to the Creative Center for the Arts. They made a very handsome offer for the right to share your music with the people of Javan."

"An offer of what? Money?"

"We use luxury credits here. We don't have to pay for food and shelter. Citizens may sleep under a tree and pick food off a bush their whole lives if they wish."

"I'd be happy doing the same," I muttered.

"You don't need to because you have luxury credits."

"*Lots* of luxury credits," Jarell said. "The Beach Boys are particularly popular."

"My iPod paid for this?" I stared at Diago, dumfounded.

He seemed to wither under my scrutiny. He said something weakly to Aizah and she nodded as he kept talking, then shushed him so she could translate.

"Diago was so grateful for you saving Suri's life that he wanted you to have this house. Everyone pitched in to help design and build it."

"Athena knew your style preferences," Jarell said.

"While she was interrogating me during my thaw," I surmised.

"And this is the result." Aizah swept her armored hands about the room.

I focused on the shaker table centered in front of the sill. A collection of Chia Pets grinned from its polished surface. Their green afros vibrated in a breeze blowing through the curtains. "I don't know what to say."

Diago bowed his head and apologized. "*Lohsin,* Jordan."

Now what do I do? The father and other elders watched quietly.

"How long did it take to build?" I asked.

"A long time, practically a week."

While I digested that impossible fact, I grappled with my mixed feelings about this incredible gift. Despite Diago's intentions, there was no way I could live here. It was more than I needed by a factor of a zillion. But to refuse the gift would insult the village, embarrass Suri, and shame Diago. I had to back out gracefully. I thought of the little house I'd owned back home and recalled what I'd done with it in memory of my wife and daughter.

I felt the father's stare. He said something to Aizah that included my name. She responded. Conversation died and all faces fixed on him as they went back and forth. Aizah nodded and looked at me. "He wants to know if you like the house."

Here goes. "Are a lot of refugees still arriving in Javan?"

"There are refugee camps set up along the borders. They are being taken care of."

"I bet this place could hold a hundred families."

"I bet it could."

"Can I donate the house to them?"

"Perhaps."

"Could you ask?"

She hesitated. I jerked my head toward the father to spur her on. Aizah translated. The father seemed shocked. It looked like I had upset him; but, insult or not, right is right.

The father asked a question through Aizah. "Is that what you wish to do?"

"Yes."

The father apparently knew the Engel word for yes. He fired

off another sentence, his face ominously stern. Aizah looked like I was about to be hung. She said, "So be it."

After a long pause, the father burst into a laugh. He grasped my hands, while the Elders smiled with satisfaction. Aizah punched me in the arm. "Congratulations."

"What's going on?" I asked.

"You passed the test."

"What test?"

"You're a citizen."

"Why?"

"Because you gave away your house!"

"I don't understand."

"When Javans are given, they give back more," she said. "You had to act like a Javan before they could make you one."

"By giving away the house?"

"You realize what this means, don't you?" Aizah said.

"I can apply for an air car license?"

"Issa-dew!" she snorted. "You and Diago share the same brain. No, it is much more important than that. Now you have the Father's permission to marry Suri. By the way, that's why she didn't say yes to your marriage proposal. If she'd accepted without you asking him first, both of you would have been in huge trouble."

Jarell had been translating our conversation to Suri's father. The Elders huddled around to listen in. Their smiles broadened.

"Why didn't you tell me?"

"What, and ruin the test?"

"Of all the crazy, insane …"

Jarell clapped me on the shoulder. "Cheer up. Now you can marry Suri, move in next to all her parents, and have a dozen kids."

"A dozen?"

"Berbai produce big families," Aizah said. "Didn't Suri mention that?"

Suri arrived a few minutes later on the arms of two ladies introduced as her sisters. Her father embraced all three of them and spoke at length. The women clapped and Suri held her hand to her chest in relief, beaming at me. I didn't need translation. We were then left in the watchful company of her two sisters, plus Aizah. Chaperones were probably going to be the norm until we were married.

Suri hugged me, then turned to Aizah urgently. "He didn't see the whole house, did he?"

"Relax, we kept him out of the sleeping wing," Aizah said.

"Another surprise?" I asked.

We did a group tour of twelve bedrooms, culminating in the master suite. The bed was immense. Thirty pillows lined an ornately carved headboard.

"I am glad you gave the house away," Suri said quietly.

"You don't like the bed?"

She shook her head quickly, "I would never be able to find you in the dark."

I spotted the drawing I'd made of Lisa and Sophie hanging on the wall next to the bed. Time seemed to lurch to a stop. Somebody had gone to the trouble of framing it. A small note was attached to the picture. Suri let go of my hand and hung back as I bent closer to read.

I hope you like the frame.
Love, Suri

I took the picture off the wall and stared at the images I'd drawn during our sea voyage. Through the windows, the willow tree on the hill lit up under a passing sunbeam. Suri's eyes met mine.

"There's something I have to do," I said. "Could you wait here?"

She searched my face. "Sure."

The master bedroom had doors leading out to the pool. I skirted the waterfall and hiked up the hill. I don't know if I was truly alone. Cloaked Guardians were probably tailing me. I didn't care. It was a long climb.

The rooftops of the village spread wide beyond the sprawling mansion. Suri's tiny form stood in the doorway. I sat under the willow and pulled out the picture. Sunlight played through the branches upon the faces of my departed family. Lisa and Suri had seemed almost identical to me when I'd first come here. Now they seemed so different. I tried to imagine Lisa's and Sophie's tombstones far away in the future. The breeze picked up. My family seemed so very far away.

"We said if something ever happened to one of us that the other should move on," I said. "At the time, it was easy to agree. I was going into combat and you were staying home." I touched Lisa's face on the sketch. The glass covering it had warmed in the sunlight. "I figured you would be the one who would have to carry on without me. Of course I wanted you to find someone and be happy. I just never thought …" I choked and wiped my eyes. "I never thought I would be the one who got left behind."

I sat there a long time, letting the wind tug at the picture while the willow branches brushed my back. Suddenly, I felt Lisa behind me, urging me to let go and move on. I would have insisted the same for her. There was no reason to hold on anymore.

I dug a hole next to the willow and wrapped the picture in a T-shirt from my pack. I placed the bundle gently in the hole, pushed the dirt over their hidden faces, and smoothed it into a small mound. A stiff wind brushed past my face. I felt her farewell as the breeze faded.

"God be by you," I whispered.

I was loaned a small cottage on a quiet street overlooking a grassy commons. The owner—Suri's cousin—was away on business and insisted I stay there until the wedding. I dropped my backpack on the floating pond bed.

"You like it?" Suri asked.

"Oh yeah."

She tugged me toward the door. We spent the rest of the morning visiting in the village. Folks greeted us from sidewalk cafes and flowered park benches. A clump of Suri's aunts shadowed us five paces back, chatting quietly.

"It is my family's custom to accompany us before we are married." Suri whispered.

Even though the entire village seemed to be related to her, there was a lot of family she didn't know. I could tell when folks were strangers to her. They'd smile and call out like she was a long lost daughter, rushing to greet us. She'd hesitate, her grip tightening on my arm.

"Nervous?" I asked.

"I haven't been here since I was five. It's a little overwhelming."

We were invited into many homes. Most had workshops. A woman was designing a town center from her kitchen table. The model formed overhead. I touched it and it spun. Down the street, in another home, a father held his daughter on his hip while he helped a colleague coordinate an evacuation in a country called Chi. A tidal wave was about to hit. Transports scrambled into position along the beach, picking up stragglers who couldn't make it to the pyramid mounds lining the edge of the city. The transports lifted as the first waves rolled ashore.

"Do a lot of people work at home?" I asked later.

"Why wouldn't they?"

We watched a couple on their porch. A transmission floating before them showed the undercarriage of an enormous six-legged machine. It pulled a boxy form from a flooded field and sprayed the thing clean. In the rubbery claws was a brand new cottage.

"Does anybody work in a factory?"

Suri's face wrinkled as if she'd smelled something rank. "Like in Payahdon? Why would we want to do that?"

"How does everything get made?"

"Like that." She indicated the machine loading the new cottage on a wide flat transport next to three others. "They get made by little machines."

"How are they powered?"

"By the pyramids in Mestre."

"And how do people get paid?"

"They get credits, as you did for your songs."

I continued to pepper Suri with questions about Javan society. She started to run out of answers. Apparently, either she or one of the aunts called for backup. A man with a red dot on his sleeve joined us. He launched into a detailed explanation of the Javan industrial system.

After an hour, I was out of questions and completely astonished. Javan society was free enterprise on steroids; unlimited energy, self-repairing tools, instant communications, creative credits, and the freedom to pursue one's dreams and disperse the rewards without fear of confiscation. It was a paradise for family enterprise. Bosses were not needed to cajole people to work. Parents made sure their offspring pulled their weight. Taxes weren't extracted. Expensive bureaucrats weren't necessary. People were so generous, they gave more than what was needed to those who needed it. Factories didn't have to concentrate labor near a power source because power was everywhere. Goods didn't have to cluster around a transportation hub. Anything could be shipped anywhere. A person could sit at home, hold a baby in one hand, and design a city with the other. Anyone could excel and succeed in whatever endeavor they desired, with however much or little technology they needed.

Could this be what Plato had written about when he claimed the ancient people of Athens were the most virtuous and down to earth people that ever lived? Perhaps, but my instinct said there had to be more to it. The system I'd seen so far didn't guarantee a utopia. America in its purest capitalistic form proved that. While many Americans exhibited the traits of Javans, it only took a few bad corporate apples or bureaucratic lemons to ruin things. Javans didn't seem enticed by the lure of excess. When they had enough, they gave the rest away. When an individual stepped out of line, the family drew them back in. That didn't always work where I came from. What happened if a family got greedy? A village? How about a whole country? Who corrected that? I got the impression from the expert who'd joined us that nobody needed to. That didn't make sense. What restrained the citizens of Javan from overachievement and over accumulation? What made them so darn nice?

CHAPTER THIRTY-THREE

LEVI

Our Darts knifed the clouds.

"A thousand miles to the ice," Aaron said.

He shadowed my wing a mile to port. We cloaked and scanned for Mer's defenses. They were legendary for their stealth.

I winged over and dropped to tree level. Aaron followed, slipping back to give me a clear view. My ship imaged the polar cap, its three-mile-high ramparts shimmering in my display. The flatlands of occupied Gomer smoldered from a hundred fires. Towns lay in ruins. None of Mer's forward lines showed any signs of life.

Suddenly, threat alerts vibrated through my controls and up my arms. Fire bases lit up behind us.

"Lead, Two, missiles cycling for firing solution."

"Confirmed. Cut forward motion and hover."

We sank into the trees and held our position. The mobile bases swept the charred trees and failed to lock on us. Mer's defenses on the icecap launched recon flights. They bracketed the area and began a methodical sweep, trying to get a fix on our position.

"What's the plan? Straight in, engines blazing?"

"No."

"De-cloak and say hi? Since we're technically on the same side?"

"Remain cloaked and inch forward."

Aaron paused a moment. "Uh, right; that was going to be my next guess."

I drifted my Dart forward between the blackened trunks. Aaron matched my pace a mile west. My teeth rattled as heavy scanner fields swept down from the sky. The gravity beams crisscrossed my hull. I heard the discomfort in Aaron's voice as his ship struggled to absorb the punishing beams.

"You want to p-p-pick up the pace, Chief? I won't have any teeth left by the time we get to Mer."

"Those scanners are upgraded. They can detect gravity fluctuations between objects in motion and the ground."

"They can tell the difference between my puny Dart and the dirt? Anak, here comes another sweep."

I bit back my discomfort. "Only if you're moving too fast. Velocity creates a gravity ripple in the ground they can read."

"All this trouble to smooth turbulence and they spot us anyway because we make the ground rise a couple molecules by flying over it. How come we don't have these new scanners?"

"Odin only gives us tech he knows he can beat. In case it gets stolen."

"He likes having the biggest and the baddest."

"Confirmed."

"Nephillim have serious size issues."

The edge of the icecap lit up with targets. Aaron whistled. "Trahl surface patrols popping out topside, heavy and lethal."

"Air patrols sweeping overhead," I said. "Reinforcements are launching. They've gone to general alert."

"This is where you're going say that's a good thing."

"Yes, it means they failed to locate us. You have a problem with that?"

"No, just speeding up the conversation since nothing else is moving very fast."

Long-range defenses emerged from hiding places in the jagged walls of the icecap. My Dart vibrated the information into the tips of my fingers, giving me range, speed, vector, and types. I zoomed in with my oculars and located the lethal machinery crawling out from the shadows of crevices.

"Spray fires have been deployed, Chief."

"I see them."

"That's a bad thing, you know."

"I'm aware of that."

The Trahls ran the deadly barrage guns through tunnels in the ice and popped them out of openings along the wall. Each gun fired a half-mile-wide spray that could shred an entire legion in seconds, regardless of whether they were airborne or came from a burrowing ground assault. The barrels pointed across the tundra. Bright red stars dotted the length of the icecap from east to west as the gun barrels heated up.

"They're going to paste the whole forest," Aaron said.

"I was counting on it. Wait one. We climb when they fire and use the bombardment for cover to crest their defenses."

"Cool plan."

"Cool?"

"A word I learned from Jordan."

Thousands of flashes cast staccato shadows on the ice as Mer opened fire. Our Darts screamed skyward as lead tracers hissed past our tails.

"Anak, I'm hit," Aaron cried.

"How bad?"

"I'm trailing smoke. So much for being cloaked."

Trahl air patrols circling above us winged over and pounced. Their contrails converged into a single spiraling mass as they flew in a coordinated barrel roll to avoid any defensive fire we might send their way. I had no intention of attacking allies. Unfortunately, they didn't know we were friends. I couldn't tell them. If I did, I wouldn't find what I sought.

"Are your suit's flight systems operational?" I asked.

"Yeah, working fine."

"If they fire at us, eject and send your Dart west."

"West. Got it."

"I'll send mine east. If the missiles follow the Darts, we might be able to fly in cloaked over the ice and drop out of sight."

As predicted, a cluster of gravity-seeking missiles flared off their wings and filled the night sky with a swirling cloud of flames.

"Oh, come on, guys, I just got this armor."

"Eject," I said.

My armor's personal flight systems took over as I separated from my Dart. My doomed aircraft materialized and banked sharply east, taking half of the missiles with it. The other half followed Aaron's empty Dart as it screamed over the Atlantic. The missiles struck simultaneously. The Darts exploded, pinprick flashes swallowed by the starry night. Far below, the distant tundra abruptly vanished as we crested the moonlit icecap. Mer's defenses swept the skies south. We were well north of Mer's frontline before they started looking in our direction again.

Aaron glided over the icecap several miles to my left. I sent him my vector and he narrowed the distance. Two red ovals of light drifted into position beside me. They were the reflections of his oculars. He blinked hello.

"Breaking into Mer is looking more challenging than first described, Chief."

"Noted."

"That means we're still going in?"

"Confirmed."

Aaron's oculars tilted away. His transmission stayed active but he didn't speak.

"What's on your mind, Two?" I asked.

"Just wondering again why we're doing this."

I concentrated my scanners on the crater in the ice, where Atlantis had dropped a massive bomb on Mer.

"Your turn to say something," Aaron said.

I checked my calculations. Five seconds, four, three …

"You're wondering why we're breaking into Mer when we could simply walk through the front air lock?" I said.

Aaron's response was swallowed by a tremendous flash directly north. The blaze lit up the night, outlining the ragged icecap in sharp detail and turning the star-filled sky into artificial dawn. A pillar of flame soared skyward, arcing gracefully through wisps of cloud.

"Mer launched a rocket," Aaron said.

Suddenly, both rocket and flame vanished.

"Are you sure?" I said.

"Anak, where'd it go?"

"It cloaked."

"Nobody can cloak a launch."

"They can."

"How'd they cloak the propellant trail?" Aaron asked.

"New tech from Odin." I chinned a control inside my helmet and patched Aaron into my scanner. The rocket reappeared, a thin streak of flame arching high over our heads. "Can you see it now?"

"Anak, how'd you do that?"

"New tech from Athena."

Aaron's suit scanner carried additional components for analysis. He fed me data on the rocket, confirming what I'd already been warned to expect.

"That ship's carrying construction equipment," Aaron said.

"And heading to what's left of the Queen's spaceship. According to my source, Mer ships are repairing its hull and life support systems."

"Who's your source?"

"Can't tell you until we're inside. In case you're captured."

"Why would Odin fix an enemy ship he tried to destroy?"

"He didn't want it destroyed. He overpowered it and intentionally left the core of the ship intact."

"So he could repair it and aim it at Atlantis?"

"Good theory, but wrong."

Thousands of miles west, my displays reported the launch of an Atlantean rocket. I patched the visual feed to Aaron. He whistled as it climbed. We tracked it as it cloaked.

"Construction supplies again," Aaron said. "No weapons. That's weird. Atlantis always arms their ships."

A few minutes later, the construction rockets flew side by side, straight for a cloaked bubble of space orbiting the moon that contained the remains of Babla's spaceship.

"Odin and Atlantis aren't acting very war-like."

"Nice of you to notice."

"What's going on, Chief?"

"Now do you understand why we couldn't go through the front door?"

"Not exactly, but I'm getting there."

Trahl ice patrols clustered under us. It looked like they had caught a sniff of our armor.

"Anak, they're good," I muttered. "Let's find a hole through those patrols and get in the ice before they get lucky."

"There's a gap in the search pattern, Chief."

"Go."

We knifed the frigid air boots-first. We passed between two patrols spaced a little too far apart, leaving a gap between their scanners' reach. A second later, we hit the ice. We used our armor to absorb the impact. By the time we stopped fracturing the floe, we were a hundred feet below the surface, looking at blue reflections of ourselves in the refreezing sheet.

We melted our way horizontally at a slight incline and breached the surface a mile from our impact point. Trahl patrols buzzed over the spot where we'd hit. We took cover behind a tilted slab the size of *Olympus* and unpacked our gear.

Aaron pointed northeast. "Mer is that way. The roof is still ruptured where Atlantis punched it open."

"Noted that on the way in. Let's go."

"We can't infiltrate there. Every kind of sensor known and unknown is watching that hole."

"Not planning to. Just getting close enough to scan the city."

"In other words, you haven't completely worked out how you're getting inside Mer."

I widened my oculars into glaring red circles.

"Just kidding," Aaron said. "You always have a plan. You're just not telling me in case some Trahl aims for you and glues me by mistake. For the record, I've never talked during an interrogation."

"You've never been captured."

"So?"

"You've never been interrogated."

"It's still a true statement."

"Move out."

CHAPTER THIRTY-FOUR

JORDAN

The bachelor's cottage was a welcome respite. I flopped onto a bed floating in the middle of a small pond. A waterfall splashed out a slot in the wall. Rocked by gentle waves, I fell asleep and dreamed weird stuff in large quantities: Kate rescued from a red cave by a bunch of civil war guys before she ran out of air; a monk paddling past a ruined bridge in a beat-up canoe; a little girl clinging to an old man's leg while he painted spaceships on a stone wall by candlelight; and Amon raising a staff at a pyramid surrounded by an endless swamp. Then I woke to hummingbirds crisscrossing the kitchen. They probed my hair for nonexistent blooms, while I tried to shake the strange dreams out of my head.

"I need a bath," I told the inquisitive birds.

That was easily resolved. All I had to do was roll off the bed and start scrubbing. After that, I went into the dreaded toilet room. It was a duplicate of the one at the embassy: a walled garden with a swiftly moving stream, a cart with little boxes, and the notched bar with a ring taunting me from the wall. That moment, I made the most important discovery of the entire trip. Hastily stuck on the wall above the mysteriously notched bar was a piece of paper with full instructions on the use of the planting room written in Engel and signed by the owner of the cottage.

"I love you, man."

Dressed and refreshed, I was halfway down the street when Suri rounded the corner with a sizable cluster of relatives and children. Becca and Liv-ya peeled off like a couple of SAMs and intercepted my hand.

I curled my arm and lifted them off the ground. They squealed while the other kids begged for a turn. Suri navigated to my side, entwined my other arm in hers and interlaced our fingers. She smiled as I lowered Becca. Liv-ya scrambled up my shoulders, solemnly informing the other kids that she was the only one allowed to ride on my back.

"I'm sorry this is happening so soon," Suri said.

"I'm ready."

"It's tradition to hold the Betrothal Ceremony when the moon is full."

"Is that for religious reasons?"

"No, it's so we can see what we're eating."

"The ceremony lasts into the night?"

"A little longer."

"You want to elaborate?"

She giggled. "If it doesn't scare you away."

"Not a chance. The ceremony can last a week if it has to."

"It might," Liv-ya said in my left ear.

"What exactly happens?" I asked.

"You go to all the villages," Becca said. "The moms hug you a lot and the dads make speeches."

"Takes forever," Liv-ya sighed.

"If that's what it takes to marry your sister, bring it on. What happens at the wedding?"

Becca's eyes lit up. "It's really cool. We—"

"Becca!" Liv-ya hissed. "You can't tell; it's a secret."

"The honeymoon is the worst part," Becca said, nodding her head seriously. "It's tons longer than the wedding."

"You're kidding," I said.

"So boring," Becca said, rolling her eyes.

"Is not," Liv-ya said.

"Is too," Becca said.

"How do you know? You've never been there," Liv-ya said.

"You climb a mountain and sit in a garden all by yourselves for a month," Becca said, smacking her forehead for emphasis. "Boring."

"You want us to come visit you?" Liv-ya asked. "I think I found a way to sneak in."

"I'm sure we'll manage," Suri said.

We crested a hill overlooking a part of the village I hadn't explored yet. The street widened, offering a panoramic view of a manicured commons crisscrossed by streams emptying into a river that wound about the base of the village tree. Fountains sprayed from islands, catching sunbeams penetrating the heavy overhead foliage. A gentle breeze swirled our clothing, carrying familiar scents: spice, fruits, earth, water, and wood. These mingled into a singular fragrance that seemed familiar. Something so primal I couldn't retrieve it, yet what I'd known my whole life. It was like the memory I had as a kid when my foster family drove me to the shore. I'd smelled the inland salt marshes from the open car window and known I was near the beach. That was this moment. I knew I was near something wonderful that once was and wanted to be again.

"Can you smell it?" Suri asked.

"Yes."

"It's the tree," she said. "Athena planted it when she founded Javan. It's slowly putting the scents of the First Age back into the air. Athena's been colonizing First Age plants on the boughs of the tree, where the sunlight and ozone can't reach them."

I marveled at the leviathan with its half-mile-wide canopy. Like the pillar trees of the Costa Rican rain forest, this giant was the re-colonizer of the First Age paradise.

Suri's ten parents met us under a colorful canvas roof that shaded a polished stone table with intricate carvings. They greeted us warmly. I had a hard time not staring at them. Even though I'd already met some of her parents, it was hard to get used to their youthful appearance. They all looked like they were in their twenties. In truth, their ages were vastly different. They were Suri's parents, grandparents, great grandparents, great-great grandparents, and great-great-great grandparents. Suri called them all mom and dad out of practicality. Calling everyone mother or father without the grands and greats saved wear and tear on the tongue. Everybody knew the birth order, and, Anak, did it go back. Maybe that's why ancient genealogies avoided the terms grandfather and grandmother. Maybe too many generations were alive at the same time to be bothered with it. That was probably why they counted their ages in decades instead of years. The same reason we measured our height in feet instead of inches.

Zadeh and her husband—Suri's actual mother and father—were four hundred and forty years old. Tara and her husband were six hundred and twenty. Zulei and her husband were seven hundred and seventy. Paris and her husband were nine hundred and twenty. Habi and Tumleh, the matriarch and patriarch of the entire Berbai colony, were an astonishing one thousand sixty years old. I was quietly told by Zadeh they were unusually old. No kidding.

Had I not read Josephus I would not have believed such lifespans were possible. But extreme longevity among people of the distant past was remembered in multiple cultures. If so many disparate cultures remembered the same phenomenon, was it possible the stories were blurred memories of actual fact? Josephus claimed people lived for centuries because they consumed food and drink that no longer existed in our age. He claimed the foods of our age were weeds by comparison, offering feeble nutrition that didn't enable human bodies to stave off degeneration. That made sense. I'd seen firsthand how the effects of poor diet in my age had stunted growth, caused poor health, and impaired cognitive abilities. We are what we eat. Were we also not what we didn't eat? Was my entire age malnourished and didn't know it because there was nothing to compare it to?

The evidence of our race's dietary adaptation to global disaster was right in front of us at every meal. Massive extermination of foods designed to perfectly nourish us had forced us to adapt. We ate whatever we could consume without being poisoned: vegetables meant for other animals, those that were perfectly nutritious for them but mildly toxic to us. Babies couldn't eat vegetables because their livers weren't strong enough to handle the toxins. The loss of our natural diet forced us to eat the unborn seeds of plants, such as grains. I'd normally relished a steak back in the Fourth Age. That was until I tasted the Second Age meat fruit. Maybe the loss of protein-rich plants, like meat fruit, had forced my ancestors to become carnivores. Vegetarians ate peanuts roasted to kill the toxins. We consumed foods meant for other animal's newborns: milk and other products cultured from it. We ate unborn animals: eggs from chickens, ducks, and fish.

I realized what an ecological wasteland my age was by comparison. Cooking to detoxify, gathering and storing against bad weather and decay, and cultivation to protect weak plants from sturdier weeds were realities in the Fourth Age. The battle for resources to stave off cold and disease, the preying on animals, nature eating itself to survive: these horrors were considered natural in the Fourth Age. I now understood why Adam and Eve had been vegetarians in the Garden. They'd had the good stuff. I understood why the Apostle Peter had been told to kill and eat animals when he'd been praying on his roof. The good stuff hadn't existed in his time. I understood why the prophet Ezekiel saw the fruit trees growing by a river gushing from the temple on top of a mountain. The good stuff would come back someday; at least one tree's worth.

As I took my seat at the table, I wondered what I would do differently with my life if I had nine hundred years to live. I thought of the bachelor's cottage. It had been full of sketches, books, and images of trips. All the things the owner had already seen at the youthful age of two hundred and twenty, all the interests he'd pursued. He could have had ten professions before he even married. Or he could have married his childhood sweetheart and had a thousand offspring grow up around him. A person could make a Fourth Age lifetime of mistakes and have nine more lifetimes to fix them. How much time did I have? Sick in a week, dead in two.

Suri's fingers affectionately stroked my back as she talked in rapid Javan to one of her moms. I felt robbed. The chance to live as long as these couples was beyond my grasp. Suri might live so long, but her time with me would be terribly brief, spent mostly in the company of a horribly aged man losing his hearing, teeth, and sight at an age slightly older than Becca. I would never know what it would be like to live for centuries without the fear of disease or the humiliation of aging.

Was it possible my body would remain stable in this environment as long as Athena kept treating me? Might I live as long as Suri? I resolved to be the dutiful adopted son, visiting my giant adopted mom every Sunday for tea and dusting.

I chatted with my future in-laws as waves of countless siblings filled rooftops around the central ceremonial terrace. Fresh fruits of several varieties were picked as needed from the surrounding fields and forests, and brought into the center of the village. As evening deepened, dancing dominated the commons. It was the best party I'd ever experienced.

Finally, people curled up to sleep on the terraces. Come morning, Suri and I were sent down river in a festively flowered raft to the next village, where the party kicked up with a whole new set of relatives and neighbors.

The Berbai at the next village were infectiously happy and seemed to enjoy playing practical jokes. There was a lot more dancing, games with kids, babies to hold, and an amusement park with a couple of rides that made Disney look tame.

Aizah, Diago, and the other Guardians kept watch the whole time. Even though they were cloaked, I was occasionally reminded they were around. On the seventh day, we landed on the shores of the oldest village of the Berbai colony. The family stayed by the raft landing and tearfully waved us up a small path. For the first time since I'd arrived in Javan, Suri and I were going to be alone.

We climbed a hill littered with stone ruins. It was quite a hike. For a long while, neither of us spoke. Honestly, I was all talked out. Finally, as we neared the summit, Suri broke the silence.

"This is a lot easier to climb than that glacier in Tevleh."

I helped her over a fallen tree trunk. "I never felt so cold before."

"I wouldn't have survived if you hadn't known how to dig a snow cave."

"When we were attacked the next day and you fell down the hill, I didn't think I'd find you in that avalanche."

"I thought we were going to die."

We reached a ledge and paused a moment to figure out the best spot to climb it.

"You told me you were glad I believed in the Creator because it meant I would be with Lisa and my daughter after we died," I said. "Then you said you wished someone loved you that much."

"I did?" She wrinkled her face up as if concentrating. "Did you say anything back?"

"I told you someone did love you that much. I didn't have time to tell you it was me."

"I wish I could have heard you."

"I'll tell you every day."

We finished the climb and looked out over the valley. The Javans had given it to the Berbai. Six villages dotted the two rivers. In their midst, an enormous tree towered in full splendor, wisps of clouds drifting beneath its canopy. Darker clouds crested the distant mountains and edged south, slowly crawling across the sky like a gray blanket.

Habi and Tumleh joined us a few hours later, followed by a procession of the entire Berbai clan. They invited us to join them on a stone bench set on an outcropping, while the others gathered on the slope.

"Nine centuries and five decades ago, I was brought to this hill with my parents," Tumleh said. "We were twenty-four refugees, strangers from a land destroyed by the Seed of Ephraim, the half-giants of Atlantis. Athena brought us here and made us welcome. She told us to make this valley our home, the land of the Berbai."

Habi smiled in remembrance. "She suggested if we were going to become a nation, we'd better get to it."

"We married that day," Tumleh said, his voice cracking. "Two strangers in a strange land that made us one and we made a home. How fitting at this time that we have the high joy of welcoming two strangers to this place where they may be one and be a home to many others not yet born."

Habi's voice strained a little as she called out to the crowd, "People of the Berbai, are they welcome?"

The cheers were deafening. After the applause subsided, Habi and Tumleh turned and placed their hands on our heads. Habi had hers on mine, Tumleh on Suri's. Habi said, "Jordan, do you now declare you're intent to be married to Suri?"

"Yes," I said without hesitation.

"Suri, do you declare you're intent to be married to Jordan?" Tumleh asked.

"Yes."

"Then, in the tradition of our ancestors, let it be known that Suri and Jordan will be wed before the tree on the evening of the next full moon."

The clan sang as we embraced. Water splashed over our foreheads. I laughed and asked, "Is that part of the ceremony?"

"No," she said.

Tumleh and Habi were wet, too. Then a raindrop the size of a softball hit some nearby kids. Another fell, and another; then thunder rumbled. People panicked as the shower intensified. A hand gripped my shoulder and I spun around. It was Aizah.

"We have to get everybody off this hill and into the ruins." She pointed toward the valley. The landscape was vanishing behind a thick curtain of gray.

The other Guardians had de-cloaked and were urging people down the mountain. Lightning lanced the clouds and children screamed. Thunder shook the ground. The wind picked up. Folks running down the hill vanished as the gray curtain closed over them. The storm swept up the slope and nearly drowned us. People slipped and tumbled down the hill.

Suddenly, a triangular wedge of black burst through the cloud ceiling and slowed above us. *Olympus* had maneuvered into position to act as an enormous umbrella, yet the rain continued to sweep us as the wind hurled it through the vines. Forks of lightning struck *Olympus'* flanks. The flashes outlined the village tree, which swayed.

Tumleh and Habi had more trouble than the others getting down the hill. Aizah and I supported Tumleh as he gingerly shuffled down the slope. Even though he appeared twenty years younger than me, he had poor balance. Suri and Diago had Habi in tow. We got them to the bottom of the hill and huddled inside a ruin.

"Stay with them," Aizah shouted over a thunder clap. She and Diago ran back up the hill to find stragglers.

"Quite the downpour," I shouted to Tumleh, trying to project calm. "How often does this happen?"

Lightning illuminated his worried face. Thunder made him wince. "Never."

CHAPTER THIRTY-FIVE

LEVI

We reached a jagged ice shelf just out of range of Mer's sensors guarding the gaping hole in what had been the city's protective ice dome. Atlantis had fired a space-based missile called a Thunderbolt that had hit the ice cap directly above Mer, guided by someone inside the city. I suspected Numu might have been responsible but I could never prove it. One cubic mile of ice roof had collapsed and buried the heart of Mer, crushing a third of the population in five agonizing minutes.

I deployed the bots. The plankton-sized machines buzzed out over the crater. The bots formed a network and linked their tiny oculars to zoom in on the city three miles down. They sent a chilling view at what had been the heart of Mer's urban center. Incredibly, the ice debris was all gone. Outlines of streets and ragged shapes of flattened buildings formed a surreal quilt of gray on white.

"How did they clear the city so fast?" I asked.

"Aizah said Odin used some kind of super-thermal device to evaporate the ice mound and shoot it into the atmosphere," Aaron replied. "One of her brothers who cleans Odin's mansion saw him carrying the device out a side door."

"Another First Age tech toy he was hiding in his vault for

emergencies," I said.

"Makes you wonder what else he's got hidden in there."

"Things your parents read at night to make sure you stayed in your hammock."

"Those Trahl-tales? You're joking, right?"

The bots zoomed back to normal view. Construction machinery and security patrols down on the ground looked like tiny insects. Their lights winked in and out as they crawled between square fields of debris that had been the city blocks of downtown Mer. A cluster of six-legged recyclers lumbered through one of the residential zones. An intricate pattern of glowing lines fanned out from each of the machines as operators targeted piles of debris. In less time than it took to recite a Javan nursery rhyme, an enormous shape twisted and undulated skyward. Finishers scrambled up the curving skin as it cooled from orange to white.

"That doesn't look like a building, Chief."

"It's not."

The finishers crawled in and out of the hull. Flashes of light erupted from the openings, starting at the bottom decks and moving up.

"Are you able to see inside?"

"Confirmed. They don't have any shielding up."

Engines formed. Cowlings opened and retracted. Lateral fins grew like leaves and solidified. Mer was in the space business, copying Atlantis.

I turned my scanner back to auto-detect. It powered down. Nothing here was new. I'd seen it all before under Payahdon.

"Guess Odin decided to borrow some Atlantean space tech," Aaron said.

"Apparently."

"Tell me again how we're getting down there without being detected and subsequently killed by their comrades-in-lethal arms?"

"I didn't tell you the first time."

"I was hoping in your old age you'd forgotten you hadn't and figured you might as well tell me again."

I turned my invisible helmet to stare at the empty space where his was located. "That doesn't even begin to make sense." I sent him a vector. "We're going in over there by that mountain peak."

"Where the ice is so thick it will take a full day to melt through, cause us to be detected and blow the mission?"

"Are you coming or not?"

"I hope Athena loaned you one heck of a piece of tech to get in."

"Of course she did."

We remained cloaked as we hiked five miles to a featureless spot on the ice. It was just outside the Trahl's defensive perimeter. I pulled out Athena's device from my sleeve pocket. It appeared to float in the air between our cloaked bodies.

"That's it?" Aaron asked. "Looks like a fruit masher."

"It's a key." I aimed the ancient device at the ice. A hole opened about a dozen yards to the east, revealing a smooth shaft of clear material angling down through the ice. It was just large enough for a Nephillim to fit through.

"Athena said this is how the first Trahls found Mer."

I showed Aaron where to grapple. Then I slid down the tube first, popped out over the city outskirts, and grappled the ceiling of the ice dome. I clung upside-down a mile from the ground. Aaron swung beside me, silent and invisible as a spirit. We relay-grappled across the curved ceiling, giving the impact zone careful berth.

The gaping hole in the ice grew as we neared, forming an oval of blue-tinted light. Clouds hovered beneath the arched ceiling that had sheltered Mer since the dawn of the Second Age. Sunlight lanced through the hole and spot-lit a new rocket. I recognized the configuration of loading platforms and limited viewing portals. The design was a cargo vessel capable of transporting animals, plants, and a small number of passengers.

"That park near Odin's mansion looks like a safe place to land," Aaron said.

I had hoped to avoid that particular woods, but unfortunately, he was correct. We detached from the ceiling and free-fell into trees that were a thousand feet tall, then shot grapplers into their ancient bark and braked inches from the ground. We touched down on soft grass as the lines zinged back into our sleeves.

Odin's mansion couldn't be seen through the dense growth, but it would be hard to miss. The rambling estate took up the entire mountainside. We just had to walk uphill.

I passed the largest tree, supposedly planted by Mer himself. It had sweeping branches that drooped low to the ground, low enough for a five-decade-old refugee kid to climb. I flipped open my visor and sucked in the familiar air.

"Your face is showing, Chief," Aaron warned.

It happened a few days after Athena had rescued me, much to the disgust of her father. She and Odin had come to my village after a border war attack to study the effects of the weaponry Atlantis had used. My little sister and I were the only survivors, holed up in the bombed-out basement of what had been our ancestor's home for twelve generations. Athena had taken us to Mer and adopted us. We lived in her bedroom, keeping away from Odin.

My sister had fallen ill to something similar to what had ailed Jordan, something nobody had seen before, what Odin had called *illness*. She'd gotten weaker. Odin had agreed to save her and spent two full days in his lab. Athena had wept in her quarters in the meantime.

I'd gone looking for Odin to see my sister and had slipped through the swinging pet door. I'd found her lying on a stone table with tubes hanging above her, her arms bent and fingers curled like dead twigs. Her head lay sideways, her tongue hanging out and eyes cloudy white. Odin was hunched over her chest, holding a jar that contained something bloody.

"Who let you in here," he'd roared when I'd screamed.

I'd fled the lab. Athena had found me hiding in the Great Hall and scooped me into her arms. Odin had pounded down the hall. He'd put on his protective suit again, like he'd worn in my parents village.

Athena had shielded me from his glare. "What did you do to him?"

He'd stabbed a finger at my face as he'd slapped his bubble helmet back in place. "Get him out of here."

"Why?"

"I told you we shouldn't have brought those human larvae here. His sister was a carrier. Ninety percent infectious. She could have killed half of Mer. He's probably just as viral. Get rid of him now."

"Are you insane?"

"No, I'm furious."

"I will not abandon a five-decade-old child no matter what his race. You're assuming he's contagious. We must quarantine him like the Trahls and run tests."

"He doesn't belong here."

"Why not?" she'd demanded. "Give me one good reason."

"Because he's human!"

"How dare you; after all Rahn did for these people."

"And look what it got him."

"Pompous, arrogant, self–"

I'd wriggled out of Athena's arms and slid down her gown.

"What did you say?" Odin bellowed.

"I said I'm leaving."

"Don't be ridiculous. Where could you possibly go?"

"Javan. I'm tired of hiding under this ice."

I'd fled the mansion. When Nephillim start throwing things, it can get dangerous, especially when what's hurled includes ten-pound goblets and forty-pound dishes. From my hiding place in the woods, I could hear their tirade through the open windows. One of the Nephillim grounds keepers had spotted me in the branches. I was pretty high up, but not for a Nephillim, even an old one well into his silver time. He walked stooped over, shuffling as he pushed his way through the tangle of foliage until his enormous wrinkled head was even with my scuffed sandals. He set me on a lower branch and settled himself on a nearby boulder, pulled out a leaf of something, handed me a piece of it, and started chewing his own. It smelled like burnt onion.

"You like to climb?" he asked and spit out a wad on the ground.

I nodded.

"She's a fine tree for that. Shame she's so distressed."

When I didn't say anything, he reached up about twelve feet and gently pulled the tip of a branch down into view. It was covered with clusters of acorns.

"See that?" he said. "You can always tell a tree is in trouble by how many acorns they make." He handed me a nut. "She knows she's going to be dead soon, so she's putting all her energy into making babies." He looked me over. "You're too willowy to be a Trahl child. You must be one of those humans I heard about."

I nodded again. He let the branch slip out of his hand, and it sprang back into place, showering acorns over his scraggly head. He made a show of being surprised as they bounced off his bald scalp.

"Ha! That got a grin out of you." He tilted his huge face at the mansion, where things had started to quiet. "First time you've been around Nephillim? I thought so. Well, listen carefully. Odin may howl like a sabre tooth but inside he's all mush, especially toward Athena. Last thing he wants is her getting whatever is killing folks out in the wilds. I'm not surprised he let you come here. He loves her. Doesn't show it right, but he does. That's why he let you and your sister come here. I caught a glimpse of her when you arrived. She's a sweet little thing. Odin's a softie for little girls, no matter what size. She'll win him over for both of you. You'll see."

I bit my lip to keep from crying. I wasn't going to blubber in front of an eighteen-foot stranger.

"Oh, now, don't worry. You and your sister just lay low for a while like you're doing. Try not to get stepped on and he'll come around. You'll see."

I reached out to touch the limb where I'd sat with that grounds keeper so long ago.

"You okay, Chief?"

I snapped my visor back in place. "Fine. Let's go find that vault."

CHAPTER THIRTY-SIX

JORDAN

The storm spent its fury and swept southwest over the cliffs into Phut. The power was out and the air cars didn't start. We had to hike back home, walking through ankle-deep water and over fallen branches. Some folks hadn't made it to cover in time and had been injured. Aizah and her Guardians carried them on makeshift litters.

We crested the last ridge and Suri's village came into view. A giant limb from the village tree had snapped off. It lay on shattered roofs and crushed gardens. Smoke and flames curled from the splintered mess. Becca clung to my back and pointed at a bit of roof under a massive twist of bark. "That was my house."

Suri and I looked at each other. She seemed to be thinking the same thing. A lot of people would have been killed if it hadn't been for the betrothal ceremony. Becca sobbed into my neck as the village elders cordoned off the area.

By late morning, the power was restored. News broadcasts reported the strange storm had swept over the Acropolis, into the capital, and had cut a wide swath of destruction west across Javan. The capital had been the hardest hit. A dozen people were dead. They'd been swept away by flash floods. One little boy had been rescued by a long-neck. The amphibian had kept the child's head above water until it could deposit him on shore.

Heavy equipment and volunteers poured into Javan from Magog and Indra. A team of hovering claw-like machines descended on Suri's village. The enormous tree limb was cut, hauled off, and mulched within an hour. The villagers rebuilt the destroyed cottages by lunchtime, except for the furnishings and gardens. Berbai preferred handmade furniture and hand planted gardens.

Guardian healers enjoying rest cycle on the Acropolis rushed into the valley and assisted with the injured. Tumleh had been hurt the worst, a crushed shoulder and severed arm.

Suri and I cancelled our outing to the capital and spent the afternoon with other family members repairing salvaged furniture from Tumleh's home. He found us hunched over a work bench, our foreheads touching as we finished painting the filigree on an intricate chest. He placed his hands on my shoulder. His new arm was thin and bright pink, encased in a rubbery film that protected it while it grew to its original length.

"You do fine work, young man. I feel badly that you two are not spending time together."

"We are, Father," Suri said.

"I heard the capital is in bad shape," he remarked.

"They're telling the tourists to stay away." She sighed. "I wanted Jordan to see the museums so badly."

"Things might improve by tomorrow."

CHAPTER THIRTY-NINE

LEVI

We reached the front gate of Odin's mansion. The ivy-draped granite walls and moss-covered roofs towered above us. A breeze set up a swirl of dead leaves. We flattened to the ground, keeping our cloaked armor from being outlined as the dervish passed over us. I scanned the immediate area while we waited for the wind to die down. The ornate entrance gaped open.

"Something's not right," I said.

"You're basing that on the unlocked door and lack of sentries?" Aaron replied.

"Confirmed."

"Maybe the Trahls took the day off since Grumpus Maximus is away."

"Odin would never leave his secrets unguarded."

"A trap."

"Probably."

"I love a challenge."

"We'll enter through an upper window."

"Without grappling, in case they hear it."

"Confirmed."

"Climbing cloaked gives a new meaning to hand/eye coordination."

We crossed the lawn with boot cleats extended to avoid crushing the grass and revealing our movement. Stick pads worked well on the smooth boulder wall. We inched up the façade to a third story window and dropped inside a dark room. Cobwebs hung from gigantic furnishings. A thin layer of dust covered the stone floor.

"Odin hasn't been up here for a while," I said.

"Aizah says he keeps to his study since Athena left, but Trahls are still assigned to guard the unoccupied floors."

"Keep the cleats deployed. We don't want to leave tracks in the dust. Anything on your scanner?"

"Not even a cockroach."

We navigated through a maze of empty chambers and halls to a circular staircase. I led the way down it. We reached a room I'd sworn I would never visit again.

"Your heart rate is erratic, Chief. You feeling okay?"

"Never better."

I took a breath, fighting back the memory, and cracked the heavy door enough to slip through. Aaron eased the massive thing shut behind us, taking care not to latch it. "Wow, look at this place."

"Don't touch anything. Odin's fond of booby-traps."

"Yeah, Aizah told me about them."

I scanned the circular lab. It was large enough to hold a legion of Guardians with transports hovering overhead. Odin's autopsy table hung from stiff chains. Memory replayed the image of my sister's limp hand hanging over the edge.

The curved walls soared a hundred feet. Faded murals depicted scenes of a distant time and place: castles floating in the sky, creatures thrashing in a green ocean, a battle being fought on a charred plain, warriors using spears and clubs against hoards of enraged animals. The fantastic scenes were crowned by a gilded obsidian dome glowing with stars.

"I don't recognize any of those constellations," Aaron sent.

"This sky hangs above another world."

"Really," Aaron said dubiously. "Nicely done."

"It's not a painting; it's real."

Aaron's oculars swirled. "Wow."

Odin's desk commanded the far wall, flanked by enormous

shelves packed with books and scrolls. Gaps with recently toppled volumes indicated where Odin had grabbed particular works to take along on the evacuation to *Olympus.*

Opposite the shelves was a carved seat with deep cushions set beneath towering lancet windows. The view was a panorama of dying forest and city ruins being recycled into missiles. In the center of the lab stood a contraption I hadn't noticed as a child. It was a long golden tube the thickness of a tree, affixed to a substantial tripod of red metal. Wires protruded and draped the device, weaving a geometric web that glistened in the dusty light. The web gathered into twisted strands the thickness of my thumb. They spiraled down beneath the tripod and disappeared into a pipe set in the floor. The contraption was tilted with one end set at comfortable Nephillim head height. The other end pointed toward the starry dome. It was aimed at one particularly large star. I zoomed in on the star with my oculars. Three planets orbited it, all in motion.

"How does the ceiling work?" Aaron asked.

"I'm planning to find out. Keep an eye out for cloaked patrols in the hall."

"Maybe I should ignore my scanners and watch for dust swirls on the floor."

"If they find us, we evacuate through that window and head for the river. Rendezvous at the falls if we get separated."

"Then what?"

"We find your future father-in-law and see if he's willing to take us in."

"That might prove awkward."

"You haven't proposed to Aizah yet?"

"It's been a little hectic."

"Anak."

My visor display linked to Aaron's scanner-bots as he deployed them into the hall. They scattered in all directions. I de-cloaked so I could see my hands and not accidently knock something on the floor, then began a careful search of the shelves.

"What are you looking for?" Aaron asked.

"The location of Odin's Vault."

"You mean you don't know where it is?"

I felt the back of a shelf that appeared cut. “Not yet.”

“You think it’s written down here somewhere?”

“According to Athena, Odin was agitated when he arrived at *Olympus*. He was upset about a book he grabbed during the evacuation. It was a journal of his explorations of the vault.”

“If he had it, why was he upset?”

“He forgot he’d made a copy. It’s still here somewhere, disguised as another volume.”

“Did Athena know what it looked like?”

“No.”

“It’s a big room.”

“Yes.”

“With lots of books.”

“Just watch the halls.”

I examined the woodwork, hunting for any sign of movable panels or secret compartments. Aaron stoically stood guard, watching his displays as his bots roamed the halls.

Five hours passed as I searched all the books in the room, then stepped away from the shelving and stared at the distant skyline.

“How’s it going, Chief?”

“Nothing,” I said.

“Maybe he put it somewhere else in the mansion and forgot where.”

“In which case, we won’t find it before Odin finds us. He’s due back tomorrow to retrieve it.”

Trahl machinery hovered around a partially standing ruin. Their weaving beams reduced it to a very small pile. I ran back to the shelves.

“Thought of something?”

“I forgot how Odin packs.”

I removed my gloves and slowly ran my fingers across the bare shelving between the books. Aaron snapped open his helmet. “What do you mean?”

My finger brushed a speck on a shelf above my head. As I hoped, the spec didn’t budge. I put my gloves back on to increase the strength of my fingers. “Found it.”

“Found what?”

"I need your help. This is going to be heavy."

He stared as I struggled to slide the speck across the shelf. "Uh, help with what?"

"Moving these books, of course."

"Yeah, you definitely need help."

"Your oculars working?"

"Of course."

"Zoom in."

He let out a low whistle. "Cool."

"Cool?"

"Jordan–"

"Just help me pull it to the edge of the shelf."

Aaron pulled on my gloves when both of us couldn't grab the speck at the same time. "Anak, it weighs a ton."

"Of course it does. It's called shrink wrap. Volume is reduced but weight isn't. Watch out; it's getting close to the edge."

"Is that bad?"

The shelf cracked.

"Potentially."

"Then why are we doing this?"

"Get ready to dive behind the desk."

"When?"

The speck tipped over the edge.

"Now."

We dove. An explosion rocked the room. Books bombarded the other side of the desk, pushing it across the floor. When the barrage petered out, we chanced a look. A box the size of an air car sat quivering on its side in front of the splintered shelves. A jumble of books had exploded from its innards and lay strewn across the floor. Leftover volumes popped to full size, ricocheting across the room. One bounced off Aaron's shoulder.

"If anybody's guarding the mansion, they're probably on their way," Aaron said.

"We're going to have to search this mess quick. I just wish I knew what to look for."

A scroll sprang to full size and ricocheted off the desk top, into Aaron's glove. He opened it and handed it to me. "Is this it?"

I examined the contents, a floor plan of the mansion with a series of arrows leading to the lowest basement. From there, a cavern was sketched out showing a serpentine path leading to a circle marked ENTRANCE TO VAULT.

"That was convenient."

"Trap?"

I slipped the scroll into an armored pocket. "Probably."

"We're going anyway?"

"Of course."

"Cool."

Aaron and I cloaked and followed the circuitous route scrawled on the map. Threat symbols popped up on my oculars: Trahl sentries, some holed up, others patrolling. Avoiding them was—how did Jordan express it—as much effort as the preparation of a simple bread product.

"You mean piece of cake, Chief."

"My version is accurate."

Walls became dustier and lights became scarce as we descended into the bowels of the mansion, crawling through places nobody had been in a long time or would want to be. I stopped to pull rat dung off my faceplate and checked the map. Aaron's cloaked armor was streaked with cobwebs.

"We might as well not bother trying to be invisible," he said. "There aren't any patrols down this low."

"According to the map, Odin's Vault is a mile down and three miles that way," I said, pointing north.

"Anak, that's deep."

"We've traversed a cavern system with enough wrong turns to confuse Ground Com," I said. "No wonder nobody could find his vault."

Masonry gave way to rough-hewn slag as the corridor ramp descended below the deepest floor, through thick layers of ancient sediment. Our oculars switched to gravity imaging as we plunged through the gloom. A flash of light raced along a distant wall. It split in twelve directions and vanished.

"Some kind of power transmission," I said.

"Probably feeding lights and lab equipment in the vault. Odin probably made it split into multiple lines to prevent anyone from following it to the vault."

"Actually, according to the map, none of them go near it. They're an elaborate decoy."

"Aizah admitted trying to trace them," Aaron said as we sidestepped a hole in the floor of the ramp. "She got lost and almost didn't make it back."

A mile short of our goal, the ramp ended on a natural stairway of cascading limestone ledges. These went through a labyrinth of massive caverns. Stalagmites towered overhead. Crosswinds buffeted my body as we grappled over steep drops. It was a good thing we didn't need light to find our way. Athena had warned of ancient creatures—some organic, some mechanical—sleeping beneath Mer. Few were tame. I thought they were bedtime stories, courtesy of Odin to keep Athena away from the vault. Then we almost walked into the side of a forty-foot reptilian device with razor-sharp spikes made of armor. Motion sensors flashed rhythmically on its idling turbine.

"Anak, that didn't show up on any sensors," I said.

"Definitely not Mer-made," Aaron said.

Even with the map, I missed turns, backtracked, and missed again. Cave-ins since the map's making were to blame. The obstructions appeared recent, probably triggered by shock waves from exploding ordinance during the invasion of Mer. Without the map, we wouldn't have found our way.

At the end of a long side cavern, hidden under an enormous granite outcropping, was where the map indicated a vertical tunnel dropped into the vault. At first, I feared the map was wrong. Gravity imaging showed no entrance. When we reached the spot, the ground felt solid and untouched. After an hour of fruitless searching, a hole suddenly appeared next to us.

"Shield cover timed to disengage after sufficient contact," I said.

"Athena's dad is pretty clever."

I sent the bots in to check for threats. Aaron peered down the hole. Wind sighed as if in greeting, spewing phosphorescent dust that outlined his cloaked body. His blurred torso turned toward me. "It goes a mile down. This thing's so deep, you'd think we'd run out of planet by now."

"Bots indicate all clear," I said.

"No guards?"

"None."

"You want to go down and get shot at first or should I?"

"You don't believe my scan?"

"You think bots you got from Odin would warn us that his vault is guarded?"

"Point taken."

"I don't get it, Chief. Why are we doing this if you're sure it's a trap?"

"What makes you think it's a trap?"

"This place is too important to be unguarded."

"Obviously."

Aaron's helmet tilted and his hands spread in apparent exasperation. "And we're still going in?"

I got in position for the descent. "I promise to leave you some targets."

"Thanks, not that I need the practice."

"No trouble."

I dropped into the hole. Odin must have used a repulser rig to soft land, a caged platform that functioned similar to a flying Walker Scout, only without armor or weapons. Ripple marks on the walls of the shaft were similar to stone warping from such a device. I didn't have the luxury of using one even if Odin had left it sitting around. Too noisy and slow.

I popped out of the ceiling and free-dropped to the floor. I hit the smooth surface and expulsed a ring of dust that would have outlined me had there been any ambient light. I side-stepped as Aaron touched down beside me. Light came on.

Correction, there were no lights. The walls, floor, and ceiling simply started to glow. We stood in a room large enough to hold a fleet of heavy Retrievers. It was hewn out of solid rock and honeycombed with storage niches. Each niche held clusters of tech. Large portals afforded views of adjacent vault chambers, their surfaces brightening.

"Bots indicate the other chambers are larger," I said.

Aaron ran his hand over the mirror-smooth granite, glowing as if it was a crystal panel over some gigantic light fixture. "How big is this place?"

We walked from chamber to chamber. Some contained vehicles of unknown function as large as houses, with appendages and devices impossible to identify. Stairs and ladders hung from the larger units. I examined one ladder, noting the twelve-inch spacing of the rungs. We came to a section of one chamber that was partially cleared out. Nephillim work tables, higher than our heads, were arranged in the open area.

"The bots are getting a whole lot of nothing, Chief."

"Confirmed. Doesn't mean we aren't being watched. Keep your weapons primed."

"No problem with that. They're recharging off these walls like they want to burst."

We climbed up on the tables. Devices were strewn across the gleaming surfaces. They were in various states of disassembly. Aaron pointed to one I didn't recognize.

"Odin just finished reverse-engineering this one last decade," he said. "Aizah's squad used them when I was Ground Com Liaison." He picked up the inert device and popped open his helmet. "Watch this."

He spoke softly into the little gadget and set it back on the table. It grew legs, whirled around like it was looking for him, skittered up his arm, and perched on his shoulder, sprouting what looked like a miniature disabler cannon.

"Cool, huh? You say a certain phrase and they become your shoulder weapon for life. They don't respond to Ephraim voices, only Trahl and human."

"Interesting," I said. "Tech Atlantis can't steal."

"Yeah, amazing how Odin got it to do that." He looked at me guiltily. "Sorry I didn't tell you about it sooner. Aizah had one. Borrowed it from Odin's lab."

"Borrowed?"

"She swore me to secrecy."

Aaron tried to coax the device off his shoulder, but it dodged his fingers and ran up on top of his helmet. "Anak, I can't shut it off." He danced around, arms flailing as he tried to catch the skittering device. "Come here you piece of . . ." He tried to grab it and smacked himself instead. It chirped happily and went down his back, poking at his fingertips with its antenna. "Could you get it off me?"

"It's obviously attached to you. I'd hate to upset it."

"Maybe I can order it to guard you."

I fired a restrainer, knocked it off Aaron's elbow, and glued it to the table. It shuddered in the flexible jelly, then folded up with a sigh.

We continued to explore. Some chambers were round, some were multi-tiered. Others were insulated and pressurized. Each contained technological wonders even legends hadn't remembered. Each device was perfectly preserved in packaging covered in thick dust, hinting at a phenomenal age. The clear packaging pulsated as if it was alive. All the vestiges of an extremely advanced civilization were on display: works of art, devices and equipment, tools of unknown utility. There were rooms upon rooms of weapons appearing to be far more lethal than anything I'd fielded, and stockpiled in quantities sufficient to arm a hundred legions. As we walked, a wild notion came to me. I shrugged it off. Only the lovers of wild controversy would entertain such an idea. Yet the thought persisted.

We reached a final long chamber holding thousands of small arm weapons wrapped in the strange pulsating packaging. Some had been removed from their niches, unwrapped, and arranged on a Nephillim work table. Others were stacked on a floating sled, as if awaiting transport.

Aaron lifted his dusty faceshield and stared closely at the packages. "I wonder what this place is for."

"Probably where Odin stores tech he's re-sized for human . . ."

"What is it, Chief?"

"What do Nephillim always say about First Age tech?"

"That it was found in vaults deep beneath the ice cap."

"Made by whom?"

"First Age Nephillim, of course."

"And what did they do with it?"

"Gave it to our ancestors to help them glue Ephraim half-giants into nice, neat piles."

"Right, but what did they do to the tech before they gave it away?"

"Miniaturize the controls so we could use it. What are you getting at?"

"You ever see an armed Nephillim?"

"I've never seen a Nephillim, period, until yesterday. But, sure, they're armed. Weapons rods, disabler balls."

"But never with weapons like these. Nothing with finger holes."

I walked over to a niche holding a dozen heavily packaged Repulser rifles that looked ancient and more advanced than anything we'd deployed in the field. I pulled one out and blew a thousand decades of dust off its packaging. The protective film instantly dissolved. I cradled the perfectly crafted barrel and it rested lightly in my arm. I activated what looked like the power gatherer and the body of the weapon vibrated.

"Notice anything strange about this un-reverse-engineered piece of First Age Nephillim tech?"

"Well, for one thing, it's resisting your cloaking field and staying visible."

"Besides that."

Aaron's eyes widened. "It's human size."

"Remember the ladders on those mobile units? Too tightly spaced for a Nephillim or a half-giant to climb."

"But perfect for us," Aaron said.

"I haven't seen a single thing that's Nephillim-sized."

"You're saying the vault was built by humans?"

"Probably Trahls, too." I picked up a tiny hand pistol.

"And dwarves," Aaron whispered. "You think it's possible our ancestors were that smart back then?"

"What I don't think is twenty-foot First Age Nephillim manufactured weapons too small for them to fire."

"Odin issues us this stuff because his fat fingers can't fit in the triggers."

"The more primitive pieces, yes. But some of these devices are inoperable for a different reason. Maybe they're more advanced. That's what Athena thinks."

I lifted my helmet and spoke the command Athena had taught me. I was still shaky on the inflections. Ancient languages were not my strong suit.

"Hello, sir," the weapon responded in perfect Engel. "It is good to meet you. How may I serve?"

The firing ring changed shape, wrapped around my fingers, and the weapon's tube glowed blue. I snapped my helmet shut. "These more advanced weapons only respond to the touch and sound of Engel-speaking indigenous races."

"Trahls, humans, and dwarves," Aaron said.

"The races that lived on Earth before the Nephillim landed."

"And bred half-giants from our women."

I nodded. "That's why Odin brought the Trahls to Mer and let Athena arm Javan and Mestre. The Nephillim needed us to fight off the half-giants."

"All this time we thought they were protecting us—"

"When it's been us protecting them."

"Those old farts. They could've just asked." He picked up a packaged rifle. His face hardened. "And given us the best stuff to fight with instead of hiding it."

"Fewer of our people would have died."

Thunderous applause filled the vault. We dove behind a stone shelf. The clapping was so loud my helmet rattled. My newly acquired Repulser rifle sensed my need for stealth and vanished inside my cloaking field. Aaron's weapons came off his legs, grav-hunting for the giant who was doing the clapping. I sent bots flying around the room in a frantic aerial search. Of course they saw nothing.

"Well done, Levi," a familiar voice reverberated through the vault. "Took you long ee-nuff to figgar it out."

"Is that Odin?" Aaron asked.

"No," I replied. "Better power down."

"We're safe?"

"Confirmed."

We popped helmets and de-cloaked.

Aaron's weapons glowed crimson. "All right, very funny. Show yourself."

The owner of the voice materialized, all twenty feet, twelve hundred pounds of him. He leaned against a wall between niches holding missiles. His left leg was tucked up behind his kilt as if he'd been lounging there for a while. His close-cropped mane was disheveled. Dried blood pasted the side of his temple. His arms hung loosely at his sides, a flask dangling from one hand. He clinked it carelessly against a metallic nose cone.

The young Nephillim lurched forward. He stumbled when his sizable head banged on the edge of a stone shelf. He hung on as his legs buckled, then straightened. Fortunately, the shelving seemed engineered to withstand stronger forces than an inebriated giant could inflict upon it.

"So, now ya know …"

We held our ears to muffle his thunderous voice. He seemed to realize he was talking too loud and fiddled with a control on his thirty-inch collar. "Oh, Anak, juss-a minute. Testing," he said, much quieter. I gave him a thumbs-up.

"Juss wanted to s'prise you." He took a long drink from the flask and wiped foam from his face. "How'r ya doin', lil brudder?"

"Wondering why you're here, Apollo."

Aaron stared at me and jerked a thumb up at the giant. "That's Apollo?"

"Unfortunately."

Apollo let go of the shelving and lurched toward us. He managed a few steps, wavered, and then straightened up in an apparent attempt to look dignified.

"You look like drek," I said.

"Ak-shully, I feel great," he said and swayed in place.

"A little too great," Aaron muttered.

Apollo's eyes rolled up inside his enormous head.

"Anak, he's going down!"

"Run!"

Apollo, intrepid explorer of outer space, half-brother to Athena and unfortunately mine as well, toppled like a chopped cedar. It takes a while for a twenty-foot-tall Nephillim to hit the ground. We sidestepped his impact. He hit face-first, rattling tech off their niches. A wave of dust rolled over us. Apollo moaned, flopped onto his back, and commenced snoring.

"Guess it didn't hurt," Aaron said.

"It will later."

"Is he breathing okay?"

"He might swallow his tongue. Best we roll him onto his side."

Rolling a giant is never easy, even with our armor assisting, but I'd had practice with Apollo. "Grab his leg and pull his knee to his chest."

"I'm trying, but he's limp as a sloth."

"Anak, he's rolling the other way. Get his other leg."

"You … try … getting … it."

"Can't you hold on?"

Aaron stopped pulling and wedged his head against Apollo's thigh to keep the giant from defeating his efforts. "You're grabbing armor joints; I'm grabbing skin."

"So?" I grunted.

"In case you didn't notice, his skin's as oily as a slobbering longneck."

After a lot of arguing, we got Apollo into a stable sideways position. Bubbles of mucus rhythmically ballooned from his nose. We leaned against his chest armor as if we were lounging against a wall at one of the clubs on the Acropolis. Aaron had his back to Apollo's face. I kept a clear view past his shoulder to make sure the Nephillim continued breathing.

"Why would he oil his body?" I asked.

"Aizah says all the young Nephillim are doing it."

"Since when?"

"Since the recordings were released last month."

"What recordings?"

"Jordan's recordings, from that iPod tech thing with all the music on it. It had picture recordings, too. They're called movies. One was about soldiers called *glad-ee-ay-tors.* According to the recording, they lived in a country called Grease. I guess they oiled their bodies to honor their homeland. Ground Com thinks they're ancient primitives from the North, but I say they're wrong. The characters weren't dressed for cold weather. They had feathered helmets and ran around practically naked, with just a little piece of cloth covering their privates. Oil covered everything else. The leader wore a cape like mine and called himself *Spart-a-cus*. Guardian maidens are nuts over him."

"Why?"

"Cause he looks like me, of course."

I rolled my eyes. "That's about the most ridiculous thing I've heard this decade."

"They think it's cool." He checked his hair in Apollo's armor.

"How did Jordan submit his recordings for creative credits so fast? He hasn't been naturalized as a citizen yet."

Aaron found a particularly stubborn part of his hairline that refused to be perfect.

"Somebody else submitted them for him?" I inquired.

"Kind of."

"With Jordan's permission, of course."

"Not exactly."

"You're telling me Jordan wasn't asked?"

"We thought he'd be thawed out by the time it got submitted to the Center, but Athena changed her mind and kept him under longer."

"Who's we?"

Aaron looked morally torn.

"If memory serves me, Diago had a certain fondness for Jordan's iPod," I said.

No answer. I understood why. Diago must have gotten his hands on the iPod and did the deed. Aaron must have found out and arranged disciplinary action with the Acropolis. They kept the proceedings private for first offenses to give young recruits a chance to make good to the offended and clear their record. I wondered what Diago had done to make it up to Jordan?

"As soon as we get back to the Acropolis, I'm going to have a talk with that Algonian."

"I tried to stop him," Aaron said.

"How hard?"

"If Jordan's going to be a citizen and hang out with that princess, he's going to need creative credits to spend on her. It just made sense to get Jordan set up so he could treat her royally."

"I was under the impression she'd had enough of the royal treatment."

"Oh, come on, Chief, that would be a historic first. You've got to try courting again one of these centuries."

"And you're an expert in these matters?"

"Well, I do get a lot more attention from the maidens."

"I was doing fairly well with those hostages I rescued from the starship."

Apollo had turned deep green by now. The mucus bubbles suddenly retreated back into his fist-sized nostrils.

Aaron waved me off. "I was giving you space."

"I suppose you're right."

"Hey, I can't help it if I'm better looking than you."

Apollo's chest heaved. Aaron turned around as I dove out of the way. The Nephallim's enormous mouth spewed. Three gallons of vomit makes a mess on new armor. Aaron did not appear pleased.

I took a whiff. "Fermented barley."

Aaron wiped his armor with his cape. "I need another shower."

"Good idea. Aizah might suspect you've taken up drinking."

Apollo roused and pushed himself into a sitting position. "Ah feel much bedder." He looked down at Aaron. "Sorry 'bout that." He spotted his flask under a shelf and reached for it.

I nudged it away with my boot. "What are you doing here, Apollo?"

"I should be askin' you the same queshion. I thought Athena was coming."

"Couldn't make it. I thought you were on Mars, supervising your Father's science labs."

"I came back."

"Why?"

He laughed long and hard. The chamber reverberated and my ears hurt. Eventually, whatever joke had gripped him let go. His face slackened. "Because it's gone."

He popped something into his mouth and his eyes cleared. A sobriety tablet, no doubt. He shook his head once, wiped residual spittle from his mouth, and focused on me.

"What's gone?" I asked.

"Everything," he said perfectly. "Scientists, plants, animals, labs. They're all gone."

"I don't understand," Aaron said.

"Anak, you humans are denser than Trahls. Mars is dead, destroyed. The planet got pounded into a wasteland six months ago."

"By Atlantis?"

"Of course not."

"Ground Com hasn't detected any such disaster," I said.

"Yeah, and they probably think Babla's spaceship was destroyed. You didn't tell them yet, did you?"

"Athena worried there might be a leak."

He looked at the smooth wall at the end of the long chamber. A double-wide door materialized and silently swung open.

Aaron stopped wiping his armor and followed Apollo's gaze. "What's in there?"

Apollo crawled through the human-sized opening. It was a tight fit. He grunted. "Something you wouldn't have found without my help."

It wasn't another vault; it was an exit into a wide cavern. The ceiling was about three stories high and spread for miles. Faint light emanated from geometric shadows crowning a distant rise. We hiked a half hour until the shadows took recognizable form. A vast urban ruin spread before us. The towers impaled the ceiling of the cavern, as if the dome had formed around them. Glints of gold shimmered as our field lights played across the ancient walls.

"What is this place?" Aaron asked.

"Don't know," Apollo said. "There's no record of it in the Vault archives. Odin's notes indicate that it's over five thousand decades old."

"Impossible. Nothing constructed can last that long."

Apollo shrugged. "This did."

I didn't realize the most important aspect of this discovery until we neared the first structures. They were arranged behind a curved canal with regularly spaced boulders down its center line to prevent silting. Water still flowed through it. Aaron took the opportunity to grapple into the water, slosh around and retract up to the other bank, clean once more.

Apollo chuckled at Aaron's preening. "Hopefully, nobody is drinking that downstream."

Aaron looked as though he'd been grappled in the chest. "Anak, I didn't think of that."

"What flows down goes back up," Apollo said. He leapt across the canal and landed on the bank. I stood in a doorway and reached a little above my helmet to touch the lintel. Beside it was another doorway, dwarf-sized. There were no doors for giants.

"This was a human/Trahl/dwarf city," I whispered.

"Predates the First Landing," Apollo said.

"So, it's true," Aaron said. "We were here first. Your ancestors came to Earth just like the legends say."

"Not quite. They landed on Mars first." Apollo smiled. "But they didn't like it there very much."

"There are Nephillim living on Mars?" I asked.

"Nephillim, Ephraim, and even some Trahls. Or, at least, they used to. Maybe they went underground, I don't know. It was too hard to see through the explosions. The comets just kept coming." He stood there looking like the world had just settled on his shoulders. "And I couldn't do a thing to save them." He shook his head and straightened. "I'm wasting time. Follow me."

He hiked through the ruins at a brisk pace, meaning we had to grapple to keep up. He ducked under leaning walls and toppled towers that soared above our helmets. We came to a circular plaza surrounded by ornate structures. A colonnaded building with a gilded dome commanded the center. It appeared completely intact except for an irregular Nephillim-sized hole melted in its side. Across a curved tablature were etched unfathomable symbols—save one. It was an ancient symbol I knew from studying the scrolls of my faith: *Shem.* Another name for Shant Dai. It meant: *the god who teaches.* The rest of the script was amazingly simple to decipher. The patterns combined basic shapes, forming word pictures common to Indra, Chi, Gog, and Salem. Even though I had never laid eyes on this script before, I felt as if I'd known it all my life. There was no slow welling of familiarity in the back of my soul this time. Their revelation sang straight into my heart and set it aflame.

For the wisdom of Shem is a hidden sustenance. For the virtuous it is a shield. Seek it while it lingers.

"You got that look again, Chief," Aaron said.

"Excuse me?"

"You actually reading that scribble or do you have a neck crick?"

"Maybe to the first question."

We followed Apollo into a Nephillim-size hole in the building's façade. A grand rotunda contained eleven devices that matched the shape and design of the one Odin had jury-rigged in his lab. A ragged hole in the ornate floor testified to where Odin had obtained his device. Apollo stopped in the middle of the room and pointed up at the dome ceiling. Unrecognizable constellations slowly rotated across the black surface.

"It's been running a long time. Odin wrote that the dust in here came up to his knees." Apollo pointed to a bundle of tubes pulsing with light. "Odin relays the images to his lab. What you saw projected on his ceiling is coming from this room."

"What was he looking at?" Aaron asked.

"Something the device chose to show him. After that, he couldn't get it to change views."

"What is it?"

Apollo crossed his arms. "Our home system, I think." He pulled a scroll out from his chest plate and handed it to me. "I hung onto this in case you blew up the lab."

"Levi has a habit of doing that," Aaron said.

"Be careful opening it. It's old."

I unrolled the scroll on the floor. It was a schematic of the room we stood in, with details of the tubular devices arrayed at the dome. The writing was in the same symbol language on the outside of the building. I parsed the beautifully scripted words and got enough deciphered to make a judgment call. "It's a telescope, but more advanced than anything we have. I think it can see anything in the galaxy."

"You sure that's all it does?" Aaron asked.

"No. There's more writing, but it's deteriorated."

"Can you operate it or not?" Apollo asked.

"Why can't you?" I returned.

Apollo narrowed his enormous eyes. "Remember all the tech in the vault? Voice and touch activated. Won't listen to a Nephillim."

"How did Odin get it to work?" Aaron asked.

"He didn't; the device activated itself. I think to warn Odin to leave it alone."

"What happens if I get this device to operate?" I asked. "What is it you're hoping to see?"

"You still don't trust me?"

"Should I?"

"I'm sorry I threw you in Athena's pond when you were seven. I was stupid. There, satisfied?"

"What's your purpose here?" I demanded.

"Athena warned me this might happen. She figured you'd assume I'd use it to destroy Atlantis, or something violent like that."

"You assumed right."

"With a telescope?" Aaron inquired.

"Any First Age tech is a potential weapon, especially tech that predates the Landing," I said.

Apollo looked in the air. "Are you listening, Sister?"

"I'm here." Athena's voice echoed through the rotunda. "Guardians, you can trust him. His intentions are the same as mine; we want to learn what threatens Earth."

"And you think this device can help?" I asked.

"Yes."

"Why don't you just turn it on?"

"Only a virtuous human can operate it," she said. "That's why I sent you."

"So much for character judgement," Aaron whispered.

"Aaron, be quiet," Athena said. "Odin doesn't know what we're attempting, but I can't keep him distracted much longer. Please turn it on. It will shut down afterwards and be completely useless to any Nephillim, I promise. You and I need to see what it does. It stayed awake all these eons for a purpose."

The scroll confirmed her words. But what if the scroll was a forgery? A prayer welled up inside me. *Please have me do the right thing or glue me fast.*

I spoke the words on the scroll. The eleven devices glowed and swung about. Their long tubes swiveled and dipped, painting an image across the dome in flames of light. The dome flared and seemed to rotate under our feet, duplicating itself and creating a sphere. The sphere expanded until all we saw was a universe of stars and a swirling galaxy beneath us.

"Well, this is cool," Aaron said.

The galaxy grew and swallowed us. We flew past star systems and through wreckage spinning slowly above lifeless planets. Then we hovered above the sun, where planets pinwheeled about. The sun shared an orbit with another star. They followed oval paths that crossed as if they were on two loosely joined rings. The other star was dark and compressed—the collapsed mother star that had birthed our sun and died in the process. Comets, planetoids, and meteors orbited the dead star, a great ring of debris concealed by the dust of countless collisions. The two stars were nearing in their binary dance. The ring of debris trespassed into our solar system and collided with the outer planets.

The device zoomed in on Mars. The planet was pounded by thousands of small meteorites and comet fragments. Its atmosphere succumbed. Life retreated underground.

The view shifted to the stream of meteors and comets. They paraded through us, a vast celestial river curling in on itself in a long sinuous helix. The sheer beauty and terror clawed at my soul.

"The stream of meteors and comet fragments are presently between Mars and the asteroid belt," Apollo said. "Based on this projection, the stream continues across Mars' path and reaches Earth in a matter of weeks."

"What happens if the stream crosses Earth's orbit?" Aaron asked.

"Imagine what a hundred small comets would do to the atmosphere," Apollo said. "Super-cold ice seeding warm moist atmosphere, storms would be spawned reminiscent of what destroyed the First Age. Winds strong enough to rip people and animals to pieces. Glaciers piling a mile high in minutes. Then you have the meteors. A hundred of them hitting Earth in a line. The axis would keel over like a swamped Baskra hull-ship. Tidal waves miles high would scour the continents. The planet's surface would slide across the deeper rocks. Friction would ignite thousands of volcanos. We'd be ripped, hurled, drowned, frozen, boiled, and buried in a day."

"Could Odin be aware of the danger?" Athena asked.

"Not this way," I said, indicating the projection around us. "He couldn't operate the device."

"He must have gotten his information from somewhere else," Athena said.

"The Queen," Apollo said. "She told him."

"First of all, Babla's dead," Aaron said. "And second, how would she know?"

"She is very much alive," Apollo stated. "Thanks to Levi."

"I watched her die," I said.

"Babla is an ancient Nephillim soul that infested a human host," Apollo said. "She didn't die; her host did. She discarded her old host and was incubating inside a new victim in one of the hibernation tubes before you arrived. Didn't you wonder why all those women in Babla's command saucer looked the same? They're compatible hosts for Babla. She's been cheating death by infecting young girls who look like she did for over two thousand decades. Depending on compatibility, she burns out their bodies in a couple of years, then infects another. That's why she needed so many women stored in her quarters on the starship. She needed a lot of young bodies for the long trip back to the Nephillim home world. She almost died on that ship, but you rescued her."

Aaron smacked his forehead. "Chief, that woman who went berserk in the shuttle. The Queen infected her before you rescued them. She transferred her—whatever she is—into the woman's body and took her over."

"Vaguely put, but yes," Apollo said.

My body chilled. I couldn't believe my stupidity. All those women had looked like Suri. "That means Suri is genetically compatible with Babla."

"In fact, she's the best match," Apollo said. "Babla would get at least a century of host life out of her. She probably realizes now that she can't escape the end of the age. If she could infect Suri, she'd be able to ride out the end and find a new host among unsuspecting survivors after they've long stopped worrying about her. Why do you think Babla's been chasing the princess all this time?"

"What's it take for Babla to infect Suri?" I asked.

"Direct contact and transfer of fluids—spittle, sweat, blood," Apollo said. "And from what I read, the host has to be willing, passive, or unconscious."

"Who would be willing?"

"The same kind of souls who became like Babla long ago," Apollo said. "People who wanted to cheat death enough that they were willing to rob others of their lives."

"Can Suri fight her off?" Aaron asked.

Apollo spread his hands twenty feet apart. "From what I read, resistance sometimes delays the crossover. But, against the Queen, I doubt Suri could resist long."

"As far as we know, Babla's in Phut," I said.

"And so is that weapon she had mounted on her spaceship to fire a parting shot at Javan before she launched into deep space. Odin tracked its plunge into Phut. I bet he lost it the same time Babla's new host vanished from our sensor sweep."

"This is my fault," I said. "If I hadn't gone up there …"

"Stinks when you mess up, doesn't it?" Apollo said. "In your Guardian zeal to save those women, you gave Babla and her infected host a nice safe trip back to Earth. Now Babla's running around somewhere in Phut while she plans her next move."

"Anak," was all I could say.

"I've been where you are," Apollo said. "Why do you think I drink?"

"What's Babla's next move?" Aaron asked.

"To figure out a way to survive the end of the age like the rest of us stuck down here on terra not-so-firma," Apollo said.

"And she's planning to do it inside Suri's body," Aaron said.

"If she gets the chance," Apollo agreed. "With her intelligence, she'd know where to go and how best to ride out the end."

"Suri has to be moved to a more secure location," I said. "A place the Queen can't easily infiltrate. She should be moved to the *Olympus*. Do you agree, Athena?"

Silence.

"Athena?"

"Her channel is still open on my com but she's not responding," Apollo said.

"When's the last time she said something?" Aaron asked.

I tried to contact Ground Com.

"Ground Com is not responding either," I said.

Apollo growled. "You flew Darts to get here?"

"We blew them up," Aaron said.

"Follow me," he said.

The device seemed to sense it was time to shut down. The room darkened as we hurried out. Apollo's ship waited on a rooftop.

CHAPTER THIRTY-SIX

JORDAN

The next morning, we boarded an air car for the capital. Aizah spun the copilot chair around and looked us both in the eye. "Here's the deal. Levi has put my team on higher security alert."

"How much higher can you get than this?" I pointed at *Olympus* floating directly overhead.

She glared back. "Try me."

"Why?" Suri asked. "What's wrong now?"

"The Ra is mad that you left Mestre. According to him, it made Amon appear weak. His standing as future leader of Mestre was diminished."

"That's his fault, not hers," I said. Suri patted my arm to cut me short.

"Regardless, Numu has propagated a cover story for the Prince." Aizah said. "You won't find it pleasant."

"What did Numu say?" Suri asked, anger edging her words.

"The official pronouncement is that you had a secret lover. Amon found out and was deeply hurt."

Suri's face turned red. "Jordan and I would never …"

Aizah held up her armored hands. "Relax. I know that. I've been watching you, remember? Numu claims Amon did the noble thing and quietly sent you away to stop the Ra's inquiry into your alleged indiscretion."

"Give me five seconds alone with him," I said. "I'll straighten out his facts."

"Numu is just saying words that will make people laugh," Suri said. "If this is what it takes to marry Jordan, then bring it."

"I like this girl," Aizah said.

"I don't get it; higher security because of a rumor?" I said.

Aizah shook her head. "Levi believes the Queen is still alive. Suri remains at risk."

"Why?" Suri inquired, "I've done nothing to offend her."

"I did," I said.

"This is not about offending the Queen," Aizah said.

Suri almost choked on her frustration. "Then why does she hunt me?"

Aizah hesitated for a micro-second, keeping her expression blank. I'd seen it before. When a nervous mom asked her kid's commander if the mission would be dangerous, it took that long to bury the possibilities and give a sanitized answer.

"Levi is still assessing that," she said. "Until we know otherwise, the Guardians will assume you and Jordan are at risk, even in the capital. We will be close, cloaked, and watching at all times." She looked at me and arched an eyebrow. "So behave yourselves."

I thought my dating years had been over after I'd met Lisa. Now I was on a date with Suri under the watchful eye of chaperones and air support. We bravely made the best of it.

Suri squeezed my hand as she discussed last minute plans with her siblings. Our convoy of air cars lifted off, scattering leaves and twigs from the storm. Suri seemed to forget we were being watched as her family drew her back into the civilian world.

"You have flying cars in your age?" a future brother-in-law asked me in perfect Engel. It seemed the majority of Suri's family had become proficient with the language.

"When I was a kid, my teachers promised we'd have flying cars, bases on the moon, and jet packs by the time I was grown," I replied. "But we don't."

"What went wrong?"

"We fought a war in a jungle instead."

"I hear the Nephillim have a base on the moon and one on Mars," he said. "Maybe you can talk Athena into letting us visit."

"That's a great idea. You're on."

He looked around his seat. "I'm on what?"

We sailed out the north gate of the village, straight toward the shimmering skyline of Deucalion, the capital of Javan. Two pairs of *Olympian* fighters orbited above us in precise figure eights. *Olympus* followed a few miles starboard, gliding majestically toward the capital.

Suri pointed port-side. Another flying mountain loomed in the clouds. "That looks like the *Valhalla*," she said excitedly. "See the long arch of rock on the bow?"

Javan forest gave way to streams of traffic. Thousands of vehicles raced hood to trunk through massive arches formed by bending slender trees. Northbound traffic flew beneath the southbound vehicles. The tree tops appeared to be fused into one.

The same future brother-in-law said, "You see? We tie the trees together when they're young. They grow together to make the arches."

"How long did it take for them to grow that big?"

"Not long, twenty decades. Do you see how each pair is different? There's a competition every century for the best design."

We passed a turn-off for a small town. The entrance arch was an elaborate bending of four flowering trees with perfectly intertwined branches. The blooms blended into a waving multi-rainbow.

"That took first prize when I was seven," he said.

I had a panoramic view of the countryside. Flowered foothills and sparkling lakes gave way to village clusters and manicured gardens. Beyond their quaint rooftops towered the distant skyline of Deucalion, sheltered beneath a fog-laced stand of enormous trees. The silver-barked ones had to be twice as tall as our village's tree. Beyond the city, sheer limestone cliffs stretched to the clouds. These were the outcroppings of the ancient Acropolis Plato had claimed extended thousands of miles from Athens to the Sphinx.

We neared the outskirts of the capital and cruised through neighborhoods of spacious homes and intricate gardens. Many were damaged. There was a lot of debris piled up outside the town walls.

"The storm was bad on the outskirts," Suri said. "I hope the center of the city was spared."

"They're getting it cleaned up," a sister said.

"The skate park is closed," another said.

"But there was supposed to be a race today!"

"Have no anxiety," the driver said, "the park officials heard that Suri and Jordan were coming and reopened it this morning."

This announcement was met with happy applause. The news was shouted to the other cars in our convoy. One of my future brother-in-laws clapped me on the shoulder. "I'm glad we're related."

"What kind of skating?" I asked.

"You'll see," Suri said.

"And you'll race," the brother-in-law added.

Suri's time at the Ra's palace seemed to have prepared her for public scrutiny. The prodigal princess' return was apparently a big story not only with the Berbai, but with the Javans.

Official cars with the Javan eagle emblazoned on their hoods joined up with us and took fore and aft positions to escort us through the thickening traffic. Folks waved enthusiastically from street corners and balconies. Parents pointed out our convoy to their kids as we glided past. A couple of guys shouted something from a passing car. Suri laughed behind her hand, pointed at me with the other, and shouted something back. They pretended to be profoundly disappointed as they swerved around a lumbering cargo carrier.

"What was that all about?" I asked.

"They asked me to marry them."

"What did you say?"

"I told them I already found the love of my life."

"You're amazing,"

"No, you are."

"Oh please," Aizah said from somewhere.

Traffic sailed into the heart of Deucalion. Suri's relatives pointed out the sights. Gleaming structures festooned with hanging gardens towered on enormous raised mounds. Pedestrian malls spanned between their canyons with razor-thin elegance. Verdant parks bounded their edges, some wide enough to host artificial rivers. Enormous canopy trees protruded through the malls, soaring into the clouds to spread their protective umbrellas of green and blue leaves over the entire metropolis. Wisps of fog drifted beneath their massive limbs.

Suri fumbled in her sleeve, pulled out a small metal rectangle and stretched it wide. A colored film expanded within the frame. "Here, try these." She held it in front of my face and pointed at a distant branch. "See the houses up there?"

The image of the branch zoomed in close, revealing clusters of vacation homes perched along its massive length. A game was in progress in a small park between the homes, involving two teams racing back and forth after a floating ball.

"The city trees were planted by Deuca," she said. "They are as old as the beginning of our age."

"Who was Deuca?" I asked, eager to learn if he was who I thought he was.

"A famous sailor," a sister said.

"He was a king, too," Suri added.

"That's not been proven," said a brother.

"Didn't you see the excavation Theos started in Mestre?" Suri said.

"No, but—"

"Well, there you go." Suri crossed her arms. "He found a carving showing Deuca's shepherd's crook inscribed over a royal crest in Rahn's study. If that's not proof, what is?"

My head was reeling at the Noah parallels. Suri tugged on the sleeve of our driver and pointed at a square in the heart of the city. "Oh, land there!"

"So much for water skating," her brother muttered to a sister. The sister shushed him.

Our caravan buzzed the rooftops of towers, dipped into the square, and circled for a landing. Everyone gathered their stuff.

"What are we doing first?" I asked as the driver leveled out and descended.

"Whatever you want," Suri said, her eyes focused on the center of the square.

"As long as it's a museum," a brother whispered in my ear. The sister swatted him.

We touched down. I sucked in my breath at the sight. The pedestrian mall stretched nearly a mile in four directions, spanning a massive void between four flat-top pyramids the size of mountains. The mall was a masterpiece of planned outdoor space, defined by graceful pavilions, flowering parks, and a sprawling amusement park. City towers edged its four sides, cut through with wide avenues linking to the urban fabric beyond. Pedestrian thoroughfares conveyed colorfully dressed crowds like floating spirits. Far beyond the city, the escarpment of the Acropolis spread across the northern and western horizons. To the south, the fog of the mighty Mestrean waterfall misted the sky. To the east, the city undulated down successive mounds to a shimmering sea.

"Would you like to see a museum?" I asked.

Suri's eyes lit up. She grabbed my hand and set course for a small brown building. The surface we stood on was translucent stone. It stretched above a jungle dotted with interconnected lakes filling a valley between the city-supporting pyramids. Each mound appeared to be a mile across and several hundred feet high. Vines and flowers clung to their flanks. Sloped construction and massive masonry seemed the rule of Second Age architecture.

"Do you get many earthquakes or tidal waves here?" I asked.

"How did you know?" a sister asked.

"He comes from the future," another sister said. "It's in his history."

"Actually, we don't know," I said. "I was just guessing from how those mounds are shaped. Looks like they're meant to withstand some major natural forces."

"When our age began, there were many tidal waves," Suri said, confirming my suspicion. "People were afraid to come down from the mountains for fear of another flood. But the highlands became too crowded. The Creator wanted people to spread out so there wouldn't be any fighting or enslavement. The half-giants had already claimed the west, so Deuca led his people to this valley and built his city on pyramids to provide protection from the receding seas."

"Rahn helped, of course," the brother said.

"Rahn didn't live that long," Suri said.

"Who was Rahn?" I asked as we walked toward the museum set in the exact center of the mall.

"You walked across his grave in Mestre," Suri said. "Rahn and Deuca were close friends."

The museum entrance was shaded by fig trees in raised earthen planters. We joined a queue of noisy visitors crowding the portico. Suri pressed up against me. An invisible hand grabbed the top of my head and slid me back an inch.

"Watch your proximity, mister," Aizah's disembodied voice whispered in my ear. "You aren't married yet."

"Where are you?" I whispered.

"I'm grappled to the ceiling. I'll be here when you want me and especially when you don't. Have a nice day."

Inside, the museum officials greeted us like dignitaries and escorted us to the main attraction: an ornate case that held pieces of Deuca's ship. Projections overhead showed carvings on the fragments made by Deuca. The line to the exhibition was long. Despite the official's insistence that we could go to the head of the line, Suri and I and our entourage of siblings quietly took our place at the end. When it was our turn, a guard opened one of the cases and let Suri and I touch the blackened pieces of wood.

"I didn't know people were allowed to do this," Suri whispered.

"Judging from the crowd's reaction, I'm betting they aren't."

The museum officials closed the case. An official with oriental eyes and snow white hair explained in perfect Engel that the fragments predated a flood that covered the Earth, ending the First Age. So there it was. I'd touched Noah's Ark.

As much as I wanted to believe, it was still hard to. Two hundred years of concerted effort during my age to turn the Noah story into a myth had taken its toll.

A large exhibit displayed a section of storage holds and the family quarters.

"Is this real or a reproduction?" I asked.

"It's real," Suri said. "It took decades to move it."

On the wall was an animated three-dimensional schematic of the ark. The design of the ship was not what I'd learned as a kid: a cute curvy boat with a house on top and a giraffe sticking its head out of a porthole. The ark looked more like a double-wide super-tanker, minus the bridge. The long low hull was completely sealed with no windows or protrusions along its sides. There was one fortified window and one very thick door set in the middle of the flat bow.

The white-haired guide explained the design. Inside, large water tanks flanked both sides of the door, fitted with filtration systems to process waste and replenish stock from seawater. Air reprocessing machinery supplied the five decks. Seed and embryo storage units floated within bubbles filled with shock-absorbing gel. The weather deck had a twelve-inch-thick tarpaulin stretched over the gunwale and secured above the waterline. Long, wide, and low, the ship looked like a black-lidded coffin.

"But where did all the water come from that caused the flood?" I asked as the animation ended and a model of the landing site lit up beyond the view screen.

"Legend says from space, but no one can prove it." Suri pointed to the rotating model of rolling hills and ice-capped mountains. A tiny dot blinked on the south face of a smallish mountain, about two-thirds up from the base. "Deuca and his family ran aground in southern Magog. A museum is built over the site. What's left of the ark is carefully preserved, as are the excavations of Deuca's village and vineyard." She pointed to six impact craters in a valley near the west end of the model. "And that's where Rahn landed. A little north of the city."

"Landed?" I said.

That afternoon, we picnicked on the shore of the Io Sea, much to the relief of Suri's brother. He happily introduced me to the sport of water skating, the equivalent of water skiing, except I wore a thin film on the bottom of my feet instead of skis, had no tow rope, and was propelled across rough water ten times faster than a sane person would attempt. Suri's brother neglected to cover certain details before launching me onto the lake, like how to stop. I broadsided a pleasure raft a quarter-mile from the beach. Fortunately, Javan clothing dries quickly and civilian heal sticks do wonders on sprained wrists.

Once I got the hang of imitating Jesus on water without flailing my arms and landing on my butt, I advanced to shuffling, then gliding, and finally following Suri's eager siblings as they raced, somersaulted, and generally pounded each other around a marked course, all to the amusement of a gathering beach crowd. I tried the jumps with Suri's brother. She watched from the shore with her hands plastered over her eyes. They were still covered when her brother fished me out of the reeds.

That evening, we drove east into the foothills of the Acropolis mountain range. The old part of the city hugged its ancient flanks. We flew through winding streets and worn masonry buildings anchored atop tightly spaced stone terraces that cascaded down the slopes. The cliffs of the Acropolis towered so close, I could have thrown a rock at them. Lush trees shaded the terraced buildings. Fast streams tumbled beside cobblestone streets and rushed under gracefully arched bridges. We landed in the middle of a busy plaza that had the feel of the Montmartre of Paris, surrounded by the stately shops of the Convent Gardens of London. Artists painted, sculpted, and wove by hand. Vendors called to folks to check out their wares. Comedians and mimes entertained clusters of tourists. Live music played from storefronts and balconies. A troupe of dancers dressed in what appeared to be traditional garb performed for a crowd. They whirled in two, intricate loops using pairs of sticks to lightly tap other dancer's sticks as their paths intersected. A tour guide wearing a brightly colored scarf led a discussion with a group of attentive children in front of impressive fountains spraying thirty feet into the air before a montage of towering sculptures. Plato had described ancient Athens as being an incredibly advanced country, her capital full of fountains fed by mountainous springs. I was convinced that Josephus's Javan was Plato's Athens.

The buildings appeared very old, built of stone with sloped facades that made them bottom heavy and stable during earthquakes. Entrances and stairs were five distinct sizes, side by side. People ranging from knee-high to flagpole navigated the town with ease. The smaller people generally stuck to the upper terraces to avoid getting trampled on. They crossed streets via bridges between balconies. Even the Nephillim could enter ground floors, which were colonnaded high enough to prevent a twenty-foot person from banging their forehead. Traffic maintained a cruising height of fifty feet as pedestrians wormed though the narrow side streets, buying stuff from shop windows and terraces.

I was trying to understand a family of dwarves' soft, high-pitched English over the din of the music when it happened. The flying traffic came to an abrupt halt. The music died and everyone looked up at flashing displays floating in the air.

Suri had drifted away to say hello to a cluster of admirers. Our eyes found each other and locked from across the square. Some kind of an announcement echoed off the buildings. A nearer version of the same announcement started, muddled by the echo. Then air car horns blared and tower bells rang. People cheered and hugged each other. Moms and dads rubbed noses with their kids. Dogs barked, cats meowed, and something hanging on the wall next to me croaked. People came pouring out of the buildings, into the streets.

I got separated from Suri and her brothers and sisters. The crowd pressed around but couldn't reach me. I jumped to see above their heads, but many tourists were eight feet or taller. The plaza was completely jammed but the mob didn't touch me. I had a five-foot perimeter around me. No matter how hard people pushed, their bodies came up against an invisible barrier.

"Aizah, you here?" I asked.

"Yes," her disembodied voice answered behind my left ear. Then she and half her squad materialized around me.

"What about Suri?" I shouted over the cheering.

Aizah had her glove to her ear, talking rapidly in Trahl to a floating mini-display of a worried Athena. The other half of our Guardian escort, led by Jarell, emerged from the crowd, depositing Suri within our perimeter. She was covered with confetti and crying. Diago was by her side, pulling bits of food out of her hair. Her sisters and brothers appeared, some cheering, some dazed.

I pushed through them to Suri's side. "Are you okay?"

She nodded and started to reply, but a huge gun fired off a volley of shots from the top of a tall building. The fusillade arched across the sky and exploded into multiple fireworks.

Civilian aircraft roared over the rooftops and barrel-rolled toward the sea. The crowd went nuts. Flower petals fluttered from rooftops like confetti. Suri's siblings jumped up and down, cheering, looking like they'd just won the lottery. The Guardians maintained the perimeter and stoically kept watch.

Suri threw her arms around me. "Isn't it wonderful?"

The crowd started chanting *'Shank-day, shank-day.'*

"What just happened?" I asked.

Suri answered but I couldn't hear her over the chanting. Sounded like she said I was older.

"What?" I yelled back.

She stood on tiptoes and yelled directly in my ear. "The war is over!"

Aizah and Jarell then bugged us out of the square, down a side street, into a taller section of the city. Jarell suggested a particular tower. Aizah gave it the once over and agreed.

"Where are we going?" I asked.

"Someplace quiet until things settle down," Aizah said. "The whole country is a bit delirious, if you haven't noticed."

We were ushered inside and taken up a lift, a circular platform that swooshed up a clear tube, past a dozen floors, depositing us in the foyer of a vast room. Metal doors stood at both ends. We hiked toward the door that was on the street side of the building. It opened to reveal a vast rainforest terrace with meandering paths and bubbling streams. Brightly colored birds huddled on branches with heads tucked under their wings. The lights and noise of the celebration far below echoed off the vine-covered ceiling.

Aizah nodded and the squad fanned out, scouring the thick growth with their helmet lights. Suri touched a flowering plant hanging from a branch and hid her mouth behind her hand. She was trying not to laugh.

"What's up?" I asked.

"I'll tell you later, *Na-hee*," she said.

Diago and two Guardians surrounded Suri and me, their backs to us, heads on swivel, mouths shut, and calm as cucumbers. Apparently, we were safe. We were celebrating the end of the war with Atlantis. I understood the need for caution. A stealthy enemy used chaotic opportunities as cover to strike.

Diago acted less like Suri's teen friend and more like a soldier. I wasn't sure I liked the change. The kid in him was fading. He seemed to be growing up fast for someone only fourteen decades old.

A few minutes later, Jarell returned. She retracted her helmet and talked quietly with Aizah.

"Do you understand what they're saying?" I asked.

Suri shook her head. "They're using a different dialect. Jarell wants something done to us here."

"Done to us?"

"Maybe she says done for us."

Their discussion suddenly turned heated. Jarell hissed a point and jabbed her finger in her palm. Aizah shook her head no, her long hair swishing.

"Whatever she's selling, Aizah isn't buying it," I whispered.

Jarell pleaded, said our names, said a sentence with Aaron's name in it, and pointed in our direction. Aizah looked at me. She actually seemed to soften, which, according to Aaron, required considerable effort for a Trahl.

Jarell urged something. The slightest of microscopic nod came from Aizah. They tapped each other's forearms and Aizah barked a command. The squad, including Diago, exited past Jarell and Aizah, fully buttoned up, weapons hot. Aizah and Jarell backed out through the heavy door, with Jarell smiling and Aizah not. We started to follow, but Jarell held up her glove.

"Where do you think you're going?" she asked.

"You're leaving us out here by ourselves?" I asked.

"It's a secure location. One door in and out. You'll be safe."

"We will be back in one hour," Aizah said.

"You agreed to two," Jarell said.

"An hour and a half," Aizah shot back.

"You said two," Jarell grumbled.

"Why?" I interjected.

Jarell checked the power setting on her weapon and slapped it into the aiming cradle on her forearm. "Because you kids haven't had a moment alone all day; not from relatives, crowds, and certainly not from invisible us."

Suri's hand slipped into mine. Jarell seemed to notice and continued, "You're getting married in a few weeks. Where I come from, couples spend months by themselves, talking things through, making plans, getting used to being together. You kids could use some time alone."

"It has been feeling a little crowded," I said.

"A little?" Suri exclaimed. Her free hand went to her mouth. She seemed as surprised by her outburst as I was.

Aizah's eyebrow arched. "I do not share my compatriot's enthusiasm for risking you to enemy exposure, no matter how remote."

Jarell moaned. "They'll be perfectly safe, sir. We're twelve stories up, with every rooftop covered and half of Athena's air force circling overhead."

"I didn't tell Athena we were doing this," Aizah said.

"She suggested the idea and gave me the location of this building. She knew you would be stubborn."

I shrugged. "Well, heck, if mom says it's okay."

"It isn't with me," Aizah said. "And I'm still in charge." She looked at Suri and sighed. "But, considering what you've been through and how little time you've had together …" She squared her armored shoulders. "We've extended our perimeter beyond this terrace and taken positions on all the surrounding buildings. We'll maintain that distance for the next hour and a half."

"Two hours," Jarell said.

Aizah rolled her eyes. "We will maintain surveillance of the area but leave the interior of the terrace unscanned. You will not be watched. Do you understand?"

"Understood," I said.

"This door will remain locked and guarded, preventing you from exiting and anyone from entering."

"Got it," I said.

She handed me a headset and what looked like a small weapons rod. "If at any time you feel yourself to be in any danger, hail me with this. She tapped the rod. "In the event of jamming, fire this into the air."

"Got it."

She pointed past my left shoulder. "Take cover in that corner of the garden. It is farthest from any penetration point. Are we clear?"

"Aye, Captain,"

"Do not joke with me, mister."

"Sorry."

"Don't get too close to the edge of the terrace. There's no railing to prevent you from falling. The nets will catch you, but then you'd be exposed. And don't—"

Suri took Aizah's glove, startling her. "We'll be careful. Thank you."

Aizah arched an eyebrow. "*Pros-sau-o, a-pros-sau-o.*"

Suri groaned and tried to shove Aizah back; but because she was armored, it was as effective as trying to push a truck.

Aizah smiled. "Back up, I'm securing the door."

After the door sealed, Suri and I clambered through the thick growth to the edge of the terrace. We were in the tallest tower on the street. The city undulated before us down to the sea, shimmering lights and bursts of fireworks illuminating the underside of the massive tree. Better than seeing Paris from the Sacré-Cœur.

"Why were you laughing about that flower?" I asked.

"You mean this one?" She picked a bloom hanging from a branch.

"Yes."

"Maidens pick it for boys they like. Smell."

I took a sniff. My heart started pounding and everything got brighter, especially Suri's face.

"What do you think?"

I tried to keep my knees from buckling. "Is something supposed to happen?"

She smiled slyly. "It's supposed to make you want to rub noses with me."

"Really?"

"Isn't it working?"

"I guess so."

Her face fell. "You can't tell?"

"No, because I've been wanting to nose you all day."

She threw her arms around me. I lifted her in the air and we had ourselves a nice slow nose rub, followed by an even longer Trahl kiss. We found a smooth stone with two wear spots indicating that it had been used by couples many times before, probably for centuries. We took our shoes off and sat with our toes dangling in the air. Suri's free hand explored my chest.

"Alone at last," I said.

Three Guardians appeared on the roof opposite our vantage point. Diago waved and we waved back.

"We could move back into the garden where they can't see," I said.

She leaned her head on my shoulder. "I don't care. The view from here is nice."

"What did Aizah say back there?"

"Back up. I am going to make the door locked."

"No, before that."

"Oh, *pros-sau-o, a-pros-sau-o.* It means good touch, bad touch."

"Have I been doing any bad touches?"

"Not yet." Her warm breath blew against my ear. "After we marry, we will spend a month alone on the mountain. Then every *pros-sau-o* is good."

"A month?"

"It's our sweet-month."

"Like a honeymoon?"

"That's a nicer word for it."

"A whole month alone together."

"Mmm."

"We can get away like that more than once."

"Of course. Every decade."

Every decade? I stared at my toes.

"What's wrong?"

"Nothing."

Her hand released mine. I felt her eyes fix on my profile. "Make it come out."

"You mean, out with it."

"Whatever."

I glanced at her. She looked as young as a college graduate. I looked back at my toes. A parade was starting down the street. "I don't know how many decades I get to live. What if my body keeps aging like it did in the Fourth Age?"

"You don't know if that's true or not."

"If it is, I'll be dead in four decades, five tops."

"Impossible."

"You'll be a widow for, what, seven hundred years?"

Suri didn't say anything. I felt her breath near my shoulder. The parade was in full gear. Musicians and floats wove slowly down the ancient boulevard. The glowing colors winked in and out between my toes.

"I love you, Jordan, son of Wright," she said. "I will love you for five decades. I will love you for seventy decades." Her hand reached up around my shoulders. "I will love you forever."

"Me, too."

She turned my face toward hers and we kissed for a very long time. Large bands filled the street twelve stories below our entangled feet. Wind and string instruments, punctuated by the pounding of huge drums, heralded its progress. The parade wound along the center part of the street like a sinuous Chinese dragon. The reveling crowd eddied against its undulating flanks. Traffic had stopped completely. Lines of air cars hung against the buildings on anchor cables so they could shut off their lights and watch the parade. Others landed on rooftops. Families jumped out and children skipped to viewing balconies to watch the fireworks. Somewhere up there, our cloaked Guardians might be having a collective cow.

"Oh look," Suri exclaimed. "They're bringing out the big lanterns."

What she called lanterns were blimp-sized illuminated balloons. They floated down the street, pulled on long ropes by legions of revelers. Some of the balloons were in the shape of animals. Others were important historical figures, according to Suri. She pointed out a floating Deuca. There were children-themed characters, too, smiling long necks, and comical turtles.

"I was Becca's age the last time I saw the Parade of Lights," she said. "Just before I moved to Mestre. Oh, this is wonderful. I missed the lanterns so much."

The turtle rotated on its side and gave us a big painted grin. A wave of sadness hit me.

No, not now. Not here.

I fought the flashback but it was too strong. I could almost hear the Sesame Street ring tone from my cell, a call from my daughter; Sophie's little voice telling me about the Snoopy balloon breaking free during the Macy's Day Parade and bumping into all the buildings; Lisa's panicked voice telling me to come home *now*; my car feeling like it had molasses for tires when I'd floored it. Police lights flashing on the corner house. Cops walking all over my lawn. EMT's with their empty stretchers. The hospital. The morgue. The funeral.

Suri had both arms around me. I hung on to her, anchoring myself here to get away from *there*. The images cascaded in a ceaseless torrent.

Her embrace was oak-solid. My heart steadied. The images blurred and receded. Tears fell off my face and landed on her wrist. Suri restrained me as a nurse at a psyche ward would have and somehow moved me several feet back from the terrace edge. Must have worried I was going to fall or jump. She wiped the sweat off my brow with her sleeve. Slowly, the flashback slithered into its hole and she relaxed her grip.

"Better?"

"Getting there."

"Athena said you would have these." She stroked the back of my neck. "A memory she couldn't smooth."

I leaned forward and panted between my knees. "Flashback."

Back in Tevleh, we'd been chased by Atlantean walkers, driven high into the mountains and caught in a blizzard. We'd dug a snow cave and rode out the storm. Sometime during that long night, I'd opened up to her about the deaths of my wife and daughter. She'd been cautious with questions, letting me skirt around the nightmare. This time, she gently but firmly coaxed every detail out.

The parade drummed beyond the terrace edge. The crowd cheered. People sang from nearby rooftops. Their jubilation framed my monotone description of my family's murder like a lush field bounding the edges of a smoking bomb crater. I felt the pain ease. Suri's flowered hair swept past my face as she brushed it behind her ear. Her swollen eyes crinkled in an exhausted smile.

We nose rubbed, then kissed. We held each other long after the parade faded. An oversized firefly buzzed our heads.

"Sorry about all that," I said.

"Feeling better?"

"Yes."

"Good."

"This was quite a night," I said.

"Want to do it again tomorrow?"

I choked back a laugh and was about to say something I hoped was witty when the terrace door burst open.

"You kids okay in here?" Aizah asked, her voice edged with worry.

"We're fine," Suri said, annoyed.

The glowing weapon rod on Aizah's forearm made a swift arc as she waved us toward the door. "Time's up."

Suri and I stood outside her cottage. An orange moon hung beneath the great canopy of the village tree, blurred by passing mists. Dawn threaded the ridge of the Acropolis. Her brothers and sisters bade us a sleepy good night. I leaned in for a good night kiss and Suri's lips parted. Her head tilted to miss my nose. My mouth came in for a landing.

Aizah materialized beside us. "You are nuts, Ground Com. Under no circumstances will I let them return to Mestre."

Suri sighed and we drew apart. Aizah's helmet retracted. Her long mane cascaded in place against her armor. A man's face floated six inches from her left eye. He looked just as angry.

"That's the stupidest idea Odin has had yet," she snarled at the face. "You tell him it isn't happening."

"You mind, Aizah?" I said. "I'm trying to say good night

here."

Aizah held up an armored hand, her eyes locked on the display. She argued with the man, then pounded a nearby trunk and sank her fist six inches into the wood. "I'll do it *only* if they agree … Has your brain gone silver already? Of course, I'm taking my team. I run this mission, not Odin. I don't care how sorry they are … As soon as the Ra signs that stupid scroll, they come home, not a second later … I don't know what they're going to say. Unlike you corpses, I don't manipulate civilians … Did I mention they're standing right here … Yes, they're listening. And growing more suspicious by the second, I might add … Would you care to explain that to them? I didn't think so … Then go slink back to Odin and complain … How should I know? I'll tell you their answer when they're ready to give it, *confirmed*?" She swung a fist at the display. The infuriated man's image dissolved before she hit it. She pounded the trunk again. "*Ic … lagdette … dwaes … fore-tadtva.*"

"That's a really old tree, Aizah," Suri said.

Aizah stopped and swept her hair back over her shoulders. "So it is."

"What's going on?" I asked.

She yanked a six-inch splinter out of her glove. "Atlantis is requesting a peace treaty with Javan."

"That's a good thing, right?"

"The treaty will be signed in Mestre at the Ra's palace. Numu has specifically requested her Highness to be included in the Javan delegation."

"No way," I said.

"Why?" Suri asked.

"The new government of Atlantis wishes to apologize to you in person for the ill treatment you suffered at the hands of the former queen. Amon also wants to apologize and offer his blessing on your marriage to Jordan."

"Tell him to send a card," I said.

"Amon said that?" Suri asked.

"According to Numu, yes. The Ra plans to thank you for your contributions to Mestre as princess during the signing. Odin believes the gesture of your attendance would be helpful for repairing relations between Mestre and Javan."

"What's Athena think?" I asked.

"She's willing to support whatever Suri decides."

"This smells worse than that sewage lake," I said.

Aizah frowned. "The Ra wants Atlantis to know they can't pry his nation away from the Eastern Alliance like they did with Phut. The Princess's attendance at the signing would be a symbol of the unshakable Javan/Mestre alliance."

"Nice words," I said. "Numu's?"

"Of course."

"It stinks."

"Confirmed."

Suri and I looked at each other.

"They can't force you," Aizah said. "Athena and I won't let them."

"Amon wants to apologize." Suri said. "I can't spurn his request."

"What if he's lying?" I said.

"What if he's not?"

"I'm coming with you."

"I want you to."

I looked at Aizah. "Will she be safe?"

Aizah's face hardened. "I'll shoot the appendages off anybody suspicious."

Suri gasped.

"What?" Aizah asked. "They grow back."

Olympus took up station over the falls. Suri and I transferred to the Palace via Athena's heaviest transport, with four escorts bracketing us in diamond formation as we swept across the Iterah River, ancestor to the Nile. The deck of the transport was fitted with portholes, affording a rolling view of the turbulent waterway as we approached the Ra's Palace. Late morning light cast long shadows from the summit, into the city below. Ornate fountains gushed silvery water and brightly attired crowds milled about landscaped walks, while flags fluttered south in a stiff breeze.

A trio of Nephillim battle-mountains held their positions above the city west of the palace, their hanging gardens undulating beneath the massive crags, each profile unique. Their bows faced east, as if Ra's Palace had three enormous arrowheads pointed at it. Their combined air screens buzzed the skies like African bees, their contrails creating a basket-weave pattern in the sky. Fighter wings flashed sunlight as they orbited the city. I wondered what powered them; certainly not big long wires dragging the ground.

We descended smoothly through the contrails and the city burst into full view. Military hardware glinted at checkpoints, snarling civilian traffic. Armored Mestrean units surrounded the base of the royal plateau. The main landing zone was crowded with aircraft of every imaginable shape and color. Diago sat behind us. He pointed out the different types and tried to explain their capabilities. Suri didn't seem interested in helping to translate. She stared out over the city. Best let her be, I figured.

I marveled at the sleek designs. Just one of these machines in the hands of a third world country in my time would catapult them to a world power. Walking anti-air defense systems clanked over, squatted, and tracked our little ship as we hover-taxied to a designated landing pad.

"A lot of firepower for a peace ceremony," I said.

"Mmm," Suri replied. She looked nervous.

I set my own uncertainties aside. Protecting her became my focus. Having armor and firepower would have helped, but lacking it didn't diminish my resolve.

Aizah's squad surrounded Suri and me before we deplaned. They closed ranks so tight I got brush burns from Jarell's armor. Their weapons were sheathed, mounted on shoulders and thighs. Helmets were open.

Aizah moved to the armored porthole of the hatch. Mestrean Guardians floated steps up to our aircraft. A cloud of flower petals fluttered to the pavement, all the way to the palace entrance. Thousands of people crowded behind barricades, which were held in check by gleaming Mestrean Guardians. I wondered how many folks considered Suri a traitor for bugging out on Amon and renouncing the throne. What would they do when the door opened?

Her hand clenched mine.

"It's okay," I whispered.

She nodded rapidly as if trying to convince herself of that.

Aizah turned and locked eyes with me. "You *will* stay in the middle of my squad."

"Yes," I said.

Her eyes darted between Suri and me. "Is that understood?"

"I heard you," Suri said.

"I don't care if the Creator himself reaches out to greet you; you stay inside our formation," Aizah insisted. "No contact with the crowd. Guardians, prepare to move out."

Helmets slapped into place. Aizah left hers open. Probably to yell at us if we did anything stupid. The hatch swung open. Suri stiffened and locked her arm around mine, while two Javan Darts hovered into position over the stairs.

The crowd erupted into cheers, waving wildly. Banners unfurled above the barricades with Suri's picture on them. The Mestrean Guardians had a hard time keeping the fences in place. Aizah talked rapidly into her helmet rim. Four of our Guardians hurried down the steps and fanned out, their helmets pivoting as they surveyed the crowd. Folks chanted Suri's name like a rock star.

"I think they like you," I yelled over the uproar. She wiped her eyes. I handed her a handkerchief.

Aizah hustled us down the steps. Bouquets arched over the barricade and landed on the path. Suri scooped one up and shyly waved. The crowd went nuts.

An hour later, we entered the throne room. It was packed with glittering dignitaries and bodybuilding security types, all who seemed to regard our arrival without much interest. It didn't feel at all safe. My inner voice was screaming at me to stay alert. Aizah kept a sharp eye on our formation. It was difficult to see past our Guardians' shoulders and helmets. Their weapons weren't blinking but I could feel the heat from Jarell's when it brushed my leg. Diago had filled me in on what was supposed to go down. We were to approach the throne. Guardians would give a silent salute and politicians would make speeches. Then Suri would mount the steps so Amon could apologize. Ra would bless our betrothal and sign the peace treaty. After that, we'd go home and I'd patch things up with Suri. What actually happened wasn't even close to that.

Aizah's squad slowed and she barked an order. They halted dead center in front of the throne and slammed their left boots against their right, making quite the echo through the chamber. The dignitaries in fancy robes and jewels were startled and shut up. Aizah clipped off a command. Her squad expertly changed formation, a kind of peel-apart into a half circle that SEALs don't drill. The formation kept Suri and I screened from the crowd, while allowing us to view the royals seated on the platform in ancient thrones. Aizah was one step in front of Suri and half a step to the right. Jarell was to my left, providing similar cover. Numu was planted left of the Ra. He looked like he'd added another chin to his neck collection. I fantasized aiming Jarell's shoulder weapon at his receding forehead and hitting the fire button.

A line of Mestrean Guardians faced us at the base of the platform. Both groups opened their helmets, revealing chiseled and youthful faces. Eyes front, the men and women shouted, *"Shank-day S'WEST."*

The startled look on Numu's face and the royals sitting on thrones told me something unscripted had just happened. Mestrean and Javan Guardians snapped palms to their chests and together shouted, *"Ell Ahbl AZIN."*

A Mestrean with shiny metals draped around his neck stepped forward. I recognized him from the pyramid standoff, Levi's friend. He saluted Aizah, slamming his flat palm across his chest, then snapped it forty-five degrees to his chin. Diago had tried to demonstrate that extra piece of the salute on the raft and almost got his arm torn off by Aaron. It was an officer-to-officer salute, rendered between battlefield veterans who'd shown exceptional courage. Guess Aizah's actions to save Suri in Tevleh, particularly the standoff under the glacier, had made a splash with the brass. It was a high honor for her.

She returned the salute with swift precision. I noticed the royals squirm and Numu turn red. Amon looked like he needed a potty break. The Ra stared down on the affair with a granite expression. These Mestreans were sending some kind of message to their superiors; but, apparently, larger concerns restrained the Ra from reacting to this unwelcome display of espirit de corps between Javan and Mestrean Guardians.

The revision to the politicians' speeches was even better. The Ra stood up, looking rabulous. The man was tall, verging on Ephraim height. Had to be pushing eight and a half feet, from his big toe to the gleaming thing on his head. He started into a preamble that I couldn't understand and nobody dared to translate while His Shininess spoke. Even he didn't seem interested in what he was saying. He went on and on and then got to a good part. Amon's face paled. Ra included Suri's name a couple of times, forcing a smile each time. He looked at me but the name Jordan never left his lips. Maybe he did mention me, but instead of my name, he might have used Suri's Betrothed or Nile Alligator Bait. Then he waved his important looking staff at Amon and said something sad and compassionate. Amon listened and nodded with a puppy dog face. It was apology time for the jilted prince. Were his eyes tearing up? Give me a break.

Ra nodded and Amon shuffled forward. Ra motioned Suri. She squeezed my hand. "Be back in a second."

"Smack Amon for me."

"Hush!"

The Mestrean Guardian who'd saluted Aizah pivoted to make way and nodded in respect as Suri glided past him and up the steps. Her blond hair swayed behind her flowing white dress. She shined like an angel before the backdrop of glittering royalty, especially when she turned to face Amon. She bowed and touched her chin in greeting. Amon coughed, looked her in the eye, and fled.

The place went berserk. Numu chased Amon to a portal and recoiled when Amon slammed the door shut. Numu's belly impacted with the heavy oak door before his face could. Everybody shouted at everyone. Aizah bugged us out during the commotion. We were halfway to our hovering motorcade before a pair of wheezing officials caught up and did a begging routine. Aizah ignored them. They pleaded even more. She ignored them again. Then she got a phone call on her helmet. The officials bent over their knees, panting, while Aizah argued into her chin display.

"Who's she talking to?" I asked.

"Don't know," Suri said.

"What happened back there?"

"Amon started to say he was sorry and then just ran away."

"Saw that part. Why did he run?"

"I guess he was sad that he hurt me."

"Yeah, right. He's mad because he can't have you."

"You make it sound as though he wished to control me."

"Of course he did."

"Jordan!"

"It's the truth."

"He cared about me."

"He doesn't give a flying squirrel about you."

"Whatever that means, it's not true."

"He wants to be the big bad prince and have you fawning all over him while he gives orders."

"Amon cares about me."

"About as much as Numu does,"

"Numu's the reason Amon became heir to the throne. He taught Amon everything he needed to beat his rivals. Numu cares deeply for him. He cares about me. Amon and I would have never had a chance at royalty without his help."

"Numu's a snake," I said.

"A what?"

Aizah interrupted us. She looked mad enough to spit nails. "Ground Com is ordering us back to the palace."

"Suri's not going back into that throne room," I said.

"I can make my own choices," Suri said.

"That throne room is too exposed," I said. "You're not going back in there."

"It sounds like now you wish to control me."

"Ground Com says we're not returning to the throne room," Aizah said. "Numu is offering an arrangement that lets the Ra save face in front of the Atlanteans without risking further public embarrassment by the prince. He suggests Suri visit the prince in his apartment. He will deliver his apology to her with the Royal Family as witnesses."

"Security?" I said.

"Same as the throne room."

"I don't like it."

"I don't either," Aizah said.

"The Prince's apartment is safe." Suri said. "I've been there many times."

"Doing what?" I blurted.

She looked confused. "State dinners, dancing at balls, attending court."

In other words, it was a downsized version of the Ra's palace, not a three-room bachelor pad with an intimate dinner for two.

Aizah was back on her helmet phone, arguing with three floating faces: Athena, Odin, and Numu. She was as concerned about Suri's safety as I was. Numu's shrill voice shouted in the background. Aizah put the hovering images on hold, which was interesting because Numu's face froze in mid-shout with his tongue lolling.

She gave me a raised eyebrow. "The Ra is very put out. Ground Com strongly suggests we agree to this condition."

"What does Athena think?"

"She counsels that it would be better if this treaty were ratified with Atlantis without any strain between Javan and Mestre. She got Numu to agree to full Javan air cover around the Prince's apartment."

Suri sighed.

"You're mad," I said.

"You treat Amon as if he wants to harm me."

"Because the whole thing doesn't make sense. All this risk for a meaningless apology."

"You don't think he's sorry?"

"Of course he isn't."

"You're calling him a liar."

"Yes."

"You barely know him."

"I know him well enough."

"I grew up with him."

I felt the stares of everyone on us. "That's not my point."

"What is your point?"

"It's a stupid Mestrean ceremony. It doesn't accomplish anything."

"I grew up Mestrean. Does that make me stupid, too?"

"Suri, I didn't mean—"

She turned her back on me and looked at Aizah. "I'm going. We need this treaty."

They fed us at the palace in a private dining area overlooking a small orchard, probably to give Amon time to pull himself together. By late afternoon, officials arrived and we were conveyed to the Prince's Palace. It lay south of the city on an island in the middle of the river. Suri and I had lots of time to ride and not speak. The silence was killing me.

The convoy sped over the rolling river, dodged raft traffic, and docked beneath swaying palms, all under the watchful eyes of pivoting guns. We walked to the foot of a three-tiered gate flanked by crouching silver lions on alabaster pedestals. Mestrean Guardians stood watch upon bannered ramparts. Their uniforms were polished armor draped with lion skins. Almond-colored manes framed their grim faces. Maybe they thought they looked regal. Perhaps the royals dressed them up like dolls. I thought they looked ridiculous.

"Are those real pelts?" I asked.

"Of course not," Suri said.

The Guardians snapped to attention, rendering a loud salute across their chests as we passed.

"The manes were Amon's idea, I bet."

Suri let go of my hand.

What was eating her? Did she feel sorry for him? Or was she nervous about seeing him? Maybe she was worried about getting out of here. Probably something my knuckle-scraping brain couldn't register.

Numu's bald head emerged from the shadows of an arch at the far end of a vast courtyard. Suri gripped my hand as he made a bee-line for us, a plastic smile affixed to his rubber face. Aizah and Jarell positioned themselves in his path. Numu slowed his gait, his smile listing starboard. He seemed to consider his chances of survival, then navigated his girth between the armored Guardians. Bless their sweet shoulder missiles, I've got to learn how to test fire one of those things.

Numu bowed to Suri. "Thank you for coming, dear Princess."

"She's not a princess anymore," I said.

Suri's full length gown concealed her heel as she stomped my toe.

Numu's smile didn't waver as he tilted back upright. "She will always be a princess of Mestre to us."

"Thank you, Ambassador," Suri said. "Where is Amon?"

"Awaiting you in his apartment, as we discussed." Numu pivoted his rotundness and got under way. "Follow me."

CHAPTER THIRTY-SEVEN
LEVI

Apollo's sleek ship sliced through low altitude clouds. I hailed Ground Com a dozen times on multiple gravity settings and finally got a rippled image of a Ground Com controller but no audio. I scrolled my message to him. His eyes followed my words as they climbed up the right side of the screen.

Where are Suri and Jordan? I sent.

... *Mestre to attend* ... Wild static flooded the display, obliterating the rest of his response.

"We're being tracked through the transmission," Apollo warned.

I chinned the rim control to cut the link.

"Athena, why did you let them go to Mestre," Apollo grumbled as he dodged snow-capped mountain peaks.

"Should have snatched that sniveling prince and hung him upside down from *Olympus*," Aaron said. "He would have apologized fast enough."

I wanted to rise to my adopted mother's defense but I was too busy trying to reach Aizah. When I made contact, her response was disturbing.

"Everything is under control," her lips mouthed and gave me a thumbs up. Jarell smiled behind her.

Aaron grunted as a duplicate image of Aizah faded from his

open helmet.

"Something bothering you?" I asked.

"The chances of seeing that pair smiling at the same time are smaller than me getting married, Chief."

Apollo threw the ship into a long curve. "Definitely trouble."

"How fast can we get there?" I asked.

"Not fast enough," Apollo said. He fooled with some floating displays. The center blinked red and a panel in the deck whisked open. Wind whistled through the cavity. Two lethal looking missiles lay in twin launch cradles. He retracted them into a storage hold, leaving the cradles empty.

"You can get there faster if you don't mind becoming human missiles," he shouted over the wind.

"Why would we mind?"

Aaron leaped into the slot almost as fast as I did. We lay face-down with our arms tight to our sides and toes pointed.

"Always wanted to try this," Aaron said.

"Good luck," Apollo waved. "This might max out your armor, so be careful."

"Define careful," Aaron said. "Wait, don't."

I slammed my helmet shut. The deck sealed above my face.

"I'll catch up …" Apollo sent over my com unit.

The launch shoved me so hard my life support failed. I was long past worrying about dying. I held my breath and waited as I hurtled through layers of cumulus cloud banks. Several gut-wrenching seconds later, the system repaired itself. I'd live but my com unit and external weapons were nonfunctioning and their repair systems were not responding. My com unit was operational but there was no link from Aaron. This left me without any idea of his location or condition.

My body buffeted and twisted, skirting mountain peaks and hugging valley floors with hair-splitting precision. Apollo must be flying my suit from his ship. He seemed to enjoy showing off his skills a little too much. I prayed Aaron was still with me somewhere.

CHAPTER THIRTY-EIGHT

JORDAN

We were escorted by Numu down an elegantly mirrored hall, past a double line of Mestrean Guardians with their fake lion skins over their armor. Aizah and Jarell had their helmets open. Images of Athena floated to one side of their chin rims. Intermittent conversations were going on between the three of them. If I knew enough Javan, I'd be able to read their lips. Probably feeding Athena a play by play.

We came to a set of carved wooden doors as tall as an aircraft hangar. I was trying to keep my cool, but everything felt wrong. I felt like we were walking into a trap.

The doors swung on massive bronze pivots without a sound. Numu bowed and waved us through. The doors shut silently behind us. Before us stretched an art gallery as deep as a football field. Most of the statues were of Amon; at least I thought they were. Some parts were exaggerated. I hoped.

"Which way to his apartment?" I asked.

"You're standing in it," Suri said.

Numu smiled and pointed a chubby finger toward an ornate doorway. "The meeting will take place in the south study."

Amon's apartment had more rooms than Versailles. Did Suri really want to give all this up? What did I have to offer her? Forty years in a cottage and she'd be a widow for seven hundred more.

Everyone moved forward except me. Suri looked back. Her hands went to her hips. "Wheels are turning in your head."

"You've got to trust me. This isn't safe."

"I've been here a thousand times. We're in no danger."

"My gut tells me differently."

"Maybe you should consider marrying your gut." She stomped off after Numu and the others. Diago lingered beside me.

"Guess that means she's okay with this," I said.

"Sorry, I don't understand."

"Still working on the Engel?"

"Sorry?"

"Danger," I said. "Uh, what's the word? Dang. Farell. Fart."

"Farlii?" he said.

"Yes." I indicated the whole place. *"Farlii."*

"I know."

"You be ready."

"Yes."

Diago and I caught up to the group. They were milling about in an airy room filled with bookshelves. A bank of tall windows opened out onto a wide garden with a reflecting pool in the middle. Suri and Amon sat on a cushioned window seat, talking like best buds. They were even laughing.

Suri turned to me and her smile faded. She motioned me to join her, them, whatever. Diago looked worried. He said something to Aizah. She casually waved him off.

Something was definitely wrong. Aizah was too relaxed. Come to think of it, so were the rest of the Guardians. They were too far from Suri. And why weren't there any Mestrean Guardians here? Were the Javan aircraft on station outside?

"Set phasers on stun, Scottie," I muttered as I approached the chuckling couple.

"Amon apologized," Suri said. "Everything is good."

"That's nice."

Amon stood, giving me a condescending smile. "No hard feelings." He extended his hand as if to shake mine.

I took it. "None."

Our hands remained locked in a fierce grip. Amon tried to match my tightening hold. He smiled calmly as a bead of sweat rolled off his nose. Suri coughed, ending the testosterone contest. Numu bulled his way between us, forcing a drink into my hand.

"His Highness wishes to apologize to you, also," Numu said.

"Why is there no security in this room?" I asked, pouring the drink into a nearby plant. Diago smirked.

"Jordan!" Suri scolded.

"Mestrean Guardians are not allowed in my chambers for the sake of privacy," Amon said in perfect Engel. Then he rattled off a long sentence in Mestrean to Suri and Numu, I guess to show off his ancient multilingual skills. They all had a good laugh. Yeah, just give me a couple more years and let's see who had more dead languages under their tunic.

Amon said something else, nodding at me. Suri said something back to him, looking a bit annoyed. He crossed his arms like a stubborn two-decade-old and jerked his head at me, as if she was supposed to hurry up and do something. Suri sighed and translated. "Amon says you should now apologize to him."

"For what?"

"He says you—"

A Javan Dart fell into the garden, crushing a fountain. Diago started to run to the window but froze in mid-stride. A bright blast shot through the window and knocked Numu off his feet. A second one hit Diago in the chest. The kid flipped backward head over heels. His leg weapon whipped through the air and bounced off the rear wall.

I lunged for Suri but something big and invisible punched me in the gut. I flew backward and slammed against a wall. Everything appeared in triplicate for a few seconds.

Suri screamed. I shook off the disorientation and tried to get back on my feet. Diago was down and I couldn't do anything for him. The other Guardians were immobilized in their armor, drinks motionless in their rigid hands, their helmets retracted. Their heads strained as they tried to move.

"Protect Suri," Aizah yelled.

As Amon was lifted into the air, I forced myself back onto my feet and staggered toward Suri. She was picked up by someone or something. The intruders must have been cloaked like Guardians.

I saw ripples in the air come at me. I ducked and felt the wind of something big swing over my head. A vase smashed off a table next to me, while Suri, Amon, and Numu were whisked out the window.

"Jordan!" Suri screamed.

I grabbed Diago's leg weapon, pounded it on the floor to get it glowing, and dove after them. I hit the dirt and rolled. Multiple shots shredded the curtains and busted the window into splinters. I landed behind what I hoped was a solid enough statue of Amon in repose.

CHAPTER THIRTY-NINE

LEVI

My systems were blind. No communication from Ground Com. Apollo directed me right through the roof of the royal residence, into a mirrored hall. Aaron landed beside me, a pile of plaster and roof tiles cascading off his armor.

"My systems are reading a power drain in the Prince's apartments," Aaron said.

"Mine, too. Protect your armor's power. Switch off your ground feed and go to internal reserves."

A Javan Dart dropped out of the sky and crashed somewhere beyond the palace roof. Shots fired. We sprinted down the empty hallway. When we rounded a corner, we saw the flash and spark of weapons fire through open doors.

CHAPTER FORTY

JORDAN

I peeked out from behind the statue's fat head and lined up on where I thought Suri's abductor might be most vulnerable. She was floating six feet off the ground. If he had her in a one-arm carry, that meant he was one of those twelve-foot half-giants.

The lawn was mashed where invisible boots thumped a path. I aimed for his leg but my shots missed. Wicked return fire drove me back behind the granite statue. The shots powdered and chipped it, but it otherwise held together.

I spotted another decent Amon statue to act as cover and dashed for it. Streamer fire pocked the ground as the shots chased my heels. I fired back as I dove behind the statue. I must have hit the goon because Suri suddenly dipped. She screamed and pounded her fists against something solid. I took aim for the other leg, watching the grass impressions of her abductor's footsteps.

Someone ripped the gun from my hands and knocked me sideways. I hit the statue hard. In a daze, I saw Numu's unconscious body bob past me. I tried to get up. Something smacked me hard to the pavement. Then invisible hands threw me over an invisible shoulder.

A ship emerged from the pool. It was visible for a short time while the water spilled off its flanks. Dripping steps extended from the hull. Amon was the first to be carried inside, then Suri. I kicked and clawed against the armor toting me afterward.

A shot struck the air near Numu. His abductor became visible. He was a thirteen-foot giant wearing the black and red dragon uniform I'd seen back in Atlantis' capital city. The giant toppled, waving his weapon wildly as he stumbled for the steps.

My captor hurried after him, pivoting once to fire back. I got a brief view of Levi and Aaron shoulder-rolling to dodge the shots, springing back to their feet and firing in response with perfect precision. My big guy went down hard and didn't move. The other giant blindly aimed at Levi and Aaron. He staggered and his weapon swung at me, going off.

Aaron leaped in front of me and took the shot in the chest. The impact knocked both of us into a heap. I rolled him off of me, grabbed one of his leg weapons, and crawled toward the ship. Its engines started up and I shot at the orange flames. The ship lumbered over the garden, picking up steam as it headed for the palm trees. Levi and a dozen Guardians with Javan Eagle insignias ran past me, firing all at once. Their shots bounced off its hull with no effect. The ship suddenly vanished in a ripple over the palm trees with the Javan air force in pursuit. I flung the weapon and yelled Suri's name into the empty sky.

A shadow appeared on the pavement next to me. A Guardian lifted her helmet. I didn't recognize her face.

"You are okay?" she asked with a thick accent.

"I'm fine, help him." I pointed at Aaron. His armor was smoking and looked inoperable. He was bleeding from the neck.

The female Guardian pulled out a heal stick and plunged it into his neck while I pressed on the wound. Soon, the green juice did its magic and the bleeding stopped. Other medics ran past us to help the others who'd fallen, while Guardians restrained the struggling giant who'd tried to abduct me. He stopped moving when Levi shoved a weapon's tube up his oversized nostril. To my relief, Diago stumbled out of the window, minus his armor, dazed. Aizah emerged without her armor as well and sprinted to Aaron, screaming his name.

I knelt on the spot where Suri had vanished. Hands touched

my shoulders.

"You okay?" Aaron asked.

I couldn't speak. Couldn't believe I'd lost her.

"Don't worry; we'll bring her back," Aizah said.

I rose to my feet and found my voice. "I'm going with you."

CHAPTER FORTY-ONE

LEVI

It was a bittersweet reunion at the Acropolis. Many teams were on the Tableland, a vast plateau set in the middle of the Acropolean Range, a thousand-mile limestone ridge that bisected Javan and stretched all the way to the Mestrean border. This was home to forty thousand men, women, and children who were the Guardians of Javan. We answered to no one but the Creator, which meant we lorded over no one and served anyone who was in need. Protect all; harm none. Our brethren to the south once shared this hallowed field. Now, a wall blocked the ancient road to their half of the Acropolis.

Aaron and I bunked with the other bachelors close to the practice fields that overlooked Deucalion. Suri's family had implored Jordan to stay with them. He'd politely turned them down. Athena assumed he would return to his apartment on *Olympus*, but she assumed wrong. There was only one thing on his mind: rescuing Suri. While I appreciated his focus, I was loath to risk a seasoned team and Suri's rescue by bringing an untested civilian along. But something tugged at me from within. Allowing Jordan on the Tableland was a concession to that urging.

Athena stationed *Olympus* over the Special Missions training field and barracks to shower Jordan with vitality treatments from her garden. I bunked him with Diago and the two trainees who'd run the salvage mission over Payahdon last season, where I'd discovered an ancient weapon of unknown origin. It had seemed alive, evil, and otherworldly. It was the only thing I had ever encountered in my miserably long life that frightened me. I still felt where it had attached itself to my chest, feeding off me during our escape from Atlantis. That feeling now grew stronger. I suspected it was in Phut, the same country I believed Suri and the Mestrean hostages were being held.

While Aaron and I stretched on the practice field, Diago and the other trainees followed Jordan through an unusual exercise routine. It included strenuous activity in one of the deep ponds. The healers analyzed it and pronounced the various exercises were beneficial. A sizable crowd of Guardian families stood along the far shore watching them pound through the water using an efficient hand/leg propulsion method I'd never seen before. Jordan called it freestyle.

"Any word yet from Phut?" Aaron asked between grunts as he pressed his forehead to his thigh.

"There are refugee rumors about something happening in an old harbor east of the capital. I dropped in a team yesterday. They scouted the docks. It was tough to get in close. A lot of military were guarding the harbor."

Jordan reached the edge of the pond first, flipped over in the water and shot in the opposite direction, cutting through the water even harder. He left all the other recruits in his wake.

"What did they learn?" Aaron asked.

"Fifty cargo rafts arrived yesterday morning. Phut insignia but Atlantean design. The pontoons were submerged deep, suggesting heavy cargo on board. This morning, the rafts floated thirty feet higher, pontoons breaching the waves."

"So? That happens when you off-load cargo. Light rafts ride high."

Jordan emerged from the water and sprinted across the field. He reached a tree, leapt, grabbed a branch, and began a rhythmic lifting of his body such that his face crested the top of the branch, using only his arms to pull himself up. Some of the Guardian children chased him. He was joined by Diago and the other recruits in short order. Diago found a neighboring branch and began making his chin go up.

"There's only one problem with that," I said as Jordan, Diago, and the other trainees dropped and carefully navigated their way through young admirers in their race back to the pond. "According to the team, nothing was off-loaded from the rafts during the night."

"That's weird."

"It becomes more alarming. Just before dawn, legion-strength Phut military boarded all the rafts, along with something else: a shrouded device of a curvilinear profile twenty-five-feet long. It floated all by itself, with nobody touching it."

"Was it the weapon?"

"The team observed the dock lights dimming as it floated down the gangway. The Phut soldiers escorting the container had a hard time walking beside it. One collapsed and had to be carried away. That thing was sucking the life out of everything near it. There's a cloaking field spread across the entire sea bed of the harbor. A military-grade power drain has been drawing from the Mestrean pyramids toward that harbor ever since."

"They were attack subs powering up."

"Or something like them."

"Why hasn't Ground Com hit them?"

"Suri's, Amon's, and Numu's life signs are coming from the formation."

"Atlantis is using them as shields. The Queen knows we won't attack if it means risking harm to them. Anak, what if she infected Suri already?"

"I don't think she would, not yet. Phut is on bad terms with Mestre. The Queen would have a hard time ordering Phut soldiers from Suri's body. Suri makes a better hostage at the moment. I'm guessing she's safe."

"Yeah, but not for long. We've got to move on this rescue."

"I briefed Athena on the situation."

"Get it past your teeth already. What did she say?"

"Our team launches in three days."

Aaron's gaze centered on Jordan and Diago practicing team hand and foot assaults designed to disable Ephraim at close range.

"I assume I'm on the mission," Aaron said.

"Confirmed."

"Aizah?"

"If you're okay with it."

"You think I'd try to say no? She'd disable me in my sleep."

"Understood."

We sparred hand to hand. Aaron threw me almost as many times I threw him. Then Aaron called time to catch his breath. His normal grin was gone. "What about Diago and Jordan?"

"The mission is too dangerous for trainees."

Aaron looked like he wanted to say something.

"What?" I asked.

"You know what."

"I have to decide what's best for the hostages and our team."

Aaron nodded at Jordan. "Good luck explaining that to him. I don't think anybody will volunteer to translate."

Jordan and the others ran along the palisades overlooking Deucalion. Jordan had them in a columned formation, chanting something in Engel.

I stood up, straightened my tunic, and rubbed the back of my neck. "I can't risk two dozen lives on a couple of trainees who aren't special mission tested."

"But Diago said Jordan served in some kind of military, doing things that might qualify."

"I can't risk a team on what someone claims they can do. Besides, he's emotionally compromised."

We took a break under an apple tree and watched the others finish their workout. They took a breather. Aizah and Jarell had joined them and were teasing Jordan. All the while, he was watching us and trying to be stealthy about it.

"Look at it this way, Chief. What if Aizah had been taken instead of Suri? Would you have kept me off the team?"

"There is no comparison. You're one of the best SMs on the Acropolis."

"Agreed, except for the *one of* part."

Jarell lay on her back, urging Diago to lean down. Aizah and Jordan cajoled him to agree. The crowd chanted Diago's name. He turned red and slowly brought his nose close to hers.

I bit into an apple and swallowed. "What's that all about?"

We joined the crowd. Jordan stood over Jarell and explained something while Diago maneuvered a smiling Jarell so her head was arched back and her lips were open. Aizah translated for those who didn't speak Engel.

"This is a technique to help an unconscious person resume breathing if you run out of heal sticks," she translated. "The same technique can also restart the heart."

Jordan directed Diago to pretend to push forcefully on Jarell's chest and breathe hard into her mouth in a rhythmic cadence. I linked a medical tech from Ground Com through my com unit and started recording. After Diago had demonstrated a few times and Jordan answered questions, the medical tech scrolled into my oculars.

"We just ran a simulation at the clinic. It works. This procedure could prove useful in an emergency."

Applause broke out. Jarell sat up and waved triumphantly to the crowd. Then she knocked Diago off his boots and gave him a Trahl kiss he'd probably remember the rest of his juvenile life.

Jordan spotted me. I nodded my approval. He snapped the appropriate salute and looked away.

"You think he can qualify before we launch?" I muttered to Aaron.

"Confirmed."

I thought hard. "He has two days to get through final weapons training. I'll test him on the third day."

"Which test?"

I bit into my apple. "Same one I gave you before your first mission."

Aaron's eyes went wide. "Anak."

CHAPTER FORTY-TWO

JORDAN

A team was assembled for Suri's rescue, including Jarell and several hardened veterans, mostly Levi's old squad from the Payahdon bug-out mission. There were slots open for two more. I upped my routine and soaked in all the training available for weapons. I attacked each new skill set, determined to master everything. Aaron didn't say much and Aizah said less.

Diago tried hard to keep up as the training intensified but he washed out. Man, did he throw a fit. Aizah walked him off the field, away from the smoldering walker he'd just wrecked, and gave him a dressing down out of earshot. The way he kept looking my way and then didn't so much as even try to stumble through Engel to explain left me with the strong hunch that I, too, had been one mistake away from washing out. I understood why. Rescuing Suri and the others without mishap was more important than who got to be on the team, no matter what the personal feelings of the applicants were.

The next day Levi approached me. His Engel had improved since we'd arrived on the Acropolis. Guess he found some time to study. "Armor up and meet me on the field in five minutes."

I suited up and hurried out to the field, where I found him waiting for me, along with the team he'd chosen for Suri's mission.

Aaron indicated that I should fall in behind Levi. When I did, we moved out.

Levi set the pace. We started running along a path following an undulating cliff overlooking the Javan capital. It was a long way to the bottom, at least a mile and a half straight down. About five miles into the run, Levi stopped and walked over to an apple tree. He picked one, took a bite, and threw the rest over the edge of the cliff.

"I dropped my apple," he said. "Get it."

I dove off the cliff headfirst. I had armor and a set of grapplers I'd been practicing with day and night. A lot of masonry had been chipped off some pretty important-looking temples the last two nights while I'd practiced diving.

I ticked off the seconds and searched for my target. I knew how to fall faster than terminal velocity from my SEAL jumping days, but I had a strong hunch simply surviving the drop wasn't going to qualify for a berth on this mission. Cloud cover was no excuse. Nothing mattered except finding that apple.

I willed it to appear. If the Almighty accepted that as a prayer for assistance, great; if not, no problem. I was too busy doing this task to worry about properly phrasing a divine intervention request.

There! Gotcha. The apple was directly below me.

I was running out of altitude. Sharp ragged peaks rushed toward me. I made a swipe. Something exploded above me. I got tossed off target. The fruit flew out of my grasp. I popped my helmet open and changed vectors, searching for the apple the old-fashioned way, using my eyes. I ripped past a nasty looking outcropping, then the rest of the jagged mess closed in.

CHAPTER FORTY-THREE

LEVI

I stood watch with the rest of the team on the edge of the cliff. A cloaked rescue Dart dove within grappling distance above Jordan the entire drop, ready to arrest his fall should he panic or abort. Then the impossible happened. The Dart struck an outcropping and flipped nose over tail before impacting in its own absorber gel. Jordon was thrown in its backwash and the apple blew out of his reach.

Jordan was too far away for us to rescue but we jumped anyway. The last few seconds ticked by. We had all jumped similar distances to know Jordan would hit the ground long before we'd be in grappling range. I lost his flailing body in the smoke from the crash. Too many seconds later, we plunged through the smoke.

"I'm sure he gave up chasing that apple, Chief." Aaron said. "Even if he hit the ground without the grappler slowing him, the suit would keep him alive."

"As long as he kept his helmet secured," I said. A sick feeling welled up within me. Jordan had the motivation of a desperate man.

"Found something," Jarell said.

I zoomed in with my oculars. Jordan's battered helmet lay on the edge of a lake in a city park. His locator was in the helmet. We had no means of tracking his body. He hadn't been cleared for implants yet.

We fired grapplers to arrest our drop and touched down, sending blue geese into a panicked flight. Aizah ran to the shoreline and picked up the helmet. She yelled and hurled it to the ground. It sparked and smoked. Tourists stared from a nearby orchestra shell. Then Jordan came around the back of the amphitheater. He was carrying a tray. On it lay my apple, surrounded by steaming beverages.

I examined the apple. It had my bite mark, plus one of his. He gave a long explanation I wasn't confident I'd heard accurately. Jarell chuckled.

"What are you laughing at?" I asked.

Jarell snapped to attention. "Sir, trainee apologizes for biting the apple, sir."

"What happened?"

"Trainee had to shove the apple in his mouth so he could laterally grapple with both arms and prevent damage to his armor."

"How did he fire laterally?"

"Sir, trainee fired one grappler at the cliff and the other at that building across the lake to arrest his fall ten feet before impact.

"Anak," Aaron grunted.

"Trainee relied on the grappler exoskeleton to absorb the lateral strain."

"He could have hit a window and caused severe casualties to the civilian population," I said.

"Yes sir. Trainee states he never misses."

"Tell him he'll have to work off the cost of a new helmet."

"Confirmed."

"Is that all?"

"No, sir. Trainee hopes we like our wine hot."

Aaron took the tray from Jordan.

"Team will take notice," I said.

Boots pounded the ground as everyone stood straight.

"It normally takes longer to be accepted within our ranks," I said. I carefully unfurled an applique of our nation's cherished symbol: the silver eagle. "But, given the character and abilities of the one before us, the brave acts of protection he carried out in Payahdon, Baskra, Mer, Tevleh, and Mestre—"

"And without wearing armor," Aaron shook his head. "You *rukta!*"

I waited until the chuckling quieted. "I believe it is appropriate to invite him into our ranks. I believe his addition will strengthen our ability to carry out the mission before us. What say you all?"

The team yelled *hoo-yah*, a phrase Jordan had shared with them during training. The meaning was strange; something about agreeing with what I'd said and willing to dive into an underground lake of eternal fire if we did not succeed.

"Very well, then," I said and applied the eagle to Jordan's armor. I pounded it once and we traded salutes.

Aaron shook his head. "That eagle doesn't look like it's on firm enough, Chief."

I pretended to examine my efforts. "Anak, I think you're right."

Jordan touched it gingerly as I nodded to the squad.

"Protect all!" Aizah yelled.

"Harm none!" they shouted.

In one mass, they pounced on Jordan. They carried him into the lake and beat on his armor until he begged for mercy.

CHAPTER FORTY-FOUR

SARAH

The long porch sheltered us as an afternoon cloudburst shed curtains of water off the eave. Its wash made the jungle a blur and the beach invisible. Krax, Kate, and Greg were at the far end of the porch playing cards. Some of the Javan refugees were watching. Many were gathered at Shamel's mansion. It had taken a lot of courage for them to come here. After what we'd been through, few of us lived near the ocean. But something had drawn us together. Even the ones we'd sent to watch over the digging by the Egyptians in Giza had a hard time staying there. They longed to come here and said so during video conferences. We didn't know what it was but we all described it the same way: a feeling that wished to grow into a thought.

The porch became clustered with people escaping the downpour. Becca taught some of the children sitting in a circle on the warm tile, while Liv-ya sat wedged between new friends, happily chatting away with other children.

"How's she doing?" I asked as we neared.

The clacking of toucans on a nearby branch distracted Laura from answering. Becca asked a question and Liv-ya leapt to her feet to answer.

"You can see," Laura said, "she is much happier."

"I heard Becca and her husband are going to adopt her."

Laura's hand tightened on my arm. "Good."

Liv-ya spotted us and darted over. Another little girl followed and stood beside her, holding hands.

"Krax taught us some new Engel words!" Liv-ya said, her eyes wide.

"English," I corrected. "They call it English here."

"Whatever," she said. "You want to hear them?"

Laura looked dubious but I nodded.

"Krax said that if I want to make somebody laugh, I can say this: Are you a smart feller?"

The other little girl grinned. "Or are you a fart smeller?"

"Um, feller is not proper English, sweetie," I said.

Laura jumped to her feet, muttering in her native Quechi. Then she called, "Michael Kraxman!"

He managed surprising speed out the terrace doors, hobbling on his cane.

CHAPTER FORTY-FIVE

LEVI

Donde-nay ouve iri Klappu ouve.
Those most lost are the longest sought,
—Rahn

We hid in the lower storage hull of a Phut sea fruit harvester. The captain was an old friend of mine with strong opinions against his country's change in loyalties. His stubby sailing raft fluttered in the stiff breeze, tacking westerly with the rest of his village's fleet over the predawn whitecaps. We were west of Mestre, deep inside Phut waters, a freshwater sea Jordan predicted would be a wasteland in his future age. Ironically, sea or desert, it would carry the same name: Sahara.

I had the team do a final gear check and ordered their helmets sealed. Then I went up to see the captain one last time. I nodded in greeting.

He pointed toward the bow, then shifted the double rudder to keep the sails trimmed. "We are close to the spot."

"You're certain?"

He nodded, pulling at his beard. "No deep sea melons could rip my nets like that. What you seek sleeps down there."

"Power generation from Mestre will cease in five minutes," I said.

"Fortunately, I own a sailing raft."

A foaming mound of sea water boiled starboard.

"The harbor patrol is early today," the captain said. "Get down."

I ducked below the rail of the raft, right when a submersible battle raft rose out of the water. Although it was of Atlantean manufacture, the Phut coat of arms glowed gold and blue on its dripping bow. Its weather deck towered high above our sails. The weapons deck, one level down, blinked and shifted as fire systems shed their cowlings and rotated lethal barrels in our direction.

I counted the remaining seconds down to zero. After that, the battle raft went dark. So did the city lights on the shore. In fact, every city on Earth would have gone dark, courtesy of Mestre shutting off the pyramids.

My friend grunted his approval. "You have very powerful friends."

We grasped forearms.

"Good hunting," he said.

My special mission party slipped out through the bottom of the elevated deck and swam for the sea floor. By the time the battle raft managed to lower a skiff and hand row toward my friend's old sailing raft, we would be long gone and he'd be tacking away into the rest of the harvester fleet.

Without Mestre recharging, our stored suit power would last twenty-four hours under nominal use, six during sustained combat. We spent precious power cloaking and maintained a random formation mimicking the long necks and giant turtles milling about the sea fruit beds just in case the enemy had figured out how to penetrate our cloaking.

Ground Com relayed news from a Guardian team in Phut. The woman who the Queen now infected had been spotted surrounded by revolutionaries seeking to overthrow the Phutian government. That meant she wasn't hiding below with the hostages. Suri had not been infected yet.

Gravity imaging bore through the blackness, revealing a bed of canyons and valleys. A thousand uncloaked containers spread across the sea floor. They were twice the mass of standard shipping containers, regularly spaced and pointing north toward Javan.

We fanned out and began our search, looking for Suri's life sign. The interiors were hard to scan. Most of the volume in each container seemed to be folded fabric that shielded thick metallic cores. Ground Com believed the cores were undersea attack subs with weapon systems evident. Life signs were clustered in cramped living quarters, but there was no sign of the hostages or the weapon we were looking for.

"Chief, I just thought of something," Aaron said. "A weapon that powerful would be mounted on the lead ship to avoid hitting anything else in the attack force."

"And probably shielded by the hostages," I said.

Suddenly, bubbles exploded from all the containers. Hatches swung open and great folds of fabric began to inflate.

Ground Com had been wrong. These were not attack subs; they were aircraft.

CHAPTER FORTY-SIX

JORDAN

We swam in a V-formation, transmitting our positions to each other since we were cloaked. Levi took the lead; I followed in the middle of the port-side leg. Aizah's shapely outline on my visor kicked a yard ahead of my outstretched glove. We'd left the harvester raft far behind, plunging past swaying stalks loaded with melon-sized fruit. Dolphins, seals, and amphibious dinosaurs called longnecks darted through the undersea forest, unaware of our cloaked passing. We hoped their frolicking concealed the turbulence generated by our armor's propulsion.

Guardian armor was my favorite piece of Second Age technology. It was indestructible, versatile, and except for the helmet and equipment sheaths, thin as a speed skater's uniform. I didn't feel enclosed in it at all. Scanning systems transmitted information to all my five senses. The life-support system extracted air from the water, while power-assisted joints amplified my foot and arm motions to propel me to the bottom of the sea. The armor shielded me from massive thorns slashing in the current. I felt water rush over me from my neck to my toes and smelled the stalks, heard a dolphin startle when I passed her. My helmet oculars zoomed in on microscopic creatures swirling through my armored fingers. My heads-up displays responded to voice and eye movement, scrolling data on both sides of my faceshield. Live audio/visual feeds of the other team members projected across the curve of my helmet's rim.

"How you doing back there?" Aizah called.

"This armor is amazing. I can feel the plankton."

"In space, I heard stars," Jarell said.

"Keep focused," Aaron said.

I was ten times the depth I'd ever gone in scuba gear. I knew from lectures on the Acropolis that the suit could take me a lot deeper. My gravity imagers spotted the containers five hundred feet below us. I stared at the color-enhanced shapes as data scrolled down both sides of my faceplate. The rectilinear containers lay across the uneven sea bed arranged in a grid thirty wide and forty deep, spaced a hundred feet apart. Each was the length of a destroyer.

Levi's three-dimensional face shifted to center position on my helmet rim. My suit translated his words. "Team, Lead,"

I waited my turn to respond. "Lead, Eight."

"Hostages are likely being held near the front of the formation, possibly shielding the weapon I briefed you on. Head for the north end of the field and begin your scanning—"

The tops of the containers suddenly cracked open. Plumes of bubbles burst upward, enveloping us in a violent whirlpool. Aizah and I grasped each other's forearms and held on. Team members and curious longnecks were hurled in all directions. My displays went nuts and my cloaking died.

Aizah fought to face me. She pointed down at a mountain of fabric bulging under us. I read her lips. "Clamp on."

The fabric billowed out of the container and rapidly expanded. My hand and boot grips sucked onto the stretching material. A low-pitched whine emanated from the container far below, climbing through the octaves. Blurred flames shot up into the bulging material, revealing it to be a giant translucent balloon. Bubbles the size of dinner plates jostled and combined within the enormous shape. The sea floor looked as if it was on fire.

Aizah latched on beside me and we rode the birthing dirigible as it rose from the seabed, pulling something out of the container. We were pushed to the surface much faster than we'd descended.

The vessels in the front were more fully inflated than ours. Their balloons resembled twenty-story lima beans standing on edge. Two smaller bean-shaped dirigibles erupted and inflated on each side. It's port-side companion rushed toward our boots.

Aizah touched helmets with me. "We have to climb higher."

We crawled up the side. The secondary balloons grew fast, hugging the main balloon. If we didn't get to the top, we'd be trapped between the dirigibles and forced to give away our positions by blowing it up. I reached the top first, grabbed Aizah's outstretched arm, and hauled her topside just before her legs got wedged.

I'd ridden on fast attack subs that had high-tailed it to the top but never on the *outside* of the hull. Thank God for pressurized armor. The enormous balloons climbed into the sunlight, avalanching sea water from their luminescent sides. The Atlantean fleet resembled rows of enormous glowing teeth climbing into a blood-colored morning sky under a ceiling of sullen clouds. I saw what the balloons cradled beneath them. Ominous reptilian shapes uncurled. Metal plates thundered into place. Metallic booms extended and locked down, garnished with complex devices. Lights sparked and things whirled to life.

"What are those things?" a lanky Javan named Seth asked.

His image in my helmet faded, along with the rest of his comments. That was the last audio I heard. My situation display showed Levi trying to communicate with the team. Then his image vanished into a field of static. Our communications were being blocked.

Aizah touched helmets with me again and shouted through our faceshields. "When this thing levels off, we'll grapple to the front of the fleet and infiltrate the lead ship."

"Confirmed," I yelled. I steeled myself. This was going to be a long grapple.

The fuselages finished forming under the balloons. They resembled titanic sea horses hung in harnesses of red cable. Rows of glowing portholes and what had to be gunnery towers fore and aft hinted at multiple decks sandwiched within each heavily armored hull. The bows and joints were translucent. Long articulated arms extended amidships to hang below the belly, festooned with a lethal array of what looked like long-range cannons. Sinuous tails unfurled and smacked the water's surface, sending up massive plumes of spray. One scoop-shaped tail smashed a pair of unlucky sailing rafts. The tails sucked up water and sent it rushing to the fuselages. Once the water reached the body of the aircraft, engines mounted on top and at the stern rotated into position and came to life, shooting searing flames into the balloons. The fleet leveled at a thousand feet, their armored tails comfortably stretched to maintain contact with the sea, which appeared to be their source of power. They were probably extracting hydrogen from the water for propulsion, buoyancy, and whatever their weapons were going to spit out when they reached their objective. So much for starving Atlantis by turning off the Mestrean power grid.

They'd picked the perfect place to launch, the northeast corner of the Sahara Sea. They were west of Mestre and only sixty-one miles south of the Javan Border. Battleships could hit anything that close. At the speed these things were charging and the technology they seemed to possess, they could ravage my new homeland at any moment.

We were three ships back from the lead. Aizah tapped me on the helmet and shot into a sprint. I kept up with her. We neared the front of the balloon, aimed grapplers at the stern of the next ship, and tossed dissolvers behind us as we launched. The disks stuck to the membrane and melted through it. The grapplers found purchase and we shot off the bow, riding our retracting cables to the next ship. Sailors from the previous bow fired shots at us. Small arms fire pinged against my armor. Moments later, their bad aim got a lot worse as their beautiful balloon sprang an ugly leak.

Aizah and I skidded on top of the next balloon, reset our grapplers, and kept running. The crippled dirigible behind us spun around in frantic circles as it deflated, hitting the sea hard and sending up a radial burst of water mixed with smoke. The two side balloons kept it afloat but not airborne. A mile to port, two more dirigibles met similar fates. Tiny figures were grappling to the next ship, leapfrogging like us toward the lead aircraft.

We dodged a sudden wave of ineffective defensive fire, apparently designed for targets much larger than fast-moving Guardians. Aizah and I sent another dragon ship into early retirement.

Suri's ship lay dead ahead. We fired grapplers and hit topside. A second later, three more Guardians landed beside us. The remaining nine hundred and whatever ships opened fire on Javan.

Defensive ordinance from neighboring ships became better coordinated, hindering the rest of our team from reaching the lead ship. The Atlanteans commenced a massive bombardment, rhythmically firing their paired cannons. Balls of swirling flame hissed over our heads and beyond the north shore. My helmet scrolled data. Nephillim aircrafts crested the eastern horizon, a hundred sorties inbound from Mestre. The *Valhalla* sent everything it had, reinforced by the *Xian* and *Salem. Olympus* held her ground over the Javan border, heroically trying to intercept incoming bombardment.

Levi decided he couldn't wait for the rest of the team to reach us. He finger-signed the attack plan. We lined up on top of the balloon and sank our grapplers into its fabric, then transferred the grapple feeds from our forearms to our waists to free up our hands. We lobbed a truckload of Javan flash-bangs over the port side to distract the crew, then pivoted and ran down the starboard side of the balloon. I had an upside-down view of the fierce fire fight pounding the perimeter of the attacking fleet.

Some kind of shielding glistened around the fleet's formation like a translucent egg. Nothing from the good guys was getting through. We kicked off thirty paces down the main balloon, ricocheted helmet-first off the secondary starboard balloon, and dove over thin air and distant whitecaps.

I played my grappler out the distance recommended on my suit's display and snugged the line. The tension spun me around, pointing my boots at thick armor forested with ten-foot-long spikes. Two monstrous metal arms with thirty-inch cannons rhythmically pulsed fireballs. My weapon rods were off my legs and in my gloves, set on dissolvers and glowing like flares. We swung Tarzan-style past the recoiling cannons and straight for the spikes.

We aimed for an upper deck, one compartment left of where our scanners showed a cluster of Mestrean and Berbai life signs. Grapplers compensated automatically. I fired between my boots and kept firing as the spiked hull got close in a hurry. The dissolvers smacked the black armor. My boots punched through like I was kicking in a spider web. Jarell came barreling in behind me. I switched to restrainer gel, flew boots-first into the smoking interior, and jettisoned the grappler cable before I hit the deck. I kept my sticky boots up and let my smooth armor skid me across the deck toward dozens of hostiles who were too busy looking at our fireworks display on the port side.

I fired fifty rounds from both rods. Jarell glued the leftovers. We slid to the center of the deck, smacked our boots to stick, and rolled into a crouch. Jarell and I faced the stern, while Levi, Aaron, and Aizah ended up facing the bow. We took out anyone dumb enough to enter the compartment, rushed the bow hatch, and found an unusually tall guy hiding behind it, shaking in a Phut officer's uniform. He tried to jump Aaron, but Aaron ducked. The guy's head connected with the bulkhead. We doused him with restrainer gel, gluing his ugly mouth and all his extremities until he looked like cheap wall art.

Aaron ripped the man's uniform open. The officer sported a ten-head dragon tattoo on his baby smooth chest. Only one race saluted that symbol and they weren't humans.

"Phut, my foot." I pressed both weapons into his hairy nostrils. "Frigging half-giant. Didn't your mama feed you enough? You're as small as I am."

"Guess that was the plan," Aaron said.

"You get extra glue for impersonating a human."

The officer looked like he was going to wet his pants. I aimed higher and glued his bald head until the expanding filaments made him look like a chia pet.

My heads-up display showed static. The enemy was jamming my comlink. I minimized the display and kept it active in a small corner in case it started working again. A lot of the challenge on the Acropolis was learning Guardian methods and boxing my SEAL training off for emergencies.

Levi chop-pointed to the bow. We moved out at a hard sprint, dissolving holes though successive bulkheads and pasting crew members before they had time to notice our presence. We breached the forward-most compartment and engaged forty targets to clear the room in three seconds. The two big guns under the ship fell silent. We must have taken out their fire control and jamming system. My scanners were operational again.

My scanner showed Suri and the other hostages directly below my boots. A dozen other targets were milling about the place, probably wondering what was going on above their heads. We formed up for an assault. Aaron dissolved a small hole in the deck and dropped in Javan versions of flash-bangs. They went *poof* instead of *boom.*

The bridge went as quiet as a library. We made bigger holes and dropped in as silent as shadows. The enemy lay strewn about us. The entry hatch was open. Angry voices came from outside, coming closer.

Suri was tied to a column between Amon and Numu, all three slumped forward on their bindings. I fought the urge to run to her and did my job with the team, clearing the enormous room of hiding targets. Bootsteps echoed beyond the access hatch. It was propped open with an unconscious sailor across the threshold. Aaron yanked him inside and Aizah welded the hatch shut. We weren't exiting that way anyway.

One of the enemy dropped out of the ceiling hole and landed between Jarell and me. He went down with a double dose of glue from both of us. Aizah sealed the ceiling to keep any more of the enemy from dropping through.

Something heavy pounded on the hatch, while something else hammered at the ceiling. Levi motioned like a third base coach. Aaron and Aizah flipped their weapons into their gloves and took cover, aiming at the vibrating hatch. Jarell ducked behind a console and aimed at the spot in the ceiling that started to turn red. I followed Levi to the hostages. They were glued to three columns facing a curved expanse of armored windows that formed the bow.

Suri was glued head to foot to the center post. Prince What's-His-Face was stuck to the column on the right, and Triple Chin was on the left. They looked like pink mummies wrapped up to their nostrils. I checked Suri for any signs of explosives or traps and found none. Her vital signs were normal. Her chest moved rhythmically as she breathed.

Levi touched my shoulder and aimed his weapon at the elephant in the room.

To the left of the hostages floated the most disgusting thing I'd ever laid eyes on. I'd noticed it when we'd dropped into the room but had steered clear of it to do my job. It was reddish black, as long as a bus, and shaped like a turnip with three spider legs forming a tripod mount. The pointy end faced the bow. The surface looked as if someone had gutted a giant squid and draped the intestines over a pulsating alien corpse. The rubbery stuff crawled and twisted, revealing disgusting cavities that quickly slurped shut.

Levi signaled us to stay clear of it. The weapon heaved against the ceiling but the legs yanked it back. It jerked again as if it didn't like gravity. Mucous-like fluids dripped where it slimed the ceiling.

I swallowed and nodded. Don't play with the alien weapon. Got it.

Levi motioned for us to free the hostages. I made my faceplate transparent and gave Suri a squirt of reviver mist. Her eyes blinked open. Then she freaked. The glue over her mouth prevented her screams from becoming audible. I put a finger in front of my faceplate to shush her.

"Calm down, *cha-na*," I whispered. "It's me. I'm releasing you. You have to stay quiet. Blink if you understand."

She calmed down and blinked intently.

I dissolved the glue holding her to the post. She flew into my arms. I let her hug me for half a second, careful not to hug her back. I was proficient with this suit but I could accidently crush a boulder if I sneezed.

As soon as Levi unglued the prince, Amon started whining. Levi clamped his mouth shut. The kid struggled to free himself. He mumbled Numu's name through Levi's armored fingers.

"Stay put," I whispered to Suri.

She grabbed the window ledge, her eyes darting to the oozing weapon. Javan fighters screamed past the glass, blasting the translucent shield to no effect. The north shore passed under the ship. The Io Sea and Javan lay beyond.

I approached Numu. Supreme jerk or not, he was a civilian victim. Orders were orders. Despite the bile rising in my throat, I aimed the reviver sprayer at his face.

Numu suddenly snapped his restraints and lashed at me. Levi grabbed my shoulder and yanked me back so hard I hit the bulkhead. Deep gouges traced across my armor where Numu had clawed me. I looked at his chubby fingers. How the heck …

Aaron, Aizah, and Jarell whipped around and suddenly flipped off their feet. Numu grabbed Levi and hurled him. Levi landed on a console, smashing it flat.

I got up. Numu needed a new lesson in humility; but with a wave of his hand, he stuck my boots to the deck. Then my arms went rigid.

Levi beat it halfway back to Robo-Ambassador before Numu froze him in mid-stride. His head swiveled as he struggled with the chin controls inside his helmet. All the Guardians watched helplessly as Numu patted Levi's rigid shoulder, then walked toward Suri. She backed away, but how long could that last? She had nowhere to run.

As if he'd had a change of heart—or he remembered his priorities—he headed for me. Good. I was way past feeling non-lethal now.

Numu waved a fat finger. My armor popped open and I tumbled out. I wore light issue pants, a tunic, and thin-soled boots. Fortunately, they didn't stick to the floor like my armor had. It felt like I was in my pajamas.

Numu walked confidently toward me. I tried to free my weapons that were still clamped in my armored gloves but I couldn't pull them loose. I took a deep breath and faced him.

"Stand down, sir, or I *will* kill you," I said.

That bad feeling came back with alarms and sirens. Who was this new Numu? I pictured a crocodile killing a gazelle, then climbing inside its skin. Ridiculous. I could take this loser without breaking a sweat.

Levi yelled something at him. Numu made a casual gesture and Levi was hurled against the bow windows.

On second thought …

Suri screamed and tried to help Levi, but she could only get her legs to move a few shuffles. Levi waved her back, rolled to his feet, and charged Numu.

Numu motioned again. Levi catapulted backwards head over heels. His body smacked the deck and didn't move. Others tried to join the fight but shuffled like cripples.

My legs felt like they were made out of granite. No wonder the others had trouble moving. Aizah tried to say something but her mouth moved too slowly. Jarell stared at me and shook her head in slow motion, her eyes wide with fear. Aaron looked like he wanted to take a bite out of Numu's face. Numu simply extended his hand like he wanted to shake mine.

Levi rolled onto his side. Blood ran down his face. He finger signed to me. The digits slowly bent and straightened like an arthritic octogenarian. He spelled letters from the Javan alphabet. One of the first things Suri had patiently tried to teach me.

"A … pros … sau … o …"

I struggled to understand without my helmet's translator. Then I remembered the phrase. I'd read it on my faceplate when he'd briefed the mission before we'd dropped. That part about staying away from the giant weapon. It was the same phrase Aizah had said before she'd locked Suri and me on the city terrace. She'd said, *pros-sau-o,* which meant good touch. And *a-pros-sau-o.* Bad touch.

The others collapsed from apparent exhaustion. Numu glanced back at Levi to see what I was looking at. He pivoted his girth back toward me and continued strolling. Levi very carefully tried crawling. He made slow progress. I had to keep Numu's attention and beckoned him in with both hands. "You want some? Keep coming. "

Numu laughed.

"Glad you're having fun," I said.

Levi kept crawling. The others watched but stayed put. They were in Numu's peripheral vision and didn't want to risk him turning in Levi's direction. Suri looked anxiously at me. I shook my head without looking at her to warn her to stay put.

"You have no idea what this is about, do you?" Numu said.

"Why don't you clue me in?" I said. "I'd hate to bust that jaw of yours prematurely and miss out on the bad guy speech."

"Let's start with what you know about me."

"You're a pompous idiot who somehow learned English. How am I doing?"

He scowled. "It's called Engel, you Fourth Age freak. Unlike you, I speak it fluently. You pathetic Americans still have that Algonian twang."

"How do you know about America?"

He ignored my question. "Apparently, the re-educator's range has diminished. Probably increased salinity in the Atlantic. We'll fix that after we arrive."

"Excuse me?" I said.

"You're curious. Good, I was starting to wonder if you were an acceptable travel host. When I first saw you bleeding on my extremely expensive desk, I hoped you were inquisitive. You had to be in order to find the Well."

Levi had crawled several feet so far.

"How do you know about that?"

"Like you, I have the gift of second sight. Unlike you, I harness it." He flicked a finger. "That's far enough, Levi."

His admonition tossed Levi over the consoles on top of Aaron and the others.

"Try that again and I will hurl you into the Thunderbolt." He nodded at the floating mass of intestines for my benefit. "The thing you call a giant turnip." He folded his hands in the sleeves of his robe and glanced out the window at the air battle. "We have time yet. I have a business proposition."

"The only thing I'm interested in is your sorry backside going out that window."

"Humor me by listening or Suri will die." He stood within arm's reach of me. "Haven't you wondered why I look so different from all the others?"

"I figured you got hit with an ugly stick."

"Colorful expression. It's because of the genetic makeup of this body, a rare blend of three races."

"You talk as if it's not yours."

"That's because it isn't. I took possession of this specimen five decades ago." He patted his belly. "Pathetic creature, Numu, but his simplicity suited me. Corporal infestation is an interesting science, very easy to learn. Your primitive Fourth Age refers to it as demon possession."

My body went cold.

"I assure you there is nothing mystical about the process. It's quite practical. He calls it cohabitation."

"Who's he?" I asked.

"That is a wonderful question. The only difficulty with the process is the host's body tends to wear out quickly. That's why I look so much older than everyone else. Every five or six decades, I have to hunt for a new host. So few are my genetic match.

"Without a suitable replacement, I began to despair that I would finally die in this body. Certainly, I could inhabit anybody I choose, but switching is so draining and a mismatched body wears out in a matter of weeks." He stopped pacing and looked at me affectionately. "Then you dropped out of the sky. Right into my pond. I am part human, Trahl, and Anakim." He looked at me hungrily. "Just like you."

I wanted to puke.

"Until you came along, I was at a loss for a new body. You see, not many Anakim interbreed anymore. They stay in the wilds, by themselves."

"Then why don't you go there and join them?"

"My wife had her match picked out." He indicated Suri. "She is the same genetic mix. Surely, you noticed how her beauty is tainted with Anakim blood, unlike all those perfect Mestrean maidens? Babla tried possessing them over the centuries, but that kind of beauty doesn't tolerate mixed breeding. When she found Suri, her prayers were answered, praise Anak."

"You touch one hair on her head and I will annihilate you and your soul-sucking wife."

"Threats? Really? If I were you, I'd listen to what I have to offer." He clamped my mouth shut and it got hard to breathe. His eyes narrowed like a snake. "Listen well, because if I have to repeat myself, I may forget to let you breathe." He paced while my lungs protested. "I have lived forty thousand years. I speak a hundred languages. I have seen countless civilizations rise and fall, walked with the greatest minds of three races. All that will be yours when I join with you. Everything I have done, everything I have learned, will be grafted to your soul as if you had been there. I even know some things about your age. My friends who have survived in your time sometimes commune with me across the void, thanks to the nearing of the Stream. Think about what it would be like to own all of your race's history, complete and vivid. No more questions about the past. The entire future ahead of you to experience and shape."

He paused and my mouth loosened. I gasped for air.

"Well?" he said.

"Was that supposed to impress me?"

I figured he'd sucker punch me, but he chuckled. "I'd be disappointed if it had. How about you and Suri living together forever? After Babla and I teach you how, both of you will be able to move from body to body, cheating death, eternally young, eternally together. Wouldn't that be better than you living a few more decades while Suri lives out her natural lifespan of six or seven hundred years as a widow? Of course she wouldn't; she'd remarry. Probably many times. Don't you wonder how many husbands she will take after you die? The children she will have with other men? Or did that detail escape you?"

Rage shuddered through me. Right now my feelings were as much of an enemy as Numu. Listening to him was torture, but I saw the technique for what it was. If we were going to get out of this, I had to play along.

"Babla and I could fix that. You could be married to Suri for as long as you wanted."

I acted like I considered his proposal. "What happens if I refuse?"

"I will possess you, regardless. But resisting ages your body. You'd lose decades. That's not a problem for Suri if she resists Babla. She'd still have four or five centuries of productive life. You, on the other hand, would be near death."

"So where's that leave you? All dressed up and nowhere to go."

Numu shrugged. "You'd live long enough for us to make it back to your marvelous age of blended races. I'd dispose of you there. My informant says Greg is quite virile. Babla would like that."

"What makes you think you're going back to my age?"

"Didn't you read Plato? We can't stay here. The Stream of Heaven is coming. Traveling to your age wasn't our first choice. I mean, look at your world. Living a tenth as long, eating weeds and drinking clear water. Pathetic. My wife and I worked patiently for millennia with one goal in mind: to return to our home world. During all that time, we re-educated the Ephraim. You can't imagine how tedious it is to advance savages from boulder-throwing to space flight. It was dicey, but we did it. Babla was fabulous. She has a knack for manufacturing and logistics. We had a nice ship, lots of food and replacement bodies, including two perfect specimens for when we arrived." He pointed at Suri and me. "And a star drive finally. That was the toughest part. All the star drives had been destroyed by the jailers when we'd been exiled. But we found enough pieces floating around the solar system to reverse engineer the design. We were all set. We loaded up the ship and stocked our replacement hosts. All I had to do was find you and join my wife on the ship. Then *they* showed up." He scowled at Levi, who was struggling to crawl off Aaron. "He destroyed the ship and nearly killed my wife." He waved his hand and flipped Aaron and Levi against the rear bulkhead. "With no time to rebuild, we moved on to plan B. Babla and I have set course for your body-shriveling, weed-eating age."

"I hate to break it to you, but I don't know even know how I got here."

"Don't worry; Babla and I know exactly how to do it. We'd go without you and Suri, but we need your bodies to make the trip. The device is discerning. It would block us. Your pure souls grafted around ours will gain us passage."

"Device?"

"No more chit chat. Last chance. If you accept my invitation and willingly submit to me, the strain will be minimal. You will retain most of your lifespan. Refuse and it will still happen, but you'll be dead in a few weeks."

My mind raced. I wasn't thrilled with my current options.

I met Suri's eyes. I wanted to tell her so much. That I cherished her. That I wanted to have children with her, as many as she wanted. That I wouldn't mind dying long before she did if it meant we could share a few more decades together. Why had I left so much unsaid?

Her eyes teared up and she forced a smile. Maybe she knew after all. The love she returned in that single look emboldened me.

I faced Numu and felt a power flow through me. My body, heart, mind, and soul closed ranks and collectively said, "Go to hell."

Movement behind Numu caught my eye. A dark shape rose up from his body, blocking everything else in the room. A form more hideous than the one I'd seen rise out of Babla emerged from him. His hands lashed out of his sleeves, green claws dripping pus. His mouth opened wider than any human's could. With an unearthly shriek, he clawed at my face.

CHAPTER FORTY-SEVEN

LEVI

Aaron struggled off my legs. I rolled painfully to the side so I could see what was happening. Numu stood in front of Jordan, holding out his hands. He said something I couldn't understand.

A voice whipped through my mind like a strong breeze. *Why are you just lying there? Guard my servant. INTERVENE!*

How was I supposed to help when Numu had paralyzed my legs?

They have no power except what you surrender. Believe and defeat.

Whether this was a conversation with the Creator or a delusion, desperation drove me beyond worrying about my sanity. *Help me believe.*

Suddenly I knew what to do. It was impossible and ridiculously simple. I sprang to my feet.

Jordan saw me. He said something to Numu and Numu lunged for him, pressing his white manicured fingers into Jordan's face. Jordan knifed his hands up between Numu's wrists and snapped them outward.

I charged across the deck as Jordan punched Numu in the throat. Numu staggered backwards, gasping for breath. I swept his legs out from under him and added a finishing touch to the ambassador's incapacitation: a triple dose of freeze-sleep, enough to incapacitate a Nephillim for a month.

It was as if a fog lifted in the room. My team re-animated and Suri ran to Jordan. At the same time, the hatch shuddered from new weapons fire.

"Guardians," I said, "armor on."

My team jumped into their armor and grabbed their weapons.

Two, cover fire on the hatch, I sent through the armor's communications.

Understood, Aaron returned.

I aimed at the bow windows and blasted a nice hole through it. The reinforced crystal blew outward.

The sounds of battle whined as Javan interdictors screamed past, their shots repulsed by the shield glowing around the fleet. We were deep into Javan territory, while ahead stretched the mountains of the Acropolis. At their foothills were the towers of the capital. Ground Com had figured out what was generating the shielding. Its slimy mass pulsed and heaved to my left. After the civilians were off this ship, I'd have to shut it down once and for all.

Three, Four, Eight, evacuate the hostages, I ordered.

Jordan didn't respond but went to the hole and looked back at Suri. "Don't touch me. I may be infected. Just come to the edge—"

Suri leapt into his arms and latched her legs around his torso, knocking him through the hole. He fired a grappler into the overhanging balloon, retracted to clear the bow deck, then dropped into the sea.

Jarell approached Prince Amon. "Your turn," she said, her voice echoing from her helmet.

He looked out the whistling hole. "Not again," he moaned.

She wagged an armored finger at him. "No screaming like you did in Payahdon. That was embarrassing."

Aizah slapped her weapons onto her legs and stood over Numu's unconscious girth. *What about him?* she sent.

Double restrain and evacuate, Levi returned. *He's still a civilian.*

Aizah sprayed him extra thick. Numu's eyes flew open. He

hurled he away and she tumbled out the hole.

The hatch suddenly exploded. Aaron and I came under fire from the smoking opening. Numu's restrainer gel vaporized into steam.

Jarell was knocked off her boots. Numu used his mind powers to toss her out the hole, too. Amon stood in the field of fire, tracers zipping past his trembling body. Aaron kept the enemy at bay while I crawled back and pulled Amon behind a console. Numu charged forward, shots bouncing off his body with no effect. He clawed at my armor.

His eyes widened as his fingers cracked on my chest joint. He staggered back, cradling his bleeding hands. I swept my leg under his feet and knocked him once again to the deck. He stared up at me, his expression a mix of hate and astonishment, his lips contorted in a scream. A dark translucent shape flew out of his mouth and filled the air between us.

The enemy ceased fire and stared at the unearthly apparition. The swirling figure had hollow eyes in a bulbous head. They blinked once, then the figure lifted into the air and circled the room as if it was hunting for something. The sailors shrank back behind the hatch. It swirled past them and shrieked in frustration. I remembered what the little girl had described back on Babla's ship. This creature had abandoned Numu and was searching for a new host. Wisps of its shape broke off as it flew, dissipating like smoke. It locked on me.

I felt its hunger and paid attention to the presence deep inside me. "Forget it."

It let out a shriek and fled through the ceiling. The sailors opened fire on us. Aaron kept them back.

Numu was shaking and pale. He cowered in my grip, his eyes wide with terror. "He's gone. You made him flee!"

"You can thank me later. Right now, you and the Prince stay behind this console." I turned to help Aaron.

"No!" Amon cried.

I looked back and saw Numu run to the hovering weapon. I pivoted and stumbled over the console just as he reached the bulbous end.

"Don't touch it," I yelled.

It was too late. As Numu pressed his ruined arms against the gelatinous mass, the weapon shuddered and stiffened into a rigid form. An energy surge threw me off my feet and hurled me against the bulkhead next to the hatch. Amon was safe behind the console but Numu's arms were swallowed up to his flabby biceps. The weapon thrummed and moaned, growing louder. Dark light swirled about its skin.

The terrified sailors ceased fire. Stunned, I could only watch my suit spark and smoke. Aaron ran over to help me up.

"Get off this ship now!" he yelled at the enemy, and they fled.

Numu laughed maniacally.

"Numu, no!" Amon cried. He edged around the console.

"Keep away from him," I commanded.

Numu shouted at the ceiling. "Anak, see how I make you victorious!"

Black lightning crackled across the ceiling. Numu's arms glowed purple. He stared at his changing skin. "Why am I still here? Anak, take me with you. You promised to reward my sacrifice."

"I don't think he's too happy with you," I said.

Numu's voice shook. "In minutes, this weapon will fire and all of Javan will be destroyed."

Aaron scratched his helmet. "Not exactly."

"It seems you didn't have all the necessary information to carry out your mission, Ambassador," I said.

"Yeah, when we were up in space blowing up that giant ship, I was watching Levi's visuals while he was examining this weapon." Aaron made a spinning motion with his glove. "You remember, Chief?"

I nodded and made a similar motion. "The pointed end was directed toward the interior of the ship."

"And the end Numu is holding onto was aimed out the nose cone."

"That means Numu's holding the wrong end of the weapon."

"Probably the end that shoots."

"Anak, that sucks."

Numu's head, shoulders, and arms were pulsing purple light.

Amon shrieked and darted to him.

"No, Your Highness!"

Amon was too quick. He grabbed Numu around the middle and tried to pull him off the weapon. He screamed and twisted as the color flowed onto his own hands.

I ripped a console chair from its moorings and threw it at Amon. The Prince tumbled to the deck and Aaron sprayed him into a cocoon. We hauled his wriggling body to the bow as the weapon roared and shook. The bulbous end that held Numu was a luminous mass of purple and black. Numu was barely visible anymore.

We could do nothing more. We jumped through the window and free fell. Word had spread back through the fleet. Atlanteans were dropping out of their ships. The shielding wavered and then vanished. The ship we'd exited was a mass of discolored lightning.

"Don't grapple the ship," I said.

"I know," Aaron replied.

We rolled so we would safely hit the water boots first. I aimed Amon's cocoon to do likewise. The gel would protect him from impact. Then we knifed the water and sank deep.

CHAPTER FORTY-EIGHT

JORDAN

I floated like a cork in the water. How could that be while I was wearing armor? The stuff had been as solid as granite when I'd gotten shot at; now it was as light as parachute silk. Suri clung to my chest and I stayed on my back to keep her above the water's surface.

My suit propelled us to shore, where Aizah and Jarell caught up with us. We took cover among some boulders and watched the fleet break formation. The lead ship was now a tiny dot on the horizon. Aizah's pupils swirled as she used her oculars.

"What's happening?" I asked.

"Levi and Aaron just jumped."

"They have somebody with them," Jarell said.

"Just one?" I asked.

"Just one."

"Is it Amon?" Suri asked.

"Can't tell. The body is cocooned in restrainer gel."

"Why aren't they using grapplers?" Aizah muttered.

"Ouch, they just hit the water," Jarell said.

"Anak," Aizah cursed, "sailors are bailing out of the ships in droves. The lead ship is … oh no. Duck!"

The tiny dot mushroomed into a substantial sphere of purple

and black. A rippling translucent sheet of violet fire fanned out across the sky, consuming almost the entire fleet. It passed high overhead and dissipated.

"What was that?" I asked.

"Somebody fired the weapon," Aizah said.

The closest of the surviving ships drifted our way on the wind. One came right over us, dragging its water intake up the beach. It caught on a thicket of trees. The engines sputtered and the balloons deflated. The hull crashed through the forest and sank to the ground, settling on a tangled pile of splintered branches and sections of its ruined tail. Glass broke and something long and thin slipped out. The brush swished as the creature fled into the water.

"We'd better head inland," Aizah said. "As far away from this as possible."

"I got hold of Ground Com," Jarell said. "They'll advise on a Retriever."

"Good. Tell them we're on foot, going north through the swamp region," Aizah said.

Suri looked frightened. We grabbed our gear and moved away from the wreck. Long sinuous shapes slapped the windows. Aizah winced at the sound.

"What about survivors?" I asked.

"There aren't any," she said.

CHAPTER FORTY-NINE

LEVI

I stood on a sandy rise overlooking the sea. A stiff wind buffeted my faceplate. Sea grass draped my armor from the protracted swim to shore. I contacted Ground Com to check the status of the rescue. They assured me a Retriever had been dispatched and the arrival time had not changed since my previous inquiry.

Aizah called in on a coded channel patched through Ground Com. Jarell, Suri, and Jordan were with her. They'd come ashore several miles southeast of my position. I filled her in on our situation, including Amon's condition. Aaron had him prone behind the rise on a bed of ferns.

Understood, Aizah said. *Our civilian is extremely agitated.*

Explain.

The civilian is familiar with locale and indigenous population. Strongly requests permission to rally to your position.

Suri was the civilian Aizah was referring to. She was afraid of the Anakim. A few clans lived in the swamps dividing Phut from Mestre.

Your assessment of threats? I sent.

Minimal. Population unarmed and unaware of our position. Eight is attempting to calm the civilian.

I tried to picture Jordan calming Suri down. He may be able to channel the Creator, but soothing Suri was a losing battle.

Conceal and await retrieval. Sedate if necessary. Retriever dispatched. Wait until Retriever is within ocular range before advising landing vector.

Understood. Can you confirm Two's status.

He's fine, just a few hairs out of place.

Confident he will remedy that before we rally.

Confirmed. Well done, Three.

Somebody had to look fabulous and distract the enemy.

Two's assessment of your perfect compatibility appears accurate.

Wait until you see our kids.

Has Two been briefed?

Negative, still in planning stage.

Protect all.

Harm none.

I shifted Aizah's display to the side of my helmet rim and returned to my vigil on the shore. I swept the horizon with my oculars and spotted a cluster of shapes. They were a half-mile closer. Amon groaned weakly. I heard the hiss as Aaron injected another heal stick into him.

"How's he doing?" I asked loud enough so Amon could hear me.

"He's holding up great, Chief," Aaron said.

Spent heal sticks lay scattered behind Aaron, yet Amon's face was still a death mask with hyper-wide eyes. Purple veins webbed his shoulders. Aaron kept a steady injection of heal sticks feeding into his neck. Each injection forced the purple to fade but not vanish.

Amon shook from the adrenaline buzz. Aaron had wrapped his cloak around the prince's lower arms. We didn't want Amon looking at his hands. It had taken a long time to sedate him the last time he'd seen them.

Aaron signaled that he was running low on heal sticks. I tossed him my last package. He caught it one-handed without taking his eyes off Amon's neck.

"H-h-how much l-l-longer?" Amon whispered.

"Rest easy, son," I said, summoning an assurance I didn't feel. "Rescue's on its way."

"How many tubes do you have left, sir?"

"Be still. We've never lost a civilian yet."

"Yeah, so don't ruin our stellar record," Aaron said. "Athena would turn us into wall hangings."

The prince attempted a smile. Convulsions mutated it into a grimace.

Aaron sent a scrolled message to my faceplate. *What's keeping them, Chief?*

Atlantis attacked from multiple fronts. Rescue's stretched thin, even for priority missions.

Why isn't the Ra sending help?

Because the Ra was in on the attack.

Aaron gave me a hard look. I was as shocked as he was. Mestre's defection was catastrophic news for the Eastern Alliance. Would the remaining countries become neutral like Chi and Indra, or would they join Atlantis? While Javan had miraculously survived the most daring betrayal in history, there was no cause for celebration. Atlantis would try again.

I waited as the ship carrying the weapon drifted closer. The fog billowed over the choppy sea, shrouding the sun. I steeled myself. Frothing water heralded its arrival. Out of the wavering gloom drifted the attack ships, their engines sputtering, their dark fuselages hanging beneath deflating balloons like limp corpses. Some of the fuselages skimmed the waves. One bow hit a rogue white cap and plunged. The crippled ship upended and exploded, blowing out its starboard hull. Its balloons flared full and burst into flames.

The burning embers drifted ashore on the breeze and settled around us. I stamped out the ones that landed near Amon. The other ships drifted past the sinking wreck, jostling and listing as evening southerlies blew them ashore. The first ships crossed the beach. Tail scoops dragged out of the water and emptied, denying the ships their fuel source. Portholes flickered and died. Strange black shapes wiggled and fell from the listing hulls. Their cries echoed down through the gloom, silenced by splashing into the water. The lucky sailors who'd escaped were hiding in the hills. I was certain none would return to the beach after what they'd swum past. I couldn't blame them. Even with armor to protect me, I was shaken by the trip. Beating them off of Amon was one nightmare

I intended to have erased as soon as I reached *Olympus*.

Aaron pointed at a ship. *That has to be it. Anak, it's coming straight at us.*

We grabbed Amon and carried him out of the doomed ship's path, ducking behind some boulders. The ship came ashore dragging its tail scoop up the beach, pivoted in a change of breeze, and flew right over us. The special insignia on the deflating balloon was distorted. The ship's tail became stuck and the balloons died. The fuselage twisted and broadsided the hill. The occupants tumbled out the opposite side, squealing and flopping about.

Aaron held a heal stick to Amon's neck with one glove and aimed a weapon rod with the other. Splashing noises indicated that the survivors were heading into the water. Others lay bleeding on the sand, their distended organs pulsing outside their skin.

The balloon settled over us like a shroud, its edges rippling on the grass and low branches. I motioned Aaron to stay put, then moved around the boulder and approached the ship's enormous hull. The bow had plowed deep into the hill. I cautiously approached the broken windows of the bridge. Something crawled out from under the keel. A skeletal hand with inside-out flesh protruding from its twisted muscle grabbed my leg.

I pried the fingers away from my armor. The creature hissed and withdrew. I climbed one of our grappler lines dangling from the bow windows and stepped over the sill, jumping down onto the bridge. The alien weapon stood intact on its tripod. It appeared dormant until the organic mass covering its surface shifted. Thin feelers extended toward me.

"Still awake, are we?" I muttered. "I can fix that."

I circled my quarry to the bulbous end that Numu had mistaken for the back of the weapon, a little piece of disinformation Ground Com had successfully disseminated. Atlantis had read Athena's mail.

I stepped gingerly around the pulsing flank and found Numu's lifeless body, his arms still sunk deep in the weapon, his back arched, knees buckled. His head was tilted back and his eyes were fixed as if he'd died in horrible agony. Dried blood and vomit had hardened around his blackened lips.

The weapon drifted toward the ceiling. The spidery tripod legs pulled it back. A purple spark surged up Numu's arms. Like twin clam shells, Numu's eyes opened and closed. He coughed out a chunk of dry bile. My suit chirped that it detected life signs. Impossible.

Numu's tongue twitched. Was he trying to talk?

"Ambassador, can you hear me?" I asked.

A shuffling noise came from behind me. Amon climbed into the bridge. Aaron was behind him.

"I'm sorry, Chief, he insisted."

Something told me it was important for the Prince to be here. I was long past questioning these messages. I motioned Aaron to position Amon behind me. Amon obeyed, giving the weapon a respectful berth.

Numu seemed to know he had company. "Amon," he croaked.

The Prince shuffled closer. I stuck out my arm. "Close enough, son."

"So sorry … your Highness," Numu rasped. "I didn't … know."

"You're going to be okay," Amon said. "They'll get you back to the Palace. Father will make you well again." He looked at us. "Right?"

"Sure, kid," Aaron said, looking away.

Numu shook his head a fraction of an inch. His eyes turned in their sockets and strained to see Amon. I relaxed my arm and let the Prince lean in. A smile curled the edges of Numu's bloody mouth. He stared down at the blanket wrapping Amon's hands and his face contorted with grief. "Do not trust the Ra-*aagh!*"

Another purple spark surged into Numu's arms. His body convulsed.

"Numu, no!"

"S-s-stay back," Numu said when Amon tried to go to him. "Keep him s-s-safe."

I pushed Amon back to Aaron and signaled Aaron to get him out.

Numu's lungs heaved. His body convulsed in agony. "Ahhhmon, s-s-stop him."

"Stop who?" Amon cried. "Stop who?"

"Raaa."

Numu contorted in agony. A deep groove formed down the center of his face. His lips and tongue split in six sections, and he screamed.

Aaron pushed Amon back to the window. I trained my weapons on Numu. His bald head spider-webbed and split into six pie-shaped wedges. His body dissolved around his ruined organs, turning them into burgeoning tubers. Six writhing serpents swayed from Numu's tattered robes, connected to pieces of his lower torso and legs. Oval heads formed on weaving tips. Six pairs of eyes opened. Mouths gaped to reveal fangs dripping yellow fluid.

I fired both weapons at all of them. The creatures dodged, absorbing the rest of Numu's carcass. Wholly formed, they slithered toward Amon.

Aaron and I emptied our weapons into their gaping mouths. Five died. Aaron hit the sixth one point blank, blowing it backwards. It dropped down a hole in the deck. We crowded the hole and fired four weapons down it. The deck glowed deep red. When we exited, there was no trace of the creature.

A Retriever landed minutes later. We handed off Amon to the medical crew with orders for immediate asylum and transport to Javan. The Retriever lifted into the cloud bank.

Athena and Apollo materialized on the shoreline, waves lapping around their thirty-inch feet. Athena inspected the damage with a somber expression behind her faceshield. She looked as though she'd aged a century since I'd last seen her.

"Hello, son," she said.

Apollo waved his hand and a Nephillim-sized hole appeared in the side of the ship. The bridge lay exposed and the weapon quivered.

"I suppose you need me to crawl under that thing and pull out its power rod out again," I said.

"Not if you have one of these, cousin." Apollo showed me a

strange-looking device. Part of it looked solid, while another part looked like a three-pronged fork made of smoke. "Found it in Odin's not-so-secret stash on the *Olympus*."

"What is it?" Aaron asked.

"A device that exists in two galaxies at the same time," Athena said.

"Thanks for clearing that up," Aaron muttered.

Apollo's enormous hand dropped the device into my armored glove. "It will disable the weapon and make it safe for transport."

"This little thing?" I asked.

"Father claimed to have re-engineered it to human size," she said.

"You didn't tell him about our field trip," Aaron said as he huddled over my shoulder to look at the device.

"Where's the ON button?" I asked.

"It's similar to that gun you examined. You activate it by speaking."

"And what do I tell it?"

"*Ack-ba dah-bra*," she said.

"Which means?"

She shifted her weight and pointed at the weapon. "Will you just do it already?"

I approached the weapon. It lurched toward the ceiling, flashing purple lightning. I spoke the Magi words and stabbed the smoky part at the weapon. The prongs sank deep into its quivering flanks and the weapon turned black, its spider legs collapsing. It crashed to the floor, where Athena and Apollo cocooned the inert weapon.

"Father was tracking that ship fragment you were assigned to intercept. He suspected this device was inside it."

"He knew about this weapon?"

"It's not a weapon," she said. "Not exactly."

I spread my arms to indicate the devastation around us. "What part of this is not exactly?"

"It came from another galaxy, sent by a civilization that wanted to make peaceful contact."

"The perfect ice breaker," Aaron said.

"Its mission was to locate an uninhabited planet and germinate a biosphere that could support a colony of their ambassadors," she said.

"Germinate?"

"It took basic minerals and added them to onboard biological templates to reproduce the other galaxy's plants and animals. The ambassadors needed an uninhabited planet they could live on without fear of becoming sick themselves or infecting any of our worlds with their biological agents. Their goal was to send a diplomatic mission and establish cultural relations with our worlds."

"What went wrong?" I asked.

"The planners made the mistake of selecting Anak as their chief ambassador."

"There's really someone named Anak?"

"Of course."

"So, the legends are true," I said.

"Partly. He wasn't a god or a demon. He was a scientist tasked with the operation of this device."

"And what went wrong?"

"He played god. He evaluated the worlds of our galaxy, considered our race inferior, and concluded we were ruining this galaxy. He turned the device into a weapon. Some outer worlds colonized by our people millennia before his arrival rebelled and joined him. Civil war broke out. The Nephillim won, but barely. We exiled Anak and his comrades as far away from civilization as possible. The decision of where to send them was difficult. Almost every world that could sustain life was inhabited. This system was selected because its fourth planet was barren but livable. We imprisoned him on Mars."

"And the device was exiled with him," I said.

Athena shook her head. "It was stored somewhere else in this star system."

"Much safer," Aaron said.

"The Nephillim were confident that Anak couldn't escape. They scuttled the star drives and posted a heavy guard around the system."

"And that worked so well. Is there anything you people *haven't* done to screw up our solar system?"

I regretted the words the moment they left my teeth. Athena looked as though I'd drawn my weapon on her. "I promise you, this Nephillim is determined to unscrew it."

"Why didn't you tell me this before?" I asked.

"Don't be too hard on her," Apollo said. "We didn't know ourselves until we raided Odin's apartment on *Olympus*."

Olympus materialized above us, its vines swaying inland from the stiff breeze. Athena and Apollo lifted the cocooned weapon onto their shoulders and carried it out to a waiting shuttle.

"You can't destroy it," I said. "It'll just rebuild itself."

"I know," Athena said.

"Isn't Odin watching?" Aaron asked.

Athena shook her head. "He's gone. So is the Council."

"Didn't even take their stuff," Apollo added.

"Where'd they go?" I asked.

Apollo shrugged.

"Your squad is already onboard," Athena said. "I request you transport Jordan and Suri safely to her home village in Javan. Return to the Acropolis and get some rest while I'm away."

"Where are you going?" Aaron asked.

"I have a weapon to hide."

Athena lifted into the air. A few minutes later, Aizah reunited with Aaron. She clung to him, pressing her lips Trahl-style to his. Aaron returned her passion. The mission must have shaken them. I made a mental note to suggest memory smoothing and stepped away to give them privacy. *Olympus* sounded klaxons for getting underway and slowly rotated east.

I kicked myself for hurting Athena. She was my mother, adopted or not. It wasn't her fault the world had fallen apart, that Atlantis existed. It wasn't her fault my real parents had been killed by half-giants descended from Nephillim. She'd been kind to me since she'd rescued me from the wreckage of my village. I couldn't blame her for what she'd stolen from the Vault to keep me alive after Odin hadn't been able to save my sister. Her impulsive action had saved me from the same disease. I would have died otherwise. Now it looked like I'd never die. Nineteen centuries later and I still had the vitality of Aaron, but with more smoothed memories than any man on Earth. All my earlier friends had silvered and died, their children the same, gone to the bliss of what followed this existence. I never blamed her for marooning me in the present. I kept it behind my teeth.

Athena had tried everything to win my affection. I returned her desperate love with cruel tolerance. And today, on the field of victory, I'd wounded her once more.

She'd been the brunt of worse outbursts from me in the past, but something told me today was different. I'd never had much of a family. Perhaps now I had none.

Low hanging clouds swirled behind *Olympus* as the stately ship got underway. As she faded in the haze, I felt very alone.

Athena either didn't receive my calls or chose to ignore them. I'd pried out of Ground Com's station on the Acropolis that *Olympus* was cloaked somewhere on the eastern border of Mestre, the whereabouts of Athena and the alien weapon unknown. Peace celebrations on the Acropolis did little to lift my spirits. I should have been grateful the war was over, but I wasn't. It didn't feel right.

I passed the airfield where returning Guardians reunited with their families. Veterans and their spouses, all younger than me, surrounded by generations of descendants. Suddenly, the scene changed. Corpses tangled in sea vines swayed above shattered Retrievers. A shark swam past, rolled, and bit off a head.

I shook the vision from my mind and the Acropolis returned to being above sea level again.

A veteran made eye contact with me. I saluted him and quickened my steps into town. The officer's tavern was somber and quiet. A lot of Guardians' names had been added to the memorial board above the fireplace. Aaron was talking with a couple of raft captains in a corner, looking a little relaxed. He must have gotten the memory smoother I'd suggested.

I stared into my wine. I sipped my drink and looked at the stars shining over the ancient courtyard. A meteor streaked across the sky. Another followed. Aaron set his mug down next to mine and asked for a refill. I felt his stare.

I swallowed. "What?"

He wiped foam from his clean chin. "Extra moody tonight?"

I stared at my reflection in the cup. "Confirmed."

"Yeah, you and the rest of this place. Everyone is acting like the world is about to end."

I nodded. Everything Jordan had predicted on the Sacred Mountain was happening. The false peace, the surprise attack. How long did we have before the big one hit? I had to snap out of this.

I forced a smile. "So, Jordan and Suri are finally going to get it done."

"Yeah, lucky kids." Aaron fingered his engagement cape from Aizah.

I raised my mug. "Long life together."

"Here and hereafter," he said.

We clanked mugs and drank.

CHAPTER FIFTY

JORDAN

Suri and I joined the clean-up and reconstruction in the aftermath of the attack. Javan forces tightened up along the Phut border so much that a flea couldn't have crossed. A contingent of Guardians, including Diago, set up camp outside Suri's village. Suri got busy with wedding preparations. Berbai tradition dictated that I steer clear whenever she had her moms over to work on something. I made myself scarce by hanging out with the Guardians.

Aaron and Aizah were in charge of our security detail. Wednesday nights became game night, creative credits at stake. Guardian games were complicated and hard on my brain. I taught them the Fourth Age game of poker. I drew the cards on my sketch pad and cut them out with Aaron's weapon rod set on low. Next time I go exploring under pyramids, I'm bringing playing cards.

The Guardians were fast learners and adept bluffers. House rules were no facial scanning and oculars had to be switched off. I still got creamed.

Tonight, a chill wind blew through the air. We had an old-fashioned campfire going. The village dogs slept under the homemade card table with one eye open for falling snacks. Diago, Aaron, and three other Guardians ringed the table. Jarell was visiting. Aizah had watch on Suri for the night.

For some reason, I was winning. Aaron and company were losing copious amounts of creative credits, as if I needed them. The camp com buzzed. Jarell took the call on her helmet while the rest of us were occupied.

She clicked off. "Jordan, Mother Zulei wants you back at her place immediately."

"But he was just there," Aaron said, snapping his fingers at Diago for two cards. The kid slid them over.

She shrugged. "Something came up."

"Is it serious?" I looked at my hand. It was a royal flush.

I scrutinized my cards. The queen of hearts was not how I remembered drawing her. I looked over at Diago, who studiously avoided my stare.

"Just five more minutes," Aaron said, frantically arranging his new cards.

"Zulie says I have to bring Jordan back immediately. Suri needs him."

Aaron looked pleadingly at me. I bit into my favorite fruit and gave the rest to the dog warming my feet. "Sorry, gang, duty calls."

The others moaned. We all gave up our cards.

"Anak," Aaron threw down a flush.

I hiked the short path back to Suri's village, hastily wiping bits of meat fruit off my chin. My security detail was cloaked except for Aaron. The Guardians kept invisible as we walked past clusters of people settling in for evening visits. As we crossed the greens, the west buildings cast long shadows. The east buildings were ablaze with early sunset. Well-wishers greeted me and thanked Aaron for his service as a Guardian. He seemed uncomfortable with the praise.

"Are you okay?" I asked.

"I'll tell you later," he said.

I enjoyed the Guardians' company. In some ways, I felt more comfortable around them than the villagers. The civilians were gracious and friendly, to a fault, but it was hard for me to wind down and go back to being one, especially after my first mission in years. And what a mission it had been. Even though I'd been decommissioned immediately following the rescue, I felt a permanent bond with Aaron and the other Guardians reminiscent of the ties I'd had in the Fourth Age. We talked about anything and everything at our camp.

Aizah met us on the gravel street outside Zulie's house. She and Aaron exchanged a long look. Then she walked us through the garden entrance. Mother Zulei was waiting for me, flanked by two of Suri's other moms, Habi and Paris. My escorting Guardians de-cloaked so Zulei could greet them. She looked like a twenty-two-year-old cheerleader. Hard to remember she was on the far side of six hundred.

"Oh good, you came quickly." Paris gave me a motherly nose rub with her finger. "She's on the roof terrace."

"Is she okay?"

"She wants to show you something. And have a little talk."

"She shouldn't be standing in that low sun," Habi said with a rasp in her throat. "It's not good for the eyes. She should come down here."

"Mother, she wants to talk to Jordan alone," Paris said, a little louder than normal.

Habi coughed. "Oh, all right. But I don't see what all the fuss is about."

I wanted to grapple to the roof, but I'd had to give up the cool equipment. Marrying Suri required that I became a citizen again. Suri's moms led me into the house at a turtle's pace. Paris steadied Habi's elbow. She seemed to be having trouble walking. I caught Aizah's eye and used the finger signing code Diago had taught me. *Is she okay?*

Aizah signed, *she's fine,* and cloaked.

I followed Zulei as she bounded up the spiral staircase to the roof terrace. Paris and Habi stayed below in the sitting room. My head cleared the landing and found Suri waiting along the opposite railing, near some fluttering silks hanging from a line. She was posed in a horizontal wash of sunset and dressed in a bright outfit of green and rose.

"It's her going-away dress. I just finished making it," Zulei said. "I thought that as long as you were coming back to talk, she should show it to you first."

Suri looked embarrassed and irritated. Zulei said something pleadingly in Berbai, spinning her fingers insistently. Suri rolled her eyes like a teenager and obediently rotated.

"I told her to stand there," Zulei whispered. "The evening sunset colors her face so nicely, don't you think?"

Suri wore a short dress with shimmering pants that extended to her calves. Her feet were bare. The dress was lightly embroidered along the waist in silver that flashed as she turned. A silk scarf draped her neck and hung off her bare shoulder.

Zulei leaned into my ear. "That's to keep the bugs off while riding. You do know how to ride a horse, don't you? I will leave you two alone now."

Suri finished her turn and flopped her arms, making the scarf flutter. "What do you think?" she asked miserably.

"You're beautiful," I said.

She held her hand to hide her mouth and looked at a spot on the floor between us. "I mean the dress."

I crossed the tile and took her hand. "You're beautiful no matter what you wear."

She brought my hand to her lips. "Thanks for coming back."

"What's wrong?"

"It's such a nice evening, I don't want to spoil it, but ... I have something I must tell you. It's not words that will make you laugh."

"Do you want to go someplace private?"

"No, I've kept this behind my teeth for too long."

"I'm listening."

She nodded at the stairs. "They are not my mothers. My mother was a slave in Phut."

"The Phuts keep slaves?"

She nodded. "My mother escaped and fled into the swamps."

"The same swamps where we came out of the water after the attack?"

She nodded again. "They are the home of the Anakim-Libai.

One of them found my mother. He did … terrible things to her. She became pregnant with twins. Zulie's husband found her in a cave trying to give birth." Suri wiped her eyes with her sleeve. "I'm sorry, Jordan, I shouldn't have hidden this from you. It brings me such shame."

I pulled a silk off the line and handed it to her. I wanted to hold her and tell her that none of it mattered, that I'd love her even if she was a longneck, but I sensed she needed to tell her story.

"What happened," I asked as gently as I could.

"The babies can be big when a half-giant is the father. Zulei said my sister was thirty pounds. She didn't survive." She took a breath and squared her shoulders. "Zulie's husband called for help, but there wasn't enough time. When my mother died, he had to get me out of her belly.

She gave me a sad smile. "All the time we traveled, you were so nice to me. Then you started to like me."

"Suri, I didn't want—"

She touched my mouth. "You tried to hide it, but I could tell." Her eyes danced over mine. "I kept thinking I had to tell you who I was because when you got to Mestre and Javan, you'd see."

"Suri—"

"But when you asked me to marry you, I was so happy. I hoped I could forget. But the kinder you were, the worse I felt. I had to tell you." She wrung her hands around her scarf.

"There is nothing you could say to make me love you less—"

"I am *Anakim*."

I kept my silence as I tried to figure out why that could possibly matter.

"Every time you and the others say 'Anak,' I want to die."

Anak was short for Anakim. I suddenly felt like dirt.

"That is what I wanted to tell you," she whispered. She turned from me. I'd never seen her look so forlorn.

"Your dad was an Anakim half-giant?

She nodded.

"I love you. I'm marrying you because I'm nuts about you, all of you, the good, the whatever, and the quirky. And if you have Anakim blood in you, well, guess what; so do I."

She looked at me in surprise.

"I found out from Numu before he died. Apparently, where I come from, most of us are part Anakim."

She blushed and held her hand to her face. She did that to hide her nose, not her mouth. It was a little larger than what other girls sported in the village. To me, she looked normal, the girl-next-door instead of a fantasy woman. Someone I could have grown up with; and in a way I had.

I gently took her hand from her face. "When it comes to beauty, you have everybody beat."

"You need oculars," she said.

I tilted her chin upwards. "Now that you know the truth about my lineage, will you still have me?"

She reached up, put her hands on either side of my face, and placed a big, wet Fourth Age kiss on my lips.

"I'm guessing that's a yes," I said as I brushed away her tears.

It was show time. Aaron, Diago, Aizah, and Jarell watched with amusement as I paced outside the village gate. I was dressed in the traditional Berbai groom's outfit, a collision of every color in the crayon box. Diago and Aaron flicked twigs at me to see if they'd stick to my feathered cloak. Diago smoothed his new pilot's tunic over his Guardian dress silvers. Aizah and Jarell stopped my pacing and did some last minute fussing on the outfit like a couple of matrons. The guys suggested hiking up on the ridge. They wondered if my cloak could keep me airborne like Aaron's had in Baskra. Standing among them, taking their good-natured jibes, I realized they were more than just friends. They were family.

I wondered where Levi and Athena were and stared toward the Acropolis. Aizah leaned in close to examine my collar, perhaps more to talk to me than to actually fix it.

"Are you ready for this?" she asked as she re-pinned a clasp at the neck of my cloak.

I was surprised how hard the question hit my gut. "Sure."

"Thinking about Lisa?"

I was.

"It's normal the second time around," Jarell said.

"You've been married before?" I asked.

She nodded.

"I'm sorry," I said.

"Don't be; part of life."

"Especially ours," Aizah said.

"You can't let it get in the way," Jarell said. "Box it up and move on."

Aizah yanked me down to Trahl eye level and gave me a nose rub. "You got nothing to feel bad about. Together is better than being alone."

"Yeah, love her well." Jarell punched my shoulder. "And have a lot of kids so we can spoil them."

"Okay, moms."

"Speaking of which," Aizah said to Jarell, "guess what Athena told me?"

"What?"

"Odin ran some tests while Jordan was strapped to that metal table."

"That's news?" Jarell inquired.

"What kind of tests?" I asked.

"He was trying to prove you were from the future by comparing genetic samples. Turns out you are the direct descendent of two people in this village."

"Who?"

Aizah smiled. "Me."

"Do tell," Jarell said.

"Who's the other person I'm related to?"

Aizah hesitated.

"Oh no," I groaned. "Don't tell me it's Suri."

Aizah choked back a laugh. "No! Somebody else."

"Who is it?" Jarell demanded. "Come on, Guardian, spill it. The guys are coming back."

"Swear to secrecy," she said.

"I swear," I said.

"Not you." Aizah wrinkled her nose. "You're a guy; you'll just forget anyway."

"Oh no, if it's who I think it is, I might not want to hear this," Jarell said.

"It's Aaron."

"Aaron, huh?" I digested that for a second. I felt closer to Levi. Always had, but blood isn't everything.

Jarell seemed to have trouble adjusting to the news. "In other words, for Jordan to exist, you and Aaron have to get married?"

"And have kids," she said.

Jarell laughed. "No wonder I never had a chance with him. The whole universe was against me."

"Poor boy," Aizah purred. "He's trapped."

The wedding was nothing like I expected. My first surprise as I lined up with my comrades was the sudden appearance of two enormous shadows crossing the dirt road leading into the village as Athena materialized in front of a blazing sunset, accompanied by a Nephillim male. They bowed in their protective suits.

Aaron looked up at the male. "Hello, Apollo."

Apollo slapped Aaron's back. Aaron didn't even flinch.

Athena knelt before me to get closer to eye level. She seemed embarrassed behind her faceplate. "We were watching up on *Olympus* and realized you didn't have a very large escort."

"So we're offering our services," Apollo grinned. "Can't get much larger than us!"

"May we join you?" Athena asked.

"Of course," I said. "I didn't know Nephillim visited the planet surface. I thought it wasn't healthy."

"It's not. But this is a special occasion, so I figured what the heck."

"What the heck?"

"Isn't that what you say when–"

I sighed. "Did you write down *everything* I said when I was defrosting?"

"I'm thinking of submitting it for publication. Fourth Age Colloquialisms."

"Yeah, that'll get you a bunch of creative credits."

Athena's smile faded. She glanced at the ground. "Sorry about the whole adopting you thing. You are a capable adult. I realize now it wasn't necessary."

"I was a bit overwhelmed."

"Nephillim have that effect on people. Always barging in and knocking everybody over."

"Levi couldn't make it?" I asked.

"He's on his way. Things are a little busy on the Acropolis."

Levi suddenly appeared. He retracted his helmet, looking careworn. He forced a smile, which on his best days looked like a grimace. I ran up and clasped his arms. *"Brosheleau."*

He nodded. "You're welcome."

Opening music sounded from the clearing. Athena stood, causing leaves on nearby trees to updraft. "Apollo and I will follow behind you so we don't block anybody's view."

"Or elbow a tree branch on your head dress," Apollo said. "Nice feathers."

"Oh, and before I forget." Athena pulled something out of her sleeve pocket and passed it down to me. It was a small bottle of deep red liquid with a ribbon tied to the cork. "This is for your first night, just the two of you."

"Thanks."

She turned and took a long step backward to stand behind us.

"Wait," I said. She looked at me. "Walk beside me."

"But that's a position reserved for your mother," she said.

Aizah met my questioning glance with an almost imperceptible nod.

"You saved my life, did my laundry, and let me jump off a mountain to get back with Suri. If that's not being a mom, what is?"

It's risky getting sentimental with a Nephillim. With no armor to protect me, their hugs can crack ribs.

CHAPTER FIFTY-ONE

LEVI

We walked toward the enormous tree canopy silhouetted by twilight. Firelight danced under the fluttering leaves. Stars outlined the rooftops, Athena, and Apollo. Each door was open, with candles set on the thresholds representing the Berbai welcome of a new wedded couple into their community, and fruit hanging in baskets symbolizing the generations that might be born from Jordan and Suri's union. Birds and insects wheeled overhead in celebration. Jordan approached from the east, the morning birth of man. Suri would approach from the west, the evening birth of woman.

Mother Habi and her husband, Tumleh, stood at the base of the tree assisted by ten children, two of them Becca and Liv-ya. Suri's eldest parents had recently entered their silver time. Their white hair and wrinkled bodies seemed to shock Jordan as he approached. Surely, the people of the Fourth Age declined in the same manner in the final month of living. If Jordan had questions, he was wise to keep them behind his teeth for now.

Suri wanted to limit her wedding party to her other parents and a handful of friends out of respect for Jordan's lack of immediate family, but Jordan would have none of it. Berbai filled the clearing and the nearby rooftops. Amon was one of Suri's honored guests. He watched from a floating bed near one of the wedding fires, attended by a Javan medical team and an array of life-preserving devices. His condition had worsened and his arms were completely covered and restrained. Jordan and Suri made a point to greet him. It warmed my heart to see them do that.

A glint of gold flashed on the horizon as the sun set. I zoomed in with my oculars. The ancient mountain shelter for the Berbai had been cleared of surface growth and its massive gold-sheathed ben-ben had been elevated for another operational check. I'd spent a lot of time overseeing the restoration of that particular shelter. Suri's and Jordan's survival would depend on its systems working flawlessly if the Stream threatened Earth as Apollo feared. Athena had not yet informed the civilians of the coming crisis. Ground Com had decided to prepare the shelters and monitor the Stream's progress. The alert would only be given when it looked like Earth was in jeopardy.

We reached the tree. The Guardians wished Jordan well and stepped back to give the children room to perform the ceremony. We knew what was coming. We'd seen it many times before. I wondered what it would be like for Jordan, since his age had forgotten the story. Surely, the memory of the first wedding could not have survived that long.

CHAPTER FIFTY-TWO

SARAH

I held Liv-ya while I rocked in the terrace swing. Her snores added to the music of the jungle. I watched the shimmering sea from my mountain home overlooking the lights of Quepos. It was now or never. Liv-ya had been the last to jump. If Jordan was coming, he would come soon.

Her arrival in Costa Rica narrowed Jordan's point of entry down to this region. We doubled our patrols to augment the Costa Rican civil air patrol since Costa Rica had no military. It was one of the reasons so many war-weary Second Agers had settled here.

Shouts from the driveway below my home interrupted my respite. Carlos dashed up the outside steps to my terrace.

"What's wrong?" I asked as Liv-ya stirred and rubbed her eyes.

"It's Shamel."

The half-hour drive down to Shamel's mansion on the beach felt like it took forever. I found him in his study, looking frightened. The Javan medic examined him as best he could with such primitive equipment available in this age.

"How are you?" I asked, taking his wrinkled hand. Others

gathered in the doorway.

Shamel hung his head. “I don’t know precisely. I was dictating into my diary when it happened. One minute, I was speaking normally and the next speak not but tried making sense.” His eyes closed in frustration, then opened again. “Not possible this wolf orange canopy sick nothing.”

The women in the doorway gasped.

“The Stream is coming!” one wailed.

CHAPTER FIFTY-THREE

JORDAN

Levi and the team greeted the parents, wished me luck, and backed out of the clearing to watch from the edge of the firelight.

Becca looked up at the parents. "Are we supposed to start now?"

Clearly, they weren't supposed to, I thought. My bride and her attendants were nowhere in sight.

"Yes, start," Habi rasped, her voice amplified by a small device hovering near her head.

The kids came at me like a wolf pack, all racing to be first. A young boy pulled my sleeve toward a spot on the grass by one of the oversized tree roots.

"Lie down there," he said, pointing at the spot.

The other kids pointed and chimed in. Becca showed me which way to lie, on my back. The kids tried to get my clothing smoothed out.

They stood in a ring about me, surveying their efforts. I flicked my eyes to Levi to scc if this was some sort of practical joke, but his reverent demeanor assured me I was in good hands. Becca gave some orders. The smallest little girl sat next to my head, said something in toddler-Berbai, and pushed on my eyelids with her fingers.

"You're s'posed to close them," a companion explained as she twirled her hair with a muddy finger.

Tumleh hid his mouth with his hand to suppress a laugh. I obeyed but kept them open just a slit so I could see what was going on. Becca stooped down and picked up a slender branch. She plucked the leaves off. "Now comes the important part."

The boy who had raced to be first pushed his way past Becca, holding a stripped branch.

"Hey, that's my job," Becca complained.

The boy pressed the branch to the base of my foot. Several of the kids laughed.

"Not *there*," Liv-ya giggled.

He grinned mischievously and poked me farther up.

"Whoa, watch it, kid," I whispered.

Becca was mortified. She grabbed the stick. A pushing match ensued. Becca took a swing. The boy complained loudly. Tumleh started to hobble over and I sat up.

"Hang on, gang." I motioned for Becca to surrender her weapon, then handed the stick back to the boy, locking eyes with him. "Do what she says, okay, chief?"

He nodded. I lay down again. The stick got laid against my rib cage.

"Now you *really* have to close your eyes," Liv-ya said.

The stick disappeared from my chest and the kids shushed each other. Shuffling feet and a few suppressed giggles, then Liv-ya called from somewhere farther away, "You can wake up now."

I opened my eyes, then quickly sat up. Suri stood before me in the firelight, wearing the most incredible dress I'd ever seen. She blushed and slowly turned for me, her feet bare. A shimmering, full-sleeve gown extended to her ankles. The dress was bright silver. Red silk peeked from sleeves and the bodice. A gold wrap caressed her shoulders, carefully clasped across her chest by a single opal pin. A dramatic rainbow spray of feathers radiated from her back, undulating as she turned. Her flowered hair cascaded off her shoulders with orchids in full bloom. When she finished her turn, a gold headband sparkled and a red diamond blazed like a third eye.

She reached down and drew me to my feet. "Surprise," she whispered.

"Meet your new wife," Habi said from far away.

"Jordan ben Athena," Tumleh said, "do you accept Suri?"

"I do."

"Suri?" Habi said, "Do you accept Jordan?"

"With all my soul," she breathed.

"We'd better get you married, then," Tumleh said. He looked to the village. "What do you say to that?"

The village cheered their approval. Becca and Liv-ya jumped up and down. Amon smiled from his bed and nodded to me. I mouthed my thanks. Tumleh and Habi offered a prayer in Berbai. Suri quietly translated as we held hands.

"Creator, before they were made, you held them in your heart. You moved the heavens that they might meet. Such a pairing is rare. I sense that as an island in the eye of a storm, you have grafted their union across the ages for profound purpose. We ask that wherever you send them, whatever task you give them, please provide safe harbors along the way. Multiply the days they can rest in the gift of your love."

Tumleh opened his eyes. A tear tracked down his sunken cheek. "For they have had so very few." He closed his eyes again. "I see a great nation rising one day from their union, marching across a desolate land; not to conquer, but to heal. This nation will spring from their love as surely as a fountain bursts from the earth. So it has been."

"So it will be!" shouted the Berbai. The words echoed across the square.

Suri looked at me expectantly. I followed her lead, leaned in, and carefully nose-rubbed her. Applause joined the crackling of the wedding fires. I drew back to stare into her glistening eyes. She threw her arms around me and kissed me hard. I was vaguely aware of gasps, then laughter. Aizah and the other Guardians hooted their approval as I returned Suri's passion.

* * * * *

The ceremony transitioned into the Berbai version of a wedding reception. Folks changed into more casual attire. Suri and I switched into our traveling clothes. We would leave for our sweet month at sunrise.

One tradition stood the test of time: Suri and I didn't get a chance to eat anything during the dinner. Many people wanted to speak to us. After the line thinned, I brought Tumleh a drink. He'd somehow aged into a wrinkled old man in the short time I'd been away. Habi appeared to be suffering from the same malady. Suri put an arm around her and let her lean on her shoulder. They were soon wrapped up in a slow conversation.

Tumleh took the drink in his wrinkled hands and squinted up at me. "Are you enduring this bewildering celebration, son?"

"Yes, thank you." I said, watching as he struggled to take a sip. I wanted to help but didn't know if I should.

"It is permissible to offer help. You don't need to worry about offending me with kindness." He grinned mischievously. "When you reach a hundred decades, it becomes easy to discern what others are thinking."

"Sorry, sir."

"Sorry for what? That I am older than dirt?"

I held back a laugh.

"You do say that, don't you?"

I sighed. "Yes, sir. Apparently, I say a lot of things."

He handed me the drink and took my free hand in both of his. "The way I consider it, getting silver and wrinkly stinks. But I never worried about it happening."

Sad advice, I thought.

"Yes, it is sad," he said. "But that is our lot while we sojourn here. May I give you a piece of advice before the night further wanes?"

"Yes, sir."

Folks within earshot turned to listen. The music quieted. Suri and Habi ended their conversation and turned to attend. I guessed this was part of the ceremony.

"You have become part of a special people," Tumleh said. "We are exiles just like you, strangers in a strange land. When our homeland was taken from us, we could have harbored resentment, dedicated ourselves to becoming strong enough to smite those who'd wronged us. But we treaded a better path. It is a way of life that only makes sense if one believes death is not an end, but a transition. The right of passage is not earned. It is bequeathed upon those who nurture a selfless heart. As it is written …"

As if on cue, the entire assembly recited:

"For those who take, the future is dim.
For those who care, the future is uncertain.
For those who give, the future is bright."

"Much was taken from you, son, yet you kept giving when you had nothing. I assure you, stay on this path and your future will be very bright."

We embraced. I felt many hands touching my head and shoulders. Something came alive in me. Suri looked over Habi through the many relatives encircling us. I had a wife. I had parents. I had a ginormous family.

A while later, as eating and merry-making resumed, two magnificent red horses were paraded into the park and tethered at the head of a trail, the one we'd followed past the hill that I hadn't been allowed to climb.

"What are they for?" I asked Suri.

"They take us to our mountain."

"You do know how to ride, don't you?" Aizah teased.

A bunch of Suri's cousins stepped onto a raised terrace, carrying musical instruments. I couldn't believe what I saw. Horns, guitars, drum set, keyboard … was that a cowbell? The band started warming up.

"Wow, they're good," I shouted over the drum solo.

"They should be," she said. "Diago made them practice a whole week."

The crowd pulled back to make a clearing in the grass. Suri took my hand and nodded to the band. They stopped in mid-jam, tuned their instruments, and the guitar started a new song.

"What's up?" I asked as everybody whooped and whistled.

"Time to dance!" Suri exclaimed.

"But I heard the Berbai don't dance and eat on the same day," I said in protest.

"They don't. I arranged this for you."

When the horn section kicked in, I did a double-take. They were playing *that* song?

"Diago said this was your favorite," she cajoled, anxious to get dancing.

Kool and the Gang's "Celebration" had been a regular kick off song at wedding receptions I'd attended during the Fourth Age. I laughed and pulled Suri into a slow spin. Folks migrated into the circle. Becca and Liv-ya darted in and grabbed our hands to make us a foursome. Aizah towed Aaron through the crowd and we became six. The clearing then filled with weaving lines of complex, synchronized movements even the best dancers of the Fourth Age couldn't have duplicated. An old song and a new dance, linking my past with the future.

Suri had another surprise. Metal clinked against glasses on the overlooking balconies. Expectant faces smiled down on us as the sound reached a crescendo.

Suri grinned slyly. "Athena told me when glasses are struck by eating utensils, it means you're supposed to kiss me."

"Where did she get that idea?"

Suri looked puzzled as our clan kept up the clinking. "But she swore you said that."

I pretended to struggle with my memory. She started to look worried.

"Wow, really? I don't know." I shook my head. "Oh, wait, she's right."

"You're in so much trouble."

"Then I'd better not do this."

She squealed as I dipped her. I held her high enough off the ground that her hair just missed and gave her a long kiss.

The celebrating went on well into the night. Impromptu speeches were made on our behalf, none serious. Aaron and Diago tied for the most creative accounts of every cultural blunder I'd made since I'd landed in Numu's lake. Then Tumleh rose from his seat and checked to make sure the hovering amplifier found him.

"This is a wonderful day for all of us," he said, his voice echoing across the square. "But I sense the newly joined are becoming anxious to get on their way."

Folks laughed.

"We have many marriages," he rasped. "Each is special." He looked at Habi as if for approval. She nodded. "However, I must be honest, the union of these two children will be one that is most memorable to us." He coughed hard. "My dear wife and I have lived many decades. Our bodies are silvering, readying us for our journey to the Creator. What better finale to our time on Earth than to witness ..." He hesitated and gestured to Suri and me, as if struggling to remember the words. "... to witness feet ..." His face wrinkled up in confusion. "... feet giving fruit not ..."

He closed his mouth and shook his head, then shrugged and sat down. There was painful silence from the crowd. Suri hugged him. Applause slowly rose from the clan. Habi patted his hand as a healer quietly made her way to his side.

The celebration resumed, gradually building into a louder, faster tempo. Suri and I made the rounds to find people we hadn't talked to yet.

Later, something spooked the village dogs. They raced around the tables, nipping and snarling at each other. Then a few got into a fight. People looked concerned as village elders tried to separate them. One of the men got bit. I looked around for the Guardians to see if I could bum a heal stick from them, but they were gone. Athena and Apollo were also missing. Something told me to look up.

"Where's Aizah?" Suri asked.

I took her hand. "Walk with me."

I hurried her outside the village. In the darkness, away from the bonfires, my suspicion was confirmed.

"Where did the stars go?" she asked.

A whole swath was missing, from east to west. It wasn't from cloud cover. The edge of a cloud bank hung far to the north, glowing like a floating wall. Young couples sat on benches, oblivious to what was happening above their heads. They were too busy rubbing noses. Gradually, their clothing brightened, but it was hours until morning and the moon wasn't up.

I was about to guess why that was when a thin flash streaked out of the black void. It came from the west, crested a zenith, and vanished in the east. Another light chased in its wake, followed by more. The occurrences increased in frequency, two or three lights every couple of seconds. Folks came out of the village and watched. Some joined us.

"They're beautiful," someone said.

"Are they dangerous?" another asked.

"I don't think so," I replied. "They aren't falling into the atmosphere; otherwise, they'd be burning up or fracturing."

"If they're so far away, they must be very large."

"They're moving so fast."

Larger objects paraded at a slower clip with green gaseous tails. The light stream thickened. Were they comets, meteors, or space junk? There were hundreds of them streaking across the starless track in a blur. The ground rumbled and my teeth rattled. Tremors vibrated up my legs.

"My head hurts," a little girl complained in the arms of her mother.

Dogs raced past us, yipping and snarling, fleeing into the hills. The ground rose and dipped. Trees swayed. The village wall cracked behind us. I grabbed the little girl's mom and Suri by the hands and hurried them away from the wall in case it fell. We sat in a meadow in a huddle. Others stumbled into the fields and clustered on the heaving ground. It felt like I rode a raft on a rolling ocean. High above, the village canopy tree groaned and creaked. My head pounded with a massive headache. Suri moaned against my chest.

"Make it stop, mommy!" the girl cried.

The sky was full of streaks so bright they cast shifting beams through the leaves and across the land. Then, like the last car of a long speeding freight train suddenly passing the crossing, the celestial stampede ended. The strange lights faded into the east, disappearing over the horizon.

We remained huddled in the darkness as the great tree's movement settled. People around us whispered and wept. The village was dark except for a few fires. The power must have gone out. Then alarms began to blare far away.

Aaron and Aizah reappeared by the village gate.

"Are you kids all right?" Aizah asked.

"Where did you go?" I inquired.

"Ground Com flashed orders to the entire corps," Aaron said. "We had to get away from the reception to view them."

Other villagers saw us talking and tentatively edged closer to hear. Aizah waved them away. " There is nothing to worry about, citizens. There will be a meeting in the village square at noon to answer your questions."

After they moved off, Aizah nodded toward the woods. "Let's find someplace private to talk."

We hiked to a grove of trees beyond the village fields and sat by a brook. Aaron snapped off a dead twig and threw it into the water.

"So, what happened?" I asked.

"That was the Stream of Heaven you saw last night," he said.

"Figured that out already."

"Ground Com's known about it for several weeks," Aizah added.

"Why weren't our people told about it?" Suri asked, taking my hand.

"They thought the Stream wouldn't be visible for another six months," Aaron replied. "They decided to delay informing the public to prevent a panic."

"A lot of good that did," I said. "Half the world is probably scared out of its collective mind by now."

"Aptly put," Aizah said. "The Stream flows between Mars and Earth. It's visible at night in areas facing away from the sun. The citizens of Atlantis are getting an eyeful right now."

"What exactly is the Stream?" Suri asked.

Aaron and Aizah looked at each other. "We might as well explain," Aizah said. "They're going to know at noon, anyway."

Aaron nodded and picked up a pebble. "This is our sun." He picked up another pebble and held them together. "This is its mother. Our sun was born and the mother star died." He pulled the pebbles apart. "The sun orbits its dead mother like this." He moved the two pebbles in wide ovals through the air, bringing them close to each other.

"You're describing a binary orbit pattern," I said. Suri looked at me questioningly. "My people in the Fourth Age understand it. Two stars orbit a blank spot in space, like two rings linked together but pulled apart as far as they can go. The blank spot is centered in the link."

"What does that have to do with the Stream?" she asked.

"Both stars have objects orbiting around them," Aizah said. "There are two solar systems, complete with planets, moons, comets, meteors, and a lot of debris."

"I get it," I said, picturing the Yin-Yang symbol with the white dot representing the sun and the black dot its dark twin. "Stuff orbiting the dead star trespasses through our solar system like a buzz saw cutting through the orbital track as the two stars draw together. The Stream is the outer edge of the dead star's orbiting objects, right?"

"Correct," Aaron said. "Normally, the chance of collision between the two intersecting systems is slim."

"Because there's lots of space in space," I said. "Planets are like specks in a lake. Specks hitting specks rarely happen."

"Unfortunately, there's not always enough space to keep even specks from colliding," Aizah said. "Ground Com has calculated a higher probability of impacts on Earth starting a year from now."

Aaron sighed. "But given what happened last night, as you would say, Jordan, all bets are off."

I probably knew best what those chances were. There was plenty of evidence in my age to indicate our solar system had been struck by invading celestial objects of either massive size or massive quantity. Uranus rotated on its side. Venus rotated backwards. Mars was suffocating from a surface layer of peroxide, a comet-born material that destroyed life. Martian rocks had somehow landed in

Antarctica. Something had blown up a planet between Mars and Jupiter. And the moon, smooth and perfect in this age, was scarred in mine, with more craters than I'd had zits as a teen. When something small hits the earth, it's a news story. If something big hits, it's an age-ender. I had a feeling the latter was imminent. Otherwise, why this crazy journey back in time? If I'd been sent here by some intelligent force, it couldn't have been to shout out loud that the world was coming to a pause.

"Ground Com thinks the world is about to be hit hard?" I asked.

Aaron nodded and Aizah took his hand. "A series of small impacts, as many as a thousand. Individually, they would do little harm; but combined, they could exterminate most of the planet."

"Just as Jordan predicted on the Sacred Mountain," Suri said.

"All I remember is a crazy flying dream," I said. "But I've seen the differences on Earth between my time and this one. The world had to have gone through some horrible impacts to have caused all the changes in my time. Most of my people thought it was due to erosion, weathering, and gradual climate change."

"Oh, there will be climate change." Aaron choked back a derisive laugh. "We'll be lucky to *have* a climate."

"If it's any consolation, at least I'm proof it's survivable," I said. "I descended from both of you, right?"

Aaron started to say something but hesitated. Aizah patted his arm. "We're getting married next week."

"That's wonderful!" Suri said. She hugged Aizah hard.

"We're also leaving the Guardians," she said.

"What?" I exclaimed.

"We'll be assigned to your security detail and board the shelters, along with other citizens when the time comes."

"Why are you leaving the Guardians?" Suri asked.

"A lot of reasons," Aaron said. "That last mission was rougher than most. Almost losing Aizah was more than I could stomach. And, well, this might sound crazy."

"We want to make sure you are born," Aizah said.

* * * * *

Suri and I skipped the noon meeting. We were too tired. Last night we were supposed to ride off into the moonlight to our honeymoon on the mountain with the intoxicating love plants surrounding our open air summit retreat. But Aizah said it was too dangerous. More thunderstorms were popping up across Javan, making mountaintops a not-so-smart place to be. Instead, a small cottage was made available to us on the edge of the village. The family did their best to make it nice and private.

Despite fatigue, my body and mind were racing with excitement. Finally, Suri and I were alone with no prospect of being interrupted. Aizah had promised to shoot the legs off anyone who tried.

Suri took my hand and led me into the bedroom. Sheep's wool and blossoms covered a taut queen-sized hammock. Presents and food covered every available piece of furniture. Her wedding dress hung on a hook, pressed and cleaned. Athena's bottle sat on a tray with two glasses. I undid the cork and poured. The red liquid turned honey colored. There was only enough for two glasses.

"It smells good," Suri said. "What is it?"

"I was hoping you knew." I entwined my arm around hers.

"What are you doing?" she giggled.

"This is a Fourth Age custom. Now we lean in and drink at the same time."

It was the best stuff I'd ever tasted.

"Next time we visit your mom, I will ask her how to make it." Suri said.

I stashed the empty bottle in my backpack for safekeeping.

"I can't believe we're here," I said.

"Hasn't exactly turned out the way you hoped."

"Of course it did. We're together. That's all that matters."

She tried to rub a smudge off her traveling dress. "I must look awful to you."

I kissed her and lightly brushed her nose. "Never."

She ran her hand over the silky material of her wedding gown. "Would you mind if I put it on again?"

"Do you want some help?"

She smirked, then carefully picked the gown off the hook and headed for the bathroom. "I'll be quick."

I knew from experience that wasn't going to happen, but I didn't mind. She wanted to look good for me and that meant a lot. When she emerged, she looked fantastic.

"Are you sure you don't mind?" she asked. "I barely got to wear it for you."

"Of course not, but I'm afraid to hug you. I might crush something expensive."

"It really isn't," she said. "It's basically four layers." She pointed to her gold wrap. "Gold for life." She pulled back the fabric revealing the silver gown underneath. "Silver for how we age." She pointed to the red bodice. "Red for the Creator."

"What's the fourth color?" I asked. "There isn't any more fabric."

She opened her bodice, took my hand, and placed it on her heart. "Me for you."

The next morning, the ground shook so bad our presents tumbled off the furniture. The hammock seemed to have insulated us from most of the tremor. Not quite the romantic morning after I'd envisioned.

"Are you okay?" I asked.

Suri stared up through her disheveled hair, looking dreamy. "Mmm."

"It must have been an earthquake."

She pulled me back down. "It reminded me of last night."

We got the bad news when we ventured out to the market to buy an air car with some of my creative credits. The tremors we'd felt had been from an impact on the other side of the planet, in the heart of the Atlantean empire. The provincial capital of Eliassipus was now a smoldering crater. The ten nations of Atlantis in the West had gone berserk. All those words I'd simultaneously babbled in sixteen languages on the Sacred Mountain about where to run and how to survive the end of the age were talked about everywhere. According to what had come out of my mouth, the heart of the Eastern Alliance—Javan, Mestre, and Magog—was safe yet. Everywhere else wasn't. Thanks to what I'd said and the Stream of Heaven airmailing a meteorite into Eliassipus, one billion people in the ten western nations of Atlantis wanted our real estate pronto. Athena and the Guardians said no deal. Build pyramids like everybody else and ride it out. The West apologized for being so rude and stayed on their side of the planet to await the inevitable.

Yeah, right.

The weather turned violent the next day. The honeymoon trip to the mountain was postponed again because of freak thunderstorms frying the summit. Strange winds blew through the village tree, dropping leaves and enormous branches. It became too dangerous to live in the village. Every other night or so, the celestial stream would return. Sometimes, it was just a terrifying light show; others, a small meteorite or comet fragment would drop out of the sky and obliterate something.

The village relocated to a temporary encampment at the base of a mountain on the north border of the Berbai reserve. At least I'd thought it was a mountain when I'd first seen it blending with the Acropolis range. That's because it had been covered with vegetation. Stripped of the foliage and restored, it gleamed from its golden tip to its pink granite base. A perfect pyramid four times the size of Giza. Why the Berbai called it a mountain didn't surprise me. The Mayans had called their pyramids sacred mountains, as did other ancient cultures from my age. The gold top was one third of the pyramid's mass. Wide steps led to a cavernous hatchway on the side of the gilded capstone. The Egyptians called them *ben-bens* and claimed the metallic capstones could fly.

We were allowed to visit the village during the daytime but we had to sleep in the camps at night. All civilian transports hovered outside the village walls, ready to whisk people back to the mountain at a moment's notice. One afternoon, just before our first drill inside the ben-ben, Suri and I were standing in line to climb the steps when a Javan trainer jet roared past the slope, banked hard, took out the top of a palm tree, and landed on the grass ten feet from our sandals. Aaron popped the canopy, laughing his head off. Diago saluted proudly from the cockpit. Aizah swatted Diago upside the helmet and vaulted to the ground, where she hugged Suri.

"Diago's a pilot already?" I asked.

"He thinks he is," Aizah muttered. "Next time, I'm walking."

"Levi sent us over to check on you," Aaron said. "How's married life? You two kids okay?"

We were kids now?

Suri's arms went around me. She nodded happily. That's when I noticed Aizah was sporting a jewel on her forehead. Instead of being set in a gold net band, it appeared adhered directly to her skin. More practical for a Guardian, I guess.

"Aaron and I got married last week," she said. "Simple ceremony on the Acropolis. Just the two of us. Everything's in a hurry these days."

"Congratulations," I said.

She shrugged. "Newly married Guardians are restricted to domestic duty for one year. In our case, until we decide to become civilians. In the meantime, we get to stay on as your security detail, though. Aaron says when we get through this, we'll invite you over to the Acropolis for poker."

"Yeah, our crater is your crater," he said.

"What do you think?" she asked, pointing to the pyramid. " I bet you never saw one of these before."

"Actually, I have," I said.

"But not in use," she said.

"In use?"

"We're not allowed to explain, remember, dearest?" Aaron said. "The smart people at Ground Com don't want to frighten the civilians."

"Would this be what you mean?" I handed her something I pulled out of my wallet.

"What's this?"

"We call it a dollar. Kind of like a creative credit."

"What does the man with white hair have to do with the mountain?" Suri asked.

"Look at the back."

Aizah's eyes got big as she studied the image on the back of a one-dollar bill; a flat topped pyramid with a floating tip.

"Is that what you aren't allowed to tell us?" I inquired.

Diago looked over her shoulder and his face fell. Aaron and Aizah pulled us out of the line. It was Aaron who said, "Keep this behind your teeth until everyone has been properly drilled. Otherwise, civilians might panic and get hurt."

"What else is going down that you're not telling us?" I asked. "I haven't seen any Guardians since the wedding."

"They've been busy."

"No kidding," I said.

Aaron sighed. "Oh, all right. I'll get in big trouble for saying this, but you did warn us, so … Atlantis is massing to attack. The Guardians are making a stand at the coast to hold them off and give civilians time to evacuate inland."

"Who else is helping?"

"No one."

"Not even the Mestreans?" Suri asked.

"The Javans stand alone," Aizah said.

"Twenty thousand Javans against half the planet?" I said.

"We can hold them long enough," Diago said. His Engel had gotten better.

"Long enough for what?" I asked.

"Until the Stream takes them out from behind," Aizah said.

"And the Guardians with them," I said.

The villagers had been filing up the steps during our conversation. The end of the line was almost at the door. Suri threw her arms around Diago. He suddenly didn't look so tough anymore. He was now like the teenager I remembered at the Embassy.

"You had better get going," Aaron said. "Levi will have my skin if you and Suri miss any of the practice flights."

"What do you mean by flights?" Suri said.

"We'll be monitoring you from here," Aizah said. "There's nothing to worry about."

"I have to join my squadron." Diago pulled away from Suri and saluted me. "Jordan, make sure she listens to the pilots."

"Pilots?" Suri asked.

Aizah and Aaron backed away from the base of the enormous pyramid, and Suri and I climbed the steps. Diago got into his trainer jet. It shot into the air and banked toward the Acropolis.

I looked around inside the ben-ben. It was honeycombed with transparent spherical chambers containing heavily cushioned chairs. People ascended ramps and hurried to any available seats, where attendants helped them strap in.

Liv-ya and Becca waved frantically from an open sphere that was nearly full. "Suri, Jordan, over here!"

Their little arms stretched to guard the seats beside them. We took them and let the attendants snug us in.

"What does our shiny mountain do?" Liv-ya asked.

"I guess we'll find out," I said.

At the center of the lowest deck stood a large view screen in front of a flashing console. Four uniformed individuals sat before it, busily bringing up displays and speaking in terse sentences they repeated back to each other. Sounded like the Javan version of a countdown.

The massive hatch swung closed and sealed with a heavy shudder. A deep vibration began to build within the cavernous ben-ben.

Weeks later, Suri and I had the bittersweet honor of standing beside Tumleh and Habi's hammock when they passed away. They went within minutes of each other. Suri said this happens when two hearts beat side by side for so many centuries. The ancient historian Josephus recounted the same process from his study of historical documents. He confessed to his contemporaries that he would be considered insane but insisted he had to record what he'd read. Historians ancient to his time had claimed their ancestors had lived ten centuries of youthfulness, aged rapidly at the end, and died peacefully in their sleep. In my age, we labeled these accounts as myths. Perhaps such a vibrant life cycle, catastrophically lost, threatened our belief in a slow changing world that steadily improved. I'd seen no evidence to support slow change or natural improvement. I was long past questioning Josephus, Plato, and Manetho. The Earth had a habit of changing suddenly, each cycle birthing a new world that was worse than the former. Was this our fate? Work our civilized tails off, only to be knocked down over and over until we were eventually became extinct?

As I helped drape the death cloth over Tumleh's face, I felt the answer deep within me. I remembered the dream I'd had on the Sacred Mountain in that near-death dream, of the scarred man who'd urged me not to give up. It felt like an answer. It gave me comfort, but I couldn't explain why.

The funeral was sad and quietly joyful. Death was still natural and gentle among the people of the Second Age, yet none of the villagers had experienced life without Tumleh and Habi in it. The wake lasted all night. I heard a lot of stories about their lives. I hope to write them down someday. I took part in the elaborate procession to the pyre in the morning, high on the mountain of the Berbai, facing the sun. I sketched and notated the ceremony. If we made it through whatever came, I hoped my account would do their memory justice.

Amon had changed a lot after the failed invasion and his subsequent asylum in Javan. The Ra exiled him, claiming he was complicit in the attack. Amon was too weak to fight the humiliation. He left Mestre and came to Javan at Athena's invitation. He was gracious and supportive of our marriage, constantly apologizing despite my best attempts to assure him that we were square. I guess his earnest desire to patch things up stemmed from the fact Suri and I were the closest things he had to relatives in Javan. Suri felt like I was reading him all wrong. Gradually, I realized she was right. At my suggestion, we invited Amon and his healers to move in next to our cottage as he continued to convalesce from his mysterious injury.

Mestre had changed. The people demanded for the Ra to step down after revelations of his complicity in the failed invasion. It became public knowledge that he'd intended Amon, Suri, and Numu to be kidnapped. Street demonstrations clamored for his glittering head, while sympathy for Amon grew. The story of the Prince's heroic efforts to save Numu and his injury was a constant topic on the Mestrean news stations. Pressure mounted to bring Amon home. The Ra realized his rule was in jeopardy. In an effort of appeasement, he granted Amon permission to return to Mestre but stripped him of his title.

If Amon appreciated the invitation, he didn't let it show. He was quiet and remorseful, still apologizing to us despite our efforts to assure him that all was well. Most days, he seemed lost in thought, staring out our balcony windows, toward the cloud plume marking the distant Mestrean Falls. He never talked about his injury. Whatever was wrong with his arms, they didn't heal. I'd gotten a look at them when his healers had put him to sleep and opened one of the armored braces protecting them. They had to replace a stint supplying constant heal stick juice into his wrists. The heavy brace was only open for a few seconds, but in that time, his wrist thrashed and curled out of it like a raging serpent as the healers fought to reinsert the stint.

I wondered how Amon was going to fare inside the pyramid if he had to be interred during an actual emergency. What would happen to him afterward? What if the world was destroyed and his medicine ran out? During one of my weekly medical visits to Athena, I voiced my concerns for him.

"I'll see what I can do," she said as she brushed excess pollen off my cheeks.

A delegation of Palace officials appeared on Amon's doorstep a few days later and announced that a new medical facility would be constructed in Mestre to protect the chronically ill during and after the cataclysm. Athena handled the design and arranged the funding for its construction. It would have its own power source and armored hibernation chambers buried in the ground to keep patients stable and hidden for centuries following a cataclysm. Her logic was that if the Stream struck full force and ended this age, civilization on Earth would collapse. Survivors might degenerate into primitive societies. The five races would need a lot of time to rebuild before people like Amon could be discovered, thawed out, and properly cared for. A means of finding them would be provided, but only an advanced civilization would be able to detect the signal.

Athena wanted the facility built in the Mestrean highlands, east of the Sacred Mountain, after I suggested the location would be the most stable region to construct in. Ra said no way. He wasn't having thousands of sick people hibernating in his back yard. A hundred thousand Mestreans protested and Ra still said no. Athena parked four battle mountains in Nephillim airspace above his bedroom and conducted nonstop training exercises each night. Finally, Ra relented. I love my giant mom.

The day before his transfer to the facility, Amon was settled on our back porch, listening with his eyes half-closed as Suri read to him his favorite poetry, the *Voyages of Seth.* I chatted quietly nearby with Amon's medical attendants. A news alert flashed in the air next to one of them. She flicked the little personal view screen to life and expanded it so the rest of us could watch. I recognized the Ra's palace behind the excited face of the commentator, but I couldn't comprehend Mestrean.

"What's happening?" I asked.

"A revolt in the Palace," one healer said.

"The Palace Guards were overwhelmed by the Mestrean Guardians," said another.

"The Ra abdicated," exclaimed the first. "The people are chanting for Amon to be the new Ra."

Alarms sounded in the distance. Something big *whooshed* up to our garden gate.

"Jordan," Aaron yelled.

I peered out the window. Aaron and Aizah sat in the front seat of a sleek air car. Suri, Amon, and the healers joined me.

"Atlantis declared war," Aizah shouted. "Their fleet is coming. The Guardians are mustering on the Acropolis."

"They're heading to the coast to stop the invasion," Aaron said. "We're going to the capital to see them off. Get in."

"May I join you?" Amon asked me.

I yelled down to Aaron. "You got room for seven?"

The healers made Amon comfortable in the back. Suri and I sat in the middle. Aaron flew down the little street, craning his neck for the first sight of the Acropolis mountain range as soon as we cleared the village wall. Aizah stared out the opposite direction. They were on one year newlywed leave: no combat missions permitted. I sensed Aaron's frustration and perhaps Aizah's guilty relief. I shared both their emotions with intensity. Letting my friends face the enemy without me? Unthinkable. Leaving Suri? Impossible. She had become a part of me. The impenetrable shield versus the unstoppable spear. I was grateful I had no choice in the matter.

We reached Deucalion, and traffic into the city was hopelessly snarled. Every Javan was trying to do what we attempted, give the traditional send-off to our troops going into harm's way. Aaron swerved off the public road and headed down an alley. Traffic bunched up. Aaron hit the accelerator and flew up onto the rooftop. Aizah followed the news on her view screen.

"Where are we trying to get to?" I asked.

"The Sacred Way," Suri said. "The Guardians take it through the city when they go to war."

"The Mestrean Guardians used to join the march in the center of the city," Amon said. "Before the Ra took them over."

Aizah moaned as she changed views on her screen. "We aren't going to make it."

"Yes, we will," Aaron said. He dodged rooftop gardens and laundry, plunged off the side of a building and ripped down a street, over the heads of thousands of people all pressing to reach the ancient roadway before the Guardians appeared.

"I see them!" Suri shouted. She pointed to one of the access roads snaking down the face of the cliffs. It shimmered with armor.

"Anak," Aaron said, "they're all the way at the bottom. We're going to miss the front of the line."

"Head for the Market Bridge," Suri said.

"Good idea."

"And stop saying Anak."

"Sorry."

The bridge was blocked off. A civilian police officer held up his hand. "Sorry, bridge is closed to civilians and military."

"What about for the future Ra of Mestre?" Amon said.

The startled officer waved us through.

"Smooth," I said.

Amon grinned weakly.

We drove right on top of the bridge. Aaron and I helped Amon out of the car while Aizah and Suri ran to the rail. The healers propped Amon up so he could see. Aaron's and Aizah's oculars swirled as they searched the far end of the long cavernous road. It was cobblestoned and lined with statuary and carved inscriptions.

"Thank the Creator we made it," Aizah choked.

A cloud of dust swirled beyond a distant rise in the road. Civilians on rooftops began to cheer. Then those closer along the walls joined in. A moment later, the gleaming helmets of the Special Missions Guardians flashed sunbursts. The ranks marched toward us like a metallic tide, helmets down and weapons shouldered, each man and woman indistinguishable from the next except for the mission stamps on their helmets.

"Where are the flags?" Aizah asked.

Aaron scanned the ranks and stabbed a finger. "There's Jarell."

Aizah clutched her husband's arm. "Jarell! Up here!"

Jarell finger-signed something to them that made Aizah tear up.

I stood watch beside Aaron. Suri leaned against me. The cheers were deafening.

"Do you see Levi yet?" Suri shouted in my ear.

I shook my head, not taking my eyes off the fast marching ranks. There were so many of them, I would have missed Diago had it not been for Suri looking up. The Javan air force paraded overhead: Darts, Interceptors, and something massive called an Armored Repulser that shook the bridge with its anti-gravs. One of the Darts dipped its wings as it slipped by. The Algonian insignia covered its secondary wings. Suri cried Diago's name as the little fighter was lost in the sea of aircraft.

All twenty thousand Javan Guardians marched under the bridge with no sign of Levi.

"We missed him," I said.

"No, we didn't," Aaron said.

The road was now empty but the crowds on the rooftops still cheered. People along the walls pointed. Levi came over the rise wearing armor with new insignia.

"They made him commandant of the Guardians," Aaron said.

"He didn't want me to tell you until now."

Levi was accompanied by a Guardian with general's insignia. They walked side by side. One was Javan and the other was Mestrean. I don't think even Amon knew. He looked as shocked as the rest of us. I learned later that the other man was Levi's old friend, the Mestrean officer who'd helped keep order on the Sacred Mountain.

"I guess he decided to ignore the Ra's command not to join the fight," Amon said.

"It seems he's not the only one," Aaron said.

Three standard bearers appeared behind Levi and his Mestrean comrade. The flags snapped smartly through flower petals cast down from the jubilant crowd. The one on the left bore the Javan Eagle; the one on the right the Mestrean Lion.

"What's that symbol on the middle flag?" Suri asked.

"I never saw it before," Aaron said.

It had the head and wings of an eagle and the body of a lion, proclaiming the restoration of two warrior societies. Apparently, I was the only one who recognized the mythical griffin.

Behind them, about a hundred paces back, marched a sea of Mestrean Guardians. Levi drew near. He and the general halted. Aaron, Aizah, and I came to attention. Levi opened his helmet and looked up. Aaron and Aizah slapped a salute across their collarbones. I stood quietly since I was a civilian now. Levi and the general returned the salute, then Levi shouted an order as if leading an entire company. He and the general pivoted toward me, snapped their palms across their chests, then angled them to their chins.

I returned the honor. If the hint of a smile crossed that weathered face, I'll never know.

Levi closed his helmet. The two warriors marched under the bridge, followed by the now closer Mestrean Guardians. As the sea of humanity's finest passed beneath my feet, I realized these two armies were sacrificing their lives not only for their people, but for me. I remained at attention and held the United States Navy salute until the last Mestrean passed.

CHAPTER FIFTY-FOUR

LEVI

Our transports settled down on the Atlantic mountains north of the Heracles pass. Each vessel unfolded into a fire base, their twelve-foot-wide struts sinking deep into the bedrock to stabilize against shock rounds. Launch strips rolled out across the bare rock of the windswept coastal cliffs.

Our air force landed and recharged. Ground Com Forward unfolded on a peak overlooking the vast Atlantic, and Athena's shuttle set down next to it. I gripped the wet railing and opened my visor. Cold mist stung my face. I missed Aaron and his cavalier comments that would have lifted my spirits.

Lead, Ground Com Forward.

GCForward, Lead.

Enemy fleet approaching flank speed due east. Contact in five hours.

Understood.

The clouds broke, revealing a strip of clear sky from north to south. Stars sparkled. Then a trio of angry flashes cut across the void, their race marked by lightning all the way to the horizon. Atlantis wasn't the only enemy approaching.

CHAPTER FIFTY-FIVE

JORDAN

Suri and I packed for the shelter. We were each allowed the equivalent of a Fourth Age carry-on. I used my backpack. I loaded my camera and sketch pad. I also threw in some meat fruit wrapped in special packaging and a couple of rocks Apollo had given me from his travels. I think they were from Titan but the moons had different names in this age and I couldn't remember the order. Everything else—the dishes, honeymoon hammock, and hundreds of small wedding gifts from relatives and the Acropolis—had to remain behind. Suri packed some of the more special wedding gifts into her satchel, along with her wedding headband, diamond, and her Jordan doll.

By the time we crossed the border into Mestre, storm clouds were rolling over the Javan valley. The Stream was active again, sending streaks of light across the sky. Aaron watched them with a nervous eye and Aizah looked equally concerned. They were in their armor with their helmets open. Displays floated below their chins, showing views of what looked like raging battles along a beach. It had to be where the Guardians had deployed. They looked like they were fighting for their lives.

Becca and Liv-ya sat on either side of Suri, chattering like magpies. Amon smiled, clearly enjoying their company. I was starting to wonder if we'd made a wise decision in bringing them along.

"Turn here," Amon coughed.

Aaron eased the air car through the nearly empty city, around a grounded transport loaded with animals. A long line of transports hovered in line behind it, all heading to the wastelands east of Javan, a place I'd suggested would be the safest if the age ended. In my age, it was Iraq.

The hibernation facility lay west of the capital. We flew past dozens of pyramids pulsing energy into the ground. So much power was charging equipment that lightning lanced the air between the sloped faces. The Alliance was preparing for all-out war.

Clouds raced across the sky as the early morning sun rose. According to the displays, it was still night where Levi and Jarell were. I said a prayer for their safety as we landed in front of a nondescript entrance dug out of the side of a hill and next to a heavy retaining wall. Aaron and Aizah closed their helmets, pulled their weapons, and positioned themselves in the parking area.

The director of the facility greeted us in the lobby. Amon's medical team transferred him to a specially-made floating bed. The lead technician explained what would happen, answering Amon's questions. Liv-ya tried to jump up and climb on, but Becca scolded her. I picked Liv-ya up and hushed her with my finger. She hushed me with hers. Becca wanted to be picked up, too, but Suri was busy listening with Amon.

"We are going to give you a special dose of regenerative solution Athena sent down before *Olympus* headed to the front," the technician said. "It will reverse your condition and restore your arms, but we don't know for how long. We think the hibernation process will hold you in this restored condition for as long as you are frozen. When you wake up, you will need to seek treatment."

I hoped there would be someone here when he woke.

"I understand," Amon said. "Thank you for your efforts."

"Our privilege, your Highness. Let's get you prepped and down below as quickly as possible."

"Will we have some time down there with him?" Suri asked.

"A little," the technician said. "It's a little hectic, as you can imagine. Everything keeps getting moved up by Ground Com."

They floated Amon through the lobby and into a processing center. Several other patients were being examined and catalogued there. Instructions to doctors in the future were transcribed and recorded in multiple languages in the hopes that whatever language Amon's finders used, they might be able to decipher enough to facilitate his recovery.

Amon looked about the room with stoic calm as various instruments prodded and scanned him. Suri stroked his face and smoothed his hair. Becca reached up and patted his restraints.

"I'd hold your hand but I'm afraid it might bite you," he quipped.

"No, it won't," Becca said.

"I'd bite it back," Liv-ya announced.

"I hope this works," Amon said to Suri.

"When we see you again, you'll be whole."

He nodded, then looked at me. "I am sorry for everything. I hope I can make it up to you someday."

"Just get better and help us manage these two," I said.

Suri hugged him. His eyes closed as she held him. "Thank you."

The hibernation capsule arrived. It looked a lot heavier than mine had been. I guess if he was going to be in it for several centuries, it had to be. Hopefully, he would only be in it for a few days.

He was floated by a team of technicians, bed and all, into the cushioned chamber. The restraints were removed from his arms. His limbs shook and jumped as the technicians shot a blue substance into them. The quivering subsided and his hands and arms changed back to normal. He held his restored hands before his face, then gleefully waved to us. Clay packs were attached to the soles of his feet. Tubes were inserted. Then the team nodded.

"We are going to close you in now," the head technician said.

I stepped up and tied a package to his tunic.

"What's this?" Amon asked.

"Going away present. Some things from my backpack that might come in handy in an emergency."

He attempted a smile. "Like if I get hit by an air car?"

They closed the lid. I held Liv-ya and Becca in my arms. Liv-ya hid her eyes. Suri held her emotions in check. Amon's eyes darted between us as the chamber did its job. Then the glass frosted solid white.

The floor trembled. The technicians looked about nervously.

"We need to get him below. And get you back to your air car now," the head technician said.

The technician escorted us across the glass lobby. Becca was asleep on my shoulder, while Liv-ya hung on Suri's hand, skipping alongside her. The sky outside was black with thunderheads. Aaron and Aizah stood watch in the parking area. Air cars rocked and dipped behind them like boats in choppy water.

The technician paused halfway to the exit. "I'll give you Amon's internment location as soon as I get it from the staff."

Suri let go of Liv-ya to touch her chin in farewell, "Thank you for all you're doing."

"My privilege. May God be by you."

I juggled limp Becca to my other shoulder so I could touch mine. Liv-ya ran to the exit and put her little hands on the door. "Hey, kid, wait up," I called.

"Hi, Aaron!" she yelled through the glass.

Aaron opened his helmet and smiled. Aizah bent down and beckoned Liv-ya to her.

The very next instant, a change in pressure sucked Aaron and Aizah from the ground, along with the grass, bushes, and trees. Lights went out. Staff screamed. The air cars snapped their tethers and pinwheeled into the air, becoming faint dots in the boiling sky.

The technician pulled Suri to the floor and threw himself over her. I yanked Liv-ya away from the shuddering glass. It must have been stronger than bulletproof the way debris bounced off it. I covered both kids. The entrance blew out, sucking plants and small objects with it.

The pressure finally equalized and the wind settled back into a stiff breeze. Staff stumbled to their feet. Lights came back on and equipment chirped to life. The director of the facility ran over, blood dripping down his face.

"We have an emergency shelter below," he said. "There's room for all of you."

"We have to find Aizah and Aaron," Suri said, her eyes pleading. Becca and Liv-ya huddled on either side of her, staring up at me.

"Suri, there's no way they could still be …" The look on all their faces made me stop. I turned to the director. "Do you have any kind of a vehicle we can borrow?"

He pointed across what was left of the parking lot at a substantial looking building still intact. "There's a maintenance carrier in that building."

"I don't know how to thank you."

He ran to a storage closet and pulled out four satchels, which he shoved into my arms. They were full of heal sticks. "If you find your friends, they'll need these."

We piled the kids into the maintenance carrier between us on a driver's seat as wide as a couch. It took two hands to pull the armored doors shut. Good. Heavy metal made me feel safer, even if the next blast could probably hurl us clear over the city.

I tried the com unit on the console. It spurted disjointed images of faces all clamoring for a response. No one responded to my shouts. I turned the sound down but left the images playing.

"That one is showing a map of Phut," Suri said.

"What are those three circles supposed to be?" Becca asked.

"Meteorites, silly," Liv-ya said.

"They could be comets."

"Same thing."

"No, they're not."

"Suri, Liv-ya stuck her tongue out at me!"

"If those were impacts, then that wind must have been the shock wave," I said.

Aizah and Aaron had been blown east, so that's where we drove. I had no clue if we could find them but I had to go in that direction to reach the road back into Javan, anyway.

The Mestrean capital was a twisted ruin. Fires roiled through its crumbled walls, up into the sullied sky. The sun hung low in the clouds, a bloodshot eye beneath a purple-green brow of clouds that stretched across the entire horizon. The Stream raced across the heavens, its couriers of death flashing through breaks in the clouds. We picked up survivors along the way and let them crowd into the cargo bay. They were the color of dust.

One was a nurse and we handed her the heal sticks. She went to work on the injured. Another was a diplomat from Phut who'd survived being hurled miles through the air, thanks to his personal armor. It gave us hope that Aaron and Aizah might still be alive. If only I had a tracker.

I tried the com unit again. It displayed three-dimensional fuzz. I almost uttered the forbidden curse word.

My rear camera flashed warning signals. People started screaming in the cargo hold.

"Jordan, look behind us," Suri cried.

A wall of black water as tall as a mountain plowed down buildings like twigs as it came straight at us.

I floored the carrier. We reached the shores of the river and churned across the bank, the engines pushing boulders and plowing gravel as the carrier pitched across the raging torrent. We got ashore and fled east. I was doing about a hundred miles per hour across open country by the time the wave reached the east end of the city. It pulverized what was left of the capital and tumbled across the river bed.

I never saw a river move sideways before and hoped I never did again. Hills, towns, forests, and bodies on the east shore were ripped up and rolled into a seething deluge of sludge. The river humped up like a liquefied ridge. The degrading wave was diverted to the northeast, slowing as it curled around us to the north. The good news was that we were not going to drown. But there was also bad news.

"We're cut off," I said. "We can't make it to Javan."

"What are we going to do?"

"We'll head for high ground. The Palace Mount," I said.

The Mount looked like an anthill. It was crowded with all manner of people. Like hundreds of other vehicles, I drove straight up the side. Maybe because I was higher, the com unit got a clear signal.

Bless its frazzled electronic brain.

... imminent ... This is an alert. All civilians to their shelters immediately. Ben-ben activation imminent. This is an alert. All civil ... st ... rt ...

"All the shelters were on the west side of the river," said the diplomat from Phut, now in the back seat.

"So much for government planning," I muttered.

"Maybe we can ride out the storm here," someone said.

I had a very clear impression of how dumb that idea was. I remembered the ruins on Malta and how far the stones had been pushed eastward. They'd been shifted by a tidal wave a lot taller than that puddle jumper we'd just escaped.

It started raining harder than any downpour I'd ever known. Call it racial memory, call it God interrupting my thoughts and giving a direct order, I knew exactly what I had to do. I raced the carrier across the mountain.

"Everybody, hang on," I yelled.

The large vehicle plunged down the east face of the slope. Our passengers, many hyped-up on heal stick juice, got agitated.

"What are you doing? Are you mad?" somebody yelled from amid the jostling bodies.

"Jordan knows where he's going," Suri said.

"Yeah, so be quiet," Becca chimed.

"Do you?" Liv-ya asked from under my elbow.

"Yes, honey," I said. "Pray we get there in time."

CHAPTER FIFTY-SIX

LEVI

The long-range guns on Atlantis' battle crafts relentlessly pounded our line. Atlantean troop rafts dropped their ramps and squads poured onto the beach. The metal deck of Ground Com Forward shook under my boots, despite the pillar struts embedded fifty feet into the ridge. Hurricane-force winds lashed the barren coast land, long since stripped of its vegetation by the ruthless pounding of Atlantis' raft-to-shore battering. Our fire bases stood like sloped sentinels, evenly arrayed along the Heracles Pass. Incoming rounds pounded them with unending ferocity, erupting into fireballs that mushroomed through the clouds. The bases held, their sides hissing steam as the rain cooled their cherry-hot armor. Remote turrets, dispersed around each base, answered the barrage by swiveling and firing so fast they resembled the glowing fingers of many hands spreading out to touch the sky. Some fired interceptors to diffuse incoming rounds; others bombarded the storm-swept beaches, hurling disabler orbs. The swift landing rafts sparked and shuddered from our hits, their onboard systems faltering as they lost forward propulsion. For every troop raft we stopped, five others knifed past and reached the beaches. Mechanical infantry galloped ashore, firing from their chests with withering precision, cutting my Guardians in the forward position to pieces.

"Heavy incoming," warned a Ground Com ensign seated in front of me.

The shutters went black. The base shook from a massive hit. Screens faltered. Systems went down. My drink bounced off the map table.

"We just lost turret control," an officer warned.

"Front lines being overrun," said another.

"Pull back mechanized troops to the ridge," I ordered. "Reform under the fire bases. I need volunteers to fire the turrets manually."

Every hand shot up. I picked five and prayed as they suited up and deployed down the floor hatches. I watched the flickering displays as forward lines withdrew from the beachheads, pulling their wounded and dead with them. They were hounded by reinforcing Walkers coming off the next wave of troop rafts. The machines leapt into the surf and galloped through the shallows. Waves smashed their unyielding metal legs as they fired on my people.

Athena rested her massive hand lightly on my back. Her fingers draped over my left shoulder, her thumb over my right. "We can't hold much longer."

"We'll hold long enough," I said.

Lines of fire on the screen showed the icecap of Mer. Three rockets had just launched out of the crater that was the collapsed dome of the ruined city. Athena watched as the rockets fought their way skyward. "Looks like Apollo is going to the moon."

"And the rest of Mer with him," I said.

"I hope they make it."

"Sir, we have inbound comets breaking from the Stream," a young sensor operator reported. "Hitting the atmosphere and descending fast."

"Give me the vectors," I said calmly. "Will they hit us or Atlantis?"

"Atlantis, sir," he said, querying his screen to bring up data. He looked up and swallowed. "Multiple impacts projected. North Eliassipus, all the way to the North Pole."

"How large?"

"At least twenty alphas. Sir, when they hit, they could fry the icecap and tilt the planet."

Some four million cubic miles of scalding water could surge into the eastern Atlantic. Super tidal waves would rip across the ocean and inundate hundreds of miles of coast land. Jordan's map of a submerged Javan and Poseidon suddenly made sense.

"Sophia," I called to my left.

My com tech looked up from her console. Her face was ashen, her expression determined. I kept my voice calm. "Tell Ground Com Acropolis that we may lose contact. They are to cut our power and divert it to the civilian shelters in the event that happens. No hesitation. Understood?"

"Yes sir." Her fingers flew across her console.

"Adrian, estimated time until the tidal waves reach our position?"

Adrian pounded his screen for the answer, "Estimated time … um, no wait … Anak."

"Take your time, son."

"Got it. Two hours forty minutes after impact."

"Sophia, advise Ground Com Acropolis to cut power two hours from now but have the civilian shelters buttoned up as soon as possible. Make sure they're seeing what we're seeing."

"Understood." She spun back to her displays and called up the faces of my counterparts on the Acropolis.

"Everybody, suit up," I said. "Charge your armor and secure personal weapons."

A few minutes later, as Atlantis pressed the assault up the slopes of the Heracles Pass, godlike streaks descended through layers of cloud and silently dropped below the western horizon, deep into the doomed Atlantean empire. Somewhere below the horizon, a rain of flaming comets, most smaller than air-cars but not all, impacted at fifty thousand miles an hour into the frozen tundra of Northern Eliassipus. The night sky lit up with the brilliance of a sun. I had a vague sense of the command center being lifted into the air.

CHAPTER FIFTY-SEVEN

JORDAN

By the time we reached the ancient city, water was surging under the carrier and lapping at the sides. I gripped the drive controls in frustration. Suri stifled a sob. There was no way we could search for Aaron and Aizah now. Too many lives depended on us to get to safety.

I drove straight down the reflecting pool even though it was hidden by debris-choked water. I only knew where I was because I drove between the flanking pyramids. They pulsed and ripped with electric fire. I prayed for the Guardians and civilians, who'd depended on these machines to pump them power as long as possible.

A wave humped under us and carried us like a clumsy boat toward the Sacred Mountain.

"Didn't think we'd be visiting this place again so soon," I tried to joke.

Suri bit her lip and looked back at our passengers. They were drenched from the backwash coming up through what was supposed to be drain holes in the floor.

"We're coming in pretty hot," I said. "Tell everybody to hang onto something."

We lurched to a stop three feet from the slope of the pyramid when the carrier caught on the footbridge. The wind blew the waterfall to the south. I prayed the wind wouldn't shift.

There was some rope in the carrier. We ran a safety line across and relayed folks over the hood of the carrier into the arms of able-bodied people on the steps to the north of the waterfall. It was a miserable business and we almost lost two people to the flood waters. I suggested we climb the pyramid in stages, stopping at each intermediate platform to rest. I wondered if this was why the ancients had built them that way in the first place.

I had the best climbers go up to the first intermediate platform and secure safety lines. Then the others either free-climbed or steadied themselves with the ropes. Kids climbed in front of adults so they could be caught if they slipped. Many were terrified, especially the smaller ones. They clung to adult chests, their little arms wrapped around necks as the grown ups carefully climbed.

"Take your time, folks," I said. "If you see someone getting scared, help them out."

Other experienced people were saying the same thing in a half-dozen languages. The wind kicked up but didn't shift. Lightning lanced the sky and thunder shook. It wasn't going to be a nice night.

Two hours later, we were halfway to the top. That's when Shamel and Carlos—Shareb and Baak—found us. They had a contingent of civilians and park service personnel with them. They'd rigged some kind of spray-in-place shelter on the side of the pyramid that looked like a giant wasp's nest. We gripped each other like long-lost friends. Little did they know.

Baak apologized over and over for not seeing us sooner and Suri translated. "He says it was a long time since anyone reached the pyramid and they assumed the flooding would prevent any more. Shareb says we can rest in there. He believes we're high enough to wait out the storm."

"Tell him he's wrong," I said. "We have to get to the top as fast as possible."

"But he said lightning is striking the summit. It would be dangerous to climb any higher. Besides, the official forecasts—"

"Will be wrong," I said. "Trust me, Suri; in my time, this whole pyramid is underground. The only safe place is at the top, and even that is going to be risky."

She translated. Shamel's eyes narrowed in the rain. He yelled to everyone, pointing upward.

We reached the battered terrace at the top a long while later. The stream flowed from the fountain as peacefully as before. Incredibly, the gardens were still here. Kids crawled into the soft planting beds and curled up next to adults, shivering and crying. The wind howled outside but didn't penetrate.

"What's keeping the wind out?" I asked.

"Shareb doesn't know," Suri said. "He has never seen a wind this strong before."

"Are we going to be safe up here?" Liv-ya asked.

Lightning cracked against the sky. She leapt into my arms and clung like a monkey.

"Nothing is going to happen to you," I said. "I promise."

That's when the terrace shuddered. We were knocked off our feet. Far below, the attending pyramids winked out. The electrical charges crawled down their sloped faces and dissipated into the flood tides. What few lights twinkled on the horizon slowly died.

CHAPTER FIFTY-EIGHT

LEVI

Cold water rushed past my faceplate. Systems scrolled static displays. When I fully awoke, I had a vague memory of dragging wounded people to a transport, then of me being loaded on top of them.

Now rock scraped my faceplate as I was carried up some kind of cave. The armored hands holding me were as large as my chest: Athena's. Her faceshield was smashed.

My left boot scraped the wall. Searing pain shot up spine. My legs were broken. Why hadn't they been treated?

Hold still, Levi, Athena sent. *I am getting you to safety.*

Where are we?

The Cave of Michah. Jordan called it Saint Michael's Cave when I probed him for Fourth Age geography during his thaw. Good thing I was so thorough.

I rolled my eyes.

Why wouldn't I be? she sent. *I got worried when he said the Javan Valley would flood. Saint Michael's Cave. They must have named it after* Rahn's *brother, Michah. Isn't that amazing they remembered him?*

Irrational exuberance made her sound like she was having an emotional breakdown.

I can help climb, Athena. Just give me a heal stick.

So many wounded, so few heal sticks. You needed one for your legs but refused. "Help the others first," you said. We used them up. Still wasn't enough to go around. Then the Walkers found us, but the wave washed us in here. Higher and higher we go. We'll be safe in the cave chimney. We just have to get high enough. Jordan said the top of this mountain stays above water. He called it Gibraltar. Isn't that a funny name?

I was about to argue when my displays suddenly sharpened. I was looking at the interior and exterior views of the pyramid shelter Suri and Jordan were assigned to.

"Berbai Shelter Alpha, Ground Com Forward," I called through my helmet com.

There was no response. I could see civilians strapped and sealed in their family spheres but they couldn't see me. The pilots were secured in their four seats facing the center of the deck. I searched in vain for any sign of Jordan or Suri.

"System power up," the north pilot said into his chin com. All four pilots slid straps over their gloves to keep the controls in their hands. Their displays came online and merged to form a three-dimensional view of their shelter sitting on its electrically conductive base, a perfect gold pyramid capping a matching granite foundation.

An outside view flashed momentarily as Shelter Alpha and its sister shelters in the distance, Beta and Delta, fired their levitation systems. Thick black clouds rolled overhead, lashing the tips of the shelter with lightning. Power surged up the flanks of the enormous pyramid and swirled about the base of the gold top.

"System powered up. Launch in ten … nine … eight … seven …"

The south pilot touched another control. Power surged up the sloped sides of the shelter.

"Shelter cradled. Ready for launch," called the east pilot.

"… five … four …"

"Safeties released," said the west pilot.

"… two … one …"

The pyramidal shelter became a blurred triangle of brilliant light. Beta and Delta flared to life minutes later. All three rose a hundred feet in the air and held steady, levitating above their power bases on a chaotic swirl of electricity. I prayed for my friends.

Athena continued to jostle me up the jagged chimney. The displays faded into static.

CHAPTER FIFTY-NINE

JORDAN

The sky flashed and thundered. Each bolt of lightning revealed a frightening reality: There was nothing below us but water and it was rising fast. Shareb and Baak huddled with us. The others clustered about. Everyone looked terrified.

"What are we going to do when the water gets to the top?" Suri asked.

To the pool you go. Stop its flow.

The thought had been so audible in my head, I thought Shareb had said it.

If our voices you trust, touch you must.

Suddenly, I had a feeling this pool had something to do with how I'd come into this age. Levi had told me he'd smoothed my memory to erase the trauma of the car accident. Unfortunately, that had blurred the details of my voyage here.

I looked up at the hole in the ceiling and had an epiphany. "Come on."

I ran to the pool. Suri and the others followed. The water calmed to a mirror surface. The four channels emptied. The other people gathered around, their bodies silhouetted by the distant lightning. I touched the water. Nothing happened.

Your shirt impedes. Skin we need.

I shed my tunic.

"What are you doing?" Suri asked.

"Are we going swimming?" Becca asked.

"Shareb, Baak hold onto me."

The men motioned Suri aside and grabbed my waist. I leaned over and pushed my whole arm into the water.

There was a trembling and a big jolt. The water level dropped like an express elevator and drained down a shaft. Shareb and Baak pulled me back up. We gathered around the empty pool.

"Look at the funny heads down there," Becca said.

"They're ugly," Liv-ya said.

A familiar glow emanated from far below. It illuminated the dripping sides of the intricately carved shaft. Each side had twelve columns of carved faces, almost identical. I suddenly remembered why.

"This is how we escape," I said, then explained everything to Suri. "Tell Shareb and Baak."

She looked incredulous and terrified. "Are you serious?"

"Suri, I have never been more serious about anything in my whole life. This is how I traveled to your age. It will take me and all of you back to the Fourth Age. We'll be safe. Tell them."

Suri nervously translated. The reaction was not what I hoped for. They shook their heads and muttered obvious disbelief. However, Shareb stepped forward. He said something to Suri.

She choked back a sob. "Shareb says that if this will save me, he is willing to test your theory with his life."

Everybody stepped back to give Shareb room. He stood on the lip of the pool. Beads of sweat poured down his face, but he remained resolved.

"Tell him to keep his eyes open and watch the carvings."

"He understands."

I looked down at the swirling light and remembered something else.

"Breathe deep," I said. "The vapors will calm you."

Shareb nodded to me, touched his chin to Suri, and saluted Baak. Without a word, he jumped.

Suri held Becca and Liv-ya close. I clung to the edge of the pool and strained to watch his flailing body for as long as I could.

The hole in the roof above the pool flashed. A brilliant bolt of swirling light lanced straight down the shaft, sucking a familiar human-sized bubble of light high into the heavens.

"Happy landings, my friend," I said.

CHAPTER SIXTY

LEVI

Water swirled around Athena's knees, rising almost as fast as she could climb. I had no choice but to let her carry me. The pain in my legs was excruciating.

I tried everything I could to get the images back on my visor. Finally, a blurred transmission came through. It was from Berbai Shelter Alpha. There was no audio or interior view anymore. Just one long shot of the exterior of Alpha and her sister ben-bens, Beta and Delta. They hovered above their granite bases, riding a cushion of pure energy. The battery vaults in the bases would keep them aloft for twelve hours. I prayed it would be long enough.

A stream of meteors streaked into my field of vision. One smashed against the sloped flank of Beta and deflected harmlessly into the water. Then an interior view fuzzed to life. The four pilots jockeyed their controls, fighting to keep the ben-ben centered over the base.

Earthquakes rent and twisted the ground and swirled flood waters. Ground fell away from the sides of the pyramids, revealing the granite foundations extending deep into the earth, all the way to insoluble rock. The survivors of the Flood knew better than to build their shelters on shifting soil.

A transmission from Diago reached me. We couldn't talk. He

was flying his Dart east while being tossed by violent gusts, accompanied by five other fighters: three Javans and two Atlanteans. Diago was doing a heroic job of keeping his machine level. The other fighters were taking cues from his course corrections. It was as if someone else of vast experience was piloting for him.

Data explained that the Stream of Heaven was slicing within forty thousand miles of the Earth's surface, dropping small meteorites and comet fragments into the atmosphere and hammering the northern realms with impunity. The Earth rocked on its axis like a drunken Anakim. The stars seemed to wheel above Diago's canopy. The sun rose and set multiple times, sending crazy shadows across his determined face.

He sent me a link to Ground Com's sensors. I brought up a view of the Earth from space. Super hurricanes swirled over the oceans, beating their way inland. Volcanoes vented like an invading army, immolating western Atlantis from the north all the way into the southern continent of Mneseus. Searing lava entombed city after burning city, burying them to depths of a thousand feet. The mighty city of Payahdon succumbed to an onslaught of tidal waves. The rising ocean dissolved its limestone strata from the bottom up until the thin dome holding the city aloft crumbled and plunged the entire breadth of it to a watery death. Only the old city with its ring of mountains and insoluble foundations held. Soon, it was a besieged island in a smoking sea of death. All this happened in the span of an hour.

Something finally took out Ground Com and I lost the link. Diago's image faded. We nodded to each other in farewell.

The ben-ben transmission came back. The pilots were in trouble. The flood waters had reached the tops of the pyramid bases and were rising fast. All three shelters now appeared to be dancing over a black ocean of rolling debris. Rogue waves swept past, just missing the shelters. The flood waters still rose. Pyramid Beta's base was slightly lower in elevation than Alpha and Delta. Its ben-ben got hit first. The electrical cradle keeping it aloft blinked and died.

I sucked in my breath in horror as the enormous shelter cradling five thousand lives seemed to drop in slow motion into the waves. When it hit, geysers shot into the sky. The shelter resurfaced and slowly rolled east, pitching and bucking. Delta fell next, relinquishing herself to the fate of the waves. Finally, Alpha lost power. I saw one brief view inside as the pilots activated manual controls. They would try to keep the ben-bens vertical by shifting the storage ballast. I hoped the three shelters would be able to stay afloat.

A two-thousand-foot tidal wave rose above the western horizon, the same wave that had chased Diago and his companions. It bore down on the helpless shelters and swallowed them like toys. I felt a sorrow unlike any grief I'd felt since the death of my parents so long ago. I once again wished Jordan and Suri a safe voyage, this time to the great beyond.

Athena had stopped climbing. I snapped out of my despair. *What's wrong?*

I'm stuck, she sent.

I looked up. The chimney extended for hundreds of feet and didn't widen.

You have to keep going, she said. *The water is rising.*

CHAPTER SIXTY-ONE

JORDAN

I tried to talk Suri into going next.

"I don't go until you go," she said, clutching her satchel. I knew better than to argue with her.

The bravest wanted to jump first. I sent several down and had everyone see how each resulted in another sphere of light shooting up through the ceiling. A lightning flash happened to show a person floating in one of the spheres. That convinced most to go for it. Those who were still too frightened were shown how high the water was rising. That got them at least to the lip. We pushed one in. That rattled the line for a while. We tried to send two at the same time, but the shaft pushed them back out.

One goes in, two's a sin.

The most heartbreaking part was when parents stood their children on the lip, smiling and encouraging them to jump, then weeping as they watched them drop. They seemed to take strength in seeing the steady flight of glowing orbs shooting into the sky. They were obviously going somewhere. I prayed it was to a place safer than this. I didn't know if the shaft was sending them back to my age; I never got a rhyming answer to that. It just kept telling me to *shut my mouth and send them south.*

God, give me five minutes alone with the nerd who designed the audio for this thing.

We sent three hundred and twenty-five men, women, and children into the unknown, then got down to the last few civilians. The water was less than fifty feet from the top at that point. I figured there had to be a super tidal surge if the water had risen so high. The entire world couldn't be inundated like this.

Baak and the other guys who'd helped with the ropes worked out who went next. We lined up: Becca, Liv-ya, Suri, and then me. Suri wouldn't leave otherwise and I reluctantly agreed. We got Liv-ya set. She gave me a brave hug.

"See you on the other side," she said.

We watched Becca's sphere shoot into the sky. I looked down into the shaft. "Okay, Liv-ya, you're next." But she was gone.

"She must be hiding in the undergrowth," Suri said.

A wave slapped the top of the terrace.

"You guys, get going," I shouted.

Baak refused and urged the others to go. I think they agreed only because it wouldn't hold us up later. Spheres of light rhythmically shot through the ceiling as we continued to search for Liv-ya. As soon as the last man jumped, Baak joined us in looking for her. Side by side, Suri and I crawled through the fragile bushes, checked under stone benches, and hunted around the bridges and dry stream channels. Several minutes later, Baak called out.

"He must have found her," Suri said.

We ran back to the clearing.

Babla stood across from Baak in the clearing beyond the shaft. She held a very frightened Liv-ya in her spidery arms.

CHAPTER SIXTY-TWO

LEVI

Athena struggled to free herself. The water rose to her chest and around my battered legs. She lifted me with one arm and pushed me over her head. I grabbed a rock ledge with one arm and reached down.

Take my glove, I sent.

It's too narrow. I'm already wedged.

The water swirled about her chin. Fear filled her eyes. *Hold on tight. I'm letting go*. Her hands slid down my body.

Anak you are. I grabbed her index finger.

Grab the ledge with both hands, she sent. *You can pull yourself up.*

I'm not leaving you. Your faceshield is damaged. You'll drown.

There's no time to argue.

She gripped my thighs and hurled me upward, ripping my hold from her finger. I heard the splash and felt the backwash vibrate against my armored legs as her behemoth body dropped into the rising pool.

My head cleared the ledge. I grabbed with both hands. Wind whistled against my faceshield.

Athena, its open at the top, I sent. *Maybe I can get help.*

My words met silence. Far below, beneath the black water, Athena's helmet lights sank in a slow spiral.

CHAPTER SIXTY-THREE

JORDAN

Babla smiled as she stroked Liv-ya's disheveled hair. "Don't be too hard on her," she croaked. "She didn't run away. I took her when you weren't looking."

I put Suri behind me. "She wants you, not Liv-ya. Whatever happens, you can't let her touch you."

A wave curled high in the air and smashed against the south corner of the summit. A whole section of the roof twisted, toppling the outer columns. It plummeted off the side into the water. Cracks spider-webbed across the ceiling. Chunks of rock dropped on us. I turned to protect Suri but something had already hit her. Blood trickled down her forehead as she went limp in my arms.

Babla sensed her opportunity. She pushed Liv-ya aside and headed toward the first bridge.

This either ends fast or it doesn't end well, I thought.

I laid Suri down and ran to cut Babla off. Babla backed away and headed for the other bridge. I pretended to stumble. She darted over the second bridge. I sprinted toward her. She reached out to claw me, but I dropped and slid into her, one leg raised. My foot smashed her kneecap and she went down. I grabbed her face and punched her lights out.

Liv-ya was cowering under a bush. I scooped her up and ran

for the pool. Waves thundered over the summit where the roof had collapsed.

"You have to be brave for me," I said.

"I will."

"Keep your eyes open."

I kissed her and dropped her down the shaft. I heard her screams and sensed the globe shooting up through the ceiling, then I grabbed Suri. She moaned.

"Suri, come on, wake up." Her eyes rolled. "Please, sweetie, I think you have to be awake to do this. Please wake up."

A thunderous sound from the west told me another mother of a wave was coming.

"Jordan?"

I scooped her up and threw her satchel around her shoulder. "I'm here."

"What happened?"

"Babla's knocked out and Liv-ya is on her way to the Fourth Age. You're going next."

"No, Jordan—"

"I love you."

I tossed her into the shaft and cringed as she screamed. But then the swirling lights enveloped her, the sky flashed, and her globe shot past my face, through the roof, and into the storm clouds.

"God go with you," I whispered.

There was a flicker of movement on the other side of the clearing. An arm twitched under a bush. It was Baak. He tried to crawl out from the debris and I dragged him clear. The wave was visible now, a massive frothing wall rearing high above the roof. Shafts of moonlight punctured through the thinning storm clouds, illuminating the impossible sight. Strength borne of desperation flowed through me. I hurled Baak over the lip and he tumbled down the shaft.

The wave crested, curled, and dropped. Baak vanished. His orb flared into the sky as the wave crashed against the summit. I held onto my satchel and jumped. Water roared through the garden. I flipped and smashed my head against the stone.

I couldn't breathe. I was rolling sideways, head over heels.

CHAPTER SIXTY-FOUR

LEVI

I crawled out of the tiny cave, my ruined legs dragging behind me, encased in crushed armor. My visor shorted out and I popped it open.

Salty rain stung my eyes as I looked out over my shattered world. Over eight hundred inches of rain had fallen in a single day. Plants, animals, people, civilization, all washed into the oceans, crushed and buried under thousands of feet of mud. What had been lush hills and thick forests were now bare rock. Jordan had said a writer named Plato would describe the hills surrounding the drowned valley of Javan as bare bones. Aptly put.

I watched the sun stagger across the sky like a flying mountain with a drunk at her helm. The Earth still wobbled from her meteoric assault. When evening came, the moon rose in a twisting curve as if it, too, was lost. Its face glowed and smoked from hundreds of meteorite hits. A bright light struck its southern hemisphere. An unbelievable eruption of molten rock silently flared into the stars and curled across the moon's face. It spread a plume of smoldering light, illuminating the dark craters beyond the crescent's edge. I said a prayer for Apollo and the Nephillim hiding somewhere in the moon's shadow, aboard Babla's pirated ship.

The tidal waves had cut a deep gorge through the Heracles Pass.

The Atlantic had subsided, but at a higher tidal line than before the Stream of Heaven had struck. Its waters swirled with mud. The scattered remains of unspeakable death succumbed to the Earth's pull, taking corpse after corpse into its thickening depths.

My armor's power drained. Systems flickered out, starting with my weapons. There was no power in the ground to recharge them. My com barely functioned. I had no word on Jordan's or Suri's fate. I'd seen their shelter go under. My armored glove gripped a rock as I resigned myself to failure and the rock exploded into dust.

There was a memory message from Diago. He'd sent it before his plane had run out of power. His flight had lost its bearings when the world had tilted. He was somewhere over Indra, along with a handful of other pilots, some allies and some enemies. Not that it meant anything anymore.

His eyes were glazed and weary as he spoke. I knew the look. He was ready to die. *Sir, if you hear this, thank you for—*

I bowed my head. My com continued to falter.

A few hours later, when it flickered a recharge request, Aizah contacted me. Her voice was faint and frantic. "Levi, if you can hear me, please answer."

No time for long sentences. "Aizah, Levi."

"Where are you? I need your help."

"What is your situation?"

Aizah did something I never thought I'd hear. She sobbed.

"My com is failing," I said over her wailing. "Tell me your situation."

"Wake up, Aaron. Please wake up. Don't die on me!"

"Aizah, is he breathing?"

"He was talking to me and now he stopped. No, no, no!"

"Did you administer a heal stick?"

"I don't have any more," she moaned. "I don't have anything."

Suddenly, it came to me. "Jordan demonstrated a method to restore breathing on the Acropolis. Do you remember it?"

"Not completely."

"I'll explain." I went through the steps from memory. A lot of shuffling sounds and grunting. I prayed as she strained and blew.

Then I heard coughing, followed by vomiting.

"Aizah?"

"It's not working."

"Keep trying."

"Help me, Levi."

"Aizah, keep trying," I yelled.

There was no response. My com died. "No, no, no!"

My armor stiffened as the joint motors succumbed. My helmet went dark. I smacked the manual eject with my chin. The suit unlatched and I crawled out. Pain lanced my legs as bare bone scraped against the open metallic flaps. I bit back the agony. Nothing mattered now. I didn't even bother to stop the bleeding.

I crawled toward the cliff but couldn't reach it. A gust of wind rolled me onto my back and lightning illuminated my empty armor. It sat frozen, like a memorial to a lost age, facing the direction I had been looking before the suit had locked up, toward my best friend dying in the arms of his bride.

My legs went numb. I knew my fate. Thanks to what my adopted Nephillim mother had given me to drink without explaining, I was practically immortal. I would be lame but I wouldn't die. It would take a decade of starvation or the flames of reentry to send my soul into the next realm.

Stars wheeled right, then left, a pointless dance. I closed my eyes and prayed. "Please protect my friends," I whispered.

The response was swift and intense.

Behold, I send you a messenger, a man of sorrow and affliction. He will carry my word to my people. Guard him so my remnant may be spared.

The words were clear and ridiculous. It was the same speech I'd heard in my Dart the night Jordan had appeared in the embassy lake. Either I was talking to myself or the Creator was playing a cruel joke. I was mad enough to assume the latter.

"Are you kidding me?" I shouted into the wind. "What about this?" I smacked my arms against the wet rock to indicate the world. "Did you notice we just got annihilated?"

The wind howled and lightning flashed. The Creator was mad. Fine by me.

"How could you let this happen? All those people; where were you?" I choked back a sob. "Why didn't you help us?"

Thunder rocked the ruined mountain. A bolt lanced the ridge below me.

My rage carried my words. "You heard them screaming, didn't you? Or were you asleep? Maybe you wanted us to die."

Thunder hammered my chest.

I leaped to my feet. "You couldn't even get that right." I flicked my thumb off my nose. "You forgot to kill me. Come on, get it done. Kill me."

The wind whirled around the mountain. Lightning struck the ocean in a hundred places. I covered my face and bowed to the storm, weeping. "Kill me."

The wind died.

"Please."

An uninvited calm flowed into my soul. Sunlight warmed my brow. That's when I realized I was standing.

I slept in a cave and woke to an erratic sunrise that started in the northeast, then set an hour later in the east, and finally tried to rise again in the southwest. This time, the sun looked like it was up for the duration.

I gathered tech from my suit, slung it over my shoulder, and started down the mountain, heading east. No matter how long it took, I was going to find Aizah. I had to know if she and Aaron had survived.

The unexplained restoration of my legs was so fantastic I worried about my grip on reality. Maybe I was delusional. Maybe I was entombed in my dead armor, slowly suffocating, dreaming before I expired.

I slipped on a patch of slime and cracked my head against a rock. I was awake.

The reality was that I had healed and Athena had drowned. A strange calm washed over me again, carrying away the heartache and guilt of too many missed opportunities to be her son. I decided to attempt another conversation with the Creator.

"Sir," I began, "I appreciate what you did for me, but why did you save me and let Athena die?" I looked at the rising sun climbing through the trailing of smoke and clouds. "If it's possible, please let her know I'm sorry for how I treated her. Tell her I said she was a good mother." My eyes watered from the smoke. "The best."

A large hand rested on my shoulder. "You don't need to trouble him," Athena said. "I heard you."

She was kneeling behind me. I reached up and threw my arms around her neck. The sun swept the summit as wind blew dust and smells of the dead. I held on, relishing the feel of her pulse against my ear. Her arms encircled me.

"You found a heal stick for your legs," she said.

"In a way."

"Sorry there wasn't time to explain in the cave. Since I couldn't follow you, I had to submerge and wait for the water to subside. It took forever to clear the cave entrance, swim to the surface, and hike up this mountain."

"How did you survive?"

"Remember those air pills I issued your team for the Payahdon mission? I always keep some with me whenever I travel over water. You never know."

"Never know," I echoed.

She looked out over the ruined coast. "We must go to the Crescent and help the survivors."

"It's four thousand miles away, if memory serves me."

She nodded. "That's three months on foot."

"Fifty miles a day?"

"I can do that easily."

"I can't."

"I'll carry you."

"Oh, no you won't."

"But if you walk, it'll take eight months."

"You're not carrying me."

"Oh, come here, Levee."

"Mother, you promised never to call me that."

She chased me down the mountain.

CHAPTER SIXTY-FIVE

JORDAN

The current pitched and rolled me head over heels. I lost my bearings. Desperately in need of air, I let out bubbles and followed them.

My head finally broke the surface. A small backpack floated past my face. I grabbed it and held on. A wave curled over my head. My body rolled. Then my feet hit sand. I clawed at shells and sticks against the undertow. The next wave shot me onto a beach. It was night. Lights flickered through the palms. Where I was and how I got here, I had no idea.

I stumbled to my feet. Helicopters pounded the skies a mile north of me. Searchlights played across the ocean, looking for something.

Carlos's restaurant was lit up as usual. I wiped the salt water out of my eyes and smoothed my hair as if that would improve my appearance. I checked my clothes, feeling like I was missing something. I was dressed in a smock and pants of a weird shiny material. My whole body was covered with scrapes and bruises.

What had happened to me? The last thing I remembered was shaving in the bathroom while monkeys scurried past my window.

The restaurant was empty when I entered it, even though music played behind the bar. The room started to spin. I grabbed the edge of the counter and toppled over stools. Glasses crashed and I hit the floor.

Something felt cool on my face. "I think he's waking up," a familiar voice said.

I blinked. I lay on a couch in Carlos's lobby. Five faces stared down at me. Some were tearful; some smiling; some both. Krax leaned down on a cane and gripped my hand. He squeezed hard. "Welcome back, buddy."

"What happened to your leg?" I choked out.

"Accident in the shaft," he replied.

Kate was all over me before I could ask what Krax meant by shaft. "Gawd, and wouldn't you be a sight for sore eyes?"

Greg gripped her shoulder while she squeezed the daylights out of me. "Dude, great clothes. Souvenirs?"

"I don't know where I got them," I said.

Carlos said something to Krax, who looked worried. Headlights panned through the front windows. Tires skidded across gravel. Car doors slammed. Krax hobbled to the entrance to intercept whoever was coming. Everybody else was silent. Kate bit her lip and patted my hand. Laura was the one who walked in—with somebody who looked like Lisa. She was dressed differently and her hair was longer, but the face was nearly the same. She rushed up to me and took my hand.

"*Cha na hee,* are you okay?"

I stared at this woman who looked like my dead wife, trying to understand what was happening.

"I'm so glad you're home," she gushed and rubbed my hand against her nose. Then she stopped and pulled back, searching my eyes. The others looked away, all except Kate.

"He doesn't know who I am," the woman whispered.

Kate looked like she wanted to pound my face. "Are you daft? This is Sarah you're looking at."

Sarah? I didn't know what to say. One minute I'd been shaving in my bathroom and the next I was body surfing in the ocean.

Now I was being introduced to my wife's look-alike. And how had it gotten to be so late? How long had I been in the water?

The woman fled the lobby.

"Sarah, wait up!" Krax shouted and took off after her as fast as he could hobble.

CHAPTER SIXTY-SIX

SARAH

I woke in the middle of a grassy field. Cold rain pelted my body. Sheep were bounding down the hill from where I lay. I must have frightened them.

My satchel lay beside me. I grabbed it and searched the inside. My marriage jewel and Jordan doll were still inside it. Across the way stood a circle of large stones. Some had lintels spanning two pillars. A rope barrier encircled the ancient-looking structure. A low building lay nearby but appeared to be unoccupied, a paved lot beyond it but no air cars.

I struggled to my feet. Vertigo gripped me and I fell on my face, sobbing. "Jordan, please find me."

A clanking, coughing mechanical noise came over the fields and a strange vehicle wound its way along a small lane. Two circles of light blazed out its flat front. Red circles of light shined from its back.

I squinted in the frigid wind. Oddly, the vehicle was rolling along the ground on four wheels. I wondered if I had been transported to a primitive settlement somewhere north, maybe in Magog. But nothing felt familiar. The vehicle reached a spot closest to my hill and stopped. A man exited it, opened a strange looking toadstool device made of cloth stretched over metal rods, and held it above his head. He hurried up the hill toward me and bent down, holding the contraption over me. It blocked the rain.

"Cor blimey," he exclaimed. "Whut's a sweet lass like you doing out here?"

I shivered. "D-d-do you speak Engel?" I asked.

"Did you say English? I should hope so." He laughed, then took off his outer garment and threw it around me.

When I stood, the world tilted. He caught me and carried me to his clanking non-air-car.

"I saw that lightning bolt hit the hill," he said. "Bloody fortunate you weren't hit."

At Patrick's insistence, I stayed with him and his dear wife for three weeks in their tidy home on a hilly street in a small town called Bath. I had landed in a country called England. I hesitated to explain who I was and accepted Patrick's first guess. It was the truth, actually. I was a refugee. Patrick and his wife had strong opinions about refugees. It was the same as the Javans.

They treated me like a daughter. I learned to watch the visual displays called BBC when people were giving information about events and weather. There were no reports of strange lightning such as what had heralded my arrival. Jordan should have appeared by now. I began to worry he might not make it back.

Three weeks turned into three months. Every Sunday night, I went to service at Bath Abbey. I sat in the back pew and prayed to the Creator to bring Jordan back. The Director of Music approached me one night and invited me to tea the next day. Eventually, I was part of a home group. I began to make friends.

Three months turned into three years. I'd been granted permission to live in England. My Engel became flawless. All the while, I kept my vigil, returning regularly to the circle of old stones they called Stonehenge, hoping my Jordan would miraculously appear out of the sky.

Then it occurred to me. What if Jordan had landed in a different part of the world? Hope replaced my despair. That had to be it. He was somewhere far away, probably hunting for me. I resolved to master a device that up until now had been more intimidating than Numu: the Internet.

I rechecked the address and followed the GPS in my rental car as it directed me through Philadelphia, into a town called the Suburbs. I swerved onto Jordan's street and slowed. It was hard to believe this could be where Jordan lived. But the detective's report was certain.

I opened my cell phone and looked again at his phone number and full name glowing on the display, then gently closed it. When I'd found out where he was, I didn't bother writing or calling; I wanted to surprise him. With the money I'd saved up working in the school as a language teacher, I'd bought an airline ticket and crossed the Pond straight away.

I was about to open the car door when a car sped past me and pulled into the driveway. I held my breath. Jordan stepped out, dressed in a nice suit, carrying a roll of paper with markings on them.

I lowered the window to call out, but my heart froze. A woman opened the front door and stepped out to greet him. She hugged him as close as her swollen belly would allow.

For four years, I stayed away from Jordan. I lived in New York, teaching ancient studies at a university called Fordham. I had learned to blend into this age. I had learned to disappear, even changed my name to the more American-sounding Sarah.

An unmarried professor began to show an interest in me. He was from the Middle East, the place my people had called the Crescent. He was very polite and fairly intelligent. I refrained from his advances. I was married; nothing had changed that. Not even Jordan's betrayal. I had made a promise and was resigned to keep it. Some things were too important to abandon, no matter how obvious the matter appeared.

"A group of foreign students are heading down to the Macy's Day parade this morning," he said. "Since you obviously aren't going anywhere for Thanksgiving, do you want to join us?"

"I'll think about it," I said, looking up from my work.

He shrugged like Jordan and held up his iPhone. "If you change your mind, call me."

I sighed and went back to my books. Then I turned on the flat screen to watch the parade. A while later, I heard a commotion from the announcers.

"Oh my, folks, looks like Snoopy's escaping!"

I watched the giant beagle float high into the air and remembered seven years and two ages earlier when Jordan had told me about a parade his daughter had been watching. A balloon named Snoopy had broken loose during that parade. It struck me then what had happened. Jordan had not returned yet because he hadn't left yet. I was living in Jordan's past. How could I have known? Jordan had never told me the year he'd come from.

My heart seized. Today was the day his wife and daughter were going to be murdered.

I grabbed my cell phone and found his number. I punched the speed dial. It rang. Then I heard it connect. I didn't wait for Jordan to speak.

"Come home now," I said.

"Lisa? I'm on my way. The mini-mart was out of cr—"

I disconnected the line and bolted out of my office.

I saw everything. I watched them carry the bodies from the house. I watched Jordan bury his wife and child. I watched him collapse in the snow in his driveway, crying their names. I watched and didn't interfere. I couldn't. If I appeared to him now, wouldn't that change what had happened in the past? I had no choice. I had to be the one who sent Jordan back in time so he might return to me. I would need money to make my plan work, a lot of it.

"This is a fantastic piece, Ms. Wright," the jeweler said. "A red diamond this size is priceless. And the gold chain is unlike anything I've ever seen. Are you sure you want to part with it?"

"As soon as the auction can be arranged," I said. "And it's Mrs. Wright, please."

*****

The final bid: thirty-two million dollars. The story of the mysterious diamond headpiece was in all the news blogs. That was how Carlos and Shamel had found me. I flew to Costa Rica to meet them. The rest was history.

Again.

Now I fled the restaurant. Shamel stepped out of the shadows and met me at the car.

"What went wrong, your Highness?"

"Please start the car," I said.

He opened the rear door and I bent to get in.

"Wait," Jordan called. He was leaning against the door post of the restaurant, the single light above his head aswirl with moths.

When I hesitated, he walked toward me, testing his steps with caution. Then he staggered and steadied himself against a palm tree, staring at me with questioning eyes. It was all I could do not to fly to him and declare my love. But what would his reaction be? I wasn't going to lose him by pushing him into madness.

"Why do you look like my wife?" he asked.

"You are very tired and I have upset you," I said. "Why don't you rest with your friends and I'll come back tomorrow?"

He rubbed his eyes and held onto the tree. "Was that you at the airport when I was getting off the plane?"

"Yes."

Kate, Krax, and the others appeared behind him in the entrance to the restaurant.

"Who are you?" Jordan asked.

"Somebody who cares about you very much." I had to tell him how I felt or my heart would burst.

To my surprise, Jordan came straight toward me. He stumbled and I caught him. Shamel was there to help me upright him.

"I don't feel very good," he said.

"You need a doctor," I said. "I know a good one. Let me take you to him."

Laura helped me get him into the car. Krax leaned on his cane, watching our efforts and looking frustrated because he couldn't help.

"Krax, what's happening?" Jordan asked.

"It's okay, just go with it."

Shamel drove carefully down the coastal road, while Jordan leaned forward and put his head in his hands.

"Are you feeling carsick again?" I asked.

"Yeah."

I gently pulled him onto his back and cradled his head in my lap. He stared up at me as Shamel drove under successive streetlights.

"Did this happen before?" he asked.

I smoothed his hair from his eyes.

"I had the strangest dream about you," he added.

My hand found his. He squeezed it and didn't let go.

"I would love to hear it," I said.

Shamel drove out of town and turned up the mountain road leading into the rainforest. The breakers rolled along the beach beneath the shimmering stars. As we left the ocean far behind, Jordan began to tell our story.